SPELLHACKER

Also by M. K. England
The Disasters

Spell Hacker

M. K. ENGLAND

HARPER TEEN
An Imprint of HarperCollinsPublishers

Library of Congress Control Number: 2019950291
ISBN 978-0-06-265770-1

Typography by Alice Wang
19 20 21 22 23   PC/LSCH   10 9 8 7 6 5 4 3 2 1

First Edition

To everyone whose struggle is invisible.
Hey. I see you. We got this.

THE PERIODIC TABLE OF MAZ

The Core Strains

Firaz—*Fire and explosive effects*

Terraz—*Earth and grounding effects*

Wataz —*Water and flowing effects*

Aeraz—*Wind and airborne effects*

Nullaz—*Nullification/anti-maz*

The Perceptual Strains

Obscuraz—*Illusion and concealment*

Songaz—*Auditory effects*

Sunnaz—*Light and darkness*

Scentaz—*Olfactory effects*

Formaz—*Shape and size*

The Augmenting Strains

Magnaz—*Raw power, amplification*

Motaz—*Motion*

Vitaz—*Health and vigor*

Linkaz—*Binding and tying*

Printed and distributed by Maz Management Company
MMC International Holdings, 341 AR

ONE

I DON'T KNOW WHY I thought the cops wouldn't follow me onto the roof.

Honestly, most of the time it's true. When I go up, the cops stay down, and I'm home free a minute later. Ninety-nine jobs out of a hundred are in, steal, out, profit.

It figures that this, our crew's last job ever, would be the one fiery exception.

"Dispatch, this is 21-501. I have the suspect cornered on the roof of the Ivon Building. Requesting backup and air support."

Cornered? Please. She knows I'm up here, but she doesn't know *where*. It's only a matter of time, though. And isn't air support a bit overkill? The officer sweeps her gaze over the rooftop, pulling threads of glowing fire between her fingers as she glances right over the nook I've crammed myself into. The low concrete wall at my back bleeds evening chill through my hoodie, and my thighs burn with the exhaustion of holding still in a crouch after running for a mile straight. I clutch my bag tighter, as if that will somehow erase the vials of stolen maz inside.

This is fine. Totally under control.

Ania is probably close by, near enough to cook me up a distraction of some kind if I ask. I sneak a hand slowly into my back pocket and click the button to turn my deck back on. It gives a slight vibration in response. I turned it off earlier so I wouldn't get distracted by messages and calls while I was busy, you know, *not getting arrested*, and about a billion missed notifications flood my vision as soon as the interface pops up in my contact lenses.

Epic Group Chat: LAST JOB EVER Edition

Jaesin: Remi and I are almost home

Ania: I'm still waiting on Diz at the meet point

Dizzzzzzzzz

WHERE ARE YOU

The client is getting pissed

He says if you bring cops down on him he'll make sure we're blacklisted

Jaesin: Good thing this is our last job anyway

Remi: you ok, diz?

don't make me come after you dizzy I will fight

Jaesin: She probably found some shiny new building to climb

DIDN'T YOU DIZ

Your vital signs for the hour: Average pulse rate, 98; Blood pressure . . .

(private) Remi: diz?

Kyrkarta weather update: Scattered showers beginning at 3:30 a.m., with . . .

(private) Jaesin: Don't be an ass, call Remi
They're kind of panicking right now
(private) Ania: Okay, we're really worried

Sera Shortner followed you. Follow them back?

(private) Davon: You decided about the job offer yet?
I sent you a little something for graduation
It's fine, I know I'm the best cousin ever, you don't have to say
(private) Ania: Diz, I'm seriousssssssssssssss.
(private) Jaesin: Do we need to turn around and come back?

I double-blink to clear the clutter from my vision, then give the deck a silent command to bring up a map. The tiny sensors that read the movement of my throat have been messing up *all the time* lately, though, so I get my bank app, a word game, and a half-read fanfic before I actually get the map I asked for. Ania's dot blinks on the map at the drop point, about two blocks from my location. Definitely close enough to create some kind of diversion for me. I start to subvocalize a message to the group chat, hesitate . . . then delete the whole thing and close the map.

3

They'll all be gone in a week. Literally moving on with their lives, to a whole new city. College, jobs, all that.

I'm not going anywhere. Besides, I know this city better than anyone. If anyone can figure a way out of this, it's me. I need to do this myself.

I let my head fall back against the wall and try to visualize the roof. In the half dozen times I've been up here before, I've used the maintenance ladder, the staff exit, or the breezeway over to the next building. This cop is between me and all of them. I ease myself up slowly, just high enough to see over the wall at my back and past the hulking air-conditioning unit behind it to the roof's nearest edge. Against the inky black sky, two faint curves are backlit by the glow of the neon signs from the street below. A fire-escape ladder.

In the distance, the whine of aircar engines and sirens grows louder.

Well. No time like the present.

As soon as the cop turns her back to me, I vault over the low wall and sprint for the ladder. Her shout goes up barely a second later—"Halt!"—which is about a second longer than I expected to have, honestly. I dive to one side, tumbling over a two-foot-wide pipe with the bag held tight against my stomach. A bright flash of orange maz blasts the metal just beside my hand, turning it red-hot in a flash. Seriously, she's just gonna sling firaz around? She doesn't know what's in these pipes. What if they explode?

Apparently, she doesn't care. Another fireball blasts at my heels, leaving a black scorch on the concrete.

Point taken.

I grab the top of the ladder where it connects with the roof and swing myself over the edge, dangling by one hand for half a terrifying second until my feet find the rungs. My shoulder screams in brief protest, but it's used to this kind of abuse by now. A quick glance below, and I spot a landing about two stories down, where the ladder turns to stairs. Perfect.

Another blast of fire connects with the top of the ladder, then two more in quick succession. Then more. What the hell is she doing? What a waste of maz. I guess when the city's paying for it, you can use as much as you want, though.

Then the ladder starts to heat up under my hands, and I understand.

Shit.

I need to hurry, outclimb the warming metal under my palms. I risk another glance down. The landing is closer, at least; less than one story to go. Above me, the cop pokes her head over the side and winds up for another blast.

I let go.

For one brief second, my chest fills with the weightless thrill of falling, falling.

Then I look down, soften my knees to absorb the shock, and exhale as I land on the balls of my feet and guide myself into a forward tumble. Perfect form, way to stick the landing, self.

Unfortunately, the platform is slightly shorter than I anticipated, and I roll straight past the edge of the landing and onto the first staircase. Behind me, the landing rattles with another blast of firaz, then another, closer. A message pops up in my vision:

(private) Ania: Our client is getting ready to murder me, therefore I'm getting ready to murder YOU

Our client can eat one thousand bees for all I care. I subvocalize a message back that thankfully translates correctly.

(private) you: Kindly FUCK OFF when your best friend is being chased by the cops

Perfect. Good rule for life.

I use my unintended momentum to swing myself over the railing onto the next set of stairs, then the next, the bag full of stolen maz thumping against the small of my back with each landing. If I were at all talented with maz,

I could have sacrificed one of the vials (and a bit of our pay) to fight back. Maz is not my thing, though. You want your ex's social media profiles hacked so they look like an ass? I'm on it. With maz, I'm useless.

Well, except for the stealing-and-selling-it thing.

Far above me, the staircase rattles as the cop makes her way down in the more traditional manner, but as soon as my feet hit the asphalt, I may as well be invisible. I'm gone, around a corner, over a fence, through a narrow alley—

—and onto an empty street with an officer at either end.

Seriously?

Both cops charge at me, but before I can find yet another alternate route, an arm darts out from the alley I just came from and yanks me back, then behind a dumpster. I'm all but thrown against the cold stone wall—by Ania. Thank the stars.

"Our client actually let you leave to rescue me?" I ask through gasping breaths.

"Kindly *fuck off* while your best friend is trying to save your ass."

I bite back a grin. Ania *never* swears like that. I'm proud to be responsible for it.

Between us, her fingers fly as she weaves together a quick and simple concealment spell. Plum-colored strands of obscuraz pour from her fingertip implants, coming together in a tightly knit pattern. She ties it off with a quick yank, then rips it in half and shoves half of it into my hands, keeping half for herself.

"Stay absolutely still," she murmurs.

The spell crumbles into faintly glowing sparks as it takes effect, and I press back against the alley wall and breathe as shallowly as I can. Ania does the same, taking my hand and holding tight as all three cops converge on the alley. The woman who chased me across the rooftops does a slow scan of the entire alley, sharp eyes looking for any sign of our whereabouts. She takes a step closer to the dumpster, squinting at something on the ground, then peeking around behind the thing until she's looking right through us.

One of the other cops calls out to her, and I flinch, my shoe making the faintest scuffing sound . . . but she pulls away and turns back to her counterparts, meeting them back in the middle of the alley. They talk too quietly for me to hear well, but it sounds like they're trying to assign blame for losing me. Just as I'm starting to go light-headed from the lack of breath, they turn to leave, disappearing back in the direction I ran from.

Once they've been gone for two full minutes, I shake off Ania's hand and step away to get some space, taking a few deep breaths.

"Thanks," I say, still keeping an eye on the mouth of the alley. "Let's get to Mattie's. I want this maz off my back and those credits in our account."

Ania nods vaguely, zoned out in that way that means she's doing something on her lenses, her slim legs crossed at the ankles, where expensive skinny jeans and low boots let a strip of warm brown skin peek out. The yellowy light from the streetlamp shines through her hazy cloud of curls, wrapping each dark strand in threads of gold. We seriously just left the sewers forty-five minutes ago—how the *hell* does she look so put together? She must have ditched her sewage-covered rain boots somewhere.

Ania snaps back to reality and dodges my gaze in a way that I know means she was just messaging Jaesin about me. She turns to lead the way back to our drop point, and I scowl at the back of her head, dashing off a quick message to Remi as I follow.

(private) you: Hey, sorry, ran into some trouble. It's fine now. Heading to the drop point.
(private) Remi: GOOD because I have something that will make you die
DIZZY LOOK

The next message is a link to a news article: "Tifa and the Flower Girls to Play Two Surprise Shows in Kyrkarta on Aeraday and Firaday." A photo quickly follows: Remi with their hands pressed to their cheeks, screaming at the camera.

(private) Remi: WE ARE GOING
I'm heckin serious I don't care what Jaesin and Ania say

I bite my lip and clear the notification away, swallowing down the knot in my throat. Of course we'll go. One last chance to dance with Remi before they leave, the bass pounding in our chests, singing in our blood. I start to reply, then delete it.

Later. I'll deal with it later.

We cross the block to the next intersection, moving slowly to take advantage of any lingering effects from the concealment spell. It won't do any good if we run screaming down the street, but if we're chill, it might help an errant gaze or two slide past us. A few minutes of tense silence later, we arrive at a nondescript elevator that takes us up twenty levels.

A quick walk across one of the thousands of breezeways connecting the buildings of Kyrkarta, and we come to a darkened flower shop with loud, busy arrangements filling the front window. The CLOSED message glows bright in one corner, but the door opens anyway, held by a guy a few years older than us with tawny skin and *way* more piercings than me. Mattie, our client for this job. He's got a siphoning crew of his own, but they couldn't get it together in time to pull off this job for whatever reason, so they contracted it out to us. Their loss.

It's a big haul, and the particular combo of maz

strains they requested took us to a part of the city we'd never hit before. Maz Management Corporation's system looks the same no matter where you are, though: pipes in sewers, hiking through sludge, Ania and Jaesin watching our backs while I hack the security and Remi draws out the maz in manageable quantities. We got it done, despite the trouble at the end.

"Where's the goods?" Mattie asks as he leads us into the back. His sweet old mother who owns the shop would skin him alive if she knew that "staying late to clean the shop" actually meant "conducting illegal business in the stockroom." I let the pack slip down my arms and swing it up onto a work top littered with trimmed stems, wilting leaves, and shed petals.

"I didn't realize I was supposed to walk in juggling the vials for all to see," I say with an eyeroll, pulling a hard plastic case from the bag. I click the latches open and lift the top to reveal five clear vials nestled in their foam padded spots. Each one glows with contained threads of maz, coiled as tight as each strain allows. Our very last haul. Thick bronze terraz, sparking green vitaz, some of the same hazy purple obscuraz Ania used earlier.

Mattie picks up each one and inspects them all carefully, like he's some kind of master maz connoisseur. I bite the inside of my lip to hold in a sigh of annoyance. A less obnoxious client would have been a much nicer way to end our siphoning career together. So much for going out in a grand blaze of glory, walking off into the sunset with our riches as a team, the latest overplayed graduation anthem seeing us off.

Then again, this group has always been a mess, and I'm pretty sure it's my fault.

Epic Group Chat: LAST JOB EVER Edition
Remi: Are you dead, Dizzy?
Ania, are they killing her?
Ania: Remains to be seen. She's getting fussy. Will report back.

Fussy? I burn a hole in the side of Ania's face with my glare. I'm actually going to be forced to murder her.

Jaesin: I call dibs on her deck
Remi: Please, she probably has that thing programmed to self-destruct if she dies
You know what she's got on there
Jaesin: No, I don't
and I don't want to

The corner of my mouth pulls up in a half smile. I quite enjoy this reputation of mine, at least partially deserved. My files are largely boring records of which public officials are breaking their spousal agreements, local celebrities' secret dating profiles, and the internet search histories of Kyrkarta's most prominent business leaders. I suppose some people might find it valuable information, but gathering it all is just a way to keep myself entertained when I can't sleep.

"Oi, what's with this one?" Mattie snaps, pulling my attention away from the group chat. He holds one of the vials of obscuraz between his thumb and middle finger, tilting it this way and that to let the light filter through the strands. I see what he means. It's a notably different shade than the other vials of the same maz, like a few of the threads have turned a brighter violet-purple.

"Did you bring me contaminated maz?" he says, shoving the vial in my face. My stomach turns, and I jerk away, putting the table between us.

"That's what came out of the tap point, Mattie," I shoot back, working to keep my expression under control. "We went where you told us. MMC's pipes are clean. It's not contaminated."

Even as I say it, as I *know* it's true, the worry begins to boil in my stomach. Remi is the only one who ever has contact with the maz we siphon off from MMC's pipes, and they were diagnosed with the spellplague when they were eight. Would they even know if the maz was contaminated? It's not like you can get infected again if you're already ill.

Mattie growls and puts the vial down with the others. "I'm only paying half for that one, and if it *is* contaminated, I'll put the word out, believe it."

Ania meets my gaze, then looks at the ceiling, her subtle way of rolling her eyes among company. We're never working a job again *period*, no matter how much I might want to, so he can shove his empty threats.

"Fine, yes, half for that one vial," I say. "Can we please close this deal now? We've got places to be."

Mattie scowls but pulls out his deck and sets to work on the credit transfer. A moment later, a transaction notification pops up on my lenses. Payment cleared. Our bank account once again has more than two digits.

"Pleasure doing business," I say, throwing the vial case back in my bag and walking away, Ania on my heels, before Mattie can find another excuse to complain. As I reach the elevator, I bring the group chat back on-lens with a grin.

Epic Group Chat: LAST JOB EVER Edition

you: Against everyone's better judgment, he did not kill me. We have our money

Remi: DIZZY YESSSSSSS
SHE LIVES

Jaesin: Thank god, now we can CELEBRATE

Ania: Let the Grand Farewell Tour commence!

you: You all were in mortal peril today too, you know

Ania: Yeah, but *we* don't inspire murdery feelings in everyone we meet

Remi: Yikes, shots fired

I shove Ania's shoulder, and the elevator fills with our laughter. I can't wait to get home, even as I feel a weird sort of nostalgia for those little vials of maz we just left behind. Ten years of friendship, two years running jobs together, and now it's over. The others are understandably ecstatic, brimming over with the thrill of getting away with one last haul and looking forward to their shiny futures. Futures that require moving away.

In seven days.

Hence our Grand Farewell Tour of Kyrkarta: seven nights, seven locations, one amazing last hurrah before we go our separate ways.

Before they all move away and abandon me here, more like.

Ania startles me out of my mood with a quick excited double clap.

"I have a surprise for you," she says, throwing an arm around me and leaning down to rest her head against the top of mine. I cringe but endure her cuddling. Might as well take it while I can.

"I hate surprises," I say. "What is it?"

She grins and holds up one hand, waggling her fingers as the elevator stops and the doors slide open. Her wrist and the inside of each finger are lined with thin metal, unassuming, but actually packed with bend sensors, accelerometers, and other techy bits. The tip of each finger ends in a small implanted extruder that, by her command, releases threads of whatever maz she had loaded into the chambers strapped to the underside of her wrist. She doesn't have the natural ability to work maz with her bare hands, like Remi does, but she's good with her hardware. She's had her maz license since the day she turned eighteen—not that the lack of a license stopped her before. Not with me as a friend. I may not be able to work with maz myself, but I can build ware better than anything her mommy and daddy can find in an overpriced shop. Her ware is a Dizmon Hela original, and I'm proud of my work.

"This is a fun surprise, promise," she says, flipping her hand over to glance at her nails instead. "I went in for an A-level maz certification practice test today, and I think I pushed it a little too hard. The fifth position flow was kinda weird and uneven during our job. Wanna fix it before we go out tonight?"

I perk right up, then narrow my eyes. "You know I do, but don't think this gets you off my list. *Fussy?* Are you serious?"

"I love you, Dizzard Lizard," she sings, syrupy sweet, and I fight down an unexpected surge of anger. She obviously doesn't love me enough to *not leave*. None of them do. I want to sink in to that anger, to let its talons grip tight and pierce and fill my veins with heat. It's right there under the surface, all the time, just waiting for the wrong turn of phrase, the wrong change of subject.

But if I say anything, I'll only lose them all sooner.

My shoulders slump, and I take three long, deep breaths, one for each word.

Let. It. Go.

"Come on, then," I say, beckoning her forward. "Let's see what poison Jaesin has on the cooker tonight, and I'll take a look at that mix sensor before we go out. You didn't notice it until we were already in the middle of the job?"

She hums in agreement but doesn't elaborate as we cross into the crowded intersection at Four Bridges, where the three rivers converge at the business sector. Too many voices clamoring for airspace, and Ania hates to shout. We pass glowing storefronts nestled in the bottom floors of bulky office buildings, offering everything from maz tech to spellweaving services, rare foods to custom aesthetic implants. We don't need any of it, of course, and I wouldn't be caught dead paying business-sector prices even if we did. We already have Ania for a techwitch, and Remi the spellweaving prodigy, and I have all our hardware needs covered. Jaesin rounds out the group with most of the mundie skills, like keeping us from starving to death. And hitting people. But only sometimes.

We pass into the slightly more run-down part of town I call home a few minutes later, and the Cliffs, the dorm complex I live in, comes into view. With the chaos of business behind us, Ania finally answers my question.

"Yeah, I had some magnaz loaded in fifth position, and by the time I finished setting up our wards at the draw point, it wasn't flowing as easily as the rest. I was having to force it a little more than normal, and I can't stop thinking I'm gonna pull on that thread so hard I'll blow my own hand off."

"Nah, I'll take care of that. If it's not the sensor, it's the extruder, and both are easy enough to fix. Should be no problem to finish it before we go out tonight."

Out to one of Ania's fancy clubs, where we've been begging her to take us for ages, for night one of seven. The beginning of the end. My stomach sours.

Then the ground . . . shivers.

Ania and I stop dead. Wait, absolutely still.

Another tremble, longer. Definitely not imagined. Our eyes meet as the ground shifts under our feet, harder this time, a threat.

A promise.

Another earthquake.

We run.

TWO

IT'S THE FOURTH EARTHQUAKE THIS month, and honestly, I'm *done*.

Ania and I book it toward the nearest bit of open greenspace, a park at the corner of the block that's the sole splash of natural color among the city's shivering, flexing high-rises. The trees were cleared away years ago—too much of a hazard in a quake—leaving nothing but a wide open area. Sirens wail in the distance, and high overhead, the aircar and RidePod traffic drifts to a halt. Mostly. Emergencies have a way of bringing out the worst in some people.

An aircar with the loud lime-green markings of Kyrkarta City Law peels off from the roof-height emergency lanes and dives, sliding to a stop near the park with a high-pitched whine of protest from its ground brakes. I groan. Didn't I just leave these jerks behind?

People pour from the surrounding buildings and streets, running in blatant defiance of every public safety advisory, because humanity sucks. Two officers climb out of the aircar, a techwitch and a spellweaver, judging by their rank patches. The tall, dark-haired one weaves a quick amplification spell, then presses the glowing tangle of threads to their throat.

"Please proceed calmly to the ward zone," the low voice booms, echoing off the surrounding buildings. "If your building is reinforced, stay indoors and leave the ward zone open for others."

Hah. Right. People are assholes, as the officers quickly discover when a shoving match breaks out between two men at a bottleneck between parked vehicles. They dive in to separate the instigators as another threatening rumble vibrates through the soles of my boots. I look toward home, my gaze magnetically drawn to the grimy window of my top-floor apartment.

At the end of the street, the hastily erected buildings that make up the Cliffs pulse with a deep reddish glow as their structural reinforcement spells activate. The sheer, featureless walls they're named for flare bright for a single second, then immediately begin to fade as they burn through what little energy is left in the spells. The buildings were cobbled together from whatever crappy materials were on hand after the spellplague, sloppy constructions of wood and brick built without the aid of maz in the days when anti-maz paranoia was at its height. They won't last much longer.

But two of my closest friends are in one of those

buildings, in the tiny flat we share, making us food and getting ready to go out tonight. The fading red spells burn a permanent warning onto my eyelids.

I can't help them. I can't do anything at all.

"Diz!" Ania shouts, seizing my arm. "They'll be fine, they know what to do. Come on!"

I wrench my gaze away from the blocky towers, so out of place among the unyielding steel buildings around them, and give in to Ania's pull.

We reach the greenspace ahead of the crowds and head straight for the warded area in the center, large enough to hold maybe two hundred people. It's marked off by small solar-powered lights that light up orange to guide people to safety. Ania and I set up at the outer edge, where she crouches down and touches one hand to a glowing line etched into the ground. The edge of the ward circle. A twitch of her fingers, a complicated movement, and she draws away with a threadbare piece of the woven spell, hanging from the tip of her finger like a ragged spider-web. It casts a sickly sort of gray-blue pall over her skin as her eyes scan the pattern, no doubt identifying weaknesses and formulating a plan to reinforce it. Shielding and warding spells are her jam.

"I really hope your ware holds up," I murmur under my breath, needing to say it but not wanting to distract her. She shakes her head.

"It's only the magnaz that's acting up. This'll be

almost entirely terraz. Watch my back?"

"Always."

It's a good thing she's got terraz in today. She can only have five of the fourteen strains of maz loaded up at one time, max, and it would be a hella bad day if she had nothing but fire in all five chambers.

I shift from foot to foot with useless, nervous energy as more and more people, civilians and officers, arrive at the ward zone. The mundies like me stand helplessly in the center, while the techwitches and spellweavers gather around the edges to hold the wards together, pouring new energy into the complex system as the quake begins in earnest. Ania's gestures are graceful and restrained as she loops tangled threads of linkaz, the maz for tying and binding, around the strand she holds pinched in her left hand. Each loop is precisely formed, providing the structure that holds the wards together.

Once she's made twenty perfectly even loops, Ania taps the tip of her thumb to the pad of her middle finger, cutting off the linkaz and activating the flow of heavy shielding maz instead. The terraz flows out in thick bronze rivulets, slipping through each loop until, with a scooping gesture, Ania cuts off the strand and pulls the binder tight around it. It flares bright, then fades as the strands lock into the overall pattern, a shield between us and the threats outside.

Without even a second to admire her (honestly perfect)

work, she pulls up another worn piece of the weave and begins again, repairing it like a thrift-shop blanket. The weave isn't as tight as the threads that make up fabric, but it's far more intricate, the patterns so much more than a simple grid. Each section of threads crystallizes as they're tied off and finished, the energy slowly bleeding back into the system.

"Reloading," a techwitch calls from down the row, holding up his hands and stepping back from the wards. He's overly optimistic, though; trying to load new maz into his delicate hardware with the ground shaking is a near-impossible feat. A middle-aged woman takes his place, her ware old and grimy but the flow of her maz strong. Her clothes hang from her bones, ill-fitting and probably secondhand, and I press my lips together with sympathy. She probably can't afford to replace the maz she's using, but there she is, pitching in to help anyway. Around the circle, the natural spellweavers work their maz in a continuous flow, the threads drawn to their fingers like iron to a magnet. They're limited too, now that maz isn't ambient and abundant like it was before the plague, but at least they can burn straight through their entire stock all in one go.

Most of the time I'm glad I'm no good with maz. I've gotten used to being around it again, after the plague, but that doesn't mean I want my hands all up in it. But times like now, I almost wish I could do . . . something. Anything.

The earthquake builds with more and more frequent tremors, and before long the ground is bucking and rumbling worse than it has in over a month. Every earthquake brings a special kind of terror to native Kyrkartians. It was an earthquake that unleashed the spellplague ten years ago, cracking open the ground and bleeding some kind of contaminated maz into the world. A building could fall on us and the wards would shrug it off like dust, but none of it would matter if a fissure opened up and leaked raw tainted maz into the air inside our bubble. Boom, Spellplague II, Revenge of the Plague, spellsickness for all. No thanks.

The ground gives a particularly hard kick, and Ania stumbles backward, losing her grasp on the complicated pattern of the weave. I catch her around the waist and ease her back down into a crouch while she snatches at the falling threads. A few slip through her grasp, but she draws a little more linkaz from her reserves and renews her focus, exchanging threads with her neighbors to weave their sections tightly together. The gauzy web of spell threads glimmers in the night like moonlight off a spiderweb, the color shifting slowly from desaturated gray to a healthier blue-bronze. It's working.

I spit Ania's textured curls out of my mouth and brace her with my shoulder as the quake tries again and again to topple her back. Jaesin and his recruitment-poster shoulders would be so much better at this, but my little five-foot-four ass is all she has right now. At least she smells good, like expensive sweet perfume and freshly cast maz. The people around us stumble and slam together like an accidental mosh pit, stinking of fear and trampled dirt instead. Gross.

As always, it's only a matter of time before things turn ugly. As the wards' protective circle fills to capacity, people start shoving, crawling between legs, bordering on violent in their attempts to get inside. One man, his eyes unnaturally bright and sharp, gets right up in Ania's face and grabs her by the shoulder.

"Don't you dare touch her!" I snap in the man's face as he tries to yank her out of the circle.

"She can weave her own wards, she doesn't need to be inside," he snarls, and shoves her hard. She rolls and hits the ground on her back, hand held aloft to protect her ware, the breath rushing out of her in an audible *"Oooof!"*

Outside the wards.

No, he did *not*.

Before I can think it through, the man's blood is on my knuckles, and he staggers back with a hand cupped protectively over his wrecked nose. I shake out my fist to soothe the ache radiating up my arm and give him my best glare to convince him there's more where that came from, rather than the only sad punch I can manage. The weaver next to us shoves the guy the rest of the way out of the circle and summons up a burning stream of firaz from the stores in her bag, twirling it threateningly between three fingers.

"Back off unless you want a bomb shoved up your ass," she snarls, standing shoulder to shoulder with me.

"Two bombs," Ania adds as she struggles to get the shaking ground and her feet to cooperate. "You wanna explode from both ends?"

"Let's do it," the weaver says with a feral grin, one that Ania matches as she takes her place back in the circle.

Damn. Ania has clearly just met her long-lost sister, and together they are *fierce.*

As I brace Ania through another particularly rough tremor, the man falls on his ass, blood pouring over his fingers, and one of the officers finally intervenes.

"How's your supply doing?" I ask Ania as another techwitch steps back from the circle, run dry.

"Fine, unless this quake goes on much longer," she replies. "I filled up between the exam and our job."

Of course she did. *She* can afford it.

"Crack forming!" someone shouts behind me, and I whirl around in horror. The ground hasn't given way yet, but spiderweb lines dance underfoot—slim and deadly promises. Three weavers break off from the main circle and push their way through the crowd, working together on a single spell to knit the broken earth. Worse than the cracks, though, is the view beyond the circle: the Cliffs. The spells protecting it pulse once, twice . . . and fail.

The building goes dark.

Remi and Jaesin are defenseless.

"No!" I shout as the first of the bricks topple from the roof, smashing to the ground in a cloud of dust. I push past a young family clinging together and break away from the circle, the muscles in my legs burning as they struggle to compensate for the bucking ground. This is a long one—when will it end?

"Diz, wait!" I hear from behind me, just as an officer yells, "Back inside the wards!" I put on speed and leap over a mess of shattered glass and twisted metal. You'd think everything that could break would have already done it, but there's always something ready to give way, something on its last gasp of life. Every earthquake chips away a little more. It's only a matter of time before it takes down the Cliffs too.

Maybe only a matter of seconds.

I subvocalize a command to my deck and bring up a voice call, an obnoxious ringtone punctuating every second they don't answer.

"Pick up, damn it, where the hell *are* you?" I shout at Remi's photo, hovering in the corner of my vision.

It doesn't help. They don't answer.

I pull up Jaesin's comm code instead, but a yank on the back of my shirt collar drags me to a stop by the throat. I gasp, choke, and stumble back into Ania, just as the ground gives one more groaning shudder . . .

and splits open in front of me.

The fissure starts about fifty feet away, a single glowing wound in the street that leaks the barest spark of beautiful, benign-looking maz. Then . . . *CRACK!* Its jagged mouth splits open, grows longer, longer, racing toward me, spilling raw maz into the air. My breath comes fast, too fast, and my head swims.

Stars, not again. After surviving this long, am I really going to die like my parents, surrounded by glowing poison and—

Ania drags me aside as the crack advances and, with the most intense focus I've ever seen from her, draws a sharp shielding ward around us. She dumps huge amounts of expensive nullaz, the maz nullifier, into the air and street around us, going for quantity over quality as the deadly maz from the fissure lashes against her hastily erected barrier. She mutters formulas and patterns to herself as she opens a second stream of terraz, its earthy scent and grounding power infusing the pavement under our feet. A trickle of bright golden magnaz kicks the mix into high gear, raw power to strengthen the whole thing. A ham-fisted technique, but—

Wait.

My gaze flies to the ware on her right hand. The flow of magnaz comes out in fits and starts, like she mentioned earlier, and gets worse with every passing second.

"Ania, you're gonna break it!" I shout over the wail of more approaching sirens. The magnaz gives a worrying sputter, a flare of golden light.

"Yeah, well, you seem hell-bent on breaking *yourself*, and Remi and Jaesin aren't here, so someone has to save you from your own death wish."

"But that flow is—"

"—a lot harder to manage with you shouting in my ear. Shut. UP."

I shut up. How the tables have turned. The shield flickers with the golden light of the magnaz as Ania holds the whole thing in place through sheer force of will. Sweat glitters on the bridge of her nose as she stands her ground, unfazed even when a van comes plummeting from the airborne traffic lanes for a hard landing mere feet away from us. Bodies in Maz Management Corporation uniforms spill out, wrapped from head to toe in faintly shimmering layers of nullaz and hauling portable maz containment equipment onto the road.

The earthquake, being the petty bitch that it is, gives one last lurching kick that sends the crew tripping over their own equipment.

Then it slows . . . and stops.

The city is silent for a long moment as, all around, people hold their breath and look to one another with the heavy and unspoken question: Is it over? For real?

The answer comes moments later as the all-clear siren blares, and all the weavers and witches in sight let their wards fall.

"Finally," Ania grinds out, letting her own barrier fall too. The MMC workers tending to the fissure barely spare us a glance through the flickering haze of their containment field.

"Come on," I say, dragging Ania by the wrist, my bloody hand still aching from the punch. Her half-hearted protests are nothing but background noise as the Cliffs take up my whole field of view, consuming all scents, all sounds.

The Cliffs are composed of seven towering buildings, and Remi, Jaesin, and I live in building three, right along the roadside. The dumping ground for the city's plague orphans. Home shit home. The front door is partially blocked by a newly fallen chunk of stone railing that *was* part of the roof until ten minutes ago, but I slip through the narrow opening and into the mess of people and debris on the first floor.

The acrid scent of too many bodies in a building with terrible plumbing mixes with the burnt tang of dead structural maz in the air. Everyone's doors are thrown open as they mill about in the halls. The more altruistic among them check on neighbors and ask about injuries, while others dig through the rubble for usable bits to scavenge. Shana, a girl I sometimes go dancing with, dabs

30

at a bleeding cut on her roommate's forehead, oblivious as the vultures circle her open apartment door, scouting for any valuables in view. The few weavers who could afford some small amount of maz had apparently set up a warding circle in the front common area and are now demanding money from everyone who availed themselves of their services. If the markup is a little high, well, they just saved everyone's lives, didn't they?

My deck buzzes as a notification pops up in my vision, and I nearly choke in my haste to open it. Remi or Jaesin finally getting back to me? Or calling for help?

I missed vid call
(private) Davon: You okay? I heard there was a crack near your building.
Vid me. I'm worried about you.

A trickle of cool relief soothes a fraction of the anxiety gripping my lungs. My one bit of real family left in this world, my cousin who's more like my big brother in every way that matters. I assumed he'd be fine, inside the well-warded Maz Management Corporation IT center he works at, but still. One down, two to go. No time to respond, not now.

I shoulder my way past our downstairs neighbor (age seventeen, pronouns he/him, straight passing grades, blares porn at all hours) and leave the whole clamoring scene behind. Ania sticks close, one hand fisted in the back of my hoodie so we don't get separated. She sticks out like a gleaming jewel in the dirt here, like an easy mark, though she's anything but. No one would dare mess with her. It is *known*—she's ours. Me, Remi, and Jaesin, we have her back. To mess with her is to mess with us.

Assuming Remi and Jaesin are still okay, that is.

My pulse is a choking throb in the base of my throat as I skip the lift and race up the stairs two at a time, weaving around occasional rubble and coughing the dust from my lungs. The whole building gives an ominous creak with every gust of wind, speeding my steps faster even as my chest burns.

Remi. Remi. Remi.

I burst through the stairwell door for the top floor and don't slow until I reach the door to our flat. My hand slips on the door controls, the handle beeping in protest when it can't read my fingerprints. I take a breath and force myself to slow down, give the door a second to read me, then throw it open.

"Remi! Jaesin! Are you—"

The words die on my lips.

Remi sits upside-down on the couch, their back on the seat and their feet propped up against the wall like always, tossing a brightly sparkling ball of sunnaz from hand to hand. A breathing mask is fitted over their nose and mouth, glittering green with the aerosolized vitaz they breathe in, but it's nothing out of the ordinary. Just their nightly treatment. They roll their head to face me, their expression turning quizzical as they slide the mask down and switch off the nebulizer.

"Oh, hey, Diz. Why is your hand bloody?"

The urgent pressure in my chest unwinds in an instant.

Anger fills its place nicely. My lip curls into a snarl.

"*Oh, hey, Diz?* Really? Did you even notice the earthquake? The building's reinforcement spells failed."

They shrug and resume their one-person game of toss.

"Yeah, but Ania renewed our interior walls earlier this week, and I kept an eye on things during the quake. Everything's fine. Jaesin's making dinner before we leave for the club, you want some? What are you wearing tonight?"

I close my eyes and breathe.

They're okay. Jaesin and Remi, they're *fine*.

And they're *assholes*.

THREE

I WIPE MY BLOODY KNUCKLES off on my pant leg and slam the door as soon as Ania is through, triggering the flat's cheerful welcome protocol, complete with my latest modifications.

"Good evening, Supreme Overlord Dizmon. The time is seven fifty-seven."

"Thank you, Uni," I reply.

I set my bag down inside the front door and take off my boots, arranging them in a neat line next to Jaesin's sleek and sporty running shoes and Remi's turquoise sneakers. A holdover from my dad, apparently a thing with my grandparents who lived in a city on the Small Continent. The front room of our apartment is a bit of a disaster, but an organized disaster, and I like it that way.

In one corner is the kitchenette, where Jaesin stands in his neatly pressed going-out shirt. His hair is done somewhere between casual handsome bedhead and total mess, and he's frowning into a skillet as he pokes something around inside. Another experiment for dinner, then. Great. It'll either be amazingly delicious or horrifically, bowel-shakingly terrible. Ooh, the anticipation. He doesn't even bother looking up from his cooking as he welcomes me home in his usual fashion.

"Dizzy. My dear. My darling. If you get us evicted for messing with the flat's network yet again, a week before we move out, I will do unspeakable things to your dinner."

I roll my eyes. "Unicorn Sparkles McSunshine, will you tell Jaesin to please eat his own dick?"

"Mister Jaesin, Supreme Overlord Dizmon requests that you please eat your own dick," the flat cheerfully relays.

Jaesin barks a laugh and replies silently with a single olive-skinned middle finger. The corner of my mouth tugs up automatically, but I force the grin away. I'm mad at him, damn it. He should learn to answer his calls. Ania swoops past me to peek over Jaesin's shoulder at the food, conveying "I am above your plebian nonsense" with every step.

None of this fazes Remi in the slightest, who still lies upside down, fishing under the couch for a vial from their maz stash. Why they won't just work at a desk, I don't understand. They've twisted the bright ball of maz they were tossing around into a web strung between the fingers of one hand, pulled thin and woven into a complex improvised pattern only they can understand. There are spellweavers, and then there's Remi, weaving prodigy, genius on a whole other level.

The string lights on the wall over the couch and the faint glow cast by the weave play on their cheekbones and the tip of their nose, and shine off lips that have been licked in concentration too many times. Their face is still a bit thinner than usual from the weight they lost earlier this summer, when their illness flared up again. It's generally well controlled, so long as they're super careful to stick to the diet, exercise plan, and many daily treatments prescribed by their care team. The end of the school year and graduation had been too much on top of everything else, though, and they'd suffered for it. I don't totally understand it—some kind of cell count gets high or something, and suddenly they're guaranteed to get the next infection that's going around, and fighting it off is *rough*. They were laid up for almost a month.

Each time is utterly terrifying. The spellplague killed so many people within minutes, hours, or days of exposure, but the few who survived the initial infection live in a precarious limbo with their illness that I can only imagine. Remi has a pretty normal life now (illegal activities aside), but it'll get worse with age. Everyone starts to decline eventually. The only question is how many years it'll be before it happens. It's rare for someone with the spellplague to live past thirty.

Today seems okay in general, though. Remi's eyes are

bright and alert, their cheeks flushed with healthy color. They came straight home with Jaesin after the job to get some rest before tonight, and it seems to be doing them good. They'll still take it easy tonight, I bet, but at least it doesn't seem to be a crash day.

"How long till dinner?" I ask, tearing my eyes away from Remi.

Jaesin snorts. "Ten minutes? Depends on if Remi can let me work."

At that, a fat golden bee zips across the room and rams itself into the back of Jaesin's head, then zips right back to Remi's hands, where it dissolves back into individual threads. Jaesin startles so badly that his cheap plastic stirring spoon flies out of his hand and splatters the wall with thin brown sauce, only just missing Ania's face.

"Damn it, Remi," he shouts, though the effect is ruined by his laughter. He wipes a bit of sauce off his cheek and licks it off his finger, raises an eyebrow in pleased surprise, and goes back to stirring.

I catch Ania's gaze and roll my eyes, then beckon her over to my little corner of the flat, flicking on the salvaged lamp mounted to the wall above my desk. Light floods over the workspace, a natural daylight sort of wash that keeps my eyes from going all crossed while I stare at extremely tiny screws and wires. A plain brown shipping box with my name on the top teeters on the one empty corner of the desk. I allow a tiny smile at the return address, letting an unusual warmth fill my chest for just a moment. Davon's graduation present. Remi, Jaesin, and I can never afford to give each other gifts, but ever since Davon aged out of the orphan care system and got a real job, he's never missed an occasion. I leave it for the moment. If I'm going to get Ania's ware fixed before we go out, I need to get started. My tools are everywhere, but my fingers find the correct screwdriver and a set of fine needle-nose pliers with barely a glance.

"Take off your ware and put your hand on the work top," I order, then slip a pair of magnifying glasses on, settling them on top of my head. A faint snort comes from across the room, but I hold up a finger to Remi without looking over.

"Not a word."

I click on the magnifier's built-in light and accept Ania's wrist cuff with a ginger touch, then sync my deck with her fingertip implants. I know this tech inside and out—I built it, after all—so I know exactly how delicate it can be. Not that Ania ever treats it that way. I set it on the tabletop, pull the magnifiers over my eyes, and lean in to focus on the minuscule screws holding the cuff's access panel in place. The precise work makes my punching hand ache, but complaining about it will only draw a lecture from Jaesin about how to throw a proper punch. Again.

Across the room, there's a sudden rush of sizzling, a pained yelp, then water dribbling in the sink. Ania's low chuckle signals an impending fight.

"You planning to poison us tonight, Jaesin?" she asks, though she always scolds me for saying the same thing.

Jaesin growls. "Don't tempt me. I don't see you over here trying to cook. Doesn't your family have a chef?"

Ania must be tired of us taking shots at her over her family's money, but she never shows it, just accepts them gracefully. Which is even more maddening, to be honest. I tune out their bickering and zone into the job at hand. Access panel off. Drain what little is left in the maz chambers into catch jars, manually trigger the extruders seated inside the tips of Ania's fingers. Watch the diagnostics spill across my vision via my contact lenses.

Ania falls silent above me, her not-flirting with Jaesin apparently finished. They're the weirdest exes of all time. When I peek up at her, though, I find her looking back at me from the corner of her eye, hesitant. I know that look.

"Diz," she murmurs, quiet enough to be concealed by Jaesin's clanging. "Why don't we all stay in to watch a movie or something tonight instead of going out?"

I speak without hesitation. "I think you should give Remi the choice and go with whatever they say. You can't just dictate what you think is best for them. I guarantee, you try to tell them what they can and can't do one more time, you'll have a hot ball of firaz in your face. Burn those pretty eyebrows right off."

Ania unconsciously lifts her free hand to smooth over one perfectly plucked brow, frowning. "I know. But we just got back from a job, and we have other things we wanted to do this week. I'm not sure it's a good idea."

She isn't getting it. I need her to really hear me, so I wipe the smirk off my face, set down my tools, and blink away the text on my contacts so I can meet her eyes uninhibited.

"Look, it's their decision. They'll appreciate having the option, I think, but if they say they feel up to going out, you have to leave it at that." I flick my gaze over to Remi, whose shirt is slowly losing the war with gravity, revealing a strip of pale stomach. I look quickly away. "Is this just your way of getting out of taking us to Nova again? You ashamed to be seen with your broke-ass plague-orphan charity cases?"

Ania huffs. "I'm not going to let you pick a fight. Besides, what if it's closed for earthquake damage? That wouldn't be *my* fault."

I bring up a quick search and hit their net site, then share the view with Ania.

"Open for business. Any other excuses?"

She pouts in silence for a long moment, so I blink the deck display back onto my lenses and analyze the diagnostics from her ware. The first two maz extruders are fine, the ones that handled the terraz and linkaz she used during the quake. She's apparently been playing with fire recently, because she has firaz loaded in the third position. It's a bit uneven, but barely so; she probably hasn't even noticed. An easy fix. Her usual position-four obscuraz is fine, but sure enough, in the final spot, the magnaz extruder fires in fits and starts, the computer sometimes simulating a strong flow and sometimes the barest gossamer thread. It's all gummed up, probably hasn't been cleaned properly in months. No wonder Ania's having trouble weaving with it on the fly. I click my tongue at her the way my mother used to do to me.

"Honestly, princess, you are the most high-maintenance slob I've ever met."

"Hey!"

Too easy sometimes. I pour a shallow dish of a gentle scouring chem and guide Ania's fingertips into the solution with easy pressure, then turn my attention back to the lines of code.

"Don't move. Gotta flush out the blockage, and it's gonna take a few minutes. I'm gonna tweak the programming in your cuff a bit so if the extruders start to clog again, it'll trigger a message to get you to bring it over for maintenance so it doesn't get this bad again."

I level a look at her. "Do not. Let it get. This bad. Again. Rebuilding this thing from scratch would take longer than you have the patience for."

"Thanks, Diz. You're the best," she says, leaning

down to give me a peck on the forehead. I swat her away.

"Thank me by taking better care of your ware."

And by not leaving.

My gaze drifts back to Davon's gift, perched on the corner of my desk. Nothing for me to do while the chems work their magic on Ania's ware, so I pull it into my lap and snag my knife to slice at the tape. With a furtive glance at Ania, I swivel my chair slightly away and pull the box flaps barely open, just enough to peek inside. To my complete horror, my lip wobbles when I see the contents. He's included some of his standard practical gifts—a new multitemp soldering iron, some assorted computer components, socks—but nestled in the bottom is something wrapped in delicate tissue paper. Written on the tape that holds it together are three short words in Davon's terrible handwriting: *I'll never forget.*

My fingers brush over the paper, hesitant, heart in my throat. Whatever it is, it won't be easy. I take a deep steadying breath through my nose and slip my finger under the tape, tugging gently, tearing the tiniest bit of paper possible along with it. I fold back the delicate tissue and smooth it away from the gift, biting my lip hard to keep control.

Three numbers, cast in silver metal. Two, one, five. At one point, these numbers were illuminated with sunnaz, all the better to see them at night, but that maz has long since faded away. I'd recognize them anywhere, though.

He'd pried the house numbers from beside the front door of the house I lived in when my parents were alive. Where Davon lived right next door, my constant companion from birth. The house where . . .

The tears rush up so fast I barely have a chance to squeeze my eyes shut before they fall. I jam the numbers and paper back into the box and take long, slow breaths in through my nose until I've got hold of myself again. My breathing is still ragged as I fold the flaps of the box back up and place it gingerly on the far corner of my desk, away from Ania. It's simultaneously the best and worst gift I've ever received, and Davon knew just how much it would mean. I can clearly imagine mounting the numbers to the wall above my new desk, in the new apartment I'll be able to afford with the salary of the job he's gotten for me.

The job I still haven't accepted.

My eyes cut back to Ania, who watches me cautiously but knows better than to say a word. I need to tell the crew about the job offer. I should've done it a week ago, but as soon as I tell them, that'll be it. It'll definitely be happening. I'll be staying, they'll be going, and the door will be permanently closed on any chance of our group sticking together.

Unless they change their minds, an insidious voice whispers in the back of my head. Unless you tell them you're taking the job, and they say, "Noooo, Dizzy, you have to come with us," and you say, "I can't, I could never leave Kyrkarta, it's home," and they say, "Fine, then we're staying here with you. Remi will go to Kyrkarta University instead, and Ania too, and Jaesin will go to work for MMC with you even though it'll make Remi mad for a bit, and everything will be fine. You'll all get a new flat together in a better part of town, and it'll be just like it is now. But better. Maybe Jaesin and Ania will get back together. And maybe, after a while, when you're ready . . . maybe . . ."

"Diz?" Ania says, her voice sharp. She's obviously already said my name at least twice, trying to rescue me from the depths of my own head.

"Sorry. Zoned into my lenses." Common enough, easy to believe.

Ania hums skeptically. "Did something happen with Davon? Is he okay? You were staring awfully hard at that package he sent."

"It's nothing," I say.

Her voice takes on a warning tone. "Diz. Be real."

Without warning, all of it bubbles up inside me, acid eating at my throat, more anger than anything else.

"Fine," I snap. "Fine. I'll tell you all after dinner."

"Oh no," she says. "Now you *have* to tell me."

"*After* dinner." I shouldn't have said anything. She's pathologically incapable of waiting.

44

"No, *not* after dinner," she snaps, and I wince at the volume.

"Shut *up*," I hiss, and pull her fingertips from the chem wash, patting them dry with a microfiber cloth. The second I have the maz reloaded and the access panel closed, she snatches her hand back and props it on her hip.

"Nope," she says, "no way, you are *not* going to make me sit through dinner and keep my mouth shut until you decide to tell us."

"Tell us what?" Jaesin says as he places a giant serving bowl of something garlicky in the center of the living-room floor with a clunk, barely muffled by the cheap, paper-thin carpet. Remi slithers off the couch with as little movement as possible, their head and shoulders melting onto the creaky wood floor until the rest of their body follows. When they finally tumble upright on their knees, their cool gray eyes immediately lock onto mine.

"Yeah, Dizzy, tell us *what*? Something else happen before Ania caught up with you today?" they ask, shifting their gaze to Ania. "I told you she needed a chaperone. Should have stuck with her after we left the sewers."

"Hey, I am perfectly responsible!" I protest, then purse my lips. "There is something I should tell you all, though."

The others look on expectantly.

Turns out those breathing exercises my therapist

taught me make a great stalling tactic.

"Can't we just sit down and have dinner first?"

Jaesin smiles as we all grab our cushions and arrange ourselves around the bowl of . . . whatever it is. He passes me one of our mismatched thrift-store plates and nods, a bit of his straight black hair falling over his forehead, still flecked with sauce.

"Sure, Diz. We can have dinner."

I sigh. *Saved.*

". . . *while* you talk," he finishes, and I sag in defeat. Curse Jaesin and his dad maneuvers.

"Can I at least know what we're eating first?"

"Food," Jaesin, Remi, and Ania all chorus together, and Remi and Ania burst into giggles at Jaesin's long-suffering expression. No one should achieve that level of dadness at age eighteen. It should be illegal.

"Okay, fine. *Fine.*" I serve myself first from the bowl first, to buy a little time to arrange my thoughts. The bowl is divided into six wedges, each piled high with a different thing. I scoop some fluffy grains onto my plate first, then add crisp baby greens, cubes of spicy-smelling tofu with Jaesin's experimental brown sauce, long threads of thin-sliced root vegetables, and drizzle a milky-white dressing over it all. It actually looks and smells legitimately delicious, and fits into Remi's immune-support diet. Go, Jaesin.

The others take turns making their plates to their own

personal tastes, all in totally unusual silence. Great. Now the whole thing has been built up so much it's primed to blow up into maximum awkwardness. Ania was right. I should have told them as soon as we got home and confirmed they weren't dead, gotten it over with. Should have told them last week.

Remi especially is going to lose it. They are *militant* in their hatred of Maz Management, which confuses me to no end. It seems super straightforward to me. Big earthquake, contaminated maz everywhere, spellplague. MMC cleaned up the contamination and rebuilt the city, helped create programs for all the plague orphans, but has to charge for maz to pay for the systems and people needed for such a huge project. What else were they supposed to do? It sucks, and people have had to learn to live with a lot less maz now that it's not just freely available everywhere, but what's the alternative? I'd think Remi, of all people, would understand.

Well, nothing for it. Time to submit myself to the will of the people. My brain helpfully dredges up every single silently rehearsed conversation I've come up with over the past few weeks, but none of them are likely to play out, and certainly not the optimistic ones. There won't be any happy-family-staying-together result here. Only one thing's guaranteed: Remi's gonna be pissed.

I take a breath and forge ahead.

"I was offered a job at MMC. In their IT department.

Cybersecurity, if you can believe it. Davon got me the interview, and they called me last week."

Nope, never mind, forget telling them last week—I should have stuck to my original plan and told them after they'd all moved to Jattapore and I'd already taken the job. When it wouldn't matter anymore. Judging by their expressions, I'm in for a long night of glaring.

"MMC?" Remi finally says, their face pinched with anger. "Maz Management, Diz, really?"

I groan. Totally called it.

"Look," I say, cutting off their tirade before it can begin. "Being all high and mighty won't pay my bills once you all move to Jattapore and I have to get a new flat by myself."

And there it is, the giant neon elephant in the room we've all been silently tiptoeing around, making plans and celebrating futures but never *quite* acknowledging the core truth: they're leaving, I'm staying, and this family's days are numbered in the single digits.

I don't want to fight, but if they're going to poke at me, you better believe I'm gonna fire back. "Besides, what was everyone else up to after the spellplague? It was MMC that figured out how to stop the contamination while everyone was dying. MMC figured out what to do with all us sad little orphans. MMC did research on the earthquakes. MMC is researching a cure. Maybe I want to be part of all that."

"Diz," Jaesin says warningly.

Remi waves him off. "I'm not just some sad little spell-sick orphan. I'm a spellweaver. Do you have any idea what it's like to be cut off from something that's like . . ." They gesture wildly at the air around them, air that once held ambient traces of maz at all times. "Like breathing, Diz. I may as well be a techwitch now. No offense, Ania. What you do is amazing, but for spellweavers it's like walking around with earmuffs and super-thick gloves on all the time. I can't *feel* it everywhere anymore. It's . . . weird."

Ania wisely keeps her mouth shut. She still has her parents, *and* their money. She has no trouble getting whatever amount of maz she needs. For us, for Remi, we have to steal it. That's how we got started siphoning maz from MMC's pipes in the first place. I sigh and rub a hand over the shaved side of my head.

"I get all that, Remi, I do. But we were ground zero for the worst plague this world has ever seen, and when the whole city was dying, MMC gave people jobs, and bought toys and books for us, and made sure we went to school. That all costs money. I'm not saying they should charge as much as they do, but I'm saying . . ."

And there's the anger, back again, fresh and hot. Remi is leaving anyway, so what do they care if I work for MMC?

"You know what, I don't have to justify myself. I need a job. I got a job offer. And I'd be damn good at it."

Remi scoffs and stands, leaving their half-eaten dinner on the floor.

"Sure. Yeah. Whatever you say, Diz," they say.

The rest of us finish our dinner in tense silence. Maybe if Remi was staying in town I would work a little harder to keep the peace. Or maybe it's better this way. Start cutting my ties now so it'll suck less seven days from now. Maybe our black-market gigs are all that's been keeping us together the past two years, and now that they're over, *we're* over. Maybe we should have drifted apart long ago.

Once the dishes are stacked and Ania is elbows-deep in dishwater, Remi comes back out of the bedroom doing their best interpretation of Ania's worship-me walk. My eyes nearly bug out of my head.

"You changed!" Ania says, her gesture flinging soapy water across the room. "You look great."

"You looked great before," I say, then quickly drop my gaze. We're supposed to be fighting. Those are definitely *not* fighting words.

But apparently it was the right thing to say, because a tinge of color blooms on Remi's cheeks. "Please. We're going to Club Nova. I'm gonna *bring it.*"

Well, I guess that answers the question of what we're doing tonight. It'll be impossible to stay mad with them slinking around, dancing in those tight wine-purple skinny jeans and that scoop-neck shirt that's already slipping off their shoulder.

I roll my eyes at myself. Woe is me, swoon. Whatever will I do? However will I manage? Get it together.

I nod decisively, get to my feet, and walk right past Remi into the single shared bedroom to pull my clothing drawer out from under my bed.

Apparently I need to *bring it* too.

FOUR

WE'VE BEEN AFTER ANIA TO get us into Nova for a year. Five minutes inside, though, and I'm already seriously doubting our choice.

There's sunnaz *everywhere*, glimmering decorative accents in the darkness, though it's the most expensive maz there is right now. Twinkling spellwoven lights cling high along the walls and hover overhead, shifting color in response to the music and falling in a glittering shower from the ceiling whenever the beat drops.

I can't help but hate the place a little bit. Their earthquake wards are probably in perfect shape too.

Maybe Ania was right not to bring us before. The gross display of excess wealth, especially after today's earthquake, gets under my skin in a big way. Remi forces me and Jaesin to listen to the morning maz update every day by blaring it so loud we can't plead ignorance. It reports the fluctuating prices and supply of the different strains of maz, and Remi's tactic has done its job. I've apparently absorbed enough of it to be righteously pissed.

It reminds me of the parties MMC throws once a year for all the good little orphans who manage to keep their grades up. I used to go every time. Free food, right? Jaesin came with me for a few years, but eventually he started staying home with Remi, who sat out in protest. Their loss. The parties always started out as civilized affairs. Speeches, bubbly fake champagne, and elderly employees looking kindly upon us poor orphan children. Two hours and significantly less adult supervision later, though, and they looked more like this—all decorum gone right out the window.

Beside me, a wide-eyed girl stares as someone goes tearing past with their hair on fire, screaming at the top of their lungs. I roll my eyes. Anyone who grew up in a group home or in the Cliffs has seen that illusion a hundred times. Maybe rich kids are on such a tight parental leash that they haven't been overexposed to every prank on the planet? But some things are universal: so long as one single person falls for it, the cycle will continue.

A techwitch from Ania's school who recently paid me to fix his hardware is repurposing the glowing maz decor for his own means. He's got a spellweaver buddy drawing the threads away from the wall, feeding them straight into his ware, and he spins the whole mess into some kind of rave hula hoop to accentuate his awful table dancing. The delicate tech protests his wild movements, but he either doesn't notice or doesn't care.

"You're gonna break it again if you keep pushing it like that, you know!" I shout over the music. I don't know why I bother. If he comes back to me for more repairs, it'll only build my post-graduation noodle fund. Seeing him abuse his (gorgeous, expensive) hardware like that hurts me deep in my broke-ass soul, though.

"What did you say was wrong this time?" Nash calls to me from his tabletop, his eyes never leaving his casting hands, completely unrepentant.

"Accelerometer needed recalibration." I flip the non-shaved side of my hair out of my eyes with a toss of my head and smile. The perfect picture of innocence. "Gotta quit jerking off with your ware on."

Nash scoffs in my general direction, swaying to the thumping beat of the music. "Well, fortunately I pay you to fix my ware, not teach me how to use it."

With an overdramatic flourish of his wrist, he activates the implant in his index finger again. It releases a thin, glowing strand of aeraz, which he weaves into a simple breeze pattern with exaggerated gestures like some kind of flailing, spell-casting octopus. Then, with a sharp snap of his forearm, he pulls the final thread taut and flings the spell in my direction—sending a gust of humid, sweat-scented wind straight at me, like jet-propelled dog breath to the face. The fragile strands of the spell crumble a moment later, but it's too late for the poor bartender. The spell wasn't that strong, but it was enough for the bottles lined up neatly on the bar to rattle, tip, and start a tragic domino effect.

I leap back as the bottles hit the floor with a loud *clink*, but thankfully don't break. A notification pops up in my lenses, letting me know that particular brand is two for one tonight, but I blink it away irritably. Thought I had ad notifications disabled. A quick glance around reveals two security guards pushing their way through the crowd, their eyes fixed on Nash . . . and me. I'm not about to be Nash's collateral damage. I quickly scoop the bottles up off the ground and deposit them back on the bar, hold up my hands to show no harm done, then step back into the crowd.

And bump right into Remi.

They stumble a bit when I knock into them, but then their eyes light up, and they start babbling something about the maz effects over the bar, a complicated weave mimicking a night sky dotted with bursting stars. The light dies out as Remi visibly remembers they're supposed to be mad at me, though. They look away, their lips pressed tight together, and start to turn their back to me with a muttered "Never mind."

Before I can really think about it, my hand darts out and catches one of theirs.

"I don't want to fight," I say in a rush. "I just . . ."

. . . don't want you to leave?

I drop their hand and make a fist to keep myself from

reaching out again. This is exactly why I didn't want to tell anyone until after they were gone anyway. "I haven't taken the job yet, okay? I can still turn it down. I'll look for something else. Can we not spend our last week together mad at each other?"

I don't know what I'm saying. I'm supposed to be keeping my distance so it'll hurt less. And I *need* that job. But their expression softens as they look me over, probably seeing way too much. This is a bad idea. I shouldn't have bothered, I should have—

But then one of our favorite songs comes on, and Remi finally meets my gaze again, their frown morphing almost against their will into a small smile. Not quite forgiveness, maybe, but a truce at least.

I'll take it.

"Come on," they say. "We gotta."

I let myself give a faint smile in return.

"Yeah. We gotta."

It might only be one or two songs, unless they're feeling really good tonight, but it's a gift either way. I'm happy to accept.

Remi drags me out to the dance floor, yanks me close by my belt loops, and then their body is against mine, moving to the beat, warm and lithe and *there*. My arms wrap automatically around their neck, my hips matching their rhythm on instinct. Over their shoulder, I see Ania and Jaesin pressed together, leaning in close to talk over the music as they dance.

When I draw back just enough to see Remi's eyes, they looked almost determined. Like there's something right on the tip of their tongue that they just can't quite say, but they're daring me to guess. We've been here before, lived in this exact moment, stood right on the cusp and challenged each other. Back away, move closer, what'll it be? Are you feeling brave tonight?

Am I?

The music pounds in my ears, rising and falling, the smell of drink and sweat and perfume overwhelming. My breath comes too fast, my vision hazy at the edges, and Remi must notice, because they go stiff under my hands, losing the rhythm.

Losing it all.

I pull away, turn my back on them, and flee the room.

This was supposed to be an amazing night. We were supposed to all be together, enjoying our last bit of time in the city that raised us.

So of course I'm alone on the roof.

The bathroom was too obvious. The second-floor catwalk wasn't far enough. But some of the employees love to smoke on the roof, and they're bad at keeping the access stairwell locked. Just what I needed.

The view is awful up here, honestly. I spend a lot of time on the roof of the Cliffs, and from there you can see the whole city spill out before you in all its false neon glory. From the roof of the club, it's walls to the left, walls to the right, a disgustingly overpriced shopping district to the front, and a bunch of rooftop storage pods behind me. But there are a few stars above, shining through the light pollution. The one constant. No matter where I am, I can always leave the ground behind and climb into the sky.

The rooftop access door opens behind me, and I drop my head onto my knees. I've been found, apparently. Too predictable. Time to fight with Remi again. At least it means they aren't down there dancing with someone else. In my head, Ania lectures me about how unfair and gross my jealousy is, but I shove it away. I don't need her preaching.

"Diz?"

I jerk in surprise and whirl around. Not Remi. It's a nondescript guy in his mid-twenties, vaguely familiar, leaning against the same door I used. He holds up his hands and stays back, which I appreciate. I'm suddenly very aware of being alone on a rooftop without good sight lines to the street below. I slowly shift my weight forward onto my feet, moving from seated to crouching in case a quick getaway becomes necessary. The man gives a disarming little smile and waves, keeping his distance.

"Sorry," he says, his voice light and casual. "Didn't mean to interrupt your stargazing. I just had a question about *acquisitions*, and I figured it'd be best to ask without the crowds."

I keep my expression level, but I can't help the spark that word lights in me. Acquisitions. This guy wants maz. Still suspicious, though, how he found me up here on the roof.

"You saw me in the club?" I ask.

He makes the universal gesture for lenses, waving two fingers in front of his eyes. "You checked in on social. It was in your feed."

Oh. Obviously. Rookie mistake.

"I can't remember if we've ever met face-to-face, but you've done some work for me before," he continues. "I've been using Mattie's crew lately, but this is a job I need you for specifically."

I reconsider the man in light of this new information, the familiarity snapping into focus. Shane Drammond. We *have* met before, and he's not quite as plain as I thought initially. His outfit is understated, a simple black button-down and tan pants, but the pieces are fine in quality. His shoes probably cost as much as one of my starting paychecks at MMC, and I don't even want to think about the watch. He reeks of money, to those who know where to look . . . which means he'll pay well.

Not that we're supposed to have any more clients. Last job ever, remember? We're out of the game. The others will be furious if I take another job.

But what kind of job could he need us specifically for? It can't hurt to hear what Fancy Shoes has to say, right?

"What do you need?" I ask, my voice automatically shifting to business mode.

The man smiles and takes a few tentative steps forward.

"Maz-15. The rare stuff."

The thrill I've been trying not to acknowledge goes right out of me.

"There's no such thing. Don't waste my time. You have business or not?" I ask. Is this supposed to be code for something? I swear, if this guy is only here to mess with me on this already terrible day, I'm gonna track down his darkest secrets and make sure the entire internet hears about them.

"I'm serious," he says. "You delivered some of it with Mattie's haul today, mixed in with some of the obscuraz. Deep violet color, high tensile strength, effect similar to magnaz. Your crew is the only one I know of who's ever managed to draw some. MMC keeps it way hushed. I need you to go back to the same spot where you found it and get me more."

Wait . . . what?

I keep my face impassive, but it's like someone's just hit the brakes on my brain. That bright purplish stuff Mattie picked out in one of our vials . . . *that* was a new strain of maz? There's a fifteenth strain, and *we* were the first ones to find MMC's stash?

Thought number one: badass.

Thought number two: Remi is going to be the *most* excited.

Thought number three: sounds super fake, can't possibly be real, but if it is . . .

Thought number four: sounds *expensive*.

How much to charge, though? I'm not about to establish too low a market value for a hot commodity out of impatience. Maybe I can get him to name a price first. For, you know . . . scientific reasons. Not because we're going to take the job. Just to know.

I turn my gaze to the shopping district down the street and keep quiet. Better to examine the guy from the corner of my eye and let him sweat a bit. His polished demeanor slips when I'm no longer looking straight at him. His skin is ashen, eyes darting, fingers drumming against the side of his leg. Obviously buying stim spells on the regular to stay awake. Not a great idea, that, but I'm no doctor, and he didn't come to me for health advice.

He needs some raw magic quietly siphoned off from MMC's stash, and that happens to be my specialty.

Was. *Was* my specialty.

"Mattie has a big mouth. We just delivered those vials to him a few hours ago," I say. Not too surprising, ultimately. Word travels fast in the black market.

"And *he* was getting them for *me*."

I nod. We knew the vials weren't for Mattie. The story tracks. I chew the inside of my lip and let myself consider it for just a moment. Remi would lose it at the chance to play with a brand-new strain of maz. They have all kinds of grand plans to study maz in college and beyond, and this would be the ultimate science project.

And what better way to go out with a bang? This is what our crew does best. One last job for the best damn siphoning crew in Kyrkarta, for real this time, bigger and better and more lucrative than ever.

Maybe even enough to make them all stay.

"You realize a job like that would cost you, right?" I say, holding my gaze on the street below. No explicit confirmation. Just an observation.

"I can pay," he says, almost too desperate. Something in my gut twinges a warning, but then he pulls out a deck, tilts the screen toward me, and brings up a new transaction: eight thousand credits. "And this is just the first payment. I'll give you the same on delivery."

I bite the inside of my cheek to keep from grinning. Wouldn't do to seem eager, or like I need the money too bad. I do, of course, but that isn't any business of his.

Sixteen thousand credits. This new strain *must* be real, if he's offering that kind of money up front. That's enough for Remi to be able to afford Kyrkarta University instead of going all the way to Jattapore. And if Remi stays, Jaesin will stay. We can get a real place in the bridges district, something much nicer than the crappy flat assigned to us in the Cliffs. Jaesin will find a job easily—he'll charm every interviewer from the first handshake. Ania will be off to her fancy private university either way, but she'll visit a lot more often if we're all in one place. It could work.

It really could work.

They're going to be *so* mad at me. But if I ask them first, there's a chance they'll say no. I can't risk it.

It's too good.

We *have* to.

Besides, it's our grand farewell week. What better way to go out than with an epic score?

"Note down how many vials you need in the memo field and send those credits over. You've got yourself a deal," I say. He hands his deck to me, and I input the info for my shell bank account. "Can't give you an exact delivery date and time. These things are risky, you know, gotta be careful about the where and when. We'll put you at the top of our client list, though."

It's a client list of one, but he doesn't need to know that. It's just . . . very exclusive.

In my head, I'm already past the guilt of screwing over my future employer again, pushing it aside to dive right into planning. Jaesin and I will need to scout around the area where we pulled our last job, see if we can figure out how the new maz got into our stash, if there've been any changes in patrol patterns. . . .

"As soon as you can," the man says, his intensity bringing him a bit too close. "I have a big project coming up, and I have to have it by then. I'll add in a bonus two thousand if you can have it done in two days."

Eighteen thousand. Keep it cool.

"Okay, okay, you got it. Two days, no more. Anything we need to know about it that might help us? What it can do, what you have planned for it?"

For just a second, something in the man's eyes slips. Something hard. "Mind your business and get me my maz," he snaps. His expression smooths barely a second later.

"Sorry, I . . . sorry," he says. And sure enough, he slips a slim glass vial with a stimspell from his pocket and crumbles it onto his tongue with a sparking glow. Called it. "This project is complex. It wears on you."

I check the status of the transaction on my lens display—paid in full, *yes*—then nod at the guy.

"We'll take care of our end, so put it out of your mind and focus on your project. You need any weaving services along with the raw stuff?"

He waves me off. "No, just the raw maz. I've got the rest."

I shrug. "Your choice. We've got the best, though, so don't go shopping around elsewhere. You change your mind, you come to me."

He raises a hand in farewell and ducks back through the rooftop door without another word. I watch him go, then flop onto my back for one last moment alone with the sky.

With any luck, next week I won't be sitting under these stars alone.

FIVE

I SLIP BACK INTO THE club with fire in my veins, practically vibrating with the thrill of another job. Maybe I'm not ready to be done with this business after all. This is what I'm good at. The hacking, the deals, running from the cops in this city that I know better than myself. Why would I give it up?

The atmosphere in the club is oppressive after the fresh night air, the sunnaz decor suddenly false and pale in comparison to the stars. I scan the room, looking between all the writhing bodies for three familiar forms, trying to disconnect my emotions in case I see something I really don't want to see.

But the others are nowhere to be found.

Did they leave without me?

I feel it start inside me as if watching from a distance. My shoulders hunch in. My breathing grows shallow. Stay calm, just look at the crowd. I wasn't gone that long, so it's unlikely they've already left. I just missed them, obviously. They're here, somewhere. I close my eyes, take three deep breaths, and prepare to scan the crowd again. When I open my eyes, they'll be there. They will.

A hand lands on my shoulder, and I nearly jump right into the burly guy in front of me. Heart racing, I whirl around and come face-to-face with Ania.

"What's with the face?" she says, lifting her hands in surrender.

"This is just my face," I practically snarl. Whoa, rein it in. I need her not to kill me when I tell her about our new last job ever. A little sucking up might be in order. Over Ania's shoulder, Remi and Jaesin are messing around, flicking things off a table at each other and laughing. I guess everyone was fine without me. What was I expecting?

Well, their attitudes will change one way or the other when I tell them about this new job I've already committed to and accepted payment for without asking them, hah. In my mind, of course, Remi is immensely grateful for the opportunity to go to their dream school, and Jaesin is secretly relieved he doesn't have to move, and Ania is glad for the excuse to break some rules and get away with it one last time before reverting back to perfect-student mode. More likely, though, is a giant temper tantrum from Jaesin that'll set everyone else off. Not exactly something I want to go down in public.

I school my expression and force some of the tension out of my shoulders. "Hey, can we head home?"

Ania's gaze sharpens. "What happened? I saw you and Remi dancing, and then you were just . . . gone, for like an hour."

Almost two hours, actually, but who's counting?

"I need to talk to everyone," I say, and leave it at that. Ania frowns, but nods. A message pops up in our group chat.

~Epic Group Chat: GRAND FAREWELL WEEK Edition~
Ania: Hey, stop horsing around and let's go
Remi: wow, that might be the most *mom* thing you've ever said
you've officially spent too much time with jaesin
I'm sorry, you're cut off
Jaesin: *eyeroll*

Remi glances over in our direction and we lock eyes for a long, uncomfortable moment. I can't seem to get anything right when it comes to them. Every time I start to fix things, I just screw them up all over again. Worse, if possible. If we do this one thing, though, if they stay . . . maybe it can be the start of something new. Maybe I can do better.

I turn and shoulder my way toward the door. Hopefully my friends will be feeling a bit more charitable toward me soon.

As we emerge onto the street outside the club, the music fades into a dampened thrum, the bass still beating in our chests long after the higher tones are gone. Ania instantly relaxes as the cool early evening air hits her skin. I didn't realize how tense she'd been since we arrived. Not so much her scene, despite the fanciness and wealth, I guess. She enjoys dancing sometimes, even though she has no rhythm, but crowds get to her.

As we start our walk home, the noise of the club and the shopping district disappear altogether, the near silence of No-Man's Land wrapping us in ghosts. The club and all the surrounding buildings were well reinforced, their structural spells solid with fresh maz and money. This old neighborhood, not so much. It was once populated by the sort of middle-class family that was typical of MMC employees. So many of them were killed off in the first wave of the plague that the neighborhood was decimated, with those few who were left eventually moving to other areas to escape the eerie silence. Lots of our neighbors at the Cliffs were once part of these families. The house numbers affixed near their front doors glint in the faint moonlight as we pass. I hate walking through here, but it's the fastest route home.

Behind me, Remi and Jaesin keep up their cheerful babble, determined to drown out my mood with their own. Ania shares my quiet, though, waiting for the hammer I'm wielding to drop. No sense in making her wait any longer.

"We have another job," I say, loud enough that Remi

and Jaesin can hear behind me.

Silence. Then, louder silence.

After a long, uncomfortable moment, Jaesin clears his throat.

"I assume you're waiting for us to comment on the fact that just a few hours ago we said we were absolutely, completely, one hundred percent done with siphoning jobs, yes?"

"Well, yeah," I say, combative, then remember my whole tactful sucking-up strategy. Are we really going to play this fake-calm-questions game, though?

"And I also assume," Jaesin continues, "that you've already committed us to this job without asking us, or else you wouldn't be so weird and shifty right now."

"Yep," I say. Ania shoots me a look, one raised eyebrow with her are-you-truly-this-bad-at-life expression. Ugh. Remi, at least, seems neutral. Waiting for the details.

Jaesin rubs a hand down his face and kicks a rock in the middle of the road with more force than strictly necessary. "Diz, we're leaving in a week."

I'm plenty fucking aware, thanks, but please, repeat that as often as possible so I can't forget for even five seconds. Jaesin pushes on.

"We have so much to do to get ready to move, Diz. We can't afford to get arrested. I could lose my job offer in Jattapore. Remi could lose their place at the university. We've played our luck this far. The whole point was to quit while we were ahead."

"Well, if we—" I start, then cut myself off.

If we get this payout, maybe you won't have to leave.

I tip my head back to stare at the stars again, much more visible in this dark, broken neighborhood. The constellation of Ailia, the ancient dancing warrior of firaz, shines overhead, precariously balanced on one toe. I feel you, man. This is a tipping point for sure, but I know just how to give Jaesin a good shove over the edge.

"It's sixteen thousand credits, and he's already paid us half," I say, completely casual. "Another two thousand if we can do it fast."

Ania doesn't even blink, but Jaesin stumbles over a chunk of broken concrete, and Remi gives a low whistle.

"We'd need a *truck* to hold sixteen thousand creds worth of maz," they say. "Who's the client and what's their deal?"

"The client is Shane Drammond. We've done jobs for him before, but usually through dead drops and middle men, and he's always paid us on time. The job, though . . ." I can't help the grin that fights its way onto my face as I look over at Remi. "You're gonna love this."

They raise an eyebrow and meet my gaze head-on. "Yeah?"

"Yeah. The job is for eight vials of maz-15."

Remi's face goes blank with confusion. They look to Ania, then back to me. "Is that . . . code for something?"

I bark a laugh. "That's exactly what I thought! But he's serious. Before you handed the vials off to me earlier, did you notice anything weird in one of them?"

Remi zones out for a moment, leaving Jaesin to watch the ground in front of them for obstacles. After a moment, Remi shakes their head. "I mean, maybe? To be honest I wasn't really paying attention. I was kinda focused on going to Nova tonight, so I zoned in to the job and went on autopilot."

I wince and breathe through the sudden surge of fear in my stomach. They're fine now, obviously. "Right. Well, one of the vials of obscuraz had something else mixed into it, a few strands kinda bonded to it like magnaz would do, but bright violet instead of the usual dark purple. He only paid us half for that vial because he was paranoid about it being contaminated. Turns out it *was* contaminated, but not with the spellplague—with a totally new kind of maz."

Remi stares me down with an intensity I only ever see turned on their maz experiments. Got the hook in now. Come on, Remi. You know you want to.

"It's not real," they say after a moment, slow and reluctant. "It can't be. If there'd been a new maz discovery, it would have been announced. There'd be research."

"It does seem suspicious," Ania adds, but without much heart behind it.

I bite the inside of my lip to keep from smiling. Yes,

step into my web. "Well, if it's not real, then he just paid us eight thousand credits up front to go ghost hunting, which I'm also fine with. But I saw the stuff for myself. So did Ania. There was definitely *something* in that vial. Maybe they figured out how to make synthetic maz or something. If it's a new strain, though, don't you wanna be one of the first to work with it? We'll get this guy his eight vials, then pull a little extra for you. Golden opportunity, right?"

Jaesin sighs and shoves his hands in his pockets, shoulders hunched in. My heart sinks.

"Why would you do this?" he asks. "Especially without talking to us. That last run almost went really bad at the end. You almost got caught. They've probably increased security there if they think someone got their hands on this secret brand-new maz. So why, Diz?"

"Because . . ."

I bite my lip. Danger and trouble aren't normally a big issue for him. He's going to make me say it.

Because you and Remi . . .

Ugh.

"Because money is good?" I snap instead. "Because we need it? Wouldn't it be nice to start off our new adult lives with some cash in our pockets? Enough for that shiny flat in Jattapore you were looking at last night?"

"Hey, you stay out of my browser history," he snaps back.

Ania and Jaesin do *such* good disappointed-parent faces. It's truly unfair.

The next bit catches in my throat, my brain frantically trying to stop me from saying the rest. Too transparent, way too close to . . . everything. But I push the words out.

"Enough to cover what Remi's scholarship from Kyrkarta University couldn't."

I purse my lips, then force myself to look at Remi. "It's not too late to accept their offer. You could study Professor Silva's work at the archives there, in the department he founded, like you wanted. With this money, it would be possible."

Remi's eyes go wide, and they press the pad of their thumb to their lips, the way they always do when tears are imminent.

The silence falls back over us as the Cliffs come into view. I do my best to fade into the background, make myself small and quiet so I won't do or say anything to dissuade them from considering my proposal. Ania is trying to send me some kind of heartfelt sad look that I dodge resolutely, and Jaesin, for all he cares about Remi and wants them to have the world, still seems deeply skeptical.

But then Jaesin stretchs his arms high overhead, lacing his fingers together and flexing in a way that draws intense staring from Ania and eyerolls from Remi and me. My heart lightens a bit. Jaesin loves to get his hands dirty just as much as I do. He craves a reason to use those enormous muscly arms. And the money is *amazing*. It'll help Remi. It'll be dangerous. It'll be *fun*. It's exactly the kind of thing he normally loves.

It's only a matter of time before he breaks.

Jaesin heaves a put-upon sigh and runs a hand through his hair, looking to Remi as he holds the front door of our building open for us all. "What do you think?"

"You *know* what I think about them keeping maz all tied up in those pipes," they say, inspecting their fingernails with studied innocence as I summon the elevator to our floor. "If they're hiding a brand-new strain of maz from the world, I must liberate it, no matter the risks."

"Yes, and the irony of that position from someone who's spellsick never fades. You just wanna play with the shiny," Jaesin says, stomping onto the elevator like a frustrated teddy bear. "But what about *this* job specifically? It's so close to our time to leave. Do you really want in on this?"

Remi laughs and leans on the wall opposite Jaesin, leveling him with a frank stare. "What I *think* is that *you* want to have one last amazing job where you get to hit things and take home a big paycheck, but you want *me* to be the one to say yes so you can act all noble and resigned to your fate."

Hell yes, call him *out*. I bark a laugh, then slap my hand over my mouth. Wouldn't do to ruin this beautiful moment. So close. Just say it, Jaesin.

Jaesin slumps in defeat just as the elevator dings our arrival to the top floor.

"Fine. *Fine.* You win, both of you. I'm in." He looks to Ania, his voice lowering to something smoother, softer, as he holds the elevator door open. "What about you? You've been suspiciously silent through this whole thing."

Ania opens her mouth, then closes it again, flicking an evaluating glance over Remi, assessing their current condition. I catch her eye and shake my head ever so slightly. Don't say it. You'll regret it.

She sighs.

"Fine. I'm in too. But I want my protest on the official record. This is a bad idea."

Despite himself, Jaesin grins like a kid about to jump off a roof. Not that I've ever seen that exact expression on his face before, and certainly not when we were eleven and living in our second group home together, with the headmistress looking on in horror. I stick my tongue out at Ania.

"Your protest is noted and discarded, princess," I say.

Remi nudges me out of the way and sticks their thumb on the door lock, then throws our front door dramatically open.

"Okay, Supreme Overlord Dizmon," they say with a sweeping gesture. "Step into my office and tell us your grand plans. If there really is a new strain of maz out there, I demand to play with it."

I grin and step over the threshold with my arms spread wide, credit signs and plans for the future crystallizing in my mind.

"Unicorn Sparkles McSunshine," I call to the flat's computer. "Play my Badass Illegal Funtimes playlist, please."

The bass drum kicks in, and I meet Remi's gaze, remembering their body against mine in the club, the beat and the tension and the promise of so much more.

Maybe the possibility was real after all.

It is *on*.

SIX

I WOULD LOVE TO GO back in time and slap
Past Diz for her terrible life choices. Two days for a job
like this? I must've been high. It's the only explanation.
Or, at the very least, too dazzled by credit signs and deci-
mal points in good places to take into account the fact
that this is our grand farewell week, and we have plans
every single night. After we talked over the job last night,
we somehow thought it was a great idea to stay up and
rewatch the entire first season of our favorite series, then
celebrate with 3:00 a.m. ice cream. Remi slept through
90 percent of it and passed on the ice cream, but my deci-
sions were not nearly so healthy.

Thanks, Past Diz. You're a jerk.

Jaesin is obviously hung over and doing a terrible job
of pretending otherwise, and I'm still mostly unconscious.
The number of unanswered notifications in the corner of
my lenses ticks ever upward, but caring is just not in my
arsenal right now. I know I owe Davon a message, and
a thank-you for his gift, but that's going to require some

serious emotional energy, and I'm tapped dry.

Not that I can complain about energy. Remi slept in way late and had to be dragged to the clinic under duress to go to their monthly appointment with their care team. Blood draws to check cell counts, prescription adjustments as needed, gold stars for daily cardio (some of which comes in the form of running from cops, not that the doctors need to know that)—all the usual maintenance care, plus a little extra poking and prodding in the name of science, since the spellplague is still so little understood.

Ania is out too, probably stress vomiting at the tech division of the Department of Maz Oversight over her A-level certification final exam. At least she isn't around to see her late-night protests proven right.

One night down, six to go. Six more things we've always meant to do or see together in Kyrkarta. Six more days with all four of us.

I'll be sleeping even less than usual. Worth it, though.

Jaesin and I hover over the latest traffic and policing reports in the back of an empty train car, the city racing by below us. I liberated them from the police database during a fit of insomnia after the others went to bed last night. Not even a 3:00 a.m. sugar crash can knock me out, apparently. Red icons litter the three-dimensional map of the city projected in our contact lenses, marking contained ruptures, collapsed buildings, blocked-off streets, and every other problem we could possibly run into.

The city is an utter mess. Yesterday's earthquake might have been one of dozens we've had this year, but it was the strongest we've had in months. So many things that were on their last legs have finally given way, and the city is aching and sore, slow to bounce back the morning after.

It's awful to watch, but it might also work in our favor. People are home from work, avoiding certain areas. Police have their hands full redirecting traffic and maintaining safe clearance around buildings deemed to be structural threats, weak enough that they might give way during an aftershock. Kyrkarta is a minefield.

Perfect for doing a little light snooping.

"So, it looks to me like the spot where we pulled our last job is isolated from the rest of the city right now," Jaesin says, tracing a finger through the air to circle a spot near the western edge of town. "The trains aren't running to the industrial sector today, and all the major landing zones are closed to the public. Essential personnel only at the factories and plants."

I nod, chewing on my nail in thought. "Good eye. And there are lots of underground access points around there," I say, my finger leaving behind cheery blue markers on the diagram everywhere I touch. "I think it makes sense to just tap the same point we hit last time. We've never encountered maz-15 anywhere else, so it might only be in that one area."

"Could be. Seems odd we've been pulling these jobs all over the city and never run into it before, but the first time we hit there, we find it." He tosses back the last of his coffee with a grimace and wipes his mouth with the back of his hand. "Also, can we talk about how awful the name maz-15 is? Can we please give it a new one?"

I snort. He's right. "What do you have in mind?"

He shrugs. "I dunno, Supreme Overlord, you're the one with a talent for naming things."

"Super Magic Ultra Plum? Special Sparkle Dream Power? Fancy Ultimate—"

Jaesin cuts me off with a finger pressed to my lips. "Shh. No. Just . . . I have regrets. Please stop."

"Whatever you say, Awesome Strongman McDad Friend," I say around his finger. He throws his empty plastic coffee cup at me (totally uncalled for, and definitely worthy of some internet revenge) and slumps back against the seat, gesturing to the map again.

"Right." I trace my finger from the marker on the map to the nearest MMC junction station, leaving a green line on the image pointing straight to station twenty-nine.

The station where my dad worked, when he was alive. Ground zero for the spellplague outbreak.

Over the past two years, we've had a silent agreement to avoid doing jobs in this part of town. Remi visits the memorial site near the station there several times every year, and Jaesin and Ania always go with. I refuse to go, other than at the new year and on Midsummer Remembrance. We broke the rule for the first time on what we thought was our last job. Now we're back again. It puts a weird creeping feeling under my skin.

I shove the thought aside and continue. "The place we hit yesterday is right near that downed building on Vin Street, though, so there might be too many eyes there. Workers and police and all that. The next access point up the pipe might work—by the bakery, right?"

"That's the one, yeah," Jaesin says. He glances at the route map on the wall and runs a hand through his hair. "Let's check that one out. As long as the earthquake didn't mess it up, it should be our ticket. Off at the next stop, go the rest of the way on foot?"

"Sir, yes, sir!" I say with a salute, and he rolls his eyes, then winces at the pain in his skull. The train blinks its notification onto our lenses: next stop, Montague Street Station. As the train begins to slow, we stumble to our feet and pull ourselves down the aisle by the vertical bars, which I of course have to swing around on. You can't be in an empty train car and not. It's just not right.

The doors slide open and we slip onto the platform, which is unusually quiet for the time of day. This stop is typically busy from the morning commute through last call at the nicer bars, but it seems the whole city has taken an earthquake vacation day. Only those who can't afford to miss work still hustle along in their uniforms, wearing name tags and harried expressions.

Once we descend to street level, the difference is even more noticeable. The sun shines cheerily overhead—it obviously hasn't gotten the memo; feel the room, bro—and the pale ghost of the moon hangs in the bright daytime sky over largely empty streets. Jaesin and I set off, getting a good distance away from the station before activating our gliders. A quick subvocal command to my deck clicks on the tiny power source in my shoes, and we're off, gliding near-frictionless over the cracked streets in the shadow of the hulking gray factories of the industrial center.

Ania and Remi think we're childish for still ordering shoes with glide tech, to which we say a kindly "Fuck off." Jaesin was on the glide team at school for years and he's wicked fast, and I love exploring the city, which is much easier with frictionless speed. I don't wear them on jobs because the sewage would ruin them, though I really could have used them on that last one, at least. I shoot a quick look at Jaesin from the corner of my eye—and he looks back. We drift to a wordless stop at the next intersection.

"Ready?" he says.

"Steady."

"GO!"

We explode off the line, racing across the intersection and into the street beyond, piled high with debris. As far as improvised obstacle courses go, it's a good one, full of holes to jump over, piles of rubble, and heavy machinery abandoned for morning coffee breaks. I kick off the wall of a run-down sandwich shop with a bright red awning and throw myself into the next alley over, bouncing from pile to pile with a little assist from my boots on each push.

Another corner, then Jaesin goes sailing past me like always, middle fingers turned up at the end of each outstretched arm as he kicks off a parked bulldozer. At the apex of his jump, he grabs a flagpole standing straight out from some city building and uses it like a gymnast to propel himself into the next intersection. Asshole. But the world doesn't give him many chances to show off the things he's good at, so I let it go. The whining is just for effect.

"Oh, come on, jock," I gasp, trusting my deck to transmit my complaint via my throat mic. I'm well used to running and climbing all over this city, but I'm more a marathoner than a sprinter. "Have mercy on this poor computer nerd. I bow to your superior strength and speed."

"Oh, do you, now?" Jaesin turns back and literally runs circles around me, first forward, then backward. Guess his hangover has been miraculously cured. "So, you're admitting defeat?"

On his next pass, I reach out and yank him to a stop by the wrist. "Yes, I surrender, have mercy, Awesome

Strongman McDad Friend. For an elderly man who complains about bills constantly, you're surprisingly spry."

"Oi!" he sputters, indignant. "I'm like three months older than you! And someone has to buy food so you don't die of malnutrition in a pile of your own instant noodle cups."

"There are worse ways to go," I say with a shrug, and an awful silence immediately ensues.

Neither of us mentions the spellplague. No one has to. The thought is never far from our minds, inescapable in this city.

"How long until Remi's done at the clinic?" I ask, subdued.

His stare goes distant, as it does when he consults his lenses. "About two and a half hours."

I nod. Not much time. But enough, maybe. "Guess we should get to work, then."

We fall silent and make our way, side by side rather than chasing each other, toward our potential pipeline. First up, though: the bakery. We can't afford it often, but they know us well enough there that it's never suspicious for us to be hanging around. Good excuse to be in the neighborhood. And to shove pastries in my face.

As we approach Ginny's Boisterous Baking (a name I thoroughly approve of), the rich scents of sugar and warm bread overtake the neighborhood's smell of dust, chems, and metal. It figures Ginny's hard at work when everyone else is shut down. I have no idea why she set up shop in this part of town, but all the factory workers adore her and her creations, lining up around the block for breakfast and lunch. Actually, maybe Ginny (age forty-one, widow, secretly wealthy, beloved fanfiction author) is a genius after all. Everyone loves a little spot of brightness in the middle of the bleak.

We wander in, Jaesin first because he comes here a lot more often and she knows him better. Ginny thinks he's "just so pretty," and he loves the attention. His hair always manages to land in the perfect intersection of proper professional and casual handsome bedhead, and Ginny never can keep her hands off it. Ginny claps her hands in delight when she spots us, sending a cloud of flour billowing into the air. "It has been far too long! Where've you been, young man?"

Jaesin rubs the back of his neck and grins. "Busy times, you know. We all graduated, so we've been making plans and getting things ready. That's part of why we're here."

He pauses for dramatic effect, cutting his gaze away with something like shyness.

"Remi and I are moving. To Jattapore. We're leaving in six days."

It's only when Ginny's face crumples with fond emotion that I realize it really is part of the reason we're here. Jaesin wants to say goodbye. My throat goes thick as

Ginny bustles around the counter and wraps Jaesin in a floury hug, heedless of the handprints she leaves on his black T-shirt.

"Oh, sweetheart, I'm so happy for you. Get out of this city while you can. It's not nearly as bad in cities where they didn't lose so many to the plague. You'll do great."

A shadow passes over her face, as it always does when something brings the memory of her late wife to mind, but she forces a smile and pushes on. "And how is Remi? They're still so young, they should have a few years before the illness really starts progressing, right?"

Jaesin nods. "The doctors always say they're one of the strongest patients they have. Remi's totally on point with their exercise, eating, treatments, all that. It used to be that surviving plague patients started to decline around nineteen, but now it's more like twenty-two or twenty-three. Remi's hoping if they can keep up with the doctor's recommendations, MMC's research will turn up something before—"

And that's when I tune out. I just can't.

I turn to the case beside the pay terminal, with sweet and savory goods laid out in neat labeled rows, though she's baked less than usual due to the lack of crowds. Buns sticky with thick white icing, tarts piled high with berries, slices of pie with candied nuts, savory mini quiches with mushrooms and greens. It smells heavenly. I can still recall the exact taste and flaky texture of the almond tart I had here last time. But even with the pity discount she normally gives us, I can't justify the cost. Maybe after we pull this job and get paid the full amount.

"And what about you, little cactus? You're back early. I only saw you two months ago," Ginny says, raising her voice to draw me back into the conversation. "Are you off to Jattapore as well, then?"

I glower at the pastries. I hate that nickname so. Very. Much. Almost as much as the assumption that I'll be trotting after Jaesin and Remi like a loyal puppy.

"I've got plans of my own."

"Well, don't be coy," she says. "What are you doing? Putting those computer smarts to use?"

She just can't take a hint, can she?

"I'm staying in Kyrkarta. Taking a job with Davon over at MMC."

Out of the corner of my eye, I catch Jaesin's look of surprise as he whips his head around to stare at me—and I realize my mistake. I told them I wasn't sure. That I hadn't made up my mind. *Crap.*

"I mean, I've had an offer," I blurt. "Of a job. Thing. At MMC."

Jaesin's eyes go narrow. I backpedal furiously.

"Nothing's firm yet, though. You never know. Jaesin, we should get to our meeting. It's almost noon."

Ginny's face does the pity thing again, and she goes

back around the counter and fishes four pastries from the case: one each for me and Jaesin, and a box with two more for Remi and Ania. Our favorites. She always remembers, even though I'm only there twice per year. My stomach twinges with a blend of guilt and hunger as she hands me an almond croissant.

"I've made way too many today," she says, waving away Jaesin's attempt at payment. "I expected at least a few of the factories to be operating, but the damage must have been worse than I thought. Don't let me keep you. If I don't see you again, I wish you the best of luck in Jattapore, Jaesin. Dizmon, don't be a stranger if you decide to stick around Kyrkarta after all, okay?"

I nod, glaring at the ground, and Jaesin raises a hand in farewell as the door's bright chime signals our exit. His curiosity about my job outburst radiates in waves I can actually feel as we walk down the block to the end of the long building the bakery lives in. The alley behind it holds the sewer access we need to get at the pipes, but there's no way I'm taking my precious rare treat down there with only a napkin to protect it. At least Ania's and Remi's are in a box. I nibble slowly at my almond croissant, savoring its flaky, nutty, buttery sweetness, stretching it as far as it can go.

Until we turn the corner around the back side of the building and come face-to-face with a group of workers

89

in full nullaz suits.

A sparking maz barrier blocks the alley off from the rest of the street. The workers haul huge piles of rubble away from a long fissure running straight down the alley, while a techwitch and a spellweaver work to stitch the crack back together bit by painstaking bit.

"Oi, this area's off limits, kids," a woman wearing a foreman's colors says, stepping up to the barrier.

Jaesin turns on the charm. "Sorry, our bad. Just wandering around while we eat," he says, hoisting his sugary fruit tart for her to see. "We'll go."

The woman nods, but her gaze follows us all the way down the road until we turn a corner, then collapse against the side of a greasy gray factory.

"Well, that plan's screwed," I say, licking the last of the almond cream from my fingers. "This job just got a lot more difficult."

"Maybe not a lot," he says. A link request pops up in my lenses, and I accept so we can study the map together again.

He continues. "If we think there's just the one pipe, then theoretically any well-hidden location with underground access along this path should work, right? We just need to get down there relatively close to where we were before."

He has a point, and there are plenty of sewer access points along the way. I've always found it a little weird that we carry something as powerful and valuable as maz in pipes running right alongside the ones that carry our sewage, but so it is. Made sense to use the existing infrastructure in the wake of the plague, I guess.

"Do you have your baby with you?" Jaesin asks, circling a few points along the projected path of the pipe, voice neutral. Good. Focus on the job and not my awful slip. I may have made up my mind about the job in my own head, but he doesn't need to know that. *I* don't even want to think about it right now, considering I'll be tasked with protecting these pipes in a few weeks. At least I'll have a thorough knowledge of all the vulnerabilities, right?

"I do, yeah." I reach into my pocket and withdraw a tiny drone, a custom model I built for a school project two years ago. I got a perfect score on the project and a private email from my teacher praising my work. I *also* got a referral to the headmaster for a week's suspension and a stern warning that building tools of espionage was highly frowned upon at Kyrkarta Memorial Polytechnic. Like it's some kind of sacred institution for supporting the learning of Kyrkarta's youth, rather than mass schooling for the city's orphans. There were always lots of teachers from outside cities, here on some kind of grant program. Go work with the sad orphan children and have your student loans forgiven! They were always obnoxiously sincere and patronizing.

Regardless of its troubled origins, I love my little drone. At the time, it was a way of getting past my issues with maz, figuring out how to work with it without being paralyzed by fear or disgust. Building machines to control and contain it definitely helps. I've tinkered with my drone a lot more since its original creation, and it's better than anything out on the open market now, in my totally humble opinion. It has a tiny maz port that can accept the smallest maz cartridge available to the general public, and I load it with raw obscuraz when we can spare it, to help it conceal itself. It's nearly invisible unless you're looking for it.

I subvocalize a command to my deck to bring up the drone's operating console and share the drone's cam feed with Jaesin, then toss the little guy into the air. It takes right off, four times faster than a fly, zipping through the alleys and blocked streets we don't have access to. I bring up its GPS tracker and overlay it on the map we've been using to plan our job, then direct it to fly along the projected path of the pipe.

So many of the underground access points, whether they're sewer holes or MMC's cleaner, security-heavy access hatches, are right out in plain sight in this district. Not as much need for aesthetics in this part of town. Obviously not a great choice for us, and another reason we never pulled jobs here. With a frustrated growl, I get rid of the cam feed and map and let the drone's vision completely overtake my contact lenses, so all I see is what it sees. It's a bit like being strapped to the nose of a rocket, way disorienting, but I have a much better feel for the space around the drone and where the potential sight lines might be. As the drone draws nearer to the junction station, I begin to despair. If we have to hit the station itself, this job will be twenty times harder, enough so that it wouldn't even be worth the credits. But then—

"There!" I command the drone to slow and hover. There's a park a few blocks from the station, a wide, mostly cleared greenspace with markers for earthquake wards, but with a few rare trees standing around the edges as well. And near those trees is a little bump in the terrain. I zoom the drone in closer, circling around to see . . . yes. The bump is a slight ridge to conceal an MMC maintenance hatch, and it's near enough to the trees that we'll have a bit of extra concealment. I check its location against the map, and unless someone was drunk-designing when they planned out the sewer system, it's definitely on the same pipeline.

"You know anything about this park?" I ask Jaesin. He shifts uncomfortably beside me.

"It's a bit out in the open, but if we hit in the middle of the day, we should be fine. This place really fills up at night, though."

"Spelldealing?"

"A bit. Hooking up, mostly. A few stimmers here and

there. Some harder stuff."

I bite my lip and restrain myself from asking further. He had a bad year when we aged out of the group-home system and moved into our first flat at fourteen. We don't talk about it.

"Maybe they'll be too distracted to care about us, then," I say instead.

"You wanna risk all those eyes seeing us slip into the sewers? All we need is for one person to call the badges, or for them to discover the missing maz later and have someone call in a tip on us. Day is our best bet, around ten thirty in the morning, when even the late folks have gotten to work, but enough time before lunch for us to get in and out before the crowds. Done with half a day left before the deadline. Extra two thousand creds, banked."

I shrug. All good points, I know, but going during the day feels like waving a giant flag to announce our activities. We've always hit at night before. We'll have Ania and Remi and their misdirection spells to help us slip by unnoticed, but it won't stop anyone particularly observant. Or anyone looking for us specifically.

I bring the drone back a few streets and find a sewer cover with a finger gap it can duck through, then fly quickly back to the access point at the park to double-check there won't be anything in our way underground. Once I hit the hatch, I turn back around and trace the pipe back to the valve we tapped last night, counting intersections against the map to make sure I'm in the right place. Straight shot, no blocks, no extra security, no issues. Looks like we have a plan.

"It's dangerous," I say, because I have to. If Jaesin's going to have a dad crisis about it, better for it to happen now.

Jaesin nods, and the corner of his mouth twitches up into the faintest grin.

My answering smirk is automatic. Adrenaline and hot blood race through my veins, making my skin tingle, my fingers twitch with anticipation. Getting away with eighteen thousand credits' worth of maz in broad daylight?

This is going to be the greatest last score of all time.

SEVEN

KYRKARTA CITY IS MUCH MORE beautiful at night and from a distance. The darkness hides all the people, though many of them are still out and about, seeking their poison of choice. If only you really could dance, screw, or drink the last ten years since the spellplague away, I would be right there with them every night. As it is, I only join in on the really bad nights.

Most nights I keep to watching from my rooftop perch. If it wasn't near the highest spot in the city, my vantage point atop the Cliffs would be useless. Our building is less than half the height of the steel spires that make up the downtown business district.

As it is, I have elevation on my side, and the city sprawls out before me, each section divided by invisible but firm borders. Rich assholes pretending nothing bad ever happened, next to gentrifying assholes who consider themselves saviors, next to oblivious assholes who just want a big house. Shopping, shopping, shopping! Trendy cafés full of well-paid young MMC employees. Shiny bland newness constructed after the spellplague. Nightlife with drugs, bordered by nightlife with moderately less drugs. Strip clubs and by-the-hour motels. Abandoned "memorial" neighborhoods overtaken by maz-mad squirrels. Bad places to be in an earthquake. Bad places to park your car. Bad places to be alone.

Much of it glows with neon, with maz, with money and desperate forward-looking optimism. The parts that don't aren't parts you want to visit anyway.

I never look to my left or rear from our roof. The Cliffs are on the southeastern edge of town, part of the orphan district. No one who doesn't live here calls it that out loud, but they might as well. The neighborhood is roughly divided into thirds: the Cliffs (plague orphans who try hard), the Caves (orphans who don't care), and the Badlands (orphans who really lean hard into the whole FML vibe).

We never go near the Badlands.

We cut stop number two of our grand farewell tour short in light of the job tomorrow morning. We went to Barret Tower, the tallest building in the city and the ultimate tourist destination, inasmuch as there is such a thing in post-plague Kyrkarta. Only Ania had been there before, so she insisted on dragging the rest of us "before the family broke up," as she put it.

Admittedly, the view was spectacular. Possibly better than my own favorite spot. It put us that much closer to the stars. We spent most of the evening pointing out constellations, rattling off schemes to get selected for the lunar living program, imagining ourselves as movie heroes who get to steal spaceships and gallivant across the stars, far away from this place. It was a gorgeously clear night, worthy of basking. We left early (for us, at least, meaning before midnight) so we could get some sleep.

Well, so the others could sleep. Sleep and I aren't on speaking terms.

A notification pops up in my vision, the green border around Davon's photo melding with the lights of the business district on the horizon. I open the message, and the words spill across my lenses.

Davon: Will you talk to me now?

I close my eyes, cutting off the retinal projection while I take a moment to become a human capable of holding a conversation again. I've avoided him since receiving his gift and telling the others about the MMC job offer. Telling my friends is one thing. If I talk to him about it, I'll end up telling him I plan to take it. Telling him is effectively accepting the job offer for real, since he'll practically be my boss. That is a whole other thing that my brain shies away from like a stray dog from loud noise.

I'm a terrible cousin. Davon's known me longer than

anyone else still alive in Kyrkarta, but the thought of having to look him in the eye, even over video, makes my palms sweat.

You: Can't vid right now. Everyone's asleep. Text ok?
Davon: Fine by me.
I was worried when I didn't hear from you after the quake.
You: Sorry. I was really focused on getting home. The wards on the cliffs failed.
Davon: I figured. I heard wards were failing all over the city. I'm sure your datemate had it under control, though.
You: They're not my datemate.
Davon: They would be, if you'd let them. You know that, right?

They're leaving. What would be the point? Time for a strategic subject change.

You: Hell of an aftershock this evening. Shook me right out of my bed.
Davon: Dizzy . . .

I almost wish I had a physical deck and screen under my hands instead of using finger tracking on a virtual keyboard with my lenses. It would feel so very satisfying to chuck the thing over the edge of the rooftop, sending Davon's words flying away with it.

You: They're not and never will be. I don't date.
Davon is typing. . . .

I very nearly go stealth mode to duck what I know is coming next. Davon is persistent, though. Best to get it over with. I start typing my reply before he even sends the message.

Davon: Fine, have it your way, as always. Have you had a chance to think about my offer?
You: Just give me one more day. I need to get through a big thing tomorrow, then I promise I'll tell you my decision.
Davon: Big thing? Everything okay? You've been kind of mysterious lately. Hell, for the last few years. I just assumed it was you growing up, but is there something else?
You: Everything's fine. I just need to tie up some loose ends and see how a few things fall before I commit.
Davon: They won't hold the job forever, Diz.
You: I know. I'm not asking for forever. I'm asking for one more day. Can you live with that?

Davon starts typing, then stops, then starts again. I catch myself clenching my teeth and force my jaw to relax. Come on, please, don't force the issue right now. Is one more day so much to ask?

Finally he replies.

Davon: Yeah. I can live with that.

Not that I have a choice, you brat. :P

You: Hey! You don't get to talk to me that way!

Davon: Please, I changed your diapers, held your hair when you got drunk the first time, and bought you tissues and pizza when the girl whose name we do not speak broke up with you.

You: I never cried!

Davon: The tissues were a gesture. The point is, I've earned the right to tease you.

You: Whatever you say, Annoying Helicopter McWorryface

Davon: Just let me know. Tomorrow night, okay?

You: Tomorrow night.

And thanks for the gift. It was

. . . a lot

Davon: You're welcome. Always.

I make my messaging status "unavailable" before he can start in again. He's right, he's been there for me forever, has known me longer than even Remi and Jaesin. He held my hand at the pickup zone for school when I was in my first year and terrified and he was already in fifth grade. He knew my parents, before the plague. He took apart decks with me and taught me to hack video games.

And he's all I'll have, come next week.

Behind me, the roof access hatch clicks, and I internally sigh. If it's one of those jerks from the fifth floor up here to smoke and throw stuff off the roof, I swear I'll . . .

But it isn't. It's Remi.

My heart rate picks up as I look them over, checking for any signs of distress. Symptoms keeping them awake again? They smile, though, as they slide down beside me with their back against the building's cooling unit, a single gossamer strand of maz dangling between their fingers. They stick their bare feet straight out in front of them and keep their gaze on the maz, spinning that one thread into a more robust string that folds and twines in around itself. The golden glow of it—some of our stolen sunnaz mixed with something else—illuminates the pillow creases on their face and the dark circles under their eyes.

With a motion too complicated for my eyes to follow, Remi suddenly folds the whole weave in half, does something while it's cupped in their hands, then crushes it. The spell explodes into a dazzling cloud of tiny stars that rush toward me, fly a lap around my head, and settle into my hair. They tickle where they rest on the close-shaved side of my head, and a smile tugs at the corner of my mouth. I pick one of the stars from a lock of hair hanging near my face and pinch it between two fingers, then crush it and sprinkle the sparkling residue over Remi's head.

"There, now we match," I say, watching the glittering dust settle on their cheeks and the tips of their ears. Their whole face glows warm. Touching maz like this would have majorly freaked me out a few years ago. Remi has helped me get used to it.

"Shouldn't you be getting your beauty sleep for our job tomorrow?" they say, their voice pitched low, for my ears only.

"Shouldn't you?" I reply automatically, suppressing a wince at the reflexive snap in my voice.

"Touché. I'm just surprised you're not hacking into the dating profiles of Kyrkarta's head of police or something. Isn't that your usual insomniac boredom killer?"

I shrug, blinking the deck interface out of my contacts altogether so my vision holds nothing but city and sparkling cheeks. "I ran out of interesting people. There are no mysteries anymore. Tragic."

"You'll have to start in on the politicians of other cities, I guess. Bring a little spark back into your relationship with the internet."

I let the hint slide right on by. I can do that just as well here. No need to follow them to Jattapore to dig up their new landlord's sick tastes and secret hobbies. Besides, if this job goes well, in a day or two they'll be formally enrolling at KyrU and staying in mystery-free Kyrkarta with me anyway. I watch as they draw a new strand of maz from the necklace I made them last summer. It's constructed from five concentric circles of fine metallic tubing that act as maz chambers, letting Remi carry a bit of maz wherever they go. I gave it to them for their seventeenth birthday, almost a year ago. The look on their face when they opened the package and heard my explanation, the way our eyes caught and held . . .

My stomach tightens, and I cut my gaze back out to the lights of the city.

"What are you doing up, anyway?" I ask.

They shrug. "I slept too much after the clinic. Wide awake now. Don't worry, I'll be fine to do the job tomorrow."

I breathe long and slow through my nose.

"Good," I reply, as if that's my only concern.

Their mouth twists into an odd shape, then smooths back to blank. They coax another strand of sunnaz from the innermost ring of their necklace and twine it around their pointer finger, then weave in the barest trace of motaz from another ring. Making something animated then, able to move on its own. Remi's specialty. They work silently for several minutes, spinning the maz into a complex tangle of light until, with one taut pull of a thread, the whole thing shifts from strings of light to solid form. A tiny, palm-sized golden bunny.

The bunny hops from their hand up their arm, onto their shoulder, pauses, then leaps straight at my face. It smacks me in the nose with its little rabbit feet, bracing against my face for the jump back to Remi, where it finally nestles into their tousled bedhead. I reach a finger up to pet its tiny glowing ears, catching a few strands of Remi's hair in the process. It's soft, so dark it's almost black, with just a bit of wavy wildness to it, a total contrast to the tame, golden bunny. My gaze slides from their hair to their eyes. And there we pause, suspended in time, under the stars and the neon of our city, locked in connection. The air becomes heavy.

I snatch my hand back and let my gaze fall to my lap.

I feel more than hear Remi's sigh where their shoulder presses against mine. They lift the tiny golden bunny from their hair and pull the maz strands apart, threading them back into the necklace.

"Do you ever wonder what the people who hire us actually do with the maz?" they ask, voice flat as they start in on a darker, more complex spell. Something for our job tomorrow, probably.

I shrug, and my shoulder brushes against theirs, warm and close. I shiver and scoot away as subtly as I can.

"Not really. Probably not making vicious attack rabbits that want to kick me in the face, unlike some people. I imagine some are cooking up stims or weaving illegal spells, but . . . I think a lot of people just remember having free access to as much maz as they wanted, before the plague. They're like you. They want to be able to live like they used to."

I pause and consider, tracing patterns in the stars with my eyes. "I don't know, maybe that's naive. The balance of innocent to illegal is probably worse than I think it is. And the people who *are* buying more maz for daily life aren't the ones who have none. They're the ones who miss the convenience and want to get around the rationing. It's not like we're maz-liberating heroes or anything. But we need the money for a good cause, right?" I ask, turning to look at them.

They refuse to meet my eyes, instead putting the finishing touches on a deep blue-black spell, then placing it to one side to settle and fuse. It'll be stronger tomorrow than it would be if we used it right away, the way the leftovers of a spicy dish are always more flavorful the next day. They stare at the spell for a long moment, then fold their hands in their lap and wiggle one foot back and forth.

"I hate the idea of you all doing this really dangerous job just for me. So I can play with this new maz, if that's really what it is. So I can go to the school I want. Maybe we should just call it—"

"Stop," I snap. Every muscle goes tense, going from bone-weary tired to thrumming with adrenaline and ready to hit something in a single second. "It's not all about you, you know."

"I know that," they say, matter-of-fact. I purse my lips and brace my hands on the ground to push to my feet, but Remi places one hand on my knee and just says, "Don't."

My whole body goes warm. I don't move. They close

their eyes and take a breath, then forge on.

"Do you want me to stay, Dizzy?"

They open their eyes again, and the world falls out from under me. I'm pinned, my lungs and vocal cords frozen, my mind perfectly blank.

Just say it, my brain screams as it comes back online. Stay, please stay, I can't come with you, but I don't want to be without you. Please stay.

My body recoils at the thought.

"*You* want you to stay" are the words that actually came out. "You want to go to Kyrkarta U."

"That's not what I asked." Their hand squeezes my leg, and they turn farther toward me, leaning closer.

"Ask me to stay."

No, no, *no*. Pathetic, I'm *pathetic*, totally unable to form any words that might actually work for this situation. I don't *need* them, I can live without them, can start my new job and get my own place, can survive while they abandon me for a new life in Jattapore. They'll only end up leaving me eventually anyway. Them staying now would only delay the inevitable.

I can't do this.

I can't.

Eventually Remi takes their hand away. They push to their feet and brush the dirt off the seat of their galaxy-print sleep pants.

"Don't stay up too late," they say. Their fingers ghost over the shaved side of my head once, lingering, before they retreat.

The door clicks shut behind them.

"Don't leave me," I reply to the empty rooftop. It's just about as likely.

I drop my head into my hands, raining glowing stars from my hair down into the night.

EIGHT

THE CONVERSATION ON THE ROOFTOP feels like a hazy, half-remembered dream the next morning. Remi stands next to me on the train, deliberately not looking at me, but otherwise chattering away. They're not acknowledging anything at all out of the ordinary. Probably for the best. This job will require us all to be our best, least-distracted selves.

The four of us ride to the Montague Street Station together like Jaesin and I did yesterday morning. We laugh and mess around like normal, but the pull of adrenaline and anticipation gives every word and gesture a sharp edge. We've done this a hundred times, but something already feels off. Maybe it's just me, though. This'll be the closest we've ever gone to the station where my dad died. Not excited for that. It'll also be our actual, seriously, not-even-lying-this-time final job ever. I'd like to think I got all the bitterness out of my system last time, but let's be real. I am *never* out of bitterness.

When we arrive, we split up and make our own

individual ways to the park, stopping to browse as necessary to look natural. I arrive at the park last to find the others lying on the shady side of a hill facing away from the street, chatting quietly and passing a frothy purple tea between them. Remi's face lights up with quiet laughter at something Jaesin says, and they collapse into Ania's lap with their hands pressed over their face. Jaesin and Ania lock eyes for a moment and share a smile. The sight stops me dead for a long moment, the three of them there all together. Most people would see three friends hanging out, relaxing, enjoying the last few days before adulthood.

I see the end of everything. I see the three people who matter most to me in the world together, *without me*, the way it's always going to be. It's a bitter taste.

I command my lenses to take a picture: Remi reaching over to grab the cup from Jaesin, Ania's expression long-suffering but fond, Jaesin outraged at the theft of the drink before he was done with it. I'll probably be embarrassed later and delete the picture. For now, I save it and focus back on the task at hand.

I pause next to one of the border trees and pull out the small concealment spell Remi made last night. The crystalline dust of it makes my hands itch as I crush it over my head, then pull out another spell for the access hatch. A minute for the spell to take full effect, then I walk straight up to the MMC access hatch, careful to move with calm, even strides. Any sudden movements or attention-grabbing sounds and people will see right through the obscuraz, no matter how good Remi's weaving is.

When I reach the maintenance hatch, I smear the second spell across the door, feeling the tiny snaps as its lattice structure crumbles. The door glimmers faintly for a few seconds as the maz takes effect. Any passing observer's eyes should skip right over it. For now.

Once the glimmer of the spell fades, I get to work on the lock. It's both password and fingerprint locked, like most things are, and I spot a tiny camera in the top corner that's likely for facial recognition. No problem. I run my custom intrusion program to sync my deck and the door's system, and I'm in less than two minutes later. One hurdle down. If they'd changed up their security protocol, I'd have been here a lot longer, trying to develop a new workaround on the fly. But they haven't—this is no different than any other job we've ever pulled.

For a brief moment, I wonder if I'm breaking through code Davon has written himself. Guilt is useless, though. I've done this plenty of times before, and this is the last. When I accept the job at MMC—*if* I accept the job— maybe I'll write some new security protocols for these tunnels, and get paid for it too.

Ah, the irony.

I've had a password cracker for MMC's systems for years. Once I'm in, it's routine to erase the last few minutes of my face on the camera, pull up one of the saved fingerprint-and-face combos in the MMC database, and feed them back into the system. Too easy. They really do need my help. I guess it's a rare person who actually wants to enter a sewer voluntarily, though. Just me . . . and every other siphoner in the city. Come on, MMC. The door whirs, hums, then clicks open an inch.

Victory.

I turn as slowly and casually as I can and wait to catch Jaesin's eye. He watches the area around me intently, squinting as if he's trying to focus on something . . . then his face relaxes, and he gives the faintest of nods when he spots me, able to see through the spell since he knows exactly what he's looking for. The others apply their own concealment spells, get up slowly and stretch, drink the last of their tea, and amble my way, tossing the cup into a trash processor along the way. I pull the hatch open for them, slow and calm, and hold it until all three of them have passed through.

Once I slip in after them and pull the door quietly shut behind me, I climb down to the catwalk that runs above the river of underground sewage. The others wait with mischievous grins. We're in it now. No point pretending they don't love it as much as I do. Jaesin holds his hand up for a fist bump, which I happily oblige, part hell-yes-we-got-this and part thanks-for-not-ratting-me-out-yesterday. He hasn't mentioned my earlier slipup about the job-offer issue, so I guess he took me at my word for once.

"Any security?" I ask, and Jaesin shakes his head.

"No sign on the usual patrol paths. We're good to go. Remi," he says, gesturing ahead of us. "Lead the way."

"You just want me to step in the poop first," they whine, but take the lead anyway, practically skipping. In just a few minutes, we'll know for sure if maz-15 is real, and their excitement is palpable. Sewers aren't the best place for someone immunocompromised, but Remi always take precautions—a mask, rain boots, disposable gloves, a truly alarming amount of sanitizer once we leave, and a hot shower with decon chems when we get home. They run one gloved hand along the pipes above as they walk, sensing for the maz inside.

"I think this is the one we want. Something's weird," they murmur, muffled by the mask, and follow the pipe deeper into the tunnels. Even after knowing them for almost ten years, Remi still amazes me. The fact that they can feel out which strains are running through the pipe when it's all mixed together is amazing. And this is the last time I'll get to see them at work, doing what they do best.

I never knew it was possible to feel nostalgic for something that isn't even over yet, but when Ania meets my gaze with a little twist of a smile, I know she feels the same.

The smell intensifies as we draw farther and farther away from the fresher air near the entrance, until

the air actually feels thick and heavy with the indescrib-
able stench of rotting waste. Scentaz is fairly rare and of
limited use, so we never bother stealing any. We breathe
through our mouths and creep along the narrow catwalks
until we find what we need—a junction point with a small
pressure release valve on one side, the same one we just
tapped two days ago. That's our cue, and we move like
the practiced, efficient team we are.

Jaesin and Ania break off and take up their respec-
tive positions. I swear half the reason Ania comes with
us on these jobs is so she can try out the new shielding
and warding techniques she likes to experiment with.
She takes her time weaving protection for us in case of
trouble, making it look like a graceful performance rather
than a practical safeguard. Jaesin begins his circuit, walking the perimeter of the wide platform and a few feet
down each connecting tunnel, listening for incoming
guards and keeping watch for any other surprises.

Remi and I get to work on the pipe itself. The security
on the access hatch was nothing, but this ice is always
much harder to crack. Unlike the other night, my attempt
at a wireless connection is denied almost instantly, so I
put my bag down and dig for a screwdriver. "Gonna hardwire in. Let me know if the world burns down."

Because honestly, when I'm eyeballs deep in code, I
wouldn't even notice.

Jaesin and Ania murmur their affirmatives without

any particular concern, but Remi frowns, pressing both hands to the pipe they've identified.

"Everything okay?" I ask, fitting the screwdriver into a groove and prying the access panel off. The junction box looks new, and much more modern than the others we've worked with in the past. Maybe they did update their security after all. Not good.

"Yeah," Remi says, distracted. "Fine. Go ahead."

Super convincing there, but what can I do? I have no idea what it's like or what it means when Remi's maz senses are tingling. That's their deal.

I snip and strip a few wires, my hands absolutely steady, then pull out my magnifying goggles and a small soldering iron. The faint tinny burning smell of the heated iron is a welcome cover for the sewage and rot, but my wrist aches with the effort of the tiny movements required. Adrenaline and my racing heart make me hyper-focused, though, as I process every minuscule thread of each wire, the solder needed to coat them. Once I've established a few temporary contact points for the cables I brought, I pull up the goggles and set them on my forehead, blinking a few times to readjust. Game time.

"It's been ten minutes, Diz. Should we be planning to take afternoon tea down here? Maybe roll out some sleeping bags?" Jaesin asks. He and Ania exchange a glance, that perfect parental balance of amused and vaguely concerned.

I clench my teeth. "I'm aware, Jaesin. Doing the best I can."

I pull out my deck and slip the other end of the cable into its port, then dive in. With the direct connection, I bypass the worst of the security in a matter of minutes. *Finally*, back on solid footing. I breathe the tiniest sigh of relief as I search the code for the valve control functions; we could just release it manually, of course, but that would be recorded in the logs and possibly set off an alarm somewhere at the station. Only amateurs do that. This way I can get in, get the valve to open itself, make it look like a normal pressure release was triggered, and start directing the flow from farther up the pipe. Much quieter.

"Get those vials ready, Ania. Remi, you ready?" I ask. Everything's set. This is the hard part. We have to be perfectly coordinated, and fast. Without Ania, we only have one set of eyes on watch, but she's done setting up her outer wards, and we need her talents elsewhere.

Ania leaves her post and retrieves the vials from her bag, lining them up on a small ledge near the valve. That done, she steps back and weaves a second set of wards, this time encompassing Remi, the valve, and the vials in one area, separating them from us. The maz in these pipes is already scrubbed of the spellplague contaminant, but you can never be too careful when it comes to the thing that left three-quarters of us without parents. Remi hovers there, eyes on the first vial, nimble fingers poised and ready as I work on the code side of things. They always love this part, but today they're grinning from ear to ear, waiting to make a discovery. Maz is a huge part of their life. Finding out there might be a new kind when it's been hundreds of years since the last strain was discovered must be like . . . I don't even know. Like the jump from screens to smart lenses? Bigger? Like the world is a different place.

I prep the final command to open the valve, then hold my breath. This guy asked for way too much, really, more than I'd usually be comfortable siphoning of any one strain. Too noticeable. And last time we barely got a trickle, accidentally mixed in with something else. We're just hoping there's more where that came from.

But after this, we're done. No more jobs. One enormous payday. Definitely worth the risk.

And then I'll see what life will look like at the end of the week for real. Who knows, maybe we'll be rocking a top-floor apartment in one of the high rises together, rolling around in ice cream and tacos, watching garbage TV and eating Jaesin's experiment of the week. Screw MMC, I'll open my own business building top-of-the-line custom maz hardware, with Remi there as adviser. And more?

If we can just get through this job, maybe we can have it all.

"Okay, opening the valve in three . . . two . . . one . . ."

I hit ENTER, and silently beg the universe for some good luck. Please let Remi be right, let this pipe have the maz we need. There's a tiny part of me that still doesn't totally believe it's real, that the stuff we gave Mattie was a fluke, but it's too late now.

The pressure valve hisses open.

Remi's on it immediately, holding back the flow with one hand while they use the other to carefully separate a handful of bright violet threads. They direct it with expert precision into the first vial, mouth open wide in an ecstatic, joyous laugh.

"Do you see that, Diz?" they say, following the flow of the strands with their eyes, the cheery violet reflected against the gray. "Do you see it? It's real. Stars, Dizzy, this is a *real* thing."

"I see it."

And I'm totally captivated.

I need to be monitoring the system, looking for silent alarms or diagnostic alerts, but this part . . . Remi amazes me every time. Their connection to maz is so thorough, so intuitive. I'll never be bored of watching them feel the flow in the pipes, drawing out exactly what we need, managing all of it with perfect technique, even when it's a totally brand-new thing and their hands are shaking with pure excitement. The strain's warm purple light puts a flush on their cheeks, glints off lips bitten in concentration, turns darkest brown hair to a purple-black sheen.

They're beautiful.

A red warning light in the corner of my lenses pulls me back to the task at hand. Pressure alert. A blockage or something farther up the pipe, driving a surge of maz down our way. Remi frowns.

"You see that, Diz?" they ask, spinning the flow around their index finger while they seal the fourth vial and prep the fifth.

"I see it." I back out from the valve we're working on and travel deeper into the system, seeking out other valves farther down the pipe, away from the junction station. No security alerts at the next one down, no personnel nearby. Safe to open. I trigger it, hold my breath.

The warning light fades from red to orange, then to yellow. And holds steady there.

"Diz," Remi says warningly.

"It's fine." I look over my shoulder and find Jaesin and Ania staring me down. "It's fine, I promise. Bit of a pressure buildup upstream. I took care of it."

"I don't like it," Jaesin says. "What if it gets worse?"

"We should go, Diz," Ania urges, but I cut her off.

"No, we're almost there. Just a few more vials. I'll open the valve a bit wider so we can go faster. The pressure stabilized, it can handle it."

Ania shakes her head.

119

"That sounds dangerous, Diz—let's just take what we've got and go. We can get the rest another day," she pleads.

"And let this guy back out of our deal, or refuse to pay the rest because we couldn't deliver all of it by his deadline? We need that money." Remi needs that money. Jaesin needs it too, if he wants that shiny apartment in Jattapore he's been drooling over. Ania doesn't need anything. I sure as hell do, though.

I'm not leaving without this maz.

I open the valve farther.

"Diz!" Ania snaps, and Remi sucks in a breath and rocks back on their heels, taking on the extra flow. The vials fill faster. Five. Six. Seven. Just one more, the one for Remi.

Then the pressure spikes, and Remi lets out a cry.

"Dizzy!"

"I see it!"

I open valves all up and down the line, but something's wrong. The pressure climbs higher instead of stabilizing, traveling down the pipe like a cannonball racing toward us. I trip the failsafes, trigger every emergency protocol, but nothing, nothing's working. My heart hammers in the base of my throat.

"Get out," I say, yanking my cable free, turning to meet Jaesin's and Ania's wide eyes. "Go, GO!"

"No time—get back," Remi gasps, just as a shrill

screech splits the air and the spigot blows off the valve, grazing Remi's forehead and drawing blood. They let out a hoarse shout, but redouble their efforts, raising both arms toward the pipe to catch the enormous flood of maz, freezing it in the air above them—and all the blood drains from my face as I note the color. It's a flickering tangle of gold-red-orange, almost entirely firaz and magnaz. Practically a bomb.

The ominous silence falls like a stone as Remi holds the giant cloud of twisting, twining threads there, their face crumpled in pain, tears leaking from the corners of their eyes. Ania holds her arms up too, but techwitch ware can't control maz outside its own chambers. She's helpless, crying as Jaesin races back toward us, his eyes wild, stopping just outside Remi's wards. Remi groans and redoubles their efforts, pushing, pushing . . . until an earth-shaking *BOOM* rocks the tunnel, sending dirt raining down, and the maz Remi was barely holding at bay is suddenly sucked back down the pipe. My ears pop with the sudden reversal of pressure, and I stumble to my knees, scraping them bloody through my trousers.

I don't even feel the sting. Because right in front of me, Remi crumples, eyes closed, face pale, slipping through Jaesin's arms to the ground.

Every single *almost* moment flashes through my mind.

The rooftop, just a few hours ago, shoulder to shoulder, stars in my hair.

Out at the club, dancing close, hands on waists and hips.

That one time, when we were barely fifteen . . . that first *almost* . . .

No.

"We have to get out of here," Ania says, voice gone calm and even. "If there's another pressure surge, we're all dead."

"Diz, help me," Jaesin snaps, and that shakes me out of my horror. One of Remi's hands flopped outside the second set of wards when they collapsed, and I leap forward to grab it and help Jaesin haul them back. Once they're clear of the protective barrier around the tap point, Jaesin and I throw Remi's arms over our shoulders and half drag, half carry them back to the access hatch, Ania jogging ahead of us to clear the newly fallen debris from our path.

Behind us, secondary explosions ring through the tunnels, with screeching pipes and a threatening rumble that feels almost like an earthquake aftershock. Remi's electric blue rain boots drag over the moist, nasty concrete, the color quickly erased by grime and clinging wet weeds.

By the time we catch up to Ania at the end of the tunnel, she's woven a quick combination of vitaz, the healer, and magnaz, the amplifier, an odd bright green glow in the cavernous filthy darkness of the sewers. Jaesin and

I brace Remi long enough for Ania to slip the tiny spell onto their tongue, where it dissolves in a wash of green static.

An eternal ten seconds pass before there's any visible effect.

Finally Remi's eyelids flutter, their breathing going uneven for a moment, then cool gray eyes stare back at me, growing sharper and more alert by the second. The relief nearly chokes me breathless. My eyes burn with the effort to hold back tears.

"Can you walk?" I ask, brisk and clipped. They pull away from me, letting their arm fall from my shoulders and trying a tentative step.

"Yeah," they rasp, pressing a hand to their temple with a wince. "Ania, gimme some of that."

Remi gestures at the vial of extra vitaz Ania has pulled from her bag, and the maz lifts out of the vial like an ivy vine, twining through the air toward them. A bit of magnaz from the stores in their necklace, a tight and complex weave, and the whole thing goes straight into their mouth. A bit of color returns to Remi's cheeks, but it's a temporary fix at best. Without a word, they shrug Jaesin's arm off and step onto the bottom rung of the ladder. Jaesin follows them up, close enough to catch them if they fall, and we climb until all four of us are back at the hatch. There's no time to make a clean, stealthy exit, not with Remi's condition and the constant threat of more explosions at our back. I push my way to the front and throw the door open, letting the late-morning sun spill over us, and step back.

When I turn to watch Remi emerge behind me, the wreckage beyond the park comes into view.

The explosion wasn't just belowground.

Fire. Debris strewn through the streets. People running, screaming, crying. Loose maz pouring into the air from a gaping wound in the junction station.

Then the contamination sirens kick on, wailing their shrill warning, a savage punch to the gut.

Is the maz spilling from the station untreated? It's moving fast, overtaking block after block, spilling, infecting.

Killing?

I wrap my arms around my middle, physically holding in noxious, nauseating dread.

What have we done?

NINE

I CAN BARELY SEE WHERE I'm going as we stumble through the park to the sight of people running through the streets, away from the junction station. My vision blurs, my mind one solid, silent scream as we run, my feet following Jaesin on autopilot as they have for the past ten years, since our first day in the group home together.

"We need to get to the train station," he says, his voice hoarse. He wraps an arm around Remi to keep them on their feet as he turns toward an alley that dumps out on the nearest main road. "Come on!"

The four of us blend into the crowd, our breathing as harsh and panicked as everyone else's. I hardly see any of it. My brain spins in endless circles, replaying every second of the hack. What did I do wrong? There were no indications that there would be a problem, no overload notices, no complaining sensors, until that one pressure blip out of nowhere. And there's no reason bleeding off the pressure at the other tap points shouldn't have worked. Even Remi didn't feel anything until it was too late, way too sudden, just—HOW?

"Diz," Ania says, her voice knife sharp. "Focus before you trip over your own feet and get trampled."

But focus is impossible. Because when we turn to cross the bridge over the river, trying to get to the train station, the elevation provides us an even better view of the disaster in progress.

Of the maz pouring out from the junction station in tangled waves.

All the people who work at that station, who go there every day to earn money and a maz stipend for their families, they're all going to be ill. And it's our fault.

My fault.

I come to a stop at the apex of the bridge and watch the different strains of maz swirling through the air over the station like a glowing, glittering breeze.

"Those people—"

I break off and gag. My dad died at work, at this station, just like this. *Just* like this. My stomach roils with hot acid, and my throat contracts, trying to force me to vomit. I'm seven years old again, drowning in the smell of death, a lifeless hand holding mine, the panic, the gnawing emptiness in my belly, the strange people, the stinking crowds, the group home, the other empty-eyed kids, it's too much, *too much*, and I don't notice I've fallen to my knees until the chill of the concrete bites into the already torn skin there and sharp blades of grit dig into my palms. I can't get a breath, can't satisfy my hungry lungs, and I gasp, gasp—

An arm loops around my waist and hauls me up, slings my arm over a strong shoulder. Jaesin, dragging me to my feet and down the bridge, catching us up with Ania and Remi, who stare up at us.

Remi. Brow crinkled in worry. Looking pale and shaky.

They reach out to lay a hand on my shoulder as we draw near, and I recoil so hard Jaesin slams into the people next to us and nearly drops me.

"Don't touch me."

The words rip from my throat, my voice inhuman and harsh, sounding horribly far away. Echoing off cheap bathroom tile in a seven-year-old's high, frightened voice.

Remi's expression goes cold, so closed off it's like a detonator spell went off in my chest. But I can't. I need to shut down, feel *nothing*, and when Remi touches me . . .

I just *can't.*

Ania takes over for Jaesin and turns us toward a side street. "We should split up, in case we were spotted. They'll be looking for four people. We'll meet back at your place, right?"

Jaesin nods his agreement and guides Remi away with a hand on their back. Before they turn, though, he shoots me a look, more furious than I've ever seen him. I catch a last glimpse of Remi's face too. Blank. Resigned. I've ruined everything. I've finally done it—well and truly pushed them away, for good this time. I squeeze my eyes shut and lean more heavily on Ania.

"Oof," she says, readjusting her hold on me. "I know you're having a hard time right now, love, but I need you to help me out a bit here unless you want me to drop your ass in the middle of Montague Station like that night with the burritos and the goat."

The memory of that night is enough to penetrate the fog in my brain. I manage to get my feet more firmly under me and do a stumbling walk toward the train station, eyes locked on the ground the whole way. One thing at a time. Get to the station. Repeat it until there's nothing else in my brain. Train station, train station, train station, until they don't even sound like words anymore, just a droning noise to keep out the rest.

But the train station isn't the answer after all. We round the last corner, only to find a ring of flashing lights and uniformed bodies between it and us. The officers hold the panicking crowds at bay, directing people toward detours and scanning the crowd with sharp eyes.

Scanning for us?

Shit.

Ania tugs me around, presenting our backs to the police, and we dive into the thickest part of the crowd. We'll have to make toward the apartment on foot until we can find a bus or train that's still running, which could take all afternoon. I need to get it together. Ania can't carry me for miles.

"Hold up," I say, pulling away to lean against the side of a brightly lit coffee shop. This whole thing is manageable. I've pulled myself together before. I've let the seams get loose, though, let too much spill out into the open. Left myself vulnerable.

I can fix that.

I open the drawer in my mind where I keep all my horrors—all the details of the spellplague, my parents—and shove it all deep, deep down. Awful memories, anger, grief, everything scrabbles at the edges with long tendrils and spindly legs, desperate to get out, but I slam the drawer shut before anything can escape.

It can never close all the way. There's always a crack. But I can pull off my usual self. Lock it away. It doesn't exist. Spellplague? What spellplague? I don't know, man, I just live here.

I take three long, deep breaths in through my nose, then push off from the wall.

"Okay," I say. "Sorry. Let's go. I'll get us home."

Ania watches me, cautious and worried, but follows me down the alley behind the shop all the same.

It takes us nearly an hour to find a bus along the right route to take us back to the apartment, then another hour of hopping from bus to bus to get around earthquake-damaged sectors before we finally make it back to the right part of town. None of the RidePods are accepting passengers, either due to overflow or because the police have shut the system down while they get control of the situation. During the ride, I compose and delete no less than twelve messages to Davon. What the hell am I supposed to say? Probably best not to involve him anyway. Don't want the police knocking down his door looking for me. The need to reach out to him thrums like a constant vibration under my breastbone, though.

I'm sure he wasn't there. I'm sure he's fine. He usually works on the other side of town. Nothing to worry about.

Jaesin and Remi are completely radio silent the entire time, which is worrying, but not entirely surprising. If I let my mind wander for so much as a second, it starts replaying that moment on the bridge, the maz, Remi, my reaction to their touch, everything it brought up. We've had so many almosts over the years we've known each other, but I'll bet anything that moment on the rooftop last night was the last one. I've finally closed the door on that possibility forever.

Maybe it's for the best.

They probably both hate me now. Doesn't stop me from worrying, though. We'll see them soon, anyway. I know this city the way I know computers, and that's saying something. Though we hit detour after detour, I get us closer and closer with every turn. We're nearly home. Nearly safe.

(Nearly somewhere I can close myself off and sit in a dark room for a few hours and breathe, breathe, breathe. . . .)

We round the final corner to the block dominated by the Cliffs, and I'm already dreaming of the dinner Jaesin will make (dumplings, he always makes dumplings when he's stressed). My delicious thoughts are interrupted, though, when I'm yanked back into an alcove next to the twenty-four-hour beauty salon and a hand clamps down over my mouth. I thrash and struggle for a second, until Jaesin's voice hisses in my ear, "Chill the hell out, Diz!"

I chill the hell out. As soon as I stop struggling, he lets me go, and I see Remi do the same with Ania.

"What the hell?" Ania hisses, backing away to get a little personal space. "Why aren't you at the flat?"

"Look for yourself," Remi says. "But be sneaky about it, you know?"

Ania scoots to the edge of the alcove and leans her head out just a little bit, then jerks back.

"Why are the police crawling all over your apartment building? How could they have IDed us that quickly?"

My stomach drops through the floor. No. No, no, NO, we love that flat. We busted our asses to get reassigned there two years ago, and for us to get run out of there is our worst nightmare. All my gear is there, and

Remi's maz stash, and Jaesin's cookware that he saved for months to buy at the thrift store. They'll confiscate everything. They'll never let us go back. Because if there are cops there, then we were obviously seen leaving the park, so they know we caused the rupture, so they're out to arrest us, and—

The cops interrupt my spiral by hauling one of the guys from the fourth floor out with his hands cuffed. Benny, I think? He's cursing his face off, his face gone completely red and splotchy. I can't catch the specifics, but in between the swearing I hear something about drugs theft. Several plainclothes officers enter the building as soon as he's gone, carrying large cases of equipment. Obviously settling in for a nice, long session of evidence collection. Just not in *our* apartment.

I blow out a long breath. "Okay. So maybe they *aren't* on to us specifically, but we still can't go home with the cops crawling all over the place."

Jaesin nods. "We have to assume we were seen and our faces are going to be painted across every newsfeed and signscreen in town eventually. Where can we go to lie low for a while and figure out what to do next?"

I turn to Ania with a raised eyebrow. "Any chance your parents want some criminal houseguests?"

All the blood drains from her face.

"Oh god, my parents." She covers her eyes and shakes her head. "If the cops ID us, do you think they'll tell my parents even though I'm eighteen? They're gonna kill me, I'm gonna lose my spot at the university—"

A faint buzz sounds, and Ania's eyes go wide as she focuses on something in her lenses. She pulls her deck from her back pocket and flips the screen around to show us the notification: I new message from Mom. She looks about ready to throw up. I take a step back.

"What does it say?" Remi asks.

Ania takes a deep breath, and her throat moves as she subvocalizes the command to open the message on her lenses. She reads it aloud.

"'Hi, sweetie, please pick up some cassava on your way home. Not sure where you're at today, but avoid the western routes near the edge of town. Some kind of maz leak over there today, and we've had several new cases of spellsickness at the hospital. It's all over the news, some big hunt going on for four fugitives. Be careful. See you tonight, love you.'"

I firmly block out the bit about spellsickness and focus on the rest. "You think she's playing it casual to try to get you to come home?"

Ania snorts. "My mom couldn't be sneaky if she tried. She honestly has no idea. My house might be an option after all."

"Give me a minute to check the news. We should know what people are saying about all this," I say, and call up a new search on my lenses. I can feel Remi's eyes on me, cold and expectant. "Kyrkarta, news only, last three hours . . . Hey, apparently Seph's Appliances down in the Crater is having a scratch-and-dent sale because of the earthquake, and Councilman Blake got caught with his pants down again. Shocking."

"Focus, Diz," Jaesin growls, and I wave him off.

"I've got it, I just had to sift through all the crap first. Here. 'The disaster is thought to have been triggered by an illegal maz-siphoning operation. Kyrkarta City Law has begun a search for four suspects, whose names and faces have not yet been released so as not to compromise the ongoing investigation. Up-to-date information can be found on the Law's net site, along with a form for submitting your tips. The death toll has not been confirmed at this time, but emergency responders on-site say the number will be in the hundreds. Meanwhile, Maz Management has stepped in to contain the disaster and lend a hand to the community in a gesture reminiscent of the early days of the spellplague, with volunteer efforts . . .'"

Death toll.

My throat closes up, cutting off the last of my words. My memories of the hack play again and again, a constant spiral in the back of my mind. Where did I go wrong? I swear I did everything right, but I must have screwed up somehow, I *must* have.

Ania doesn't notice my sudden mental departure. She

just sighs in relief. "Okay, so they haven't named any of us yet. If we can sneak you all in, I should be able to hide you for a while. At least, long enough for us to figure out what to do next. I have my own room in the basement, and my parents rarely come down there anymore."

"And you've never taken your scrub friends home to meet Mommy and Daddy," I can't help but add. "So they won't recognize us even if they do eventually show our faces on the news. Good. We have a plan, then."

"Whoa, whoa, wait up," Ania says. "We still have to get you all to my house without being seen, then get you inside. It might be . . . you know . . ."

She hesitates, and all the mixed-up, messed-up, roiling anger and everything inside me comes out in a fearsome glare.

"I'm going to kindly assume you were going to say that it's not smart for us to walk around showing our faces openly, not that our broke-ass selves will stick out like sunnaz in a shit storm in your neighborhood."

Ania winces and turns her back to the road to hide the faint glow of her maz as she begins to weave.

"Let's just use some concealment spells, okay?"

I take the offered spell wordlessly and crumple it over my head, watching the faint purple-black sparks drift to the ground like embers of burning paper.

I wish there was such a thing as a concealment spell

for your own thoughts. I have it together for now, but the threads are fraying, the awfulness lying just below the surface, watching. Waiting.

Death toll, they said.

The barest crack in the surface is all it will take.

TEN

WHEN ANIA SAID HER ROOM was in the basement, she should have said "rooms." And when she said basement, she should have said "luxury apartment suite that happens to be on an underground level and yet still manages to be just as nice as the rest of the house that we weren't allowed a tour of." I've known her for six years and this is the first time I've seen any of it.

The walls are painted a cool, relaxing blue, the same color as the water maz Ania's family is named for. The bel Wataza family crest is framed on the wall, next to a string-woven tapestry of their home city back on the Small Continent, near where my dad grew up. The room holds two sleek, modern couches in clean white, accented with a brighter, more vivid blue, with end tables sporting carved sculptures and drink coasters. Gauzy curtains hang over the windows, and light fixtures adorn nearly every wall and surface. It's so bright I never would have guessed it's mostly underground. The front room is bigger than our entire flat.

I'm not bitter. Really.

"So, what are we not allowed to touch and where are we allowed to sleep?" I sneer, then mentally slap myself. Everyone is stressed. This isn't the time to harass Ania about her fanciness.

Ania takes it in stride, though, as always. "I think it would be best to stay out of this main sitting room—"

"Sitting room?" I say before I can help myself, then cover my mouth and gesture for her to go on.

"Since this is where the staircase from the first floor leads, this is the first thing my parents see if they decide to come down," she finishes. "There's a gaming room back here, a guest bedroom, my bedroom, and a kitchenette. You can survive down here without being seen for quite a while, I think."

I let that sink in for a moment. It's a bitter pill to swallow, knowing Ania has been living in such spacious luxury the whole time we've known each other, while the rest of us shared one bedroom in an apartment in the orphan district. Not that I want any of it. It feels weird, like I'm going to break something or get it dirty if I touch it. I've always known, of course, but there's a difference between knowing and seeing.

I *knew* the second she walked into the tech shop where I worked six years ago, with her fancy babysitter. I was newly twelve, barely able to work two hours a day by law. The babysitter looked around with her nose in the air, obviously appalled at the cramped quarters, dust, grease, solder fumes, and whatever else. Ania, though, looked around at everything with wide eyes, her expensive training hardware clipped around her wrist and her curls bouncing as she scrambled from one display to another. Her clothes were new and clean, her steps light, the heels of her fancy boots pinging like falling coins across the shop floor.

Twelve-year-old me was enchanted, and immediately wanted to show off. "Are you here to have your ware fixed? I'm the best there is, promise."

The babysitter cleared her throat delicately. "This shop was recommended to us by a friend of the family, but I see she must have been mistaken. Come, Ania, we won't be letting a child fix your techwitchery hardware."

She said "techwitchery hardware" like she'd read the term once in a textbook long ago, the verbal equivalent of holding dirty laundry pinched between two fingers as far from your face as possible. The shop owner, Mr. Ailiano, gave a big belly laugh. "Oh, your friend didn't steer you wrong, and Dizzy there won't be doing the fixing, though she is certainly smart as a whip and will probably be better than me before much longer. I'd be happy to take a look at your ware and give you an estimate, free of charge. Let me see, girl. I'll give it right back, promise."

Ania removed her ware with gentle grace and placed it in the man's hand without seeking the approval of her babysitter first. In fact, when she turned around, she had a bit of a smirk on her face. She rolled her eyes and jerked a thumb back at her nanny.

"Ugh," she mouthed, and I had to cover my face with both hands to hide my giggles. It was the first time I'd laughed all week, and though I normally hated rich people, I found I couldn't stop myself from chatting with Ania. Before she and her nanny left with her expertly fixed ware, Ania had slipped me a comm code and mimed typing. Message me.

And I did. And we've been friends ever since, even through my nasty comments and bloody knuckles, even through Ania's acceptance into a fancy private school while I was stuck at Kyrkarta Polytechnic, a zombie drone in front of a computer terminal in a classroom with three hundred other kids. Even through Ania's discovery of my little side hobbies: crawling through locked and abandoned buildings, hacking the accounts of public officials for fun, and stealing maz for Remi to use in their weaving.

We've stuck together. A fancy bedroom (even bedrooms, plural) shouldn't change that. And yet, I feel it more intensely than I ever have before. Ania lives here. *Here.* And as she leads us into the next room and removes her shoes to place them delicately on a hand-carved shoe rack, a new thought occurs to me. She probably brings her school friends here.

My gaze flits across the room: gaming systems with multiplayer games, a holodeck board game system, more couches that look too pristine to sit my lowly ass on . . . and framed photos of Ania sitting in this very room with two other well-dressed, perfectly styled people our age, wearing the uniform of her private school.

Yep, that stings. But nowhere near as bad as the photo of Ania and a lean, blonde girl in winged eyeliner, wearing matching university sweatshirts and holding up their acceptance letters.

Ania is going off to university with this girl. She's leaving me in the dust, alone, but she'll be anything *but* alone.

She's my best friend, but I'm apparently not hers.

And why should I be? I'm the girl who gets in fights. I'm the girl who can't have an emotion without wanting to punch a wall. I'm the girl who screwed up our last job so badly that I *killed* people.

While I'm having my private meltdown, Jaesin and Remi remove their shoes and set up shop in front of Ania's wall array, which holds an enormous screen with curved sides. Remi sinks to the couch and scrolls through the collection of games with an open mouth and unblinking eyes, arms limp with exhaustion.

"Oh, you are so going down," they say to Jaesin, who snatches up one of the wireless controllers and syncs it to his deck and lenses.

"Please. I played this game all the time back at the home and you know it. I dominated in our intrahouse league."

"That was years ago, and I've been playing the deck version for months. You're gonna eat it so hard." Their words are strong, but only their eyes and the tips of their fingers move. They've gone into full energy conservation mode.

I bite the inside of my cheek to keep from lashing out. We all have our own way of dealing with things, and they apparently need a distraction more than they need to know how we managed to screw up and kill people. Those two are like bickering siblings on the best of days. Put a video game between them, and we'll be lucky if they don't bring the cops down on us from all the shouting, no matter how tired Remi is. Speaking of which . . .

"Aren't your parents going to be able to hear us down here?" I ask, finally meeting Ania's gaze.

"It's pretty soundproof. We should be okay if we can keep those two under control," she says with a sharp side-eye at Remi and Jaesin. "This isn't a long-term solution, though. We need to talk about what we're going to do. Even if the news cycle dies down and they stop actively looking for us, you won't be able to get a job or an apartment in this city, and you won't be able to show your face out on the streets."

I sit down hard on the couch and put my head

between my knees. "Damn, Ania, just lay it all out there, why don't you?"

She winces. "Sorry, but it's all true. I know it's a lot, but the longer we wait, the harder it's going to be to get out of this mess."

The noise escalates as Jaesin and Remi get deeper into their game, shoving each other's avatars off moving platforms and dashing for the same powerups. Ania looks to the ceiling and shakes her head, then stomps over to them.

"You're going to get us caught the second my parents get home! Should I just call them and tell them you're here? Do I need to take the video game away from you like a babysitter?"

Jaesin and Remi both duck their heads with sheepish looks. Remi pushes their controller away and hits the power button.

"Yeah, you probably should take it away, actually," they say, the picture of innocence . . . until they lower their voice and mutter to Jaesin, "This isn't over."

How are the two of them so . . . uncaring? Are they just that good at blocking out the awfulness? If so, they should teach me, because I obviously can't handle it.

Ania sits on the plush couch, her face shadowed with concern. I flop down beside her and throw one of the fancy cushions at Jaesin, way harder than I mean to.

"Okay, can we be serious for a second?" I say. "A

bunch of people just died because of us and we should care. The cops are out to get us, the media will be all over us the second they release our info, and the guy we were doing this job for is probably gonna be pissed because, unless one of you thought to grab it, *we don't have his maz.*"

I pause for a minute to swallow against the constriction in my throat. "I don't know what happened. This is such a mess. Nothing like this has ever happened to us, and it's just . . ."

Somewhere above us, a muffled thump echoes, followed by what are unmistakably footsteps.

Ania glances to the corner of her vision where her lenses show the time. "My parents are home. I'm serious, though, they never come down here. They never even speak to me unless spoken to."

Her expression grows pinched, and she changes the subject.

"I guess first thing we should do is try to get in contact with the guy who gave us the job. Return his money, tell him the deal's off. We can't have him after us, too."

She's right. This is the first job we've ever failed to come through on, and the funny thing is it's absolutely the least of our worries. Now that we're murderers. Now that we've let loose a new plague upon the Industrial District. Now that we've irrevocably damaged the lives of thousands of people. All the guilt and shame Jaesin and Remi were trying to avoid shows plainly on their faces, in the way they sit slouched over, shoulders pressed together. I'm tempted to hack into the hospital's records and see if Ginny from the bakery is among the ill or dead, but I don't.

I can't.

"I have to figure out why it happened," I say, trying so hard to keep my voice from shaking. "Yes, I made a mistake. I pushed it too hard, but that shouldn't have caused such a huge rupture up the pipe unless there was already something else wrong. You felt it, Remi," I say, pleading for them to back me up.

They only shrug, avoiding my eyes as they wipe a tear away. "I definitely felt something surge or change right at the end there, but I have no idea what it was or where to go about looking for it. Besides, I think Ania is right here. I hate that it happened, but what will knowing change? It still will have happened. Those people will still be ill. Or dead."

I blink, stunned. I want to protest, to say *something* in reply, but I can't force my brain to comprehend. I know Remi can't mean that the way it sounds. They must be hurting, hurting *so bad*, thinking of all the newly ill. So how can they not want to figure this out? I look to Jaesin to back me up, but he only nods, leaning forward to brace his forehead on his folded hands.

"I think what we really need to do here is take

whatever money we can pull from our accounts and get out of town," he says. When he lifts his head, his eyes are shiny with tears, but hard. "We head to Jattapore a few days early, that's all. Ania, you come with us for a week, just to lay low and let this pass. And we forget this ever happened."

My vision whites out with a surge of anger.

"No. NO!" I shout, momentarily forgetting about Ania's parents. "We have to figure out what we did wrong. What if it happens again? Or what if it wasn't our fault and there's something wrong with the system down there, just waiting to set off another spellplague?"

Ania's expression is pained, but she shakes her head. "I'm with Jaesin here," she begins. "They'll be investigating for a long time. If there's something wrong, they'll find it. We need to—"

"You're a bunch of fucking cowards!" I spit, my throat raw and tight. My hands clench into fists, the knuckles going white. "Hundreds of people dead or dying, they said, and you just wanna skip town?"

They're so fixated on leaving, so constantly ready to just abandon Kyrkarta and leave everything behind. We grew up here, Davon is here, our parents *died* and are buried here, and they can just walk away? Just ditch our home city to fend for itself in the wake of a disaster of our own making? How can they find it so easy to leave this place?

To leave me?

They should *know*. I shouldn't have to ask them to stay and deal with this, they should *know*.

We were supposed to have more time.

"I won't leave," I say, quieter, low and furious. "I won't run away from this."

Jaesin, the perpetually patient one, finally snaps, that fury I glimpsed on the bridge boiling over.

"Why not, Diz? Isn't avoidance your default way to deal with *everything*? You never wanted to leave with us anyway. You cared more about yourself and this city than about our ten years of friendship. You decided to take that job with Davon instead of going with us, but you're too much of a coward to just say it. Don't think I didn't notice that slipup yesterday. So what's the difference? You don't want to join us? Fine. Stay here and rot in everything you refuse to get over, become an MMC zombie and look over your shoulder every single day, wondering if anyone's going to figure you out. Go out in the middle of the night and hang out with Davon and dance with random girls, even though there are people right here who care about you, who are offering you another option."

He pauses, then shakes his head. "I've always known where we stood with you. I guess I just thought you might change your mind before we actually all fell apart."

I laugh, harsh and unkind.

"Well, you should really know better by now,

shouldn't you," I say. Joke's on him. I fell apart years ago.

"Yeah," he says, quieter. "Yeah, I guess I should."

He takes a long breath in, then blows it out slowly.

"Well, we're leaving tomorrow. With or without you. Right?" he asks. The others nod their assent, tears running down their cheeks, Remi's eyes pleading.

I can't look at them. I can't look at any of them. My blood boils hot under my skin.

"Fine," I say. *"Fine."*

My chest tightens, the vise grip around my heart squeezing until it crumbles away to ashes.

"Goodbye, I guess."

It comes out rough, the last syllable barely audible, because a little dignity is apparently too much to ask for.

A notification pops up on my lenses as I snatch my boots up off the rack and tug them roughly onto my feet. Davon.

(private) Davon: Hey, I've been buried in code all day and only just heard about the maz accident. You weren't on the west side of town today, were you?
Please get back to me
Please Dizzy, gods, where are you?

I almost laugh. At least someone's still in my corner. Until I screw that up too. Until he finds out what I've done.

I walk over to the shoulder-height window that borders on a back alleyway, tuning out the muttered argument going on behind me. It slides open easily when I touch the controls, because of course everything in this house is in perfect, pristine working order. I take a steadying breath and place my hands on the windowsill.

"Dizzy, wait," Remi says, breaking through the fog, their voice high and strangled.

I jump and lift myself up, my boots probably leaving scuff marks on the wall as they brace my climb. The cool evening air stings my tear-stained cheeks as I force myself out. Free. Burning for answers.

Alone.

ELEVEN

MY HIPS BARELY FIT THROUGH the narrow basement window, but after a long, awkward moment staring out into the empty evening streets with my ass stuck inside the house, I finally tumble free. Extremely graceful exit—I'm sure everyone's impressed.

I get slowly to my feet and keep low to the ground, scurrying down the side street where the trash drones do their pickups. Stars forbid these people have to have trash bins out front of their houses like the rest of us slobs. It works to my benefit, though, because it gives me a narrow alley no one wants to look at to run down in the fading light.

My entire front is uncomfortably damp, and I brush the grassy bits off as best I can. It rained as we made our way to Ania's house earlier, slowly and carefully over the course of a few hours, and it didn't occur to me the grass would still be wet. Genius. It won't matter for long, though. Without Remi's or Ania's concealment spells, I need a disguise. A dry disguise, preferably.

I spend the next two hours walking four miles to a thrift shop I know, mostly unstaffed but for one oblivious attendant there to monitor all the self-checkout stations. Once there, I flit among the dusty, too-crowded racks of clothing for something as different from my normal everyday wear as possible.

A dress or a skirt is out of the question for so many reasons, foremost because I plan to be running through the sewers later. I settle on some tighter-than-normal jeans, a frilly and flowing black shirt, and some deep green wellies to keep my feet dry and moderately less nasty down in the tunnels. The on-again, off-again rain gives me the excuse to wear them and not stand out. I also snag a half-used cosmetics kit that I have no idea how to use, a comb to part the longer half of my hair so it flops over the shaved side, a threadbare backpack, and a plain old umbrella with none of the usual smart features.

Once I've made my purchases and gotten changed, I study myself in the mirror, avoiding my own eyes. This disguise won't fool anyone who gets a good look at me, but hopefully it won't come to that. I've killed a lot of time shopping, so I have the newly fallen darkness on my side.

I stand there, staring at the green wellies on my feet, my mind full of static. I've been so thoroughly distracted by getting here unseen, then by putting together my disguise, that I've managed to avoid thinking about my situation completely. In the silence of the dressing room, everything comes rushing back, and my hands begin to shake. I clench my fists and bite my lip, hard, then sit with my back to the dressing-room mirror.

I glance under the thin curtain to make sure I'm alone, then bring up the message thread with Davon on my lenses. He's probably worried sick that I haven't responded yet. Yet another dick move on my part. I close my eyes and command my lenses to leave the interface up, so the words are all I see as I lean my head back against the unyielding glass.

You: Hey.
Davon: Stars, Diz, I was full-on panicking over here
You all right?
You: Yeah.
Sort of.
Actually . . . no.
I'm not hurt or anything. But can I meet you somewhere?
Davon: Yes
Of course
Where are you at? I can pick you up.
You: Let's meet halfway.
I'm coming from the thrift shop on Deckard Street.
Davon: And where are we going?

I hesitate.

You: I'll tell you in person.
Davon: Fine, Super Sneaky McSpy Diz

For the first time in hours, the corner of my mouth twitches into an attempted smile.

You: No
Just
Don't try.
You can't master the naming.
Davon: You're right, I apologize. I bow to your superior skills.
You: Damn right.
Let's just meet at Nellie's on U Street.
Davon: Be there in ten. Stay safe, Dizzy.

Outside the changing room, the shuffling of sneakers over carpet catches my attention. A pair of feet in ragged, stained hightops comes to a stop just beyond the curtain.

"Hey," a voice says. The shop monitor. "You can't be like . . . getting high in there or sleeping or whatever."

I push myself to my feet and blink the chat out of my lenses, feeling slightly more functionally human than I did ten minutes earlier. Davon will meet me and hear me out. He won't be happy with my extracurricular activities, but he'll be on my side, at least. He'll want to know what happened. He'll help, like he always does. No matter what I get into, he's always there.

More than I can say for some people.

The shop guy grunts as I slide the curtain aside and push past him without a backward glance, stalking out into the misting rain with my new-old backpack slung over my shoulder. I pop open my umbrella, jog across the street, and sharpen my mind, blocking out the internal noise. The low-level constant screaming of wrongness and guilt. It's time to focus.

I have a job to do.

Davon is already waiting for me outside Nellie's when I turn the corner onto U Street. His eyes slide right over me at first, then widen when he does a double take, looking me over from head to toe and getting stuck on the green boots.

"Uh," he says. "Are you okay?"

I roll my eyes. "It's a disguise."

"Clearly." He looks at me sidelong for a still moment. Then his lip quivers, and he reaches for me. "Dizzy, I know you hate this kind of thing, but—"

I don't let him finish. I throw myself into his arms and bury my face in his shoulder. His military-cut jacket is a rough canvas material, scratchy against my cheek, the sensation grounding and immediate. He's probably half choking, I'm squeezing so hard, but I need it, need to crush us together until my heart can crawl out and curl up with his, safe and protected. Despite his lack of oxygen, he wraps his arms around me and holds me close, rocking me like my mother used to when I woke up from a nightmare.

"Hey, it's okay, Dizzy," he croons, rubbing a soothing hand up my back. "I've got you. Whatever it is, we're gonna figure it out."

He eases back and turns his attention to the people entering the club behind him, to give me a moment to wipe away my tears. Gratitude surges in my heart for this cousin of mine, the one person on this planet who just *gets* me, doesn't try to change me, who always gives me exactly what I need. No more, no less. Space when my thorns are out, love when I'm falling apart, independence and support in perfect balance.

I give one last sniffle and pull all my shattered pieces back together, then clear my throat.

"Hey, eyes forward," I say with a gentle shove. "I didn't ask to meet here so we could go dancing."

Nellie's is our favorite club, the place we always go when I need a night away from the others. Needed, I guess. Chill, safe, good music, plenty of queer folk of my particular persuasions. But tonight isn't a night for fun. My mind couldn't be further from it.

"Come on," I say, taking Davon by the arm and walking us down to the end of the street. "Call us a pod."

"Okay," he drawls. "Happy to, but I have no idea where we're going. Why can't you do it?"

"For reasons." I close my eyes and breathe hard through my nose. This is why I hate crying so much. Once you start, round two is always right behind your eyes, just waiting for the slightest provocation. "Please, Davon, I'll explain everything once we're inside. Will you just call a pod?"

He huffs, but his eyes go unfocused as he navigates the menus of the ride app. A minute later, a two-person pod descends from the traffic lanes overhead and slides to a stop in front of us. The door pops open, and I dive in first, half out of nerves and half to keep anyone from Nellie's from recognizing me in this horrible half-assed disguise.

Davon slides in after me, and when the pod's nav system asks, "Where can I take you this evening?" he gives me an expectant look.

"Junction station twenty-nine," I say, then sit back and fasten my seat belt.

"Junction station twenty-nine is unavailable at this time," the pod responds.

"Get us as close as you can on the southern side of the station, then, please."

"Acknowledged. Please prepare for acceleration."

Once we're both settled, the pod takes off, rising into

the air and weaving itself back into the light nighttime traffic.

Davon gives me all of thirty seconds before he pounces. "Okay, we're in. These things are forbidden by law to have any kind of recording devices, so you're out of excuses. I'm worried about you, Dizzy. Spill."

I look down at my lap and fiddle with a loose string at the bottom of my new-old shirt. I've done my best to keep Davon mostly separate from my friends, for a lot of reasons. The others like him just fine, mostly because he can semi-control me and because he sometimes bought us takeout. He's older than us, which means he has his own apartment outside the orphan district anyway. Natural separation. But he also knows me better than the others, a product of our growing up as neighbors, cousins closer than siblings. And despite that, he actually thinks well of me. It's been nice, having someone who cares unconditionally, who I can always go to when things with the others were rough. When I still had others.

So I've never wanted him to know about our side gig. I've lied for two years, let him think I was a better person than I really am, let him think I got my extra money doing longer shifts for Mr. Ailiano. In reality, I quit the tech shop a year ago to focus on siphoning and fixing ware on a freelance basis. I'll have to spoil his opinion of me. Maybe even throw away the job at MMC he promised me, if he's mad enough. That job offer is all I have going for me in Kyrkarta. Davon's all I have left, now that my friends have ditched me for good.

Nothing for it, though. I have to know what happened on the job today. What went wrong. And I need someone watching my back while I search.

I take a deep breath and begin.

"You know that big disaster at the junction station earlier today?" I ask. Obvious; of course he does. I barrel on. "That was me."

Davon frowns, his brows knitted together. "What . . . I don't understand. What do you mean?"

I glare at him, focusing all my anger and frustration and helplessness into beaming the information straight into his brain so we don't have to play this game, so I don't actually have to say—

"I did it. I was responsible for the junction station explosion. Jaesin, Remi, Ania, and I, we've been running a side business for two years, siphoning maz from MMC's pipes and selling it off, or taking orders from clients for specific amounts and strains. That's how I've really been paying for my tech and food."

I close my eyes and wait. Davon's silence is heavy with the weight of his disapproval, his horror, and it presses down on me in a way I haven't felt since . . .

Since I was seven. Since my mother was alive.

To my horror, my eyes grow hot and stinging again,

and I open them to find Davon blurry through a sheen of tears.

"I didn't mean to hurt anyone," I say, my voice thick with the aching in my chest and throat. "I don't even know what happened! That's what I need to find out tonight. I know it wasn't just us. We've done this a hundred times and I've never seen anything like that. Never. Something went wrong."

But you opened the valve more, you tried to rush the job, you took an order for a kind of maz you knew nothing about, a little voice in the back of my brain tells me. I shut my eyes again and grit my teeth. "It may have been us that did it, but it wasn't our fault. I'll never believe it. I can't."

A faint rustling sound, then a hand on my knee, warm and gentle.

"Honestly, Diz, I'm not actually surprised about the siphoning thing," Davon says, his voice low and calm. "I did wonder where the money was coming from, and with your and Remi's particular skill sets, it's a natural choice. And I know how Remi feels about MMC."

I do my breathing exercise, slow in through the nose, counting until I feel like I can open my eyes without shattering. Davon looks at me with such simple understanding that my heart aches with gratitude. I love Jaesin, Remi, and Ania, but Davon is my family. The only family I have left. I lift my hand, hesitate, hover . . . then slowly lay it over Davon's where it rests on my knee and squeeze it tight.

"You don't hate me?" I ask, though it comes out as a whisper.

He turns his hand over under mine and laces our fingers together.

"I could never hate you, Diz. You know I've always got your back. Just the two of us against the rest of the world, remember?"

The pod dips toward the ground, and my stomach swoops along with it. He doesn't hate me yet, but we'll be on the ground soon, near the site of the junction station disaster, where hundreds, maybe thousands got ill today, where some even died. Looking at the reality might be harder than he thinks.

Or maybe . . . maybe this is what family is supposed to be. You just . . . count on each other. Forgive. Love.

I close my eyes and rest my forehead on his shoulder, letting myself have this one tiny indulgence.

"I wish you'd been my brother for real," I whisper, a near-silent confession.

He rests his cheek on the crown of my head, and I feel him smile. "Why can't cousin mean just as much? Why does a certain mix of blood get to decide?"

And that, more than anything, loosens the knot in my chest, makes me think that maybe, just maybe, things might be okay soon.

The pod comes to rest on the ground and beeps its cheerful acknowledgment. "We have arrived at your destination. The charge is fourteen credits. May I charge this to your primary account?"

"Authorized," Davon says, and opens the door to climb out.

I sit there, frozen in my seat.

The pod beeps again.

"Thank you for choosing RidePod," it says, gently chiding. "Have a pleasant evening."

I don't budge.

"This pod will be leaving in one minute. Additional charges may apply."

Davon's hand lands on my shoulder. "Diz, it's okay. I'll be right here with you. I know it's hard. I know."

He does know. We were neighbors most of our early lives, right up until the spellplague hit when I was seven and he was eleven. We'd been home with the same babysitter, playing video games on Davon's couch, when the time our parents usually came home passed unnoticed. Ten minutes, and our babysitter had gotten huffy. Twenty, and they'd tried to call my dad, then my mom, then Davon's moms. Nothing.

Thirty minutes, and the babysitter finally thought to turn on the news to see if there'd been something to affect the traffic.

It was the first-ever coverage of the spellplague, though

they weren't calling it that yet. They were mostly calling it the West City Epidemic, a disease that was wiping out people by the hundreds, then thousands, all in the factory and mining areas or the bridges district. The areas where most of the parents in our neighborhood worked, headquarters of the biggest employers in the entire city. Those who were near ground zero of the epidemic died almost instantly. My dad. Many more died within hours. Davon's moms. And an unlucky few managed to hang on for days, weeks, or months, only to die at home, in front of their children, with no one around to help.

My mom.

There aren't many plague cases still around. The mortality rate was so high, and no one can figure out why the ones who survived *did*. MMC managed to keep new cases from occurring with its maz scrubbing tech, and they contracted with the city to research the new disease, too. There aren't many people left for researchers to study, though. Remi is one of the few, and they're required to submit to extensive testing and questioning during their clinic visits to give scientists even the barest amount of data. So far, the research has turned up some techniques for keeping the illness at bay, but not for curing it. Of course, the hope was that there wouldn't *be* any new infections.

No one knows why the maz turned toxic after the

big quake. But it did, and it killed off half the adults in Kyrkarta, took away parents and grandparents and community leaders and neighbors. It made a lot of orphans.

Some of us more slowly than others.

And today, through my actions, I created more.

"This RidePod will depart in thirty seconds."

I take one last deep breath, squeeze Davon's hand, and climb out of the pod. My eyes stay fixed on the ground until Davon joins me, his warm presence at my shoulder the only thing keeping me from calling the pod back and getting the hell out of here. But I stand fast, and bring up the map Jaesin and I used to plan the job.

"Are you ready?" I ask Davon, peeking at him from the corner of my eye. This close to the station, to the worst spellplague disaster in ten years, does he feel differently?

He only nods.

I lead us onward.

TWELVE

EVEN THIS LATE AT NIGHT, the junction station isn't completely abandoned. It sure feels like it, though. We spot three guards over the course of five minutes, silently standing watch over what's essentially a graveyard, a crime scene, a new tragic entry into the history of the spellplague. If anyone needed a reminder that the plague is still around, that it can still kill people at any time, we've certainly provided the proof.

The structure itself is a bombed-out mess, one whole wall blown out on the street side of the building. Black scorch marks line the edges of the ragged hole—the initial explosion from the pressure must have triggered a secondary explosion, something incendiary, to make marks like that. I wonder if that was the cause of most of the deaths today, or if it was the maz? Were all the people who died employees at the station? People who came day after day to work their shift, eat their lunch, chat with coworkers, then head home to family? Or were there people on the street, too, random passersby in the wrong place at the wrong time?

I think I'd rather not know.

The perimeter of the building still flutters with caution-tape lines and shimmers with recently refreshed wards. The guards, when they walk by every few minutes, glow faintly with nullifying armor. The site is still contaminated, then. So much for marching right in there.

Davon bumps his shoulder against mine. "Hey. What are you thinking?"

That I'm a terrible excuse for a human being who shouldn't be let anywhere near maz ever again?

I bite down on that thought and force my voice to be steady and sure. "I wanted to look at the actual site of the explosion, but it looks like that's not gonna happen. Not fully decontaminated yet. Follow me."

Referring occasionally to the map, I lead us back away from the station, sliding like a shadow from one building to the next. The wards and contamination signage end about a block away from the station itself, but we don't find an opportunity to descend to the tunnels until we're nearly to the same hatch we used to make our giant horrific mistake. We finally come across a sewer access in the middle of a quieter-than-usual street bordered by factories that only operate during the daytime hours. I send my little drone out for a quick scout, and when it doesn't find anything, I lead us to the entrance. With a regretful glance at Davon's pristine black sneakers, I yank the cover off (holy stars, it is heavy—how did Jaesin always manage this so easily?) and slide it to one side to expose the ladder down.

"You have got to be kidding me," Davon says, pressing the sleeve of his jacket to his nose to cut the ripe scent of flowing sewage.

"I never kid when it comes to crawling around in sewers." And down I go.

A few long moments pass as I climb down the ladder alone, but then the ring of sneaker on metal sounds above me, rhythmic, as Davon starts climbing, then replaces the cover over his head. Once our feet are on solid ground, I check the map one last time to get my bearings, then lead him deeper into the sewers.

I've never been in this part of the tunnels before, yet every step is familiar, hauntingly so, carrying with it the memory of two years' worth of siphoning. Jaesin, Remi, and eventually Ania, all four of us, dashing through the sewers in those early days before the first time we nearly got caught, laughing and pretending to shove each other into the sewage, showing off for each other and reveling in our newfound power. Remi was radiantly happy to have access to maz outside school again, and their weaving became more creative and powerful than ever.

The whole thing was my idea, a discovery made during one of my insomniac hacking sessions. It was right after Davon got hired at Maz Management, ironically. I thought I'd test the waters, see how good this IT department he was joining really was. I dove deep, deeper than I thought possible, and what started as a fun exercise to distract my exhausted brain led to the discovery of one little bit of code. The bit that opened the pressure release valves from inside the system instead of outside. That gave precise control and didn't set off any internal alarms. Way more subtle than most of the other siphoning teams out there. I did the first hack by myself, getting a few vials for Remi's sixteenth birthday, of all things. It was foolish. Risky. But I had my reasons.

And it worked.

Then it led us here.

Finally I have to fill the silence as we walk, so I explain our usual siphoning procedures. We're obviously never going to pull another job again, and Davon, at least, is in a position to make sure something like this can't happen again in the future, that the system will be protected from people like me. I tell him everything, from how we chose which jobs to take to picking our access point and the exact techniques I used to crack the digital security on the hatches and tap points. He mostly listens, making disgusted noises once in a while as we slosh through the sewers, picking our way closer and closer to the junction station. We'll get as close as we can, right up to the inevitable contamination barrier. I just hope we can get close enough to find what we're looking for.

Davon asks a few technical questions here and there, obviously taking mental notes for work. Good. If it turns out my job offer is officially off the table, at least I can help somehow. The deeper we get into the tunnels and the more I outline our tried-and-true process, though, the more my frustration rises to the surface, speeding my steps and locking my jaw in a permanent clench.

What happened here? We're good, *really* good, at what we do. There's no logical explanation.

I pull up a diagnostic app on my lenses and look over the mechanical workings of the MMC infrastructure as we proceed farther down, stopping to examine each pressure valve along the way. I need something, anything. The pipes were damaged, or someone was lazy in their maintenance. Some accident that triggered the explosion. *Something.*

The closer we get, the more the walls around us show evidence of scorching from recent fire. Nothing else.

Did we actually cause the explosion? Did the pressure backup from farther up the pipe affect this area? Did some firaz get forced out and meet with some sort of combustible?

My steps slow, then stop, as we turn a final corner and find ourselves face-to-face with the faint thready glow of a barrier ward just beyond the final valve, marking the border of the contaminated area. This tap point is our last chance. I close my eyes and breathe in . . . out . . .

until the hot pressure behind my eyes recedes. There's still a chance. This one, tiny, final chance.

"Diz, look," Davon says. His voice sounds odd.

My eyes fly open, and I see it.

Something that wasn't there on the last tap point, or on any of the points we've hit in the past.

It's like a small box wired directly into the pressure management system, its casing shiny and unscathed, other than the signs of the recent explosion. A new installation, then. What is it, some kind of upgrade? A new augmentation for the system, something to help it better regulate the maz-15? Is it more unstable than the other strains?

I slow as we approach, cautious around the wreckage. It's eerily quiet; the faint sound of maz flowing through pipes mingling with trickling water and the occasional scurrying rat feet is the typical soundtrack for our jobs. Now, all that remains is the water. Even the rats are unlikely to have survived the blast, and the system of maz pipes sounds . . . empty. Maybe they diverted the flow while they make repairs. I turn to Davon with pursed lips.

"This maintenance point is the kind of place we'd normally tap. We have the pressure release valve, which means we have a way to access the maz without damaging the pipe or setting off an alarm, and each maintenance point has a small digital control system I can splice into.

Typically I'd sync wirelessly if possible, or solder in some cables if necessary, then open the valve while Remi directs whatever maz we need into vials for transport. Normally we do a little recon to find a pipe that's both easily accessible and holds the strains of maz we need, but for this job we were hired to come here specifically."

I step forward carefully, sinking into the logic of it all, letting my diagnostic app be a shield between me and the damage. Be an investigator, solve the crime, find a suspect, and assign some blame. *Someone* has to be to blame.

"I keep a constant eye on the pressure readouts as we siphon off the maz, mostly to make sure we don't drain it so fast that it triggers a leak warning somewhere else down the line. But today the pressure didn't drop. It spiked. And that should be impossible. How can the pressure increase when you're removing material from the system? That's not how physics works."

"Maybe it really wasn't related to you at all, then," Davon says, stepping carefully over a blackened pile of twisted metal. "Maybe something was wrong with the system and it was just wrong place, wrong time for you."

"But the news said MMC is blaming it on us," I say. Why can't I just accept the life preserver he's throwing me?

Davon snorts. "Of course they are. I love working for MMC, Diz. They treat us well, pay us well, and do a lot of great things for the city. But if they accidentally unleash a second spellplague, and they have easy scapegoats in the form of people who weren't supposed to be doing the illegal things they were doing anyway? Why *wouldn't* they use that? It's the logical thing to do."

He steps over to me and rests both hands on my shoulders, forcing me to look at him. "Dizzy, even if this disaster wasn't actually your fault, what you were doing was still illegal and really dangerous. They're well within their rights to send the cops after you. Especially if it keeps the blame off them. Despite all the people mad about their pricing and restrictions, they're like saints to a lot of people in this town, with the way they stepped up after the plague. Can you imagine what this would do to their reputation? I can't even entirely blame them. It'd be hard for them to do the good work they do without that reputation."

It makes sense. It's logical, and it ticks all the boxes.

I hate it.

I let his hands fall away and creep closer to the digital control system. The case is charred and the access panel hangs loose on one end, but it's otherwise intact, and identical to the one I tapped in to earlier today. Identical except for the little box tucked away against its far side, hugging the wall of the tunnel.

My gaze sharpens. I pull out my mini soldering kit and cables and put together the same setup from this morning, then pull my deck from my back pocket and get to work. Davon watches over my shoulder as I query the access node about all the devices currently occupying its ports. It happily retrieves the information I need:

PORT 26—TK421 AUX PRESSURE REG UNIT MODEL 992654821

And there.
Right there.

```
IF valveID(XS416682:XS416698) status = 1 AND datetime ≥
07:18:344:11:59:00
THEN call(PORT 26) AND RUN(dir/sub/go.exe)
```

Translation: if one of the valves along the maz-15 pipe is opened after a certain day and time, then talk to the pressure regulator and tell it to run the file called "go."

The date listed is the day I took the job while we were at the club.

A suspicion blooms in my mind.

I hold my breath against the growing dread and dig into the pressure regulation unit to look for the file go.exe. I already know what I'll find, I *know*, but I have to have proof. The code spills across my view as I open the file.

```
leakpoint1 = (GET valveID for (valveID status=1))
IF pipeID(247-24) pressure < 100%
WAIT 30000
```

TRIGGER(TK421AUXPRU) AND SET(leakpointl) pressure = 400%

It takes a moment to parse. If the pressure in the maz-15 pipe drops below 100 percent, meaning if someone taps the pipe and causes that slight drop in pressure, wait and see if it's short, like an automatic triggering. If not, figure out which valve it's at, trigger the new pressure regulator box they installed, set the pressure . . . to 400 percent. At that pressure, all the maz in the pipe would come gushing out from the tap point, right in our faces.

That was what happened, *exactly* what happened. The pressure spiked for no reason at all, and venting the other points only helped briefly. That was the surge Remi caught, held, protected us all from, right before the explosion. It was *designed* to trigger an overload as soon as someone tapped the pipe. And the makeup of the maz in this particular pipe was 60 percent firaz. With that amount of pressure behind the raw maz, it would have ignited in a flash. We would have been killed instantly.

It was *designed* to kill us instantly.

The only reason we survived was because they didn't count on Remi, who is far more skilled and powerful than their size or age would suggest.

Someone wants us dead. Us specifically.

Because we were *sent* here, to the only known source of maz-15. If I hadn't taken that job, that awful too-good-to-be-true final job, we wouldn't have been tapping this exact pipe, in exactly the right area to be caught in this trap.

This whole thing was a setup.

My brain whirls into high gear, suddenly a thousand times lighter and flying a mile a minute. I download a complete dump of all the data to my deck, then share the relevant code with Davon.

"You see what I see?" I ask as I yank my cables free. When I look up, his expression is dark.

"Someone broke in and installed that device specifically to target you all," he says.

"Specifically to *kill* us," I correct. "Thousands of units of firaz to the face isn't all that conducive to living."

He checks the code again and his mouth presses into a hard line.

Yes, someone actually tried to kill us. They probably sent the guy who offered us the job to find me, made sure we'd be coming back to this spot. Those *bastards*.

They could have killed my friends. Remi, Ania, and Jaesin, they almost *killed* them.

But why?

"I have to get back to the others," I say, shoving my deck in my pocket. "They have to know."

Davon shakes his head slowly as I push past him to get at the pressure regulator—the evidence—with my screwdriver.

"Whoa, whoa, can we slow down for a second?" he asks. "Let's stop and think."

I pause with my cables half coiled to stuff back in my pocket and look up. "What's there to think about?"

He sighs, looks to the ceiling for a moment, then comes forward and puts both hands on my shoulders again, the way my mom used to when she had something serious to say.

"I think you need to leave that unit right where it is." I open my mouth to protest, but he cuts me off with a gesture. "Hear me out. Right now, it's a critical piece of evidence that proves you weren't responsible for the disaster at the station. If you remove it, then when the MMC crews come to investigate, they won't find anything to exonerate you. I just . . ."

He pulls me into his chest like he did earlier in the night, but this time it makes my skin itch. I'm vibrating with the need to move, to run, to do *something*.

"Someone tried to *kill* you, Dizzy," he continues, voice strangled. "And you did something really illegal. You're in a bad position, maybe even more than you realize. This city is just looking for reasons to put orphans like us in custody so they can serve us with mandatory work orders, force us into the factories or into sanitation or whatever. A court could ban you from touching a deck again for years, Diz."

It's like a hook in my gut, tugging me open and spilling

me out over the filthy sewer ground. I can't go without my deck. Coding is complicated, immersive, powerful . . . distracting. It's what I'm good at. It's everything.

But my friends . . . they're everything too. If they aren't already gone.

I have to get back to them.

I shake my head and shove the cables in my pocket, but step away from the auxiliary pressure unit. "Fine. I'll leave the box, but I at least have to let my friends know. I can't let them carry this around, thinking they killed all those people. And they need to know that someone's after us."

"And then? After that?" Davon asks.

"I DON'T KNOW," I snap, far louder than is really smart, given the circumstances. But I don't care. Can't care. It's all so much. My head's louder than the most crowded club in town, and I can barely think.

Davon watches me with a careful expression, automatically switching to Diz Gloves mode. Caution: Watch for thorns. Handle with care. He purses his lips, then nods. "MMC could take care of you, you know. If you take the job. You wouldn't be the first black-market siphoner they've hired. They could use your skills."

"Before, yeah, sure." I bite my lip and look away, taking one breath, two. Time to let myself admit it out loud. The truth that doesn't matter anymore.

"I was gonna take the job, you know. I really was.

But now that my last siphoning job blew up one of their stations and killed some of their employees? Not gonna happen."

"But it wasn't you. The evidence is right here. I know the people in charge of IT, Diz, and they'll be reasonable. I'll tell them where to look for the evidence, and they'll look. They'll find it, and they'll come to the same conclusion you did. And they'll hire you, because you're amazing at what you do, and they'll protect you, because MMC protects its own. They need people like you, and you need them. You have a sweet deal here. And it's not off the table yet."

"DOWN HERE!" a harsh voice shouts from the direction of the station. Far down the tunnel, three lights bob and grow larger as the sound of splashing boots draws closer. The ominous click of weapons being readied sends a jolt of adrenaline straight to my heart. Davon's eyes go wide, and he takes me by the shoulders.

"Go," he says, nearly a whisper. "I have my badge with me. I'll tell them I was investigating the accident."

"No, you'll get in trouble, you'll lose your job," I say, gripping his sleeves and trying to drag him with me. I can't have that on my conscience too. His job means so much to him.

"I won't," he says, giving me a gentle shove away. "I've got good security clearance. It'll be fine. Go!"

I hesitate another second longer, then finally turn and

take off with reluctant steps in the opposite direction.

Please let him be okay. The rhythm of every footfall is filled with my silent begging. Please, please, please, please. Once I'm far enough away, I reach into my pocket and lob my tiny drone into the air to scout the tunnels ahead for more MMC security guards. A moment later, a notification pops up in my lenses.

Davon: I'm fine. They believed me, and we're cataloging the evidence together now. They'll know it wasn't your fault.
Please message me later, Diz. I'm serious.
I still want you to stay here and work with me. We're family, right? It'll be fine. Your job offer is still safe. I'll take care of you. Promise.

I bark a harsh laugh in the echoing cavern of the sewer tunnel.

Yeah. Right. I'm sure Davon believes all of that with his whole heart, but I wouldn't take that job if they offered me a million credits.

Because I'm pretty sure it's Maz Management that wants us dead in the first place.

THIRTEEN

THE SUN IS WELL ON its way to full morning, turning everything to golden softness, by the time I finally get back to Ania's neighborhood, ready to collapse.

I walked. The whole way. My feet ache with blisters, and my legs are screaming at me to just *sit the hell down already.*

I nearly caved and called a RidePod no less than seven times, thinking I'd just risk creating a new profile to link to one of our shell bank accounts. Too dangerous, though. Not when I'm still the only one of our group who knows what happened. Call me paranoid, but I even kept silent on messaging and calls all night too. Didn't wanna be tracked or intercepted. The downside of being a hacker—you know exactly how insecure all your info really is.

I slip through the trashcan-lined backstreet behind Ania's row of houses as quickly as I can, trying to play it as natural as possible, like I totally belong here. As if anyone could ever believe that, especially with me stained and stinking like sewage. Again. History repeats itself in truly obnoxious ways sometimes.

The ground-level window I left through is still open when I get back to Ania's house. I can picture exactly how it went—Remi would have turned on Jaesin and reamed him out as quietly as possible, Ania would have stepped in to defend him, and the whole thing would have devolved until they all went to bed early, everyone too pissed and too proud to be the one to close the window. A tiny smile tugs at the corner of my mouth as I picture the scenario, perfectly clear in my mind. I know them all a hundred times better than I know myself, so their edges are sharp and defined, their voices practically audible. I need to hear them all again for real.

With a quick glance around, I sit on the still-wet ground and stick my feet through the window opening, bracing my hands on the expertly masoned brick exterior of the house. Hips next, then boobs (ow), shoulders, and finally my head as I fall to the couch beneath the window, smearing the delicate white fabric with the caked mud from my boots. I got way messier than usual in the haste of my uncoordinated escape, and Ania's couch is paying the price.

The room is silent, peaceful and still. They're probably all still asleep, nestled in among Ania's soft, expensive bedsheets and pillows. Good; that gives me a minute to pull myself together and figure out how to tell them everything. I wipe my sleeve over my eyes, the fabric coming away smeared with the grime of the sewers and some of the cheap makeup disguise I applied. I probably look an utter mess, but they've seen me at my worst. Besides, priorities.

I take a deep breath, hold it for a moment, and let it out as I walk over to the spare bedroom.

"Remi?" I whisper, gently pushing the cracked door open. "Jaesin?"

I stop dead in the doorway.

The bed is made. The pillows look untouched, undented by sleeping heads. There are no discarded clothes, no vials of maz, no traces of habitation at all.

Nothing.

My breath comes in burning gasps as I stumble back out of the room and burst through the door to Ania's.

A handwritten letter lies atop her perfectly made comforter of purple and blue flowers, the barest edge of lavender sheet folded over the top. My eyes sting, and my legs are wooden as I make my way over, lifting the expensive plum-edged stationery off the bed.

Mom and Dad,
I tried to get in touch with you, but couldn't get through for some reason. Morning rush hour, maybe? Anyway, I've been second-guessing the choice I made for college, so I'm going to visit the University of Jattapore. I'm taking a tour of their

campus and meeting the head of the department to
see if I want to go there instead of Lon Flaum, just
to make sure I made the right decision. Sorry for
ditching you at the last minute! I should be back
in a few days. I've got everything I need and will
call you when I get there. Have a great time at the
gala on Firaday, if it's still happening after that
horrible accident. I emailed this same message to
your secretary, too, so I hope you'll get it today.
See you soon.
Love,
Ania

I let the letter fall from my fingers and drift back to
the floral bedspread.

They left me.

They really did just leave me behind.

They said they would, but some part of me apparently
didn't believe it, because my chest feels like a black hole,
caving in on itself with a swirling mess of shock and pain.
And fear. Total, petrifying fear.

I really am on my own now.

I sit down hard on the edge of the bed, heedless of the
mess I must be making, and hold my head in my hands,
burying my fingers in the longer portion of my hair. The
strands feel greasy and disgusting between my fingers,
and probably look just as bad. Dirty tears slide through

the grime on my cheeks and drip onto my stained pants, leaving little dark circles. I'm disgusting, a mess, inside and out. Ruined.

Why did I ever expect anything else?

I haven't truly cried in years, which I've always considered a point of pride for some reason. In the last day, though, I've cried more than I have since my mom died. Yet another thing gone. Another thing I've held on to that's lost, over, ended, gone in the span of one heaving sob.

Fuck absolutely *everything*.

Filthy droplets splash onto Ania's pristine wooden floors, pooling where they fall with not even the barest gap between boards to settle into. I cry until my throat is raw and my nose is too clogged to breathe, until my chest aches and I feel wrung out, exhausted.

Empty.

I pull my hands back from my face, blinking against the sudden brightness on my swollen eyes. My hands are washed clean where I had them cupped them over my eyes, but the rest of me is still crusted with dirt and worse, my smell a nauseating contrast to the room's pure, clean scent.

A shower. I can at least use Ania's shower before her parents get home, then figure out what to do after that. A clean head is a clear head, or so my dad always used to say. It can't hurt.

I sniffle and dash my tears away with an angry swipe.

Enough. Pull it together, Diz. You're harder than this. You grew up in group homes. You lived in the Caves for a year before you got into the Cliffs. You've gotten by your whole life. This is no different. You knew they were going to leave.

You don't need them. You *don't*.

Let. It. Go.

I wipe my nose on my sleeve and stand, pressing my tongue hard against the roof of my mouth to push the last of the tears away. Sitting there and crying about it isn't going to help anything. It's time to move forward, on my own two feet. Take care of me, like Davon always says I'm so good at. I have to look after *myself*.

With that thought, I square my shoulders and rip the now-filthy cover off Ania's bed, stuffing it down her laundry chute on my way to her en suite bathroom. My boots come off first, toed off so I don't have to touch them, and my socks follow, with much wobbly balancing. The alternating blue and white tiles are cold under my feet, solid and grounding. I toss my boots into the shower to rinse them off first so I won't have to handle them after I'm clean, but just as I reach out for the hot-water knob—a rhythmic *thump, thump, thump* overhead.

Footsteps. Ania's parents are still home.

My heart hammers against my rib cage. If I'd turned the water on, that would have been it, they'd have found me and called the police, and no job with MMC would have saved me. I hold my breath and strain to listen for more indications. Are they leaving soon? Or do I have to wait for hours? Or leave in my current state and find a shelter that'll let me use their shower?

I'm so screwed.

I tug my socks and boots back on hurriedly, swearing under my breath as my fingers get tangled in a threadbare hole. I have to get out before they find me, have to call Davon for a ride—

Another *thump*, *thump*, *thump*, then a stumble, a crash, and peals of laughter.

Familiar laughter.

They haven't left yet.

I crumple in on myself, arms wrapped around my torso like I'm holding my own organs in. They *haven't left*.

My heart in my throat, I dash for the staircase leading up to the main floor of the house and burst through the door, leaving my dirty footprints everywhere. As I stumble through, everyone turns to look at me, their eyes wide, confused, concerned, and in Jaesin's case especially, still angry.

Remi and Jaesin are showered, shoes on, dressed in new clothes. Considering we had to leave all our things behind, I bet they ordered new ones for drone delivery last night. Remi looks well, all things considered. Like they got a good night of sleep, recovering from yesterday.

Ania's eyes are narrow as she takes in my appearance, a few curls popping out from under her satiny purple head-wrap. Everything about her body language says furious, from the folded arms to the raised chin to the one foot stuck out at an angle. All three of them sit at the kitchen island with bowls of fruit in front of them. Three travel backpacks sit to one side, two of them brand-new.

Because they *were* planning to leave without me.

They just haven't gotten there yet.

Jaesin opens his mouth to lay into me, but I hold up a hand, forestalling his scolding.

"I know you're—" I cut off, my throat thick. With every blink I can feel how swollen and red my eyes are, and I'm sure they can see it too. Mortifying. Damn it, get it together. They're here, I'm not too late, they're right in front of me. I breathe. "I know you're mad at me."

Ania takes a few steps toward me, then stops, wrinkling her nose. "Diz, what happened to you?"

I laugh, weak and hoarse. "I found out what happened."

"Are you wearing makeup?" Remi interrupts. I scowl.

"That's what you're going to zero in on here?" Ania says, incredulous. "Though yeah, while we're at it, what the hell, Diz?"

"I was trying to disguise myself!" I sputter, scrubbing my shirtsleeves over my face. Probably just smearing around whatever isn't waterproof even more.

"And that's what you went with?" Jaesin asks with a

sweep of his hand to indicate my general awfulness, but Remi comes around the island to stand beside me, studying my face.

"You said you were looking into the explosion," they say quietly. "What did you find out?"

"Thank you for asking," I say, voice dripping with sarcasm. *Finally*, let's get to the point. "Look, I . . . I'm sorry for earlier. And I fully admit that I screwed up during the job. I pushed it too hard. I never should have taken it in the first place, considering we know nothing about this maz-15 stuff or what it can do. But what happened . . . it wasn't actually our fault. We were set up. The line was sabotaged."

At that, Jaesin and Ania look at each other and turn to fully face me, finally listening. A tiny bit of the tension in my chest eases. Maybe I have a chance to redeem myself.

"Sabotaged how? What did you find?" Jaesin asks.

I pull out a chair from the nearby dining table and all but fall into it, the others towering over me on their breakfast stools at the island. I rest my elbows on my knees and brace my chin on my folded hands.

"We started at the junction station and traced our way back—"

"Who's we?" Jaesin asks, sharp, and I wince. Should have left that part out.

"I called Davon and told him everything. I was alone and I needed backup, what was I supposed to do?"

Jaesin scowls, obviously not thrilled at his illegal

activities being revealed—and to an MMC employee, at that. He keeps silent, though, when Ania lays a hand on his arm. I forge on, recounting the night's discoveries and showing them the code I found, but when it comes down to it, there's really only one point to hammer home: "That particular pipe was rigged to blow, and the whole point of this job was to lure us there. Friends, we were set up."

Part of me relishes the stunned looks on their faces as they absorb my words, the proof that I was right to investigate further, right to storm out in the face of their cowardice.

Ania taps one manicured fingernail against her bottom lip in thought. "So, all that firaz and magnaz, it really was supposed to be like a giant bomb exploding right in our faces."

I nod. "Fortunately, they didn't count on us having an amazing spellweaver like Remi to save our sorry asses."

A touch of a smile ghosts over Remi's lips, but it quickly wipes away.

"Did you figure out who set us up?" They ask.

The glow of being right fades from my chest. "Maybe. This is where it starts to get weird and complicated. I walked here from the industrial district after everything went down—"

"Diz!" Ania scolds, horrified.

"I know, I know, I didn't have any other safe way to get back, but listen. I had a lot of time on my hands, so I got to thinking. Who could possibly want us dead, and why?" I have their attention now. They stare, rapt, all traces of lingering anger suppressed for the moment. I push on. "We were lured there with a job to pull maz-15, which we've never encountered during any other job, just the one time in this one pipe. Seems like a bit of a coincidence that the first time we see it, we're immediately given a job to get more, then nearly killed for it. You see where I'm going?"

Remi's eyes go wide. "Someone doesn't want us knowing about maz-15."

"*No one* knows about maz-15, it seems," I add. "No one but us, the guy who gave us the job, and . . ."

"MMC," Ania finishes, her hands flying to cover her mouth.

"Got it," I say. "They have control of this new maz, *and* control over information about its existence."

"And they're willing to kill for it," Jaesin adds. "It seems so out of character for them, though. Sure, they price gouge, and their hold on maz is way too tight, but other than that they've done a lot of good things."

Ania says nothing, but she stares at the wall over my shoulder, nodding vaguely. Reviewing the facts and coming to the same conclusion, no doubt. When she finally snaps back to the present, she meets my eyes and nods.

"We need information," she says. "I highly doubt they're going to stop coming for us after one failed attempt, so we need to learn more."

"Agreed," Jaesin says, finally on board. "Where is MMC getting this new strain? What's so important about it that they'd be willing to kill to keep it secret? Once we know that, we can figure out if there's any way out of this, something we can do to get them off our backs other than just . . . disappearing to live in the middle of the ocean or something."

He winces and braces a hand against his forehead, rubbing in small circles. "Ugh. Sorry, this is making my brain hurt."

I shake my head. "No, I'm with you. It's a lot to take in."

The ensuing silence is broken only by my audibly growling stomach. I haven't eaten since . . . wait, when did I last eat? Ania passes me her bowl of fruit with a sigh.

"So, what now?" she asks.

Remi taps their bottom lip with one finger, then . . . smiles.

"We pay a visit to Kyrkarta University."

My heart leaps into my throat. Are they planning to accept the offer there, even though we didn't get the money from the job? Are they really going to stay and . . . oh. No. Obviously walking into the admissions office to create a nice, easy-to-follow paper trail is a terrible idea for someone hiding from the police.

"The archives," I say, nodding.

Remi pumps both fists in the air. "Yes, the biggest

archive of maz research in the world! I can't wait to roll around in Professor Silva's research notes. Maybe literally. That's how osmosis works, right?"

Jaesin and I lock eyes, and for a second, it feels like we're about to burst into laughter together, sharing in our adoration of Remi like we always have. But at the last moment, the mirth fades from Jaesin's eyes, and he looks away, mouth tight.

My heart sinks.

I guess bringing back vital information doesn't exactly erase the past twelve hours. Jaesin will probably stay mad at me for a while. Ania, too. Remi, though . . .

"I think you and I should go alone," I say to Remi. The others start to protest immediately, but I cut them off. "The university has a lot of random security patrols. The more people we take, the more obvious we'll be. I can get us in the back way and bypass the security. Remi can look through the materials for the information we need. We'll be quick and quiet."

"I've done tons of maz-related research work, I can—" Ania begins, then trails off at the stern looks she catches from Jaesin and me.

"Remi's been obsessed with Professor Silva's work forever. I'm pretty sure the day his obituary hit the news feeds was the second saddest day of their life. They should be the one to go," I say, and Remi nods with an exaggerated tragedy face.

Ania's mouth clacks shut. She shoots one quick pleading look at Jaesin, hoping for backup, but he shakes his head. *Yes.* Blessing of the parents secured. Mission is a go. I turn to Remi with my hands clasped before me.

"Can I maybe shower first? Please?" I beg.

Remi looks me over head to toe, then wrinkles their nose. "Yes. You will *not* desecrate the late, great Professor Silva's work with your filth. Also, please burn that shirt immediately."

I lift one arm with its formerly flowing sleeve. It hangs stiff and heavy with grossness.

Honestly? No arguments here.

"I'll be quick," I say, and meet their gaze for a long beat. "Get ready to break into your dream school."

FOURTEEN

ON SECOND THOUGHT, NEVER MIND.
Ania was right. Pairing Remi and me up for this little
side quest was a terrible idea. Sure, Jaesin or Ania would
have spent the whole time being angry at me, but that I
can take.

It's the sheer, skin-crawling awkwardness that's killing me.

Kyrkarta University is about as far away from the
Cliffs as it's possible to get without actually leaving town.
Wouldn't want those sad little orphan kids getting any
ambitious ideas. It's strange, kind of like a mini city, a
district all its own. Many of the buildings are plain and
utilitarian, built or rebuilt in the wake of the earthquake
that set off the plague, and named for wealthy donors.
The Katheryn A. Sherrinford School for Business. The
M. Ridings Social Sciences Building. The Park-Torres
Department of Technical Maz Studies.

A bit of the school's original historic charm lingers in
the older structures that have survived the last ten years

of earthquakes, mostly fountains and other low-to-the-ground features. How were the builders supposed to know that this previously earthquake-free area, tucked away in the mountains, would suddenly become one of the most quake-prone places on the planet?

Remi and I chose to wait until night to make our break for the archives. Honestly, I needed the day to clean up all the nasty footprints I'd left and to get some new clothes and other supplies delivered by drone, courtesy of Ania's credit account. And sleep. So much sleep. Turns out the cure to my insomnia problem is walking halfway across the city, soaking in my own sweat and fear. Gross, but effective.

Once full dark fell, Remi and I left Ania and Jaesin watching a movie on the couch and slipped out the same window I left through before. Though the cops still haven't shown our faces or names on the news, we have to assume they have both, so we had to get creative moving through the city. Walking there and back was definitely *not* an option. Even with gliders, it would take all night.

We ended up calling Davon. I hated to do it, but what other option did we have? Davon picked Remi and me up in a RidePod a few blocks from Ania's neighborhood, and off we sped to the university district. Cue the awkward.

The ride there is thankfully brief. I sit in between

Remi and Davon, trapped as they make the kind of polite small talk I despise.

"The Hawks are your glideball team, right?" Remi asks over my head. "Heard they made it to the finals."

Sports? Seriously, that's what we're falling back on here? I crane my neck to peek through the window at the streets far below. Too far to jump. Probably.

"Yeah, they made it, then totally blew it. Too many key players injured," Davon answers.

"I'll injure *your* key players," I grumble.

They quite charitably ignore me, carrying on with their chatting over, around, and through me while I sit on pins and needles. Any second now, Davon will ask what he *thinks* is a thinly veiled question about my and Remi's relationship (or lack thereof). Or, Remi will make a politically charged comment about MMC and the people who work there. Either way, it won't matter that we're wanted for the pipeline explosion, because I'll end up wanted for *murder* instead. Layer the weirdness of seeing Davon for the first time since I ran from him in the sewers and this is just . . . the *best*. I *love* it.

But finally, blissfully, the pod begins its descent, and eventually comes to rest next to an old half-crumbled building near the archives. I thank Davon for the ride, but the memory of breaking down all over him last night has my cheeks growing hot, so a nudge with my elbow is all the affection I can manage. He catches my hand as I slide across the seat, though. He's never been all that good at letting things go.

"Hey. You okay? Do you need anything?"

Yeah, I have no idea what to say to him. *I'm pretty sure your employer wants to kill me? I can never take that job you stuck your neck out to get me because I don't want to die and/or work for attempted murderers?*

"Fine. All good" is what I manage. His mouth twists with skepticism, but he lets my hand go.

"Call me if you need a ride home, no matter what time. Be careful, Dizzy."

I grunt an affirmative and back away from the pod, leading Remi across the street and onto the university campus.

The former school of music building is nothing but three barely standing walls aboveground, but below is a different story. Before the earthquakes started, the school made use of an underground tunnel system for the winter months, when Kyrkarta gets unbearably cold. Aboveground isn't feasible due to aircar traffic and the train lines running throughout the campus. Instead, a spidery system of tunnels—much nicer than the sewer systems we're used to—extend beneath many of the school's major buildings.

Only problem is, many of them have collapsed over the past ten years, and the parts left are unstable at best. Fortunately, I've crawled through these tunnels dozens of times since I first learned about them, and I generally know what's safe and what might crush us to death. At least, I did before the most recent quake. For the crushy parts, Remi has a shielding spell at the ready, just in case falling rocks try to kill us. Slight inconvenience.

Remi and I are silent as we make our way through the rubble of the old music building and into the basement. The wreckage has long since been picked over by university cleanup crews and scavengers alike. There's a bright flash of gold or a splintered piece of wood here and there, shining out from where a crushed musical instrument lies beneath rubble too heavy to move. It's a painful sight. My father used to play clarinet, and he got me started young on recorder, as soon as my fingers were big enough to cover the holes. I kept his clarinet and played at school for a little while after he died, but by the time I turned twelve and was allowed to have a job, it just didn't seem *practical* anymore. I sold the clarinet for sixty creds. A ripoff, apparently, but I was too young to know better.

Once we're underground, Remi draws closer to me and weaves a bit of sunnaz into a little ball, one for each of us to light the way. Their arm brushes against mine as they pass the little glowing sun to me, but it's gone just as quickly. Is it my imagination, or are they standing farther away from me than before?

They're still mad, probably. Maybe? Are we fighting? Are we not fighting? After I told everyone what I had learned, I thought we were calling a truce over the whole me-storming-out, them-abandoning-me thing.

I guess that was wishful thinking. I should have known better.

Farther up the tunnel, the sound of a slamming door echoes through the cavern, freezing us both in our tracks. We pause for thirty eternal seconds.

Epic Group Chat: We are SO UTTERLY SCREWED Edition
Ania: How's it going?
Everything okay?

The notification is so sudden I nearly shout in alarm. Ania and her awful timing, I *swear* she does this on purpose. But it does give me an idea. Remi won't talk out loud, but maybe they'll reply to a message.

(private) You: Do you know anything about what's in this archive?

Nothing, not even a flicker of acknowledgment. Maybe they have their notifications turned off?

Epic Group Chat: We are SO UTTERLY SCREWED Edition
Remi: Fine so far. We're being all sneaky though, so give us a bit before messaging again.
You nearly gave Diz a heart attack
Ania: Whoops

Oh, okay, they were just replying to Ania first. They'll reply to my message any second.

Any second now.

Any minute now.

Okay, yeah, they're *definitely* still mad. *Really* mad. Maybe I should have invited one of the others along as a buffer. It's like an itch in the front of my brain. Obviously, there's only one answer here.

Ignore it completely.

I put on a burst of speed and pull ahead of Remi, walking faster down the broken-down tunnel, taking far less care than I probably should around the crumbled remains. The whole place smells musty, mostly of dampness trapped in an enclosed space, but somehow a bit of that gym-sock dorm-room smell too, even after all this time. Wall-mounted screens with the university's logo on the frame, dark and cracked, sit at regular intervals, and a few laminated student-made flyers for clubs and parties still litter the ground. A lot of things can decompose in ten years' time. Apparently a lot can still be left behind too.

If I could stand to slow down for a second, I'd have my little drone fly the tunnel to make sure it's stayed clear of major debris since the most recent earthquake, but oh well. We'll go as far as we can, and if we need to pop above ground, so be it.

We're lucky, though. We turn one last corner, following

my mental map of the university, and the tunnel opens up into a small foyer with a branch tunnel marked by a half-fallen metal sign: THE PARK-TORRES BUILDING, jointly named for the families that funded the original department and the new building. We're here. I glance quickly over my shoulder to make sure Remi is still with me, then continue on.

No message from them. Not a word.

This is fine.

FIFTEEN

THE DOOR INTO THE MAIN building looks like it hasn't been disturbed in at least a year. Heavy dust has settled over the whole thing, and broken links and sections of chain still lie in front of it, like the door keeps getting broken into and whoever maintains it just shrugs and slaps a new chain on each time. Super effective, obviously. Once we're inside, the archives are only a few doors down, and Remi's anticipation is like a third presence in the hallway with us, peeking over my shoulder.

Okay, breaking into the archive, step one: make sure no one else is in the room. I can't tell for certain—not like I have access to camera feeds from here or anything—but I *can* query the door's locking system and see if anyone has entered since closing time. The answer is no. There's always the possibility some professor or student came in before closing and simply stayed to work after hours, but we'll just have to take that risk. When I finally pop the lock, Remi sucks in a nearly inaudible breath beside me.

I crack the door slowly, carefully, my eyes doing one

quick sweep of the room, followed by a slower one to look for things I missed. Nothing. Open the door wider— still nothing. The air vibrates with the force of Remi's restraint as they graciously refrain from shoving me out of the way and bull-rushing the precious manuscripts. I slip inside and to the left to make way for them before they lose their patience, closing the door after them and relocking it. When I turn back to the room, though, the look on Remi's face steals my breath.

They stare up at the shelves and shelves of books, files, and old data storage media as if seeing the face of a goddess, awed and humbled and glowing with some inner light.

As determined as I am to keep up my end of the passive-aggressive silence, I just can't. Not with them looking like this is the best day of their life. I need to share it.

I step to their side and shift my weight just a hair closer. "Is it everything you thought it would be?" I ask, silently begging them to just *look* at me.

And they do, turning to offer a shadow of their usual beaming grin. My own half-mustered smile fades too. Have I really gone so far as to ruin this for them, something they've been wanting for years?

They turn back to the stacks with a hum and nod. "Yes. It's . . . a lot. I'm going to hit up one of the search terminals and see what the database can turn up about maz-15 and the spellplague. We might be here all night. I hope you brought something to entertain yourself."

I roll my eyes. "I don't need entertaining. I *can* help, you know. I wasn't as good in school as you, but I can still read and stuff."

They don't rise to the bait, only turn and stride toward the nearest terminal. I stare at their retreating form for a moment longer, nursing the disappointed ache in my chest. What will it take to get back to normal?

While Remi types away, scribbling down call numbers on the provided scraps of paper, I take to wandering. I think I was expecting dusty shelves with ancient paper books, maybe, or a clunky old early model deck with barely functioning computer files. Instead, the shelves are completely free of dust, and reading stations along the outer walls hold boxes of white gloves for handling delicate objects. Heavy-duty dehumidifiers churn away, keeping moisture levels low, and UV lights glow from inside the air vents, where they kill off mold spores before they have a chance to enter the room.

My eye catches on a map on the back wall, focused on the southern part of our continent. Jattapore features prominently, a bright coastal city with stylized dolphins cresting in the sketched ocean. A plaque next to it explains the date and provenance of the map and includes a note about the shape of the coastline, which apparently does not reflect the present day due to sea-level rise and the hurricanes that slam into the city every few weeks.

Part of me wishes Jattapore would wash right off the map. How are we ever supposed to get back to normal when my friends always have it as their backup plan? What even *is* normal anymore? A few days ago, they were on the cusp of moving to Jattapore for good. Then I thought maybe I'd gotten them all back, with the money from the job. But a few hours ago they were ready to flee town without me.

One way or another, they're going to leave eventually. Maybe I should recalibrate my sense of normal once and for all. It obviously shouldn't include Remi, Jaesin, and Ania. I need to stop hoping for change if I have any chance of getting over this.

I resist the urge to spit at the map, and move on.

I follow the wall around the stacks until I reach the entryway again, where, tucked away in the far front corner, a little office is piled high with crap and labeled PROFESSOR SEANAN KAYMA, SENIOR ARCHIVIST. The room is dark, the lock intriguingly complicated for a room inside another already-secure room. The locks are digital, so I pull out my deck and go to work. Surprisingly tough for a professor's office, but nothing compared to the MMC security I'm used to cracking. It takes less than a minute for the door to yield to me.

The lights in the office come on automatically as I step in, easing smoothly to full brightness rather than flash-blinding me. The place is an utter mess. Three different cups of coffee are clustered together next to the built-in deck screen on the desktop. All three are different levels of partially drunk, and one is topped with a thin film of greenish mold. I wrinkle my nose and step behind the desk, moving slowly so as not to disturb anything or trip on the piles everywhere. A photo of Seanan Kayma and what I assume are her husband and kids watches over the coffee cups with bright smiles, all a bit slouchy and disheveled, but brilliantly happy.

The cups and the photo claim the only part of the desk not completely buried under books and papers covered in cramped, barely legible handwriting. I've only seen physical books a few times in my life, and no one uses loose paper much anymore—except this woman and Ania, apparently. I can't judge her much, since my own desk looks much like this if you replace books and paper with tools and parts, so I have to assume she has a system and knows where everything is.

I sit down at her desk and access her terminal, taking some time to dig through her files and emails. Her digital records are fortunately much more meticulously organized than her physical ones, but dreadfully boring. I don't really know what I'm looking for, but a cursory search of the computer returns no hits for maz-15, and way too many hits for Maz Management Corporation, spellplague, and spellsick. Nothing useful. I look up from the terminal and am about to stand—but there, in the opposite wall, in exactly the place where you can see it if you glance over the top of the screen, is a seam. It's mostly blocked by another pile of books, but when I get closer to peek behind, there it is: a small, digitally locked door in the wall, barely noticeable unless you're looking from the right angle—and just large enough to hold a single book.

Curious.

The security on this lock is much stronger than anything I've encountered to this point. It's a challenge, a fun one, and I happily sink into the work, zoning out totally until a notification jolts me with its sudden appearance.

(private) Davon: Everything going okay in there? You going to need a ride?
What are you doing, anyway? I know I said I wouldn't ask, but the curiosity is killing me. What does the archive have that can help your situation?

I blink the notification away with a scowl. I swear, if it's not Ania, it's him. They have the *worst* timing.

I work at the lock for another twenty minutes over wireless sync—hardwiring isn't an option here, not without doing noticeable damage to the casing—and I'm about to despair when it finally whirs and releases.

Victory.

Inside is nothing more than a few handwritten letters.

Who writes letters anymore? All are dated from within the last year and contain scrawled formulas and observations, but the thing that catches my eye is "maz-15." It's mentioned in every letter. I flip one over, looking for a signature. Who's writing to the archivist about maz-15, and why letters? Untraceable, I guess, but—

I gasp aloud, then clap a hand over my mouth.

Yours truly,
Aric

I rush to the doorway of the office to double-check my memory, and sure enough, there it is. An enormously long sign hangs from the ceiling just in front of the stacks, in clear view of every single person who walks through the door: The Professor Aric Silva Memorial Archives.

Not so much of a *memorial*, I guess.

Holy. Shit.

I triple-check the dates on the letters, but they haven't changed. The most recent one is from two weeks ago.

I'll bet anything this is from THE Professor Silva. Remi's ultimate hero. Dude literally developed the tech that scrubs contamination from maz for MMC, basically saved the world in the middle of the worst maz crisis ever, and he's *not dead.*

We *need* him.

I run out into the main part of the space, pulse

pounding in my ears. Remi is going to *flip*.

"Remi, stars, you won't believe—"

"Diz, I have to tell you some—"

We nearly collide in the middle of the room, both clutching papers to our chests.

"Remi, you'll wanna hear this first—"

"Diz, this is huge, I don't . . . I can't . . ."

I shut my mouth and take a step back, looking up from the papers for the first time. Remi is deathly pale, their eyes wide and frightened. Whatever it is must be bad.

"You go first," I say. "Are you okay?"

They shake their head, biting their lip, their eyes squeezed shut.

"I found a doctoral thesis supervised by Professor Silva from eight years ago, right before he died. It was ordered to be deleted, so there's no digital record of it. But the archivist had a printed copy hidden behind the service desk. They were studying maz-15." They pause for breath, then finally meet my eyes. "Dizzy, they proved *conclusively* that maz-15 is what makes people ill. Maz-15 isn't new—it's the spellplague. And their research was censored by MMC."

Oh *shit*.

"Maz-15 is the contaminant that was released underground after the first big earthquake ten years ago," they continue, flipping through the papers in their hands. "It's attracted to other maz and binds to it, kind of like magnaz,

208

so it just . . . got into everything. They still couldn't figure out how exactly it acts on the human body except that it enters through the maz receptors, but—"

They break off and tip their head back, a few tears leaking from the corners of their eyes.

"His doctoral student got ill and died from the spell-plague. Because of his research."

My stomach lurches, and I take a step back away from Remi. Their eyes flash with hurt, but they just shake their head.

"I was so excited, Diz," they say. Their grip tightens on the bound manuscript. "When you told me there was a new type of maz, I thought, how lucky that I get to live in a time when there's a discovery like this! I can't wait to get my hands on it and study it myself."

They laugh bitterly, and it's like a knife in my gut. I put Remi directly in contact with the cause of their illness. I took that job, I made everyone do it. After what the spellplague did to them, to my family, I turned around and made everything worse.

I can't talk about this.

"So, wait," I say, trying to salvage the situation, managing to sound almost normal. "What do you mean, they censored the research?"

Remi sighs. "Like I said, they wiped it from the records, but also, just look at the timing. This was right before Professor Silva was declared missing, then dead.

And now there's us. We discover maz-15, and we're immediately targets for an attempted murder."

I shake my head. "What I don't understand is why they don't want this public. Shouldn't they *want* everyone to know that maz-15 causes the plague? The more people who know the cause, the more people can work on a cure, right? The scariest thing about the plague has always been the unknown factor. Where it came from, what exactly it was, you know?"

Remi shrugs. "I mean, I kind of get why, if it was eight years ago. Even two years after the plague, everyone was too terrified to even walk into a room with sunnaz-enhanced lights. If it had gotten out that the plague was caused by a new type of maz, I'm not sure anyone would want to touch maz ever again. Bad for their booming post-plague business, once they got it rolling. You know how I feel about MMC, but even I can see the logic there. But why keep it up after all this time? After they started to filter and sell clean maz, proved it was safe?"

A horrible image plants itself in my mind. "Remi, imagine if our last job had been real. If some rando really had discovered maz-15 and hired us to get some, then used it to make people ill?" My stomach lurches at the awful possibility of what could have been. "After two years of tapping pipes all over the city, we only found it in one place. At least while MMC controls the knowledge of it, they can keep it contained. Killing to protect the secret still seems too extreme, but . . . I don't know."

There's a long pause filled with the rustling of pages as Remi flips to the back of the thesis document.

"There's a handwritten list of names in the back here, too, but I don't recognize any of them. Maybe one of them would know more?"

I glance at the list, then make a few queries to my deck via subvocal command. Nothing useful, though. Except . . .

"They're all ex-MMC scientists, and they all disappeared around the time the professor did. I mean, officially they resigned and moved away, but that's kind of suspicious."

Remi, who's been taking a series of photos of the thesis with their smart lenses, closes the folio and goes behind the service desk to put it back. "Definitely suspicious. MMC probably killed them all, you know? They probably killed Professor Silva and every one of his colleagues, then covered it up. At this point I wouldn't even be surprised."

I raise an eyebrow and waggle the papers in my hand. Finally, something good to focus on. I seize the chance like a life preserver. "Actually . . ."

Remi pops up from behind the counter and plants their palms on the desk. "What is it?"

"Letters," I say, sliding them onto the desk in front of Remi. "The archivist, Professor Kayma, has been writing

211

back and forth with someone about maz-15. Someone named Aric. The most recent letter is only two weeks old. I found it locked in a vault in her office."

Remi lets out a startled laugh. "And you think it's Professor Silva?"

"One way to find out. This archive is full of stuff with his handwriting, yeah?"

Remi holds up a finger and whirls around, then comes up with one of the boxes they'd pulled from the stacks. It's labeled A.S. LAB NOTES—FRAGILE in giant bold letters.

"One of the benefits of being in an archive," Remi says. "They keep *everything*."

They lift the lid carefully, pull out a single sheet of paper, and lay it out on the desk for comparison. The resemblance is obvious. Identical.

"He's alive," they say. "And I can still meet him. Professor Silva really is alive!"

Remi's head whips up, their eyes shining. "He could tell us *everything*."

"And he escaped when MMC wanted him quiet. We could probably use his expertise about that too."

Then Remi wilts, their forehead hitting the desk with a *thunk*. "But how are we going to find someone who even MMC can't find?"

I grin and shuffle through the papers, producing a plain envelope. "There's a return address. It's just a P.O.

box at the university in Jattapore, and the name on it isn't his, but it's a place to start."

I swallow hard, low-level panic filling my veins at the thought of our next step. I swore I would never do this, but the universe has left me no choice.

"Looks like you're going to Jattapore after all. But this time, I'm coming with you."

Their excited smile flickers, then fades at that last bit, and I can practically *see* them remembering they're supposed to be mad at me. Ugh. Always one sentence too many. I glance at the time—how have we been here all night?—then open our group chat with a sigh and change the name.

Epic Group Chat: We are GOING TO JATTAPORE BITCHES Edition

You: Ania, buy us four tix for the 7 a.m. train to Jattapore

Jaesin: What, did you have a change of heart or something? We running?

Ania: What did you find?

Remi: a lot

like, both literally and spiritually A LOT

You: Grab our bags and meet us at the old elementary school near the station

I'll send over the photos of what we found so you can recover from having your minds blown by the time we get there.

I look up to share the last bit with Remi out of habit, but as soon as our eyes meet, they look away.

Damn it.

Twenty-four hours ago, I walked out. Just said "Bye forever," and left.

Things will probably never be the same.

How do you come back from something like that?

Can you?

SIXTEEN

THE OTHERS LAUGHED AT ME for my disguise yesterday, but they're eating their words now.

While we finished up at the archive, Jaesin and Ania dug through Ania's wardrobe and cosmetics for something to hide us all long enough to make it onto the train. We're using concealment spells, obviously, but we'll have to walk past several security guards, including one right as we walk on the train. If anything draws their attention enough to break through the concealment, we'll be glad for the extra layer of protection. Can't be too careful when you're wanted by the police.

Remi is easy enough. Plain jeans and a World of Battle Tournament X T-shirt (Ania swears she has no idea where it came from), their dark hair parted and slicked back, a cheap deck loaded with video games in their hands, and they're a totally forgettable nerd buried in their virtual world, barely aware enough to hand the security guard their ticket. Ania generally doesn't stand out too much in her everyday clothes, though it can't hurt to tone down her utterly polished beauty. She opts for an outfit similar to Remi's, though it obviously pains her to wear her work-out sneakers outside the gym.

Jaesin, though . . .

It takes everything in me to hold back a grin as we walk through the halls of the abandoned elementary school, Jaesin slouching along in the lead. Ania set her sights on him earlier, and she made good use of the time. She worked oil into his hair so it looked limp and greasy, lined his eyes in dark kohl, and dressed him in all black from head to toe, right down to black painted fingernails peeking out from his too-slim black hoodie sleeves. It started out as a disguise, but I think by the end it turned into some kind of revenge. For what, I don't even want to know.

I prance up behind him in my flowing pastel shirt-and-skirt combination (coming off as soon as we're on the train) and lean close, waggling my fingers. "You are no longer Awesome Strongman McDad Friend. I now pronounce you Super Edgelord McRaven Dark." I fold my hands together and give a little bow, solemn. "It is so."

Jaesin glares at me, then walks faster, pulling away. I look to Remi and Ania, hoping Jaesin is just keeping in character, but find the same annoyed stares from them.

Even naming jokes aren't working. They really do hate me now.

Maybe they'll always hate me, and tagging along for this ride is pointless.

"I still don't understand," Ania murmurs, smoothly ignoring me. "If the professor were alive and in Jattapore, there'd be some trace on the net. No one can truly disappear, right?"

"True." Jaesin glances over at her with a small smile. Apparently he *is* still capable, after all. "Unless you go off the grid entirely."

Ania shakes her head. "Is that even possible? Even toilets are networked to check contents for disease markers now."

"It wasn't too uncommon, before the plague," Jaesin says, his eyes lighting up at the memory of his earliest childhood. Has he never told Ania about it? I don't know what happened while they were dating, but there are some weird gaps in their knowledge about each other.

I think back to when Jaesin first came to the group home, when we were all only seven or eight. I made fun of him because he had an accent and had never used a deck or smart lenses before. What can I say? I was even more of an asshole as a child. Remi was the patient one, showing him how everything worked. Maybe he hadn't wanted to admit that to Ania.

Jaesin continues. "Out in the Freelands between cities, it used to be possible to live a pretty great life. My parents moved out of Kyrkarta after they got married, and I was born out there. Ambient maz levels were really low, so far from a big source like the ones cities are built around, and lots of families couldn't afford smart lenses and other tech, or just didn't want to use it. We just did everything by hand and kept everything local. I think some people were there specifically *because* it made them hard to find."

His face falls, and he blinks several times in quick succession. "Once the plague started spreading, though, even our trace amounts of maz turned toxic. MMC sent evacuation teams to the outland towns, but they only had room to take the kids. By the time they went back for our parents . . ."

He swallows hard, and Ania lays a hand on his arm, warm brown fingers tracing soothing patterns on his olive skin.

"Anyway," he says, pushing past it, "it's impossible to live out there without maz now, for wards and barriers and all that, but if anyone could do it, Silva could, right?"

Remi hums their agreement. "I mean, he literally invented MMC's maz scrubbers, so yeah, I imagine he could figure something out."

"Nerrrd," Jaesin says under his breath, and Remi gives him a none-too-gentle shove.

"But then he could be anywhere," Ania whines as we pass a fading bulletin board still decorated for a lesson on weather with a calendar from six years ago.

"True," I say, forcing myself back into the conversation. "But we have a starting point. The P.O. box at the university. We'll find him."

That effectively kills the conversation. I tell myself it's because no one had anything else to say. End of topic. Moving on.

We exit the barely still hanging doors into the alley behind the school, then turn the corner out onto the main street. The looming entrance to the train station fills the end of the road with its gleaming steel face, full of rounded arch windows and tasteful neon accent lighting. It almost covers up the vague run-down feeling of businesses barely afloat that set in a few years after the spellplague. People were afraid to travel outside the protective wards around the cities for a long time, and even after travel slowly resumed, the volume of passengers has never quite been the same.

Even still, most people prefer to fly, to be far above any potential source of contaminated maz, but that isn't an option for us. Security at the Kyrkarta Air and Space Port is *thorough*, including a nullaz barrier that would strip away any concealment spells we attempted to use. The number of trains running is way down from what it used to be, but they've managed to keep the doors open. Kyrkarta is still connected to the rest of the world by ground, if only just. Shockingly, not many people want to visit the city that was ground zero for the deadliest plague the world has ever seen. Can't imagine why.

As we approach the station, Ania tenses beside me. One guard stands on either side of the entrance doors, casually observing every person that walks past. Okay, this is the hard part. Buying tickets online? No problem, thanks to Ania's money. Actually getting on the train? Fine . . . unless the police have shared our photos with security to guard against us fleeing the city, like we're currently attempting to do. Ania's the only one of us who's ever left Kyrkarta by train, and she said there would be two layers of guards to pass: one here, at the entrance, and another as we get on the train. No ID checks, but that won't matter if they look too closely at our faces.

Jaesin does his emo shuffle toward the middle set of doors, as far from both guards as possible. Remi buries their face in their game, and I turn to Ania, letting my voice drift higher and my laugh come easier. Just two friends chatting about the latest season of a popular vid series. Nothing to see. Jaesin reaches the sliding door first, hesitates for a second on the threshold, then moves on without us. I hold my breath as the rest of us approach, closer, the door slides open . . . and we're in.

Round one: uneventful victory.

The train station is as busy as it ever gets, the early morning crowd in line to present their electronic tickets for boarding, while friends and family stand off to one side to wait for their arrivals. I let myself relax just a fraction. With it being this busy, we're less likely to get stopped. We shuffle into line together, our tickets loaded onto cheap throwaway decks completely disconnected from our regular net presence. No identifying information whatsoever, just a few games to make them look used, and a single train ticket each.

The eternal line works in our favor, like I thought. By the time we get to the front, the guard next to the ticket taker looks bored enough to fall asleep. With a grunt, Jaesin holds out his deck to scan, and the woman waves him forward without a second glance, eyes glazed over. Ania and I get similar treatment, and it takes everything I have not to breathe a relieved sigh as I step over the gap and onto the train, the floor vibrating with pent-up power under my feet.

"Hey, you," someone says right behind me, and I turn automatically. The guard is waving a hand in Remi's face. My blood turns to ice in my veins.

"Yeah?" Remi mutters, not looking up from their deck.

"Oi, will you look up from that thing for five seconds?" the guard snaps.

Remi looks up, their expression baleful. Good acting. I hold my breath.

The guard studies them for what seems like an hour, then nods in satisfaction. "Get your face out of that thing when you step on the train. You fall through that gap, you break your leg. Got it?"

"Yeah, fine," Remi says, and holds their deck out for the ticket to be scanned.

Then they're on. And so is the next person after them, and the next. Some of the stiffness finally bleeds out of my shoulders as we follow Jaesin from car to car, looking for an empty compartment. By the time we find one, the loudspeaker is already announcing our impending departure. My brain hits the brakes hard.

This is not where I thought I'd be. This was supposed to be our grand farewell week. Parties, concerts, food, *Kyrkarta*. I'm supposed to be celebrating in the city I love, with the people I love. I've never left my city, not once. Neither has Remi. Jaesin hasn't left since he first arrived after the plague. At the end of this week, they were supposed to leave and I was supposed to stay. That's not what's happening at all, though.

My butt has barely hit the cushion when the train hums gently as the maglev activates, then sails smoothly into motion. The world outside the window slides past slowly first, then faster and faster until it's nothing but a blur. We sail along, nearly frictionless, past the wards guarding the city from the contaminated wastelands beyond and out into craggy mountains. On our way.

My head is a mess. I want to scream, want to tell them to stop the train, because this would be great, an adventure, but for two things.

I want to share this moment with Remi. Our first time leaving Kyrkarta, and they're right by my side, like I always thought they would be. But they won't look at me. They may as well be on the other side of the planet.

But more than that, it's the sick certainty in the pit of my stomach.

When we get to Jattapore, the others are going to stay.

And I'll be going back alone.

In the days before the plague, the high-speed train to Jattapore would have taken an hour at most. It's less than four hundred miles away, connected directly by rail. With the decreased train service, though, we're forced to ride a loop that circles through several surrounding cities. Stop in Batista, take forty-five minutes to load and unload passengers, on to the next city, rinse and repeat. What used to be a one-hour trip now takes almost six, and once we're locked in a compartment together, it takes barely twenty minutes for the anger and resentment to boil over.

Remi stares out the window, silent, with their forehead pressed to the clear acrylic. They're utterly disconnected, save for the occasional heavy look they shoot in my direction. Jaesin somehow manages to turn sitting next to them into worried hovering without saying a word, shooting glares at me every time I so much as shift in my seat. Ania stares off into space in a way that I know means she's reading a book on her lenses, her face twitching into slight smiles, frowns, and confusion along with the story.

The atmosphere is oppressively awkward, and I'm about sick of it. I get it, I screwed up, but am I going to be ignored and punished forever? Even while we take on this huge investigation into something that *I* discovered? I was the only one willing to figure out what happened, and I was right, and we're finally doing something about it—but somehow I'm still the jerk everyone hates.

Right as I finally decided to pull up a movie on my lenses and zone out, Remi stands from their seat, shoves past us all, and slips out of the compartment, shutting the door behind them with a solid click.

I stare at the closed door. My fault, probably. Everything is my fault. I glare at the door and turn back to face forward . . . only to find Ania and Jaesin staring me down expectantly.

"What?" I snap.

Jaesin practically snarls, and Ania rolls her eyes. My skin prickles with the hostility radiating off them both, putting my hackles up.

"What do you mean, *what*?" Jaesin says, terse. "Go after them."

"Why me? I didn't do anything. They just left."

Ania slaps her hands on her thighs, shockingly loud in the small compartment, and actually stands so she can glare down her nose at me.

"You didn't do anything? Are you serious?" she says, about five seconds from actually shaking a finger in my face. "You are such a hypocrite, Diz, always like 'Let them make their own choices' and 'It's up to them what they feel well enough to do,' but you're the one that acts like they're contagious. Do you even remember what happened on the bridge after the job? You ditching us right after the worst experience of our lives was only the most recent in a long line of terrible things."

Remi's hands on my hips, dancing close, me pulling away.

Remi's fingers brushing my knee, the stars bright overhead, the words "Ask me to stay" heavy in the air as my brain goes blank.

Remi reaching for my shoulder, the touch of their skin like poison, recoiling, slamming into Jaesin, into the crowd, fighting back nausea—

Wait, is that what everyone thinks? What Remi thinks? That it's about their illness? That's not it *at all*.

I shove the memories away and scoff to cover my moment of hesitation. "Obviously they're not contagious. The spellplague can't be spread by—"

"Oh my gods, Diz, I could actually slap you right now," she says, cutting me off. Jaesin laughs bitterly.

"She's right," he says. "Get out of this compartment and go after them."

"You can't just tell me—"

Ania steps closer, crowding me toward the door.

"Get. Out."

I leap to my feet with a growl and throw the compartment door open. "Assholes."

I slam the door behind me and stalk off down the hall. They may have chased me out of the compartment, but they can't make me actually talk to Remi about whatever problem they're having. What, I'm not allowed to have some personal space? I'll just walk around for a bit, explore the train, enjoy my first train ride.

Or not.

Because there's Remi, standing alone in a long stretch of hallway, peering out a ceiling high window with their forehead resting against their arms, stacked on the glass. Something in my chest gives an aching little tug.

Damn it.

I chew on the inside of my lip, then sigh and walk over. Remi doesn't acknowledge my approach, or even look over as I slide to the floor beside them, my back against the wall of the train and my knees pulled up to my chest.

"Hi," I say several eternal minutes later.

Silence. Great. The quiet game is my favorite.

"Jaesin and Ania made me come talk to you."

And that's obviously the wrong thing to say, because Remi barks out a harsh laugh.

"Yeah. Of course they did. Obviously you'd never actually talk to me on your own."

"That's not what I meant—"

"No, but it's the truth, Diz. It's the truth and I'm tired of it."

I scowl and yank at the hem of my borrowed skirt, wishing I'd thought to change when we first got on the train. I feel like I'm sitting here trying to have a conversation while wearing a costume.

"I don't know why I'm the only bad one here," I finally blurt. "I went out and investigated the problem we caused, all of us, and I come back with something real, and you were all just ready to DITCH me—"

"You left *us* first—"

"You were planning to leave anyway!" I shout, loud enough that a train attendant pokes his head through the doorway, then leaves again. I breathe hard, the air never quite enough, my eyes burning, burning. I try to pull it all back inside, but it's out there now, spilling over and raw and plain to see.

We're silent for a long moment, my words echoing like the ring of a hammer strike, like the lingering rumble of a bomb blast. Finally, Remi turns and slides down the wall, sitting beside me with a careful twelve inches between us.

"It doesn't have to be like this, Diz. We used to have

so much fun. The concerts, the stars, the movie nights. All of the . . ." They swallow. "All of it. I get that you have issues. We all do, after what we've been through. But you don't have to let it keep you from . . . from the things I think you want."

And that sends a shot of pure panic through me. Everything's exposed, naked and bleeding, and people always say they'll stay . . . but it's not true, it's *not*. No one can really say, not for certain, so what's the point of anything, of—

I drop my head forward between my knees and clamp my hands over the back of my neck and breathe, breathe, in, out, slower, slower.

Say something.

"I know," I manage. And those two words cost more than I have to give.

Remi leans closer, dips their head so their lips brush my shoulder as they whisper once more.

"Ask me to stay, Dizzy."

I close my eyes again and give in for just a moment, picturing all the things they want. Things I want. We've been so close so many times. My heart clenches, panic speeding its beating back to double time. Just *say* it. I know this is wrong. I know *I'm* wrong. I do want this. I should tell them. I should say it. Please, Remi, just stay with me, stay in the city we met in so we can start the next part of our lives still together, so I can figure myself out and when I do . . . if I'm ever okay, then we can . . .

When I finally manage to speak again, it's barely a whisper.

"I can't."

Rather than shrinking in defeat, Remi sits up straighter, staring straight across the hallway. They nod, once, firm.

"Well, that sucks. But I understand."

I bite my lip and force slow breaths through my nose. Panic shifts to anger and back again, faster than I can keep up, a swirl of awfulness, speeding cars on a collision course.

"I understand," Remi says again. "But I can still be mad about it. I don't have to like it. I don't have to think it's fair or right for you to lash out at us for not doing something you refuse to admit to wanting. We're not mind readers, Diz. If you want something, you have to say so. And we can't hang in limbo until you decide you're ready to actually have an emotion."

Oh, *fuck you* entirely. My hands ball into fists unconsciously.

Great. Just great. What am I supposed to do, give them permission to hate me? To be mad forever? What exactly are they expecting? I don't want this mess. I don't want any of this.

What I do is push to my feet and stare hard at the ground, my mouth twisted in something between a frown and a scowl. Anger is winning, as always.

"Cool. Well. Have fun being mad, I guess."

I turn and continue down the length of the train, listening for them to call me back, for a half-hearted "Dizzy . . ." to give us another shot, to take us back to our uneasy equilibrium.

They say nothing.

I walk on, my heart heavy from the awful freedom of finally knowing.

It's over. Once and for all.

SEVENTEEN

BY THE TIME WE'RE WITHIN half an hour of Jattapore, I've walked the length of the train three times, bought a sandwich, napped in someone's empty seat, and generally done everything I can to avoid going back to the compartment. The train company's weather alert system pings me with ever more concerned notifications the closer we get. Yes, I get it, Jattapore has high tides or something. We don't have tides in the mountains, so that means nothing to me, go away.

When I feel the train start to decelerate for its final approach to Jattapore, though, there's nothing for it. I have to go back. We made this MMC mess together, and we're gonna fix it together.

A new message from Davon pops up as I thread my way through the crowded market car, resisting the urge to stop and buy all the therapeutic junk food I can carry. There have been a dozen more messages since the ones I ignored at the archives last night, but I've been too busy and head-explodey from the night's revelations to say more than "I'm fine. Don't wanna talk right now." Guess I owe him a slightly longer response.

(private) Davon: Doing okay today?
Are you still at Ania's? You could come stay with me if you want.

I snort. He had the chance to gain custody of me when he turned eighteen and I was still fourteen. He said no. To be fair, he wasn't really in a good enough financial situation to take care of us both, and I *said* at the time that I didn't want it either, that I was fine on my own. Who believes a fourteen-year-old when they say stuff like that, though? Obviously he should have known that was code for "Yes, please, adopt me, I'm a mess."

(private) You: I'm fine. Going to Jattapore for a few days. Will let you know when I'm back.
Talk to you later.
(private) Davon: Okay. Please be careful. Come back in one piece so we can watch the season finale of The Rare Ones together.
And by that I mean come back *soon* because otherwise I might watch it without you.
(private) You: Don't you DARE.
(private) Davon: Then hurryyyyyyyyy

I go invisible and blink away the chat before I can get drawn into a deep discussion of our season finale theories. Dangerous topic. No time for that now. I make the final approach to our compartment on lead feet, as if it's full of MMC guards waiting to kill me instead of my pissed-off friends. I'm heading into hostile territory. My angry half truce with Remi notwithstanding, I know Jaesin and Ania would only accept one outcome: shit sorted, emotions had, kisses exchanged, everything shiny. But that's the one thing I just can't give them.

When I enter the car with our compartment, though, the whole hallway rings with muffled laughter and shouted conversation. My chest gives a little pulse of warmth at the noise, the familiar soundtrack of the Cliffs. Home. An unconscious smile tugs at the corner of my mouth, and I quicken my pace, pulling the door open to let some of that goodness wash over me.

I'm met with silence.

My smile dies away as everyone avoids my eyes, the ghost of their mirth still fading from their expressions. Something in my chest withers and curls in on itself as I slide into my seat, eyes locked on the floor.

"Hey," Remi says, voice flat, not looking at me.

"Hey," I answer. A small effort. I appreciate it. "I guess we, uh . . . need to talk about what to do when we arrive."

I hate how weak and pathetic I sound. My cheeks burn as I stare holes in the floor, the prospect of eye contact too much to process.

"Yeah," Jaesin says, cool and neutral. "Remi, you were

looking up information on the university?"

They hum an affirmative. "They're not in session right now, so the only people on campus are professors and grad students. More than likely the name on the envelope is one of them. If it's a real name, of course. I tried looking for a directory online, but no luck."

Ania turns to me, the first one to actually look me in the eye. "Diz, you think you can find that info?"

I shrug, my gaze sliding away from the creases on Remi's cheek from napping against the window. "Given enough time, yeah, but I might need to be on the school's network to do it, depending on their security. Maybe we should start by going to the university's post office. We might be able to just ask someone if they recognize the name. It could be it's the professor himself, using an alias."

"It's different handwriting, though," Remi points out. "There's at least one other person involved in this letter exchange, if only for that."

I shrug. "It's still the only lead we have. How far is the university from the train station?"

Remi shares a map with us all, and at first I can't even tell what I'm looking at. Jattapore looks completely different from both Kyrkarta and the much older version of itself on the wall in the archive. The ocean crashes in on the western side of the city, and portions of the coastline are highlighted in red with a do-not-travel warning.

Apparently all those weather warnings I've been ignoring were trying to tell me about the hurricane currently dumping rain on the city, on its way up the coastline. The hurricanes have been increasing in strength and frequency for years, and Jattapore is finally giving way in the face of the constant battering. Just like Kyrkarta and its earthquakes.

"The university post office is right here," Remi says, placing a marker on the map. "It's not too far from the train station, and well away from the coast. The worst of the hurricane has moved on, and it wasn't a bad one, so it shouldn't be a problem."

Shouldn't be, but probably will be, now that they've said it. Way to jinx us. We were lucky the train wasn't canceled due to the weather, but that luck will probably balance out with something awful later.

Angry rain lashes at the windows as the train pulls to a smooth stop at Jattapore Station, fat droplets that fall harder than anything we ever get in Kyrkarta. It's nearly as opaque as fog.

"How are we supposed to get anywhere in this mess?" I ask, expecting to be completely ignored. Ania deigns to provide an overly knowledgeable response, though, as she leads us off the train.

"Jattapore has a rail system we can use," she says. "The flooding and wind are too bad for anything else. They only started having hurricane problems recently, when the ocean started heating up, so they mostly aren't built to handle it. The rail is the only thing that still runs consistently."

"I bet the wind makes RidePods fun," Jaesin says with a grimace. He can jump off buildings and do backflips in boost shoes, but put him in a bumpy RidePod and he turns totally green.

Once we're on the platform, the others halt in place with their luggage, taking in the humid, salty air, the crowded train station, and the sheets of water pouring from the sky just beyond the edge of the platform ceiling. The architecture around us is different from the buildings in Kyrkarta, more ornamented, and somehow conjuring the swell and fade of the ocean just beyond. My hands itch to climb all over this building, to explore its hidden back hallways and secret rooftop doorways. Maybe some other time.

I catch Remi looking at me, gray eyes a perfect match for the roiling clouds above, but they quickly glance away. They know me so well, though, that they probably read my thoughts.

I don't want to be curious about this city, though. I don't *want* to feel that need, to run through its abandoned buildings, go everywhere I'm not supposed to go, let everything else fall away other than the next stair, the next rooftop, the next flying leap. It feels like cheating on my home to think it, but even in a strange, unfamiliar city, the thrill of exploration would be glorious.

Pointless to imagine now.

"Come on," I say, waving the others after me. I spotted a sign that said RAILWAY, with a little train icon next to it. Don't need to know my way around this city to get that. I lead the way up to the raised platform, never once glancing behind me.

That's the biggest benefit of being in the lead: you never see all the glares directed at your back.

The University of Jattapore campus is beautiful, waterlogged though it is. The trees (so many more of them than in Kyrkarta) sparkle with hanging droplets of rain, glimmering in the few tentative rays of sun that dare to peek through the angry clouds overhead. The storm is moving on, leaving behind fallen branches, storm drains clogged with leaves, and calf-high water in low-lying areas. The university buildings stand proud and unaffected above it all, built of bright metals and stone carved in beautiful curling waves, and bustling with people even in the wake of the powerful storm. According to the net, it was the lowest category of hurricane, though I don't exactly have the context to judge. It's earthquakes and oranges. Or something.

We stop for a quick bite at a café called Speedy's right as they're pulling their little red awning back out from its storm-tucked position. Two employees bicker back and forth as they retrieve tumbled tables and chairs from across the bricked courtyard, complaining about some other guy who was supposed to bring everything inside before the wind picked up. I guess the people of Jattapore and Kyrkarta do have one thing in common: we've all had to figure out how to structure our lives around disaster.

We order our food, then commandeer one of the outside tables to wait for it. I spend an uncomfortable few minutes trying to watch Remi without *looking* like I'm watching Remi, scanning for any sign of how they're feeling after our fight. I get nothing, though. It's like the fight never happened and I don't exist. They're totally normal, except for the fact that they won't look at me. Eventually they ditch us to run to the bathroom, which of course leaves me sitting around with Mom and Dad. Great.

I manage to endure a whole thirty seconds of strained silence before I crack. Playing nice, making jokes, apologizing—it doesn't matter what I try, so screw it. Not trying anymore.

"So, this is Jattapore!" I say. "Gotta say, not really feeling it so far. Not impressed at all. You sure you wanna live here?"

The way Ania's and Jaesin's expressions darken gives me a vindictive little thrill. Wanna shut me out of the family completely? Fine. But I'm not gonna just lie back and make it easy for you.

"Awfully soggy, for one," I say. "And what the hell are those obnoxious birds circling up there? Do they ever stop screaming?"

Jaesin closes his eyes and tips his head back with a sigh. I silently hope for a bird to poop on his face.

"This is fun, though," I continue, because I'm on a roll and can't stop myself. "The three of us here like this. It's just like when you two were dating! Lots of obnoxious tension, the two of you being all huffy and superior, and me as the third wheel, just hanging out over here while you two take yourselves suuuuper seriously and roll your eyes a lot."

Ania huffs an irritated sigh.

"I know what you're doing, Diz, and I'm not going to let it—" she begins, but Remi walks back out to join us, their arms laden with bags of food. The smell of buttery biscuits and charred veggies shuts Ania right up, and we quickly divvy up the food to scarf as we walk. It's probably better that I shove a biscuit in my face and stop talking.

Everything is fine.

We throw our wrappers in the trash receptacle outside the student union building, then slip through the entrance, into the chill of a building air-conditioned for computers, not humans. A bored student wrapped in a thick hoodie sits at the front desk with her feet up on the counter, obviously zoned in to some kind of deck game, so we walk straight past her and follow signs for the post office.

We round a corner and spot the post office window set into a long lobby wall. The others head straight for it. I hang back a bit and let them handle the talking. With my track record the past few days, I wouldn't be surprised if I managed to blow up the post office or something with my mere presence. Jaesin takes the lead, the envelope clutched in his hand, and marches straight up to the clerk at the window.

I turn away to toss my drink in the recycler, then turn back just in time to see the clerk walk away from the window where the others stand waiting. A moment later, the guy comes out a side entrance, out of their line of sight, and stalks back toward them . . . with one fist brimming over with firaz.

"Look out!" I cry, and the others whirl around just in time to see the clerk round the corner and lift his fireball.

In the blink of an eye, Remi steals the maz straight from his hand and wraps it around their own, cocking their arm back like they're ready to throw a flaming punch. Jaesin beats them to it, seizing the guy by the collar of his shirt and slamming him into the wall. Ania recovers from her shock quickly enough to scan the empty courtyard for witnesses, then starts in on a quick concealment weave. I run to Jaesin's side and look the clerk over. His name tag reads VAN, and his expression is hard. Not with anger or violence, though. With determination. This guy has a cause to fight for. Means we're on the right track, I'd guess, one step closer to the elusive Professor Silva.

"Hey, look, Van," I say, glancing down at his name tag again to double-check. "You obviously know who we're looking for, and you're feeling protective. No need for that, okay? The same people who are after him are after us."

Seriously, we're four half-drowned teenagers still wearing our awful disguises from the train. Jaesin's eyeliner is running, Remi's shirt is nearly transparent from the rain (not that I've noticed), Ania's curls are sagging, and my terrible skirt feels like it's going to slide right off with the weight of the water it's soaked up. Do we really *look* like MMC assassins come to murder the good Professor Silva?

Van pauses in his struggle against Jaesin's pressing forearm. He studies me, but still doesn't speak. I step back to include the whole group in my next words.

"Maybe we should take this chat into the office?" I say, nodding toward the door the clerk used to get the drop on them.

Van scowls.

"Fine," he says, holding up his hands. "My badge is on my belt. You'll need it to get through the door."

Remi snags the badge in question, and Jaesin hauls the guy off the wall and around the corner with Ania following, still pouring concealment maz into her shield. We all awkwardly squeeze ourselves into the tight space of the post office back room, where Jaesin finally lets the guy go, but not far. Van straightens his shirt and huffs, then sits back against a desk.

"Well? Why are you here?" he asks carefully, his eyes on Remi. I shift closer to Remi's side and watch the guy. That was a carefully worded question, fishing for information while failing to actually confirm our own. The answer, now that I try to summarize it in my head, sounds utterly absurd. I snort a laugh before I can help it.

"Remi, do you want to explain our situation to this gentleman?"

They glance over at me with a tiny smile, and my traitorous heart stirs with hope. It's more than I ever expected to see directed at me again. It lasts barely a second, though, before Remi steps forward to confront Van.

"You obviously know who Professor Silva is. You know what maz-15 is?" Remi asks.

Van's eyes widen, and he looks away for a long moment, then finally nods.

"Okay, well, so do we," Remi says. "Long story short, we found out about it, MMC tried to kill us because of it, we went to the archives in Kyrkarta to try to learn more about it, and that research led us here. We know

Professor Silva is alive. We know he discovered the cause of the spellplague. We need his help."

They pause and smile the bright, infectious grin that grabbed me and refused to let go right from our first meeting as kids. "But also, I've been such a fan of his work my whole life, and just the chance to meet him would be . . ."

They trail off with a flail of excitement, then seem to remember the circumstances and shove their hands in their pockets.

"That's pretty much it, right?" they ask, looking around to the rest of us, even me.

"That's the basics," Ania says, stepping up to lay a hand on Jaesin's shoulder.

Van braces his palms on the desktop and looks at the ceiling for a long moment, then back down at Remi.

"You're spellsick, aren't you?" he asks.

"Sure am," Remi replies without missing a beat, though the rest of us turn hot glares on the guy. How *dare* he bring it up without their permission?

"Why do you still weave?" Van asks, oblivious to the ire directed at him. "Knowing that it's maz that made you ill. How can you stand to look at it every day? Why don't you stop?"

"Could you?" Remi says, matter-of-fact. And apparently that's the right response, because Van finally relaxes, nodding.

"I'll tell you where to find him," he says. "If you make

it there, I know he'll be happy to help you."

If?

Van zones into his lenses for a moment, then a map share notification pops up. Jattapore fills my view once again, but on the opposite side of the city, near a crowded merchant district, a single marker blinks outside the faint blue line of the city's wards. Remi zooms in and checks the box to show distances. The marker is approximately two miles outside the wards, but it may as well be two hundred, for all that anyone can get there.

Beyond the city's wards, around the whole world, contaminated maz is dispersed in the very air, the way clean, natural maz used to be. In the past, a spellweaver would have been able to draw trace maz from thin air and spin it into threads to use on the spot. Free, like it should be. To be fair, they could still do that . . . but they'd probably die of the plague before the day was out.

"Ahhh, this might not be too bad," Ania says. "I can buy us some nullaz, and Remi and I can get the suits and wards set up in an hour or two."

It's so nice to be able to just money your problems away.

Jaesin nods, already bouncing on the balls of his feet. "It's not as far as I thought it would be." His eyes are aglow at the talk of being outside city wards for the first time since childhood, his grin already slipping back into its boyish seven-year-old version, all toothy and unrestrained.

"It's not far, no," Van says, leaning against the desk with his arms crossed.

Then he winces.

"Um. Good luck?"

I wave a dismissive hand. "Please. We got this."

After all, we're the best siphoning crew in Kyrkarta. We've got skills. I'm pretty sure we can handle a two-mile walk.

EIGHTEEN

ONLY TWO MILES, WE SAID.

Should be easy, we said.

I flinch as the boom of another cannon shot rends the air, but I'm not fast enough—I take another sunnaz blast straight to the face, my vision whiting out in a wash of stars.

"These *godsdamned cannons*!" I shriek, as near to hysterical as I've ever been in my life.

It's the third direct hit in ten minutes. I'm starting to worry about permanent vision damage.

A two-mile walk shouldn't have taken more than thirty minutes. Twenty-five minutes in, we're barely halfway there, and I'm about to collapse.

"I'm running low on everything," Ania calls over the sound of another cannon blast. "I'm already out of firaz!"

"How the *hell* are you already empty?" Remi shouts back, dancing around a mine and jabbing a fist into a charging gorilla so realistic I can barely make out the weave that holds it together. Remi's fingers find the seams just as the beast's jaws slam shut an inch from their nose, and with a rough yank, they pull the whole thing apart like a threadbare sweater.

"I'm a techwitch," Ania snaps, her partially suppressed accent back in full force under duress. She's in her total concentration mode, where she forgets to be poised and ladylike. "I can't just cannibalize one of these—*fuck*—one of these *demon rabbits* for its maz."

Two swears from Ania in less than a week. This is just a day full of unicorns.

And then I trip over a maz mine, which summons a literal charging unicorn, and I deeply and instantly regret every thought I've ever had in my life.

"Look out!" Jaesin calls, then puts his shoulder down and rams into the unicorn's side, knocking it just far enough off course that I don't get kebabed. I hit the ground and roll in a puff of sandy coastal soil, coming up on my toes to spring away from those stomping unicorn hooves. An ominous *CRUNCH* comes from my backpack as I roll over it—I don't even want to know. Jaesin throws himself at the unicorn again, his arms flexing around its neck, slowing it down until someone can get a good shot in.

Ania comes through with a blast from her fast-diminishing stores of nullaz. The maz, so black it seems to radiate darkness, hits the unicorn and breaks apart, individual threads wrapping around the woven motaz and vitaz that give it the appearance of life. The creature stumbles like it's stepped into quicksand, struggling as it goes down in a tangle on top of Jaesin. His nullaz suit flares as it makes contact with the maz, and Ania hisses a warning.

"Watch yourself! We don't have enough to patch your barrier if you wear it out."

"I know that," he grinds out between clenched teeth, heaving himself up onto one side. I offer him a hand and pull, hauling him to his feet, then turn back to the field before us and compare our position against the map. It's all I can do. I'm fast and agile, but not beefy like Jaesin. I'm not good at wrestling things. I can't use maz.

I can navigate, though. I can run, find us a way around obstacles, blaze a trail to the point on the map that hopefully marks the professor's secret wasteland fortress. Just like running the streets and rooftops of Kyrkarta, right?

"This way!" I call, leading us around a patch of dense beach scrub and scrabbling over a waist-high boulder without even slowing down. It's a bit longer to go around the scrub instead of through it, but at least this way we can see where we're putting our feet. There've been trip wires, mines, ankle-twisting holes, and even the occasional aggressive crab. I've never been more aware of my feet in my life, and I jump off buildings on the regular.

"Try to step where I step," I say, adjusting the opacity of the map overlay so I can clearly see the ground while staying on track.

"You know, I'm not sure I want to meet Professor Silva anymore," Ania says, panting with exertion. Remi barks a short laugh.

"You have to admit, his work is genius," Remi says. "Twisted, but genius. I think I admire him even more now."

"Who's shocked," Jaesin deadpans.

The next quarter mile is deceptively quiet. I call out the locations of mines and other traps, and Remi spends a few slow, careful minutes feeding a bare trickle of terraz back into Ania's ware, trusting me to guide them as they do. The ware really isn't designed to be loaded that way, and Remi can't accomplish much while we walk, but it's something. Enough for Ania to keep the structure of her shield strong around us while Remi feeds energy into the system, just in case a giant missile falls out of the sky or something. At this point I won't rule out *anything*.

We crest a sandy dune and step through a curtain of seven-foot-high beach grass, which seems determined to get in my mouth. I bat it away and spit, my nose itching with some kind of unfamiliar pollen. I'm not sure I like this nature shit. It's so empty, too much nothingness on the horizon, and it's so *quiet* when there's not a cannon going off next to my face. About a mile in the distance, the gray-blue ocean churns against the coastline, eroding the land little by little. And a quarter mile away and to our right is a little cottage nestled in a dune valley, surrounded by rock gardens and flowers and rogue tufts of waving grass. It's adorable.

Between us and the house is a curtain of fire.

"Well," Remi says, matter-of-fact. "That's effective. What do you think, Ania?"

Ania grunts and stumbles down the front of the dune to get closer to the fire, oblivious to the razorweeds slicing at her trousers and ankles. At the bottom, she steps up to the wall of fire until her nose is nearly touching it.

"It's not giving off much heat. Try the usual stuff?" she says, turning to look back at Remi.

"May as well," they reply. "Might tell us more about it, at least."

The two of them put their heads together and chatter back and forth, trying combinations of aeraz and wataz that have no obvious effect, but which always prompt some kind of muttered, "Hmm, interesting." Jaesin and I glance at each other and roll our eyes, and I fight down a surge of warmth. Just because we can share humorous appreciation of Remi's and Ania's complete and utter nerdiness, that doesn't mean he's going to forgive me. I can hope, though.

This whole stars-forsaken experience reminds me of being on the playground in my first group home, where I met Remi and Jaesin, but before I met Ania. I was so confused about Remi for so long, following them and Jaesin around, sneaking food from the kitchens with them and sharing in the blame when we got caught. Whenever they managed to steal a bit of maz, though, I'd turn tail and run, hide on a roof somewhere and not speak to them for days on end. Jaesin had the total opposite reaction. Growing up without much maz around, he was totally fascinated, and he made Remi drill him on all the manual-dexterity exercises they taught us in school. When we all got tested for maz aptitude in fourth year, he was heart-broken.

I'd never been more relieved in my life. I didn't want that crap anywhere near me. Remi, of course, was fast-tracked for every advanced placement maz course in the catalog. I avoided them for two weeks straight after the test. I guess I'd been hoping, somewhere in my irratio-nal child brain, that their weaving was a fluke. That it wouldn't really *stick*, and they'd be in mundie classes like the rest of us.

There was never anything mundane about Remi, though, not from the start.

We were ten when Remi and Jaesin came and found me hiding on the roof of an abandoned factory across from the group home. They'd used some stolen maz to fight off a girl who'd been threatening them both for weeks, and the whole thing had scared me so bad I'd seri-ously thought about running away to a new group home, somewhere far across the city where people were still properly afraid of maz. Remi pulled themself up on the roof, panting with the exertion and obviously overtired, but refusing Jaesin's help all the same. Even though I was terrified, and therefore angry, because even at ten years old I was still *me*, I remember being so worried. They looked like they were ready to collapse.

Remi crawled across the roof and sat down cross-legged in front of me, expression unusually solemn for them. They reached inside the front pocket of their ratty blue hoodie, pulled something out, and pressed it into my hands. Their palms gently cupped mine as together we held what looked like a mottled egg the color of melting chocolate-chip ice cream. As Jaesin knelt beside us, the egg rocked once, twice, then split open to reveal . . . a tiny golden puppy?

But puppies didn't hatch from eggs. And they didn't come in brilliant glowing shades of silver and gold, though it felt real enough as its tiny paws scrabbled at my arm, climbing as high as it could before it started licking me furiously. When I finally realized what it was, I froze, nearly bolted, but the two of them soothed me, drew gentle fingers over the puppy's floppy ears and scratched its fuzzy golden belly. Eventually I relaxed enough that we all made a big triangle with our legs for the puppy to run around in, making it do tricks and play fetch. By the time the maz lost its energy and the puppy crumbled away, I was sad to see it go.

I climbed down off that roof and went home with

Jaesin and Remi that night, and we threw our blankets and pillows on the floor between two of our beds and slept in a pile of limbs and snoring. I've never totally lost my fear of maz, but I guess I absorbed the fact that Remi and maz were a package deal and I had to get used to it. And I did, well enough to be around Remi and their little maz creatures, at least. Eventually I figured out that I could work with maz too—to contain it, control it. Make it safer. I started to work on ware, then build my own. Maz gloves, drones, stable storage vials, everything I could think of. I was good at it. If Remi and Jaesin had given up on me back then, I might never have found my talent.

Surely we can't be broken forever when we have history like that, right?

A sudden "Ha!" of triumph breaks through my melancholy just in time for me to catch Ania and Remi pulling back the edges of the fire wall, broken threads of fraying firaz drifting through the air like ash and embers. Jaesin and I race down the hill to join them, and barely a minute later we're through to the other side, nothing between us and our goal.

Nothing except a pack of spellwoven berserker rabbits that pop into existence the second we crossed the firaz threshold.

Mother. Fucker.

The rabbits charge, their powerful legs propelling them forward like a herd of angry terriers, teeth gnashing and whiskers quivering. Professor Silva apparently has an imagination like a horror-movie version of children's cartoons, and the end result is legitimately terrifying. Ania empties the last of her nullaz straight into the front line, the first few rabbits dissolving into a cloud of threads for the others to leap through. Jaesin punches a rabbit that dares to go for the jewels, then punts another straight at Remi, who catches the thing and uses its maz to take out another.

We push forward, Ania throwing tiny shields out as needed, Jaesin kicking and stomping like some kind of dancing murder bear, and me chucking rocks to goad the rabbits into chasing me as I leap over rocks and holes, my legs burning with the exertion.

And then there's Remi, totally in their element, slinging spells left and right, tearing these damn rabbits down into their component parts and shoving the maz right back in the face of the next one. By their sheer ferocity alone, we fight through the final quarter mile, leaving a trail of scorch marks, dissolving maz, and despair.

By the time we reach the front door of the little house on the wasteland, we're panting, exhausted, and scraped bloody, alive thanks only to Ania's talent with shields and Remi's overall awesomeness at weaving on the fly. Remi honestly seems thrilled by the whole thing, eyes shining with curiosity even as they prop themselves up against one of the porch pillars, totally wiped out.

"I mean, I could weave a rabbit like that if I had, like . . . all day? I've done plenty of smaller ones. But for it to just be triggered like that, and to retain its potency after being bound up in that trigger spell—"

"Shut. UP," I say, wiping a trickle of blood from the heel of one hand. It must be from when I braced for my shoulder roll during the unicorn incident.

It says a *lot* that neither Ania nor Jaesin gets after me for speaking to Remi like that.

Remi takes no notice of our moods and, with triumphant precision, brushes the sand off their clothes and begins to put their hair back to rights. Ready to meet their ultimate hero.

Screw that. I'm ready for this to be done.

I walk straight past Remi and knock three times on the heavy wooden door. Shuffling steps approach from the other side, and I hold my breath. We've fought our way over two miles for some answers, and we're about to meet the person who can give them. The knob turns, the door creaks, and *finally* we're welcomed in . . .

. . . by a man with a giant fireball in his hand.

Should have known.

NINETEEN

THE FIRE GLINTS IN THE man's black eyes as he opens the door wider, the light deepening the shadows of his gaunt cheeks and making his rich golden-brown skin glow with ominous red highlights. He murmurs something under his breath and, with a twitch of his wrist, sets the fireball to spinning, the weave stretching, and I stumble back, throwing my arms wide to shield Remi behind me—

The flaming ball of firaz in the man's hand bursts into a sparkling flower that settles into the center of his bow tie, glittering cheerfully.

"Good evening!" the man chirps, as if greeting an old friend. "Come on in! Do you take honey in your tea?"

"Yes!" Remi says. They grab my arm to steady themself, bright-eyed and eager. "Honey is great! Thank you! It's so great to meet you, Professor!"

Whoa, dial it back there, Remi. The professor doesn't seem to mind at all, though. He waves us inside and escorts us through a dowdy old sitting room, past another elderly man in an armchair. The man's head is tipped back against the headrest, mouth open, with soft, rhythmic snores filling the small sitting room. Is the professor not even going to ask what we're doing here?

"Don't mind my husband," he says instead, with a dismissive wave of his hand. "He takes a nap once an hour, it seems. He'll be awake in time for dinner, though, the old bastard, don't you doubt it. As soon as the food is ready, poof! Alert as a cat stalking a mouse." He pauses in the kitchen to fill a kettle with water and set it on the stove, then leads us onward without turning on the burner.

I turn to share a snicker with Jaesin, completely charmed by the man's chatter, only to find him already waggling his eyebrows at Ania. The two of them share a near-silent giggle, hands pressed to their mouths. My shoulders sag, but I continue on, still supporting Remi as we walk. They practically glow with excitement, despite their visible exhaustion.

Once all this is over, if we aren't dead or in jail, they'll probably all go right back to their grand plans. Ania to university, Jaesin and Remi right back here to Jattapore. Especially now that Remi knows their dream professor is here. Silva will probably take them on as a student. Who could resist? Anyone who meets Remi can tell within ten minutes the kind of talent they possess.

Suddenly the old man isn't quite so cute. I glare at the back of his head as he leads us back to a disaster area of a workroom. Three long tables dominate the space; one covered in vials of maz, one piled high with old paper books, and one so covered with potted plants leaning toward the nearest window for sunlight that the tabletop is barely visible through the foliage. One wall is lined with heavy wooden bookshelves cluttered with more maz and books, and even more spill out onto the floor. We can barely take a step without clinking bottles together or tripping over some overturned pot of dirt, though one area of the floor has been kept completely, meticulously clear: a giant hatch that reads IN CASE OF EMERGENCY.

Well, that's not ominous at all.

Professor Silva shoves a pile of folded towels off a stool and sets it down in front of Remi, then looks up and blinks at the rest of us, as if surprised to see us there.

"I'm sorry," he says. "I'm afraid I don't normally get this many visitors at once. I . . . oh, here we go!"

And with one grand sweep of his arm, two strands of maz fly from somewhere in the room, so fast I can't even identify them, then twine together in midair and burst into light with an audible *snap*. All the books on the half of the table nearest the door jump up in sync, slap together in neat rows, and hurl themselves at the nearest empty bookshelf, nearly taking Jaesin's head off in the process. I want to laugh at the wide-eyed look on Jaesin's face, but I can't make my face obey. That was incredible. I've never seen maz used like that, so effortless and effective, in my entire life. And I live with a spellweaving prodigy. I finally feel a bit of the awe that's always colored Remi's voice every time they talk about Professor Silva.

"There!" he says, obviously delighted with his solution. He gestures at the table.

"So we're supposed to . . . sit on the table?" Ania asks.

"Yes, yes," he says, flapping a hand at her, then he turns to his own stool and sits primly atop it, folding his hands on his crossed legs as we awkwardly clamber up. "Now, what can I do for you. You wish to study with me, yes?"

"Yes!" Remi says, then bites their lip, glancing back at the rest of us. "I mean, I'd like to, really, but we're actually here about something else. Something more important."

The professor's posture stiffens, and he lifts his chin, waiting.

Remi swallows, but pushes on. "We're here to ask about some of the research you supervised while you were at Kyrkarta University."

The words are barely out of their mouth before the professor is up off his stool, shooing them away.

"No, I'm sorry, absolutely not. I've signed an agreement, I'm legally tied, I'm sure you understand."

Remi leaps off the table, palms held out in front of them. "Wait, I know, but—"

"Then you know I can't help you." The professor throws open the door to his lab with a bang and ushers us out with a little tailwind of aeraz at our backs. When it's my turn to leave, though, I brace both hands in the doorway and hold on.

"We know that maz-15 caused the spellplague," I blurt.

The professor stops and holds himself against the hallway wall with one hand, leaning over as if to catch his breath.

"What did you say?" he wheezes.

Remi, sensing an opportunity, puts on their most solicitous student act and turns back to the professor. "MMC has it out for us too. Because we stumbled across maz-15. And now that I know it's what made me ill . . . I can't just not do anything about it, you know?"

Silva looks up sharply and locks his gaze on Remi as if seeing them for the first time. A lump catches hard in my throat, and I step forward.

"We're going to keep investigating this, one way or another. But I think you know things that could help us understand our situation . . . and the spellplague. Not just for Remi, but for everyone. What is maz-15? Why does it make people ill? Can it . . ."

I can't finish. The professor gets my meaning anyway, though. He turns and leans against the wall, suddenly looking every hour of his seventy years, rather than the spry leprechaun of a man we first met. Footsteps sound at the end of the hallway, and the concerned face of Professor

Silva's husband peers around the corner.

"You okay?" he asks, staring the rest of us down warily.

The professor waves a dismissive hand. "Fine, I'm fine, John. You heard?"

"I heard," John confirms. He pads forward on slippered feet and takes the professor's hand. "I'll get some dinner started for you all."

The professor snorts. "No you won't, you old goat."

John's grin is lopsided and charming. He must have been quite a heartbreaker in his youth. "It sounded good, though, didn't it?" he says.

The professor's eyes crinkle with warm mirth. "At least put a pot of water on to boil, will you?"

"That I can manage, my life," John says, giving the professor's hand a squeeze. He shuffles off down the hallway, and once the clanging of pots and pans sounds from the kitchen, the professor turns, blinking as if resurfacing from a daze, and leads us back into his study in silence. This time, instead of messing with stools and improvised table seating, he walks straight over to the IN CASE OF EMERGENCY door.

He leans over slowly, pressing a hand to his lower back with a wince, and pulls the door open with a groan, propping it against the wall. The passage below lights up, and at first glance I think it's string lights lining the staircase. As we step into the narrow stairwell, though, I get a closer look at the tiny glowing balls of sunnaz in the shape of lightning bugs, adhered to the wall at regular intervals.

"They're beautiful," Ania says, reaching out to touch one of the tiny fireflies. It twitches away from her finger, then takes flight, settling higher up on the wall. Ania lets out a delighted laugh, eyes shining in the dim light.

"But where do you get enough maz to run all this?" Jaesin asks, ever the practical one. "There's so little ambient maz out here, and to buy this much would be so expensive. In Kyrkarta most people can barely afford the maz to keep their houses standing."

"Because Kyrkarta is a cesspool," the professor says with disdain. "I'm the one who invented the scrubbing technology that separates out the maz-15 from the rest of the freely occurring maz. MMC may own that patent because it was created in their labs, but I'd love to see them try to stop me from setting up a private system in my own home. We have no competition for maz out here, and we're barely two miles from Jattapore's maz source, the caves down by the shore. We have all we need and more."

The staircase dumps us into a room with a single door and nothing else. The professor presses his palm to the door, and the metal under his hand glows a faint steely blue, followed by an echoing *click*. The door swings open, and the room beyond flares to brilliant life.

The ceiling looks as if it's been painted with pure sunnaz, the whole thing emitting a soft daylight glow throughout a room exactly the size of the one above our heads. Fourteen vast cylinders line the far wall, brimming with the fourteen common maz strains, more maz than Remi and Ania could go through in five years of daily use. Another smaller cylinder sits at the end of the row, glowing with eerie violet light. Maz-15. A deck screen the size of a bay window occupies another wall, displaying spell design sketches and calculations that are way over my head.

"Does this extend under the entire house?" I ask.

The professor nods. "Mimics the layout exactly. The kitchen is fully stocked with nonperishable food and enough water for a year. There's a bedroom, a bathroom, everything we have upstairs. Once that door shuts above us, it triggers a concealment spell on the other side. Even if someone who means us harm manages to cross the wasteland and get into our home, the chances of them finding us or my work are slim."

"Brilliant," Remi whispers, reaching out to touch one finger to the giant cylinder of magnaz. The sheer amount of power contained within those glass walls is honestly unsettling. To *me*, at least. Remi looks ready to lick the glowing golden magnaz chamber.

"How long did it take you to gather this much?" they ask.

The professor strides forward and lays a hand against the cylinder of firaz, sighing. "I started collecting shortly after MMC ran me out of town. I built this place as soon as I was able, and once both levels were finished, I kicked on the extractors." He raps a knuckle against a series of pipes that run into the ceiling next to the cylinders. "They've been full for the last two years. Feel free to replenish whatever you used to get out here."

He notably does not apologize for the berserker rabbits.

Ania paces over to the deck screen to study the formulas while Remi refills their stores, but Jaesin hangs back for once, at a loss and out of his depth. I feel much the same way, honestly. The whole place positively drips with maz, more maz than any of us has seen since we were children. For Ania and Remi, it's like something out of a fantasy. For Jaesin and me, it's a whole vast world of power and knowledge we'll never be part of. Our eyes meet, and for once, he doesn't glare at me. He just shrugs, and his gaze returns to Remi, watching their attention bounce from thing to thing, bright-eyed and amazed. After a moment, though, he clears his throat and steps forward.

"Hey," he says, voice gentle. "I know this is a lot, but we should probably do what we came here to do, right?"

Remi deflates a bit, but nods. "You're right. Professor?"

Professor Silva sighs and gestures to the table nearest the deck screen. We all take up spots around it, leaning on the cold black tabletop, watching the professor expectantly. He seems to wilt before us.

"Okay, yes. What do you need?"

Remi looks to Jaesin, who shifts uncomfortably and shrugs.

"We found out about maz-15. MMC wants us dead. We'd rather not give up our lives to be on the run forever—no offense—and now that we know what caused the spellplague, we're hoping there's a way to . . . I dunno, stop it?"

The professor's gaze alights on Remi, who, now that we're sitting down, looks near collapse from the exertion of the fight to get here. They let their bag fall to the table, then rummage through it for a moment, coming up with their nebulizer and mask.

"Do you mind?" they ask.

"Not at all," the professor says gently. "Let me know if you need more vitaz."

My chest squeezes tight with a suddenly desperate feeling as Remi fits the mask over their nose and mouth, settling in for their nightly treatment, a cocktail of medicines aerosolized with vitaz. We'll have to take it as easy as possible for the next day or so, let them build some strength back up, unless they want to catch the next cold or flu or whatever other infection happens to wander by. Last time, it meant a month in bed and at the doctor. What would it be this time? And would we be able to find a place to hide out long enough for them to recover?

The words spill out of me before I can control the ragged tone of my voice.

"How do we fix this? How do we keep them from coming after us?"

The professor gives me a pitying look. "My dear, the only way to stop them is to stop the spellplague at its source."

Ania slumps back against a work table and covers her eyes. When she speaks, her words come out watery and low. "We can't go back in time and stop the big quake. No maz in the world is strong enough for that."

At that, Professor Silva looks up sharply. "You have your cause and effect a bit backward there, child. Maybe you know less than you think about these matters."

"What?" Ania wipes her eyes and scrunches up her forehead in confusion. "That big earthquake ten years ago. It cracked something open underground, released the contaminant. We knew that as soon as it happened."

"No, no, no, no," the professor says, picking up a deck interface from the end of the table. "You have it all wrong."

He settles on a stool and brings up a document on the wall screen. It's on MMC letterhead.

MEMORANDUM
TO: MMC Executive Board
FROM: MMC Research and Development Division, Lab Nine
CC: R. Wolfram, MMC Chief Operating Officer; M. Hart, MMC
Chief Financial Officer
SUBJECT: Summary of Effects of Maz-15 and Recommendations

The research team in R&D Lab Nine, led by Professor Aric
Silva, has completed a full analysis of the newly identified
fifteenth strain of maz, proposed name kyraz. Complete
findings are contained in the attached report. Our primary
recommendations are as follows:

· Immediately cease drilling operations at all stations
  worldwide until new safety guidelines can be established
· Take corrective measures to seal the core breach at Kyrkarta
  junction station twenty-nine
· Divert additional R&D funding to the development of a cure for
  the spellplague

We request the opportunity to present our findings to you in
person at an emergency meeting of the executive board. We
look forward to your swift response.
Regards,
Aric Silva
Kamil Morad
Vi Huang

Darrin Washington
Tamar Kohl
MMC Research & Development Senior Staff

Page 1 of 50

Ania, the fastest reader of us, blows out a hard breath when she finishes.

"Those names . . . they're all the scientists who were suddenly laid off two years after the plague, who disappeared just like you. They were the ones listed in the back of that dissertation you found, right?" She glances to Remi for confirmation, and they nod.

"You discovered the truth, and they fired you for it," Remi says, muffled behind the mask. "Didn't they?"

The professor's mouth firms into a hard line. "Yes. They didn't just fire us, though. They tried to have us killed. They did it quietly, once we'd all been forced out of the city. They succeeded with the others. I'm the only one left. Because this is how the spellplague really happened."

Ania's hands fly to her mouth. Jaesin turns and walks away, pacing the length of the room with pent-up frustration. Remi just looks sad. Unsurprised. They've always hated MMC, so I guess it isn't much of a stretch for them to believe the worst. That the company would literally commit murder to cover up something that devastated not just our city, but the world. That killed our parents. They tried to have *us* killed too, after all. What else are they capable of? My whole body goes hot, then cold, shivering.

The professor scrolls through the document until he comes across a cutaway diagram of the planet, the same six-layered image we've all seen at school.

"Crust, outer mantle, inner mantle, outer core, inner core, and here." He traces a finger along the narrowest section, a thin, bright green layer between the outer and inner mantle. "The Maz Sea, where the planet converts heat and pressure energy into the fourteen previously known strains of maz. Twenty years ago or so, before you all were born, a little company called Maz Management Corporation began drilling deeper than anyone ever had, all the way down to the Maz Sea, to create greater flow and access to high levels of the freshest, most potent maz. Their idea was that if the drilling worked, we would be able to build new cities around drilled maz wells, rather than being restricted to constructing settlements around natural maz points like geysers, canyons, the caves here, and so on. It was a decent idea, though some of us were opposed. We were concerned that too many of these human-made wells might result in more maz being used than the planet could produce. It turns out that was the least of our problems."

My fingernails dig into my thigh as I force myself to breathe, breathe. I can already see where this is going.

"MMC managed to drill deeper and deeper, advancing

drilling technology in the process and making good money off of it. When they finally reached the Maz Sea, it was . . . amazing. We knew of its existence through subsurface imaging, but had never interacted with it. It was the most important discovery of the century. I felt honored to be alive for it."

I glance over at Remi, who has their eyes closed, breathing steadily as the vitaz mist swirls around inside their mask. They said almost the same thing about maz-15. It was a marvel, a fabulous opportunity, a gift to be able to study it. How bitter real life is in comparison— and the professor isn't even done.

"The maz they harvested was incredibly potent, half again as effective as the stuff that made its way to the surface naturally. After a few months of observation, when it appeared that the planet naturally reestablished an equilibrium by adapting its maz production, the MMC engineers got curious. They wanted to drill even deeper. See what else they could find."

"And they found maz-15," Remi says, quiet.

"They did," the professor says, with the air of a man leading a funeral service. "They pierced the inner mantle, and out poured this new, powerful form of maz with incredible properties the likes of which we'd never seen before. But it killed the drill operators who discovered it on contact. And there was no one to spread the word. No warning."

Parents there. Parents gone. No warning. None at all.

"Thousands, then millions of people died before we put together that it was this new strain of maz that was killing them, but by then the entire Maz Sea was contaminated. Kyrkarta got it the worst, obviously, being the site of the original rift. Huge amounts of maz-15 spilled out of station twenty-nine and the fissures in the bridges district. The currents of the Maz Sea carried the contamination far and wide, though, so that even Wisst City, on the opposite side of the planet, was affected, albeit to a lesser degree at first. Soon maz-15 made its way to the surface across the whole planet."

Ania shakes her head, face twisted in horror. "I can't believe they would just . . . let this happen."

Can't she, though? After everything else we've seen from MMC, after they tried to kill us to hide this secret, is it really so surprising they'd take things so far?

"Why is maz-15 so deadly? What is it that makes it so different from other maz?" Remi asks, their voice muffled by the treatment mask.

The professor sets down the deck interface with shaking hands, his eyes haunted. "This is maz that planetside life was never intended to touch. My colleagues and I believed that maz-15 is the fire at the heart of our planet, the source material for all other maz. What we do know for sure is this: the longer the rift stayed open, the more maz-15 poured out, the more the oceans started to warm, and the more frequent the disasters became. Hurricanes here, quakes in Kyrkarta, volcanic eruptions in Tolenne and Nuramoto. Correlation does not imply causation, as any good researcher will remind you, but the evidence is damning, no? These natural disasters spiked sharply in frequency after the spellplague, and have been getting worse year after year ever since, to the point where I fear the planet will rip itself apart. And MMC caused it all."

I yank at the hanging thread at the end of my sleeve harder and harder until it snaps, and with it, my anger. Nausea roils in my stomach, and my vision blurs, black and white sparks dancing at the edges. In my ears, my mother's voice: "Your father died at work, baby. But I'm okay. It'll be okay. I'm not going anywhere."

Before my eyes, her body slumps in the corner of the grimy bathroom she'd lost the energy to clean, her face mashed against the filthy tile floor with a trickle of bile at her lips, her skin so ashen, and her arm twisted under her in a way that couldn't be comfortable, but she was dying at the time, or dead, *dead already*, and who cares about comfort then? Who cares about a seven-year-old girl alone in a run-down subsidized apartment with a dead body, too frozen and beaten down to do anything but vomit into the toilet, add to the mess, but not cry, never cry, not until Davon came and made the call and made a promise and held everything together.

A gentle touch on my knee brings me back to the

present, and I realize I'm hyperventilating, noisy, ragged gasps, with sweat dotting my forehead and the table before me gripped hard between both hands. Ania pats my knee again, but otherwise stays back, grounding me but giving me space. I can feel the eyes of the others on me, but can't bear to look up, to endure their pitying gazes. Remi and Jaesin were both orphaned even earlier than me, but their parents just never came home. They didn't have to find them, lie next to them, dead flesh touching live flesh. My stomach lurches.

"I can't . . . I need—"

I stumble down off my stool and run.

TWENTY

I BURST THROUGH THE BATHROOM door and vomit, my mostly empty stomach contracting again and again in painful spasms. This bathroom is so different from that one, so many years ago. That bathroom had a big frosted window. This one is part of an underground bunker, lit with maz but closed off from the rest of the world. The tile here is a cool, clean, neutral marble of white and gray. Back then, it was green, or it was when it was clean. Blue towels here. Ragged, threadbare things with ugly patterns there. Bathtub here. Single shower stall there. Empty here. There . . .

I squeeze my eyes shut and take three deep breaths before pushing myself to my feet and stumbling over to the sink. There's mouthwash in the cabinet, thank the stars, and I rinse once, twice, three times, four, before I finally drink deeply from the tap and shut the water off. I avoid my own eyes in the mirror, already knowing what will greet me. Light brown skin gone ashen, just like hers.

Rich brown eyes, just like hers. Black hair. Hers. Limp, sallow, wrecked.

I'm okay. It'll be okay.

Liar.

She was never okay. She *lied* to me, and nothing was ever okay again.

With that thought, the world snaps back into focus, back into sense. I straighten, meet my own eyes in the mirror, shadows and all.

Three more breaths.

I unlock the door, close it behind me, and walk back to the study where the others wait. Remi stares straight at the deck screen, glazed over and unblinking, while Jaesin's and Ania's eyes snap to me as soon as I arrive.

"Sorry," I say curtly. "What did I miss?"

The professor frowns. "Are you—"

Ania catches his eye and gives a slight shake of her head. Good. Normally I'd chafe under her coddling, but now of all times, I really need to not be asked if I'm okay. I lean against the edge of the table, bracing on my forearms and letting the long side of my hair fall across my face.

Professor Silva clears his throat and turns back to his deck interface.

"Well then. I was just telling the others that I began researching a cure immediately after we sent that memo, but not long after, my entire lab was unceremoniously served with terminations and very firm reminders from the MMC lawyers of the nondisclosure agreements in our employment contracts. Then I lost my teaching position at the university. From what I've heard, that was due to pressure from MMC as well, and it happened to another colleague of mine too. And one by one, we were forced out of Kyrkarta altogether."

"I don't understand," Jaesin asks, pinching the bridge of his nose like he does whenever things get academic. "They did all that just to cover up the fact that they were responsible for the spellplague? And they were so desperate to do it that they wouldn't even let you work on a cure that would help absolve them?"

The professor shakes his head. "No, if that were the only factor, then MMC might have fessed up and used the cure research to earn public forgiveness, like you said. Why does a company like that ever do anything?"

"Money," Remi says, hollow.

Professor Silva nods. "Yes, always money."

"Besides," Remi says, "there may not *be* a cure. Just because we know the source of the plague doesn't mean we can automatically reverse the effects."

That punches a nice hole in something I didn't realize I'd been holding on to. "But there could be. It's a possibility."

"Maybe." Remi flicks off the nebulizer and removes the mask once the flow of vitaz and medication stops swirling around inside, looking straight at me as they do. "But also, maybe not. Don't get attached to the idea. Assume there's *not* a cure. I'd hate for anyone to wait around for something that might never happen."

I wrench my gaze away. Can we not do this here? I thought we were done with this fight.

"Sorry," I mutter.

The professor sighs, running a hand through his wispy white hair. "I feel guilty for this part. It took us too long to fully separate and identify maz-15 and to confirm that it caused spellsickness. It took us nearly a year, then another six months to have our findings independently verified by one of the other MMC labs, then another month to get all the data assembled and ready to submit to the board. And in that time, MMC had already done two crucial things."

He ticks them off on his fingers. "One: they stepped in and became the world's saviors. Even though many of their own employees were the first killed, they were the ones to organize community cleanups, assist local governments in creating orphan care programs, donate to public relief funds, bring in outside aid workers from less affected cities, all that."

I glance at Ania, who nods along. Her own parents were some of those outside aid workers. "Yeah," she agrees. "We were just kids then, but I still remember all the shiny happy vid ads."

Jaesin barks a laugh. "They used to have MMC

employees in uniform visit the orphanages for photo ops with all the poor, sad plague orphans. They loved Remi. Even back then, they were too good-looking for the cameras to resist."

Remi rolls their eyes. "Please. They may have loved to point a camera at me, but especially back then, no one wanted to come anywhere near me. Don't you know spell-sick kids have cooties?"

I wince. Even I had been like that, at first. And then, sometime later, I started keeping my distance again. For different reasons, though. Hormones. Feelings. Attachment is dangerous. Remi was always planning to leave eventually. No point in wanting what I couldn't have.

Yeah, clearly that went well.

The professor's lip curls. "Yes, they put on quite a public face of goodwill and charity. And don't get me wrong, they really did do quite a bit of good in those early days, and there were many people at MMC and beyond who truly did want to help. But the very highest leaders at MMC knew from day one that they had somehow caused the spellplague. It was too big of a coincidence to ignore. The plague just *happened* to begin at station twenty-nine, right as they pierced the inner mantle for the first time?"

My stomach lurches, and I nearly run for the bathroom again. For the first time, it occurs to me to wonder—was my dad part of the drilling crew that did this? Was he just collateral damage? Did he know what was going on? I don't remember what exactly he did for MMC, I was too young, but I know he wasn't a scientist or engineer or anything. Something that made him come home smelling of sweat and dirt and machine oil.

Until he didn't come home at all.

The professor talks on and drives the knife deeper, oblivious to my private crisis. "Everyone who witnessed it was killed instantly, obviously—"

Obviously.

"—so it was only too easy to spread the idea that the first big earthquake caused the plague, and make no mention of the *earthquake* being caused by their drilling."

Ania waved a hand to get our attention. "Okay, so you said two things. What was the second thing they did?"

The professor's expression darkens. "They've been actively making it worse ever since, making the breach wider and deeper every year, training the planet to make more maz-15 and totally ignoring the effects. It's disgusting. They didn't manage to kill us all when they released maz-15, but they just might finish the job with all these hurricanes and such. They used the tech we developed to separate maz-15 from the other strains to expand their reach. They built satellite stations all over the world, one in every city, and used that technology to collect more and more maz-15. And why do you think they bothered to do that?"

I finally find my voice again, clearing my throat to

speak past the acid-scraped rawness. "There's only ever one answer to that question."

The professor scowls. "Too right you are. Here's where the money comes in. They couldn't sell it directly without revealing their secret, but they *could* use it to power all of their buildings cheaply and develop new products, protected by their internal patents. All that legalese kept maz-15 tied up beyond reach. Even our lab teams were forbidden from doing anything with it or about it without MMC's permission. Immediately after the plague, all ten research and development labs were focused on the spell-plague problem. But slowly, after we isolated maz-15, the labs were diverted to work on developing new profitable uses for it. Over the next few years, the MMC executive board turned into a dragon perched atop a truly enormous mountain of treasure, and there was no way they were ever going to give that up."

So that's what we're really up against. All this time, I had thought Kyrkarta was just a struggling city trying to bounce back after a disaster, doing its best to adapt and salvage its reputation, held aloft by the goodwill of the few who could afford it. Apparently, though, it's a criminal empire built on ten years of lies and death, bound by one company, controlled by a handful of people exploiting its citizens for bottomless profits.

Maybe we should just burn it down.

The professor spreads his hands and shrugs, helpless.

"And that's where we are today. MMC has their money, their power, and their secrecy. At this point, even if someone does tell the truth, who would believe them? Their reputation is ironclad, and they've got law enforcement and governments all over the world eating out of their hands."

Jaesin shakes his head and runs a hand through his hair. "We really don't stand a chance, do we?"

"No. None," the professor says, sounding defeated for the first time.

Ouch. Don't pull your punches, old man.

A thump, then a loud crash sounds from above our heads. Professor Silva's head whips up, eyes wide.

"I'm fine!" John's muffled voice calls through the floorboards, followed by another clang. The professor sighs and shakes his head.

"Put some damn pasta in the pot and get out of the kitchen, you menace," he yells up.

A beat of silence.

"Where do we keep the pasta?"

The professor drops his face into his hands.

"Oh, for the love of—you're a bloody genius, John, I'm sure you can figure it out by process of elimination."

The whole thing is so hilarious, so sickeningly heartwarming, that it manages to crack through some of the heavy awful despair hanging thick around us. Remi finally meets my gaze for the first time since the train, their hand over their mouth to stifle a laugh, their eyes crinkled. I smile back, a helpless tug in my chest. I wish there was a cure for this, too.

Ania grins, but her smile fades when another crash sounds overhead, louder this time. The professor throws his arms up and stalks back toward the staircase.

"Damn it, John, just put everything down and I'll—"

Somewhere above us, a door bangs open, and John yelps.

Professor Silva's eyes go wide, and he bolts for the stairs, already summoning maz to his hands.

"John!"

TWENTY-ONE

THE FOUR OF US DASH up the stairs after Professor Silva, Remi and Ania already calling firaz to their hands. Jaesin's fists clench, prepping to strike. We burst into the upstairs laboratory and out into the hallway, and as we round the corner into the kitchen, the professor stops dead in his tracks.

Two people block the kitchen doorways, dressed in solid black unmarked uniforms and holding woven maz at the ready. A third holds John, with an arm wrapped around his throat.

Professor Silva's hands drop to his sides, shaking. MMC left him alone for eight years. Eight years . . . until we brought them here. Because of course it *has* to be MMC. Yet another disaster caused by us, one way or another.

"You four," the woman holding John says, looking past the professor to the rest of us. "Release your maz and kneel on the ground with your hands behind your head.

I'm sure I don't have to actually tell you what will happen if you don't."

She increases the pressure on John's throat, and he makes a harsh strangled sound, his eyes bulging. But through it all, he manages to shake his head, ever so slightly.

"Okay," I say. No choice. These men didn't ask for us to drop in and wreck their lives. They're happy. Healthy. Living out their days together. They don't deserve this. "We'll comply."

I shuffle forward where they can see me fully and turn to look at the professor as I pass. His gaze is hard, his mouth tense, determined. Just like John, he shakes his head. I don't get it. Why don't they . . .

Then I realize. Yes, these men are happily spending their days researching and napping. They're also the men who built an entire underground bunker beneath their house. Two of the most accomplished and brilliant scientists of their time. And their faces say they aren't letting this go without a fight.

I shrug, playing up the defeated look, then turn back to the others. "Just do it, everyone, okay?"

I wink, turn back to the commandos, and slowly lower to my knees with my hands behind my head. I'm useless as a combatant in this kind of situation, but there's one thing I can always do: piss people off.

"Okay, MMC Zombie McDoucheface, what's the deal?

You really gonna beat up on a couple of sweet old men just to get to us? Pretty damn low, my friend. Preeeeetty low."

The woman holding John curls her lip in a sneer, and the two guarding the doors shift on their feet, irritated. Good. I push on.

"We must be pretty special if you followed us all the way out here. I'm feeling kinda valuable right now, aren't you, Ania?" I say, glancing back at her. She nods, hands behind her back, the picture of an innocent princess. That draws the guards' eyes to her, while Jaesin slowly slips a knife off the kitchen counter and tucks it up his sleeve.

"And so," I continue in my most obnoxious voice, "if we're so valuable, then there are a few things we can assume. One, you can't kill us right now. You have to take us alive."

"False," growls the man guarding one of the doors. I quirk a little smile at him that I've been reliably informed is incredibly smug and irritating, and the man's expression darkens. I summon every ounce of nerve I can muster, despite the fear liquifying my knees. *False.* They're here to kill us.

"Ah well. Reason number two is still true, though. MMC apparently has something big to hide. Do you even know what that is, Gary?" I ask the next soldier, whose name is probably not Gary. "Did they tell you what you crossed a contaminated wasteland for? Do you even know what they've done? How they've poisoned the world? I bet you don't. You wouldn't be here otherwise. Unless you're a total jerk. Are you a total jerk, Gary?"

Behind me, Jaesin snorts. I grin, relieved I can still make him laugh even at a time like this.

"Yeah, I thought so. Okay, how many things has that been so far? That was one, two . . . three!"

And thank the stars for this amazing crew, which has been together long enough to know the drill, because on the count of three I drop to the ground, and Jaesin launches himself over me, knife in his hand, followed by two flaring spells, one silvery blue and one bloody red. The silver one hits John square in the chest and spreads like crawling sparks over his whole body—a shielding spell, so that when the goon holding on to him tries to make good on her threat, the knife slides harmlessly through the air a half inch from John's throat. The second spell hits her in the arm, burning through cloth and skin with a sizzle like bacon in a pan, followed by the scent of charred meat.

Jaesin is in full fearsome warrior form, finally in a situation where he can use his skills to the max. He feints a slash at a guard's face, then slams a boot into the man's kneecap instead, taking his legs out. It's Professor Silva, though, who finishes the takedown. Without John being used as leverage, the man snaps back into focus, his expression fierce. Maz from his laboratory leaps down the hallway, twining around him in bright, writhing tendrils.

His hands spin in complex patterns, weaving something intricate and multicolored, more and more maz flowing into his grip with every second.

He needs time for whatever he has planned. I'm not much of a fighter, but I don't need to be to give him that.

I rise up from my knees to my toes and dart forward to cut off not-Gary, who fires arrow after arrow of tight, sharp aeraz in Remi's direction. Hell no, you will *not*. Remi blocks them with shield after shield, but their face is starting to drain of color, a clammy sweat matting their dark hair to their forehead. The fight to get here was too much, and they're near collapse.

Not on my watch.

Mimicking Jaesin's move from earlier, I run at the guy and swing my leg in a low arc, going for the kneecap. And miss, horribly, getting our legs hopelessly tangled together in the process.

We both go tumbling to the floor, locked together at the knees, but apparently it's enough of a distraction. A sharp crackle, a whiff of ozone, and the man slumps on top of me. Out cold. I pull myself out from under him and glance up to see Remi's tired but victorious smile.

Then I catch sight of John, shaking and clutching his chest at the feet of the hostage taker as she fights off blow after blow from Ania. I shove the passed-out man the rest of the way off me and crawl to John, beckoning to him. He reaches a trembling hand out to me, and I manage to yank him out of the fray, our backs up against the lower cabinets, just as Professor Silva brings the fight to a dramatic end. He whips his maz into a frenzy, higher and higher until the air fills with a hum, a vibration, almost sizzling in the air between us—then lashes out with both hands. The maz shimmers with reds and golds and burnt orange, rushing forth in a great glowing stream of energy that slams into both remaining soldiers, knocking them instantly unconscious.

A beat of silence. Then Professor Silva quickly weaves another, less complicated spell, one for each of the assailants. He presses the shadowy, faint weaves into each of their foreheads, where the spell crumbles away like it was never there.

"That should keep them out for a few hours," he says, his face stern but his voice trembling. "Let's get them outside."

Together, we manage to haul all three of the MMC guards out through the front door and lay them out side by side, just inside the house's wards, though not without knocking over a shadow box of pinned butterflies and a ceramic elephant statue. That done, the professor's arms fall to his sides, and he meet John's eyes with a tight, tremulous frown.

John nods with a watery half smile, and the two crash together, holding each other so tight it honestly hurts my heart to look at them. They clutch each other with shaking hands, whispering with heads bent while the rest of us avert our eyes from their private moment. I can't even imagine how terrifying that must have been for them. I glance to my left and catch Remi looking at me, their face pale, expression raw. They make an aborted movement toward me, seeking comfort, maybe. My heart leaps into my throat, and I somehow try to move closer and pull away at the same time. The result is a total standstill, and before I can get it together, they turn away.

Finally, the professor and his husband break apart, but stay linked by the hands as we all head back inside. The professor looks around the front room, studying each photo as if seeing it for the first time, then turns to us.

"Thank you for what you did back there. It's a shame we've had so little time together, but I'm sure you'll want to be moving on after all that."

I look to Remi to let them make the call about traveling, and they nod.

"Yeah. We don't want to bring anything else down on you, and after what we've learned, I think we have some work to do. Right?" they say, looking around at the rest of us.

"Right. We have to do something about this," I say, as solid and confident as I can. "We'll never be able to live our lives otherwise. They'll always be after us. We could never go home."

"And they're still hurting the planet, too," Ania says.

"How many people are hurt, or killed, or have their lives ruined by these constant disasters? We need to get into MMC and stop their drilling operation. If they don't screw up and cause another spellplague, then it'll be the earthquakes that kill us all, or the hurricanes, or the volcanoes. This world will tear itself apart."

My eyebrows shoot up. "Wow. You aren't normally the one for going in with guns blazing. Not that I disagree at all—just surprised. In a good way."

She shrugs primly. "Well, there's finally more at stake than just our pocketbooks and the chance to have some fun with my ware. Remember who my parents are? When people need help, all-out guns blazing is what we do."

I laugh, and it sounds harsh and strange after all that's happened. After everything that's gone down among us all.

Ania continues. "Besides, there might be a cure for the spellplague out there. If there's even a chance, we should take it. Let the world know and see what happens. You know I'm in. Jaesin?"

Jaesin's brow furrows as he looks us over, concerned-dad face on, but he nods. "I'm in. We have to do something, right? Otherwise we just go into hiding forever."

"And that sounds *so* boring," Remi says, then smiles grimly. "I think you're gonna need someone who's already spellsick down there to do some dirty work right at the source of the plague. Plus, I love you, Ania, but I think this is gonna take some on-the-fly weaving under pressure."

Ania holds up her hands. "Hey, I know my limits. I'm the math, you're the poetry."

"Wow, that's kinda beautiful," I say, drawing faint grins from all the others.

Our eyes meet, the four of us, and for the first time in days—maybe weeks—it feels like we're on the same page.

The professor frowns, but nods. "Please be careful. Getting into one of MMC's most heavily guarded facilities won't be easy. The drill site is deep underground, and only the executive board has the codes to unlock the drill's controls. I'll bet anything it's heavily guarded. Just . . . take care of yourselves. You know now how vicious MMC can be."

My gaze drifts to the chat icon in the far corner of my vision. I bite my lip, an idea forming despite the wave of fierce protectiveness trying to kill it. I don't want to involve Davon in this any more than I already have. This isn't his mess. He's already risked his neck enough for me.

But this is fate-of-the-world-level stuff here. There's really no choice at all. Besides, he'd *want* to be asked. I owe him the chance to help.

I blow out a slow breath and resign myself to the inevitable.

"We have someone on the inside who can help us, actually," I say.

Jaesin's eyes narrow. "Are you sure? Will Davon really help us go against his employer?"

I pause, letting scenarios play out in my head. Will he? He loves his job, and he's dedicated to doing his best work for them. He recently got promoted, and it meant a lot to him.

But he went down into the tunnels with me. He wanted the truth almost as badly as I did. And he cares about me. He's the only family I have left. If it came down to me versus MMC, he'd choose me every time, hands down.

I nod decisively.

"Yes, absolutely. Once I tell him what they've been doing and what we want to do about it, he'll be on board. He always has my back when it matters. He'll be horrified once he learns what MMC has been doing."

"Okay. That gives us a starting place, at least." Jaesin zones into his lenses for a moment, then reports back. "There's a train back to Kyrkarta leaving in two hours. If we hurry, we should be able to catch it."

The professor calls a tangle of maz to hand and spins it quickly into four concealment spells, one for each of us. He passes them out, then summons more maz to refill Ania's ware and the emergency stash in Remi's necklace. He even disables his traps in the wasteland. How *generous*. Jerk. I'm still mad about the unicorn.

Once we've collected our things and are ready to go, the professor lays his hands on Remi's shoulders.

"I watched you cross the wasteland, you know. You're incredibly talented. I truly would be honored to work with you, if we all come through this alive." The professor zones into his lenses for a minute, then gestures to send something from his deck to Remi's. "Here's my info so you can contact me anytime. I do hope you will."

"But what about you two?" Remi asks. "They know where you live now. They know you helped us."

The professor looks to John and takes his hand.

"Oh, they've always known where we lived, I think. They just didn't care so long as we kept quiet. We weren't worth the bother. It's okay, though," he says, meeting John's gaze with a grin. "We've always had backup plans in case of something like this. We'll destroy this house and lay low for a while."

"Destroy it?" Ania says, stricken. "But it's your home! And it's so . . ."

I have no idea how she planned to finish that sentence, but this place could not be more different from her parents' catalog-worthy, polished style. It's more my kind of place: bits of tech strewn over every available surface, mismatched dishes, pillows on the couches that could have come from four different sets, digital frames with photos of friends on every wall. Cobbled together, lived in. Beautiful. John gives a sad smile.

"I know. But it's all just stuff. Home is right here," he says, tightening his arm around the professor's waist and pressing a kiss to his temple. "And we still have duplicates of all the best stuff from up here underground, copies of all the photos and such. It won't be permanent. We've always had a more long-term getaway plan, just in case. Call it a second retirement. It'll actually be quite nice, I think."

Professor Silva smiles, though it doesn't quite reach his eyes. "Yes. Our next adventure. Leaving my lab behind will be hard, but we'll be fine. Don't worry yourselves about it."

And with that, we head back outside for one last look at the house. The professor turns and summons maz between his hands, spinning together a spell with incredible speed and dexterity. It glows red in his hands, larger and larger, the weave gaining complexity until it's nearly the size of his head. Then, with a final nod from John for confirmation, he hurls the maz at their house.

The outer walls glow for a brief moment with that red light, so similar to the glow from the structural spells used in Kyrkarta—but with the opposite effect. The roof cracks, then collapses inward, followed by the left wall, then the right. We can see straight into the kitchen as the cabinets crumble, their contents (including several boxes of pasta) spilling to the ground. As an interior wall covered in family photos disintegrates, the professor turns to Ania, who bites her lip to fight back tears.

"It's necessary," he says. "This way, when the soldiers wake, it'll look to them and any investigators who follow like we have nothing to come back to. It'll look like we're gone for good. We'll go underground, let the wards up here decay, and pack our things. When we're ready . . . well, there's a lot of world out there. We'll be fine."

Ania dashes her tears away and nods. Jaesin throws an arm around her shoulders and hugs her to his side. I stare down at the ground as the remnants of their eight years in this house crumble like so much dust. The same thing almost happened to our apartment a dozen times, thanks to Kyrkarta's earthquakes. MMC's earthquakes. If our building had crumbled like this, with all of Remi's bright sneakers and Jaesin's don't-touch-my-spatula spatula and my cobbled-together tech equipment . . . I don't know what I would have done.

A notification pops up in the corner of my vision. A message from Davon.

> **Davon:** Hey, are you still in Jattapore?
> Some major stuff is going down at MMC here. Things are about to get so much worse.
> I hope you're looking out for yourself.

I bite my lip and look to the professor and John, then to Remi and the others. We're definitely looking out for each other.

> **You:** We're still here. We're coming home on the next train, though
> Can I call you once we're on the train?

So you can tell us what's going on

Davon: Yeah, fine. But hurry. You'll need to be prepared when you get back.

Well, that sounds delightful. I feel slightly better about involving him in all this, though. Apparently he's already involved himself.

You: Okay. Call you asap.

Davon: Love you, Dizzy.

When I tune back in to reality, Jaesin is watching me closely while Remi says their final goodbyes to the professor. I force a small smile.

"Ready to go?" I ask him.

He gives it a moment of serious consideration, then nods. "Yeah, I am. Let's go home."

TWENTY-TWO

THE TRAIN RIDE BACK TO Kyrkarta is even longer than the last one, but the time passes much faster in the fancy sleeper cabin Ania splurged on so Remi could get some rest. Though . . . that may be because I'm not exiled within the first ten minutes. Instead, I spend the entire time processing how deeply and utterly screwed we all are.

We need a plan. Step one: call Davon, find out what new stuff is going on at MMC, and maybe beg for help. An uncomfortable prickling sensation crawls under my skin at the thought, but I shove it away. Now's not the time to get precious about accepting help from people. Not when our lives are on the line.

As soon as the train pulls away from the station, I make the call.

With a few quick commands to my deck, the window pops up in my lenses and dials Davon's comm code (number one on my favorites list). The call connects after barely half a ring.

"Are you okay?" Davon says by way of greeting. My entire body relaxes a fraction at the sight of him.

"I'm fine," I say. "Do you mind if I share the call with the others?"

He shrugs. "Saves you having to repeat everything, I guess. Sure."

I add the others to the call with a heavy sense of impending doom, like I'm about to receive a death sentence. Hell, maybe I am.

"Can everyone hear me?" Davon asks, expression grim.

Four affirmatives.

"Just spit it out, the suspense is killing me," I say.

He nods. "Yeah. It's just . . . MMC is planning something big. They're evacuating all personnel from station twenty-nine, and they had the police block off the whole district due to 'structural issues' from the explosion. But I've done some digging, and I'm not finding any reports on these structural issues from our civil engineers and building inspectors. R&D, though . . ."

He pauses and runs a hand through his hair. "A few of the R&D labs have just been assigned extra staffing, and their predicted total maz inventory counts take a huge jump two days from now. But the individual unit counts for each strain don't add up right. There's a *huge* difference. So they're expecting a big influx of . . . something? Right as one of the primary catch stations gets closed down? I don't know, I keep running up against classified files even I can't decrypt."

I nod, the pieces slowly clicking together. "They're doing *something* at the junction station to get a lot more maz-15. I have no idea what, but if they're blocking off a whole neighborhood . . ."

Ania claps a hand over her mouth with a squeak. "They're going to widen the rift even more," she says.

"Of course," Remi says, matter-of-fact, the *most* unsurprised. It's a good thing they aren't insufferably smug by nature, because they've earned massive gloating rights. They were so right about MMC all along.

Jaesin chews on his thumbnail, eyes darting all over the compartment as he thinks. "The professor said they've been slowly drilling deeper and wider from the start, so the planet would release more maz-15. Do you think they're planning a big push? Something that might threaten the neighborhood?"

"Wait, back up," Davon says, shaking his head. "Maz *fifteen*? What's this about drilling?"

"You don't know?" Remi asks.

Davon's face is utterly blank. "I don't know . . . what?"

The others look at me, which I guess means it's my responsibility to fill Davon in on all we've learned. I keep my breathing slow and even and do my best to detach myself from the words, their meaning, their history, even as my stomach threatens to rebel once again. When I finish, even over the video, I can tell how pale Davon has gone.

"That has to be it, then," he says. "They're going to widen this rift thing they caused, capture all that new maz, and let the neighborhood collapse so they can be free to do even more in the future."

Jaesin snorts. "Awesome. Great timing, really."

"No, seriously though," Davon says. "It *is* great timing—for them. They're going to blame it all on you."

"Wait, what?" Remi says, surfacing somewhat from their exhausted daze. "How is it our fault?"

"Don't you see?" Davon says. "They're already laying the groundwork for it by saying the neighborhood is unstable because of the explosion at twenty-nine. The one they're saying *you* caused, even though they set you up."

"Fuck," Jaesin says, and I grunt in agreement. When MMC goes for you, they go *hard*.

It kind of is our fault, though, isn't it? If I had never taken that last job, we would never have caused that explosion. If we hadn't been thieves in the first place, the neighborhood would still be fine. It *is* our fault.

But if we hadn't gotten ourselves into this, MMC would still be flying under the radar. They'd just be making this worse a little more slowly, instead of capitalizing on this opportunity to blame someone else for their douchery.

They won't get away with it for much longer.

"Okay, nothing's really changed," Ania says, leaning

forward to prop her elbows on her knees. "Priority number one is still to stop this drilling operation and seal up that rift."

Remi settles back against the seat, exhausted. "But even that won't solve the problem of MMC coming after us. We have to try to get the word out somehow."

"Won't work," Jaesin says. "Media, mayor, police, remember? All MMC controlled."

"Then we blackmail them or something!" Remi says, desperate. "You've got dirt on everyone from your insomnia hacking, Diz, surely you can figure something out."

"I'm sorry, you *what*?" Davon interrupts, but I wave him off.

"Never mind, you didn't hear that. You're right, I might be able to put something together. I'll use the rest of this train ride to figure out what I've got and what else I might need."

I turn to stare out the train window for a long moment, the beautiful and untouchably deadly terrain rushing by outside. My mental catalog of blackmail material is extensive, from the former chief of police who said his daughter's dog ran away but really he sold it because he hated it, to some truly sick and disturbing stuff I wish I could unknow about the president of MMC's executive board. Unfortunately, the latter is the kind of thing I'll need here, and there's plenty more where that came from.

I shudder and look up at the others, a hollow pit in

my stomach. "There really isn't a clean, safe option here. I don't think blackmail alone will be enough. It's not a guarantee. And if we're gonna keep the entire industrial sector from collapsing, we have to get there before they start widening the rift. We can't let an entire district of our city be destroyed again, not when we can prevent it. Right?"

Jaesin nods. "Kyrkarta is our home."

"We have to do all of it," Remi agrees. "Take out the drill. Seal the rift. Blackmail the assholes. And hopefully get back out afterward, of course."

"Yeah, let's not neglect that bit," Ania says. "I like that bit."

"Same," I say, trying to hold back a grin. *"Kyrkarta is our home,"* Jaesin said. A part of me had been truly terrified that the others wouldn't care enough. That they'd write off the district as a loss, get me to try the blackmail and call it a day if it didn't work.

But we're all in, it seems. Finally united, and not just against me. But there's one last thread loose.

"Davon. I know this is a lot, and I completely understand if you can't be involved," I say, swallowing my pride and looking his image straight in the eye. "But we could really use your help with this. Will you? Can you help us?"

Davon drops his head into his hands with a heavy sigh, but when he looks up it's with a nod and a determined expression.

"Okay. I'll do what I can. I'll get you into the station. You can crash at my place while you get everything ready. Just let me know what you need."

I don't really do hugs, but right now, I totally would crawl through this video call to give him a hug if it were possible. To have him still be there for me even when things are this bad, when it means betraying the employer who's given him everything, brings me all kinds of warm family feels. It's just . . . *nice* to have someone like him in my life, the one person I can always count on to never abandon me.

"Thanks, Davon," I say, then clear my throat in embarrassment. Bit watery sounding there. "I really appreciate this."

"Anything for you, Dizzy." He gives me a half smile, then looks over his shoulder and back at the camera. "I'm gonna see if I can lose my roommates for tonight so there's space for you all. Call me when you get back into town, okay?"

"Will do," I say. "Bye, Dav."

Silence reigns for a long time in the wake of the call.

Even after everything else we've learned, it's a lot to take in. We've all grown up annoyed at MMC in a vague sort of way for controlling maz and charging for it, but it was always tempered by the good they'd done for our city. For us.

But they've killed scientists. They caused the plague.

They *profited* from it. And they've been actively making it worse. Now they're about to destroy an entire neighborhood—*again*—because their greed is out of control, and we seem to be the only ones who have the information and the stones to do something about it.

Ania opens her mouth to speak, then closes it again, and repeats the cycle three times before I finally snap, "Spit it out, Ania!"

She presses her lips together in a thin line, then nods. "Okay, I just . . . I'm not backing out. I'm still all in. I'm just worried. MMC is huge. We're just *us*. I know we have to try, I'm just afraid we'll fail, and then where will the world be?"

I study Ania, her concerned frown, the tightness around her eyes. She needs reassurance, but Jaesin is quiet, gaze fixed on Ania's hands where they wring together in her lap. Remi is quiet too, just watching and listening, still in energy conservation mode. I'm not exactly the sunny cheerleader of this group, but someone needs to say something before this doubt grows infectious and brings our resolve crumbling down. We have to do this. We have to rally. And I have to be the one to get us there.

"I get it. I'd be lying if I said I didn't feel the same, at least a little bit," I say, willing Ania to meet my eyes. "But look at it like this: it's the same thing we've been doing for years, but bigger. We crack some MMC security, do a little sneaking, Remi waves some maz around—all stuff we know. We've essentially been training for this for the past two years."

"But with intentional explosions this time," Remi adds, mustering the energy for a quirked eyebrow.

Jaesin laughs. "I mean, that's a bonus, for me. I've always wanted to blow something up on purpose."

He reaches out to run a single finger over Ania's wrist, slow and soothing, and she twists her hand to clasp his. I raise an eyebrow and bite the inside of my cheek to keep from smiling, but Ania does no such thing. She looks up at Jaesin, lit up from the inside by his touch.

"Well," she says with a watery laugh, "I'd hate to deprive you of a chance to achieve your dream. Let's blow up a drill."

We spend the next hour of the train ride in deep discussion, talking out our plans for breaking in, sealing the rift, dealing with the drill, and somehow not getting immediately caught and killed. Not gonna lie, it's all worryingly vague, but we have time to refine them. Maybe Davon will have some insight. I'll be able to ask him soon.

Remi kicks their feet off the window and lets them fall to the floor with a *clap*, then leans in. "Our best bet is to just go for it, right? We get on the ground, get some food, prep some spells, get your drone ready to go, Diz, and . . . we go. Tonight, if we can be ready by then. Sound good?"

I meet Ania's gaze briefly, then chew the inside of my lip. "We don't have to go so quickly if you need some time, Remi. He said we have two days—"

"Do we really, though?" they snap. "That's just a guess. It's two days until the labs get their new stores of maz-15. What if it takes them a while to collect it? We have no way to be sure."

They sit back and draw some vitaz from their stores, then start in on a complicated weave I've seen them pull off dozens of times. A little boost, a stopgap for when they're feeling poorly between treatments. Can't be used too often, but if ever there were a time . . .

They take a deep breath and continue.

"I appreciate your concern, and I know this isn't great. We still have a good twentyish hours until go time, though. I'll sleep all the way back to Kyrkarta, eat well, and sleep more at Davon's apartment. It's totally possible the sheer stress of all this will screw my immune system anyway, and I'll get pneumonia or something for a month again. I can't just *will* my body to behave. It's a risk I'm willing to take, though. And when this is all over, I promise, I'll take it easy. This is my choice and I'm making it."

My fingers itch to reach for Remi, to run through their hair, feel the pulse in their neck, brush over their bottom lip . . . but no. I don't get to want that. Can't. I've closed that door for good.

"Okay," I say, voice flat. "We go tonight."

I turn away and slump in my seat, staring out the window.

Sure enough, Remi sleeps for the rest of the ride home, but I must drift in and out too, because the blurred early morning dimness outside is already beginning to break up into patches of shadowy trees and far-distant buildings gleaming in the faint just-rising sun. The approach to Kyrkarta seems to take forever, in the same way I imagine walking to your own execution must. We gather our things in silence and stand at the door, ready to disembark as soon as the train stops. Minutes to go until we set foot back in our home city.

Hours to go until we break into one of the most highly secured facilities in Kyrkarta.

Less than a day until we change the world, or die at the bottom of a very deep hole in the ground, never to be seen again.

I always thought I'd die in a suitably dramatic way.

TWENTY-THREE

THE TRAIN DOORS SLIDE OPEN, and our plan falls apart almost immediately.

Jaesin hops down onto the platform first, bag slung over his shoulder, and is seized by his right arm before he can take a single step.

"Jaesin Kim, you're under arrest for the theft of MMC property and the deaths of—"

They should have grabbed his other arm. Jaesin's a lefty.

He hauls off and slugs the officer in the jaw with an audible *crack*, then shoves him back into the two officers right behind him. Over Jaesin's shoulder, I see four more officers coming our way, fighting through the crowd to get to the train. Really? Is our luck *this* bad?

"Diz?" Jaesin shouts as he throws some lady's luggage at the pile of officers on the ground.

I slap him on the shoulder as I hop off the train, gesturing for him to follow. And I trust he will. This is my deal. We may both be mundies, but we have our uses.

He's our strength and people skills. It's my job to know things. People. Locations. Current events. He may have been ready to run off to Jattapore, but Kyrkarta is *my* city, and I know it inside and out. This is exactly my kind of moment.

I sprint toward a staff-only door that I know holds a staircase to the roof, ducking low to cut between waiting passengers. Most people happily get out of my way, not wanting to get involved, but there's always one person who just has to be a hero.

A large girl about my age in a flowing skirt drops her bag and darts into my path, looking like she means business. She's wearing an Aeraz Warrior 3 shirt (only available as a pre-order bonus through GameGo) and has badass blue streaks in her hair. I wince internally. She and I would probably get along famously under other circumstances, but right now she's in my way, and I am not about to be arrested. Not with so much at stake.

I square off with her and prepare to attempt something ridiculous, but a bright bolt flies over my shoulder and hits the girl square in the face before I can lunge. She drops, out cold, and I leap over her crumpling form with a guilty grimace. If I ever bump into her at the club, I'll have to apologize. I raise a hand in thanks to Remi or Ania, whoever managed that quick stunner, and push onward. The door to the stairwell has never been locked during my nighttime wanderings, but that could have changed.

It's possible. I put on a last burst of speed and yank on the door handle, fully expecting it to be locked—

—and it flies open so easily, I stumble backward and almost bust my ass.

I risk a quick glance back. Ania catches up first and ducks inside, with Remi next and Jaesin watching their back right behind. All present and accounted for. I yank the door shut before the cops can clear enough of a path to start slinging maz, and push past Ania. This whole dashing-up-the-stairs thing is way too reminiscent of the day of the earthquake and my frantic rush to make sure Jaesin and Remi were okay. (Still mad about that.)

The station is thankfully only three stories high, compared to the nine floors I had to run in our apartment building, but by the time I hit the third landing, shouts of "Halt!" and calls for backup echo up after us, along with pounding boots on the stairs.

We burst out onto the rooftop, the door banging open with a sound the whole neighborhood must hear. The sound of cocking guns follows us out, and my blood goes cold. Apparently we're done messing with maz and have moved on to guns. Fabulous.

"Now what?" Jaesin asks. He slams the door shut and slumps against it while Ania draws a quick spell to bind it shut.

Remi and I look around helplessly, studying the roof. Pipes, billboards, neon, lots of long, flat nothingness.

Last time I was here, maybe three months back, there was a walkway between the roof and the strip mall next door, used mostly by the employees at the station to go grab lunch.

The walkway is in pieces on the street far below, along with half the mall. The earthquakes. Thanks, MMC.

We're so screwed.

"Do you trust me?" Remi asks in a firm voice.

I turn to them with a questioning glance. "Of course we trust you. But what—"

They point to the opposite side of the roof, to the building on the station's other side. "Then I need all of you to give me ten seconds, run for the edge of the roof, and jump for that red building next door."

"What?" Ania says, the blood draining from her face. I don't blame her. I jump between the roofs of this city all the time, and even I would never attempt that distance.

"Don't argue!" Remi says, pulling strands of maz between their fingers and weaving furiously. "You said you trusted me!"

As soon as the spell is finished, they slice it into fourths with several quick slashes, and throw one at each of us. The fist-sized deep purple spell crashes into my chest like a tiny burning explosion, followed swiftly by a shove from Remi.

"Go, I said!" Remi shouts, and the four of us turn as one to make a mad dash for the edge. Oh stars, I would *never* attempt a jump like this, it's way too far, the angle all wrong, and it could so easily go badly, impressively badly, but then the lip of the roof is there and I coil my muscles for a leap just as gunfire explodes behind us and I jump . . .

. . . and spring so far I let out the most high-pitched sound I've ever shrieked in my life. I don't jump over the gap so much as bounce over it, flying through the air like one of Remi's woven birds, and I land well past the edge of the next roof. I overbalance and catch myself on the heels of my scabbed hands, then scrabble out of the way to watch the others make their own landings. Jaesin, jock that he is, lands like a superhero, and I half expect rocks to float skyward around him as the ground cracks at his feet or something. Ania, on the other hand, tumbles into a scraped-up heap, her curls flopping over her face. Remi comes last, and I catch them as they nearly land on top of me.

"You're a genius!" I shout, still clutching their forearms.

"About to be a dead genius. They still have guns!" Remi grabs my hand and drags me down as bullets whiz over our heads, splitting the early morning silence with their loud cracks. We run hunched over, making ourselves smaller targets, until we can put on some speed and leap to the next building over, and the next. Shouting drifts from the streets below us at first, but that's fine, because the gunshots have long faded into the distance.

The sound of the speeder jets closing in provides a whole new problem.

"Any new ideas?" I shout to the group as the tiny dots in the distance roar closer.

"We need to get off these rooftops!" Ania shouts back, her long legs eating up the distance much better than my short stubby ones.

Jaesin points at the next building ahead of us. "Aim for the fire escape instead of the roof! We can run down and try to lose them in the alleys."

"And I guess we just hope they've called off the ground search," I mutter, but do as he says. I spring off the rooftop and grab for the railing of the fire escape, and my stomach lurches as the whole thing shudders and leans. Jaesin and Ania are already running down by the time I manage to haul myself up, just in time to see Remi run for the edge and leap . . . but it's going to be too short, they didn't push hard enough, or the maz is starting to wear off, and they flail in the air in what feels like slow motion, nowhere near the fire escape, nowhere near enough for me to reach out and grab them. Their eyes go wide, and we lock gazes.

"No!" I shout, arms outstretched as they begin to fall, fall, fall. . . .

Far below, a bright golden glow flares out, and I race down the rickety fire-escape stairs, barely landing my footing before flinging myself over the railing of the next set. My breath burns in my lungs, strangling my heart. They have to be okay, I will never forgive myself if Remi . . . if they . . .

On the street below, Remi lies sprawled out, arms and legs akimbo and head lolled to one side.

And laughing?

As I near the ground level, I see the faint glow of light between them and the ground, a cloud of maz cushioning them. I collapse with a hard exhale, the cold concrete biting into my knees as the neon lights of the city burn themselves permanently into my retinas.

They're fine.

Everything is fine.

I reach out, feeling for their hand on the ground beside me and letting my fingers dig into the pulse point at their wrist.

"I'm fine, Dizzy, I'm *fine*," they insist, but their breathing is shaky, and their fingers feel for and catch mine, squeezing tight.

"We're not out of this yet, you two," Ania says, tugging at Jaesin's hand. "They'll know we went to street level. They'll mobilize the ground crew again, have this place flooded with officers in two minutes. We need a new plan."

Why does it feel like we're doing nothing but running, running, running these days? We've had our fair share of jobs over the years that ended with us fleeing the tunnels, but . . .

I have an idea.

"They know we're at street level," I say, pushing to my feet and gingerly pulling Remi up with me. "But I bet they won't expect us to go underground."

"No, they'd never expect us to go back to where we committed all of the crimes they're after us for," Ania says sarcastically, but Remi shakes their head.

"No, I think she's right," they say, squeezing my hand. "They're not expecting it. I'll send a few diversionary spells down a side street, make them think we're still on ground level. Diz can disable the security in the tunnels and I can keep a feel out for any maz trouble."

"Sounds like that's our plan, then," Jaesin says, pushing gently at Ania's shoulder until she starts running again. "I'm not hearing any other ideas, and this one makes sense. Probably."

Ania sighs as I bring up a map on my lenses, splitting my attention as best I can between guiding us and not breaking my ankle while I run. "Okay, there's an access six blocks from here. Follow me."

As we jog, Remi begins to spin something into being, whispering to themself as they do. First formaz, to provide shape and structure, then motaz, adding motion, then another, and another. At some point they glance up at Ania, who promptly raises a hand and threads more magnaz into the spell when Remi's stash starts to run thin. Finally, the last strand pulls taut, and the spell takes the form of a little golden bird that wriggles and struggles in Remi's grasp. At the next intersection, Remi hurls it down a perpendicular street, then quickly spins a lasso of darker obscuraz around our heads. Shouts and a crash erupt from the direction of the maz bird, so I pick up speed and lead us in the opposite direction, taking a roundabout route to the access point.

We stick to the shadows and back alleys as much as possible, casually strolling across intersections when we can't, Remi weaving as many birds as they can. The roar of the speeders and shouts of the police fade far into the distance, as they presumably track Remi's birds instead of us. Just as we reach the access point, Remi winces.

"They've caught all the birds," they say. "We're out of time."

"That's fine, we're almost home free," I reply as I run my usual intrusion routine on the tunnel access door.

And I'm promptly iced out.

"Shit," I say. "Shit, *shit*!" It's all the eloquence I can muster. I forgot I told Davon about all the holes in their system, thinking we'd never be doing this ever again. He's probably already implemented some initial security patches. This is going to be much harder than last time.

"They changed their security protocols," I say, digging

into one cargo pocket for my cables. "I gotta hardwire in. Sorry, everyone."

"Not your fault," Remi says. "You got this."

It *is* my fault, but I appreciate the sentiment anyway. I take a breath and let their words settle in my chest, try to believe them. I've done this a hundred times. The cops are nowhere near us right now. We'll be fine. Remi will be fine. And after all this, after everything, they still believe in me.

I have this.

I pull my multitool from my pocket and pry the panel off the security system with the flat-head screwdriver attachment, exposing the wiring. There's a specific data cable I need, usually—yes, solid black with a white line up the center. I snip it in half and strip one end to expose the tiny wires within, then twine them together with the bare end of my own cable. I don't have my soldering iron with me to really secure the contact, but I pull a small roll of black electrical tape from another pocket and tear a strip off with my teeth, wrapping it securely around the join. The other end plugs straight into my deck, and my diagnostic program automatically detects the new input and brings up a command prompt.

I start basic—no need to waste time getting fancy if simple will work—but I'm stonewalled at every turn. Damn, I can't believe I told Davon, one of MMC's *IT managers*, everything about my exploits out of sheer guilt. He's a good guy, so of *course* he immediately put that knowledge to work. I should have saved it for when I took the job with them, made them bow before my awesomeness. Not that *that's* happening anymore, either. Instead, I have to sit here and play get-to-know-you with their new protocols. I growl in frustration and slam my deck down in my lap, looking up at Jaesin through the code in my lenses.

"I'm gonna have to brute force my way in, otherwise we'll be here for half an hour. It's gonna trip all kinds of alarms, probably, but I should be able to set up some decoys at other spots down the pipeline. We'll have to haul ass once we're down there."

"What else is new?" Ania says. "At least we can replenish our maz again while we're down there. I'm totally bled dry."

I huff a laugh. "A good night for another last job ever, I guess."

The others crack exhausted smiles at that, and with the thrill of that tiny victory, I get to work. A few minutes later, the latch clickes open, and my lenses flood with warning notifications in response.

We're in.

Jaesin holds the door open as I detach my cable and replace the access panel. It's not perfect, but it'll withstand a cursory glance, at least. Not that it matters much, with every MMC security system in the city screaming about this break-in, but every little thing counts.

Once we're all inside, Jaesin lets the door close and I slump back against it, my head throbbing from the stress of intense focus.

"Well," I say. "That could have gone better. I need a nap. How about you all?"

"Definitely wishing we could have nap time," Remi says, "but maybe not in a sewer. We can sleep once we get to Davon's."

I nod and point down one tunnel. "That way to Davon's block. I scheduled some alarms to go off in the other directions. We can stop at the first tap point we pass to fill up, and I'll call Davon, tell him we're on our way."

Remi nods and turned to follow the tunnel I'd indicated, lifting their fingers to trail along the pipes overhead and feeling the flow of the maz within. Ania and Jaesin follow, and once they're a few paces ahead of me, I continue after them, commanding my deck to voice-call Davon. I hate to do it, truly hate to involve him in this mess to such a degree, but what other option do we have? This is bigger than me and what I want to do. Bigger than Davon and the danger I'm putting him in. Bigger than my issues, bigger than deciding to take a job I don't truly want or pathetically following my friends to a city I know nothing about. Not like Kyrkarta, whose streets are like the lines of my fingerprints.

The call tone sounds four times before Davon finally answers.

"Hey," he says, his voice thick with sleep. "Are you okay? Are you downstairs?"

"Sort of?" I say. An alarmed noise and sudden rustling comes from the other end of the line, and I hurry to backtrack. "No, I mean, yes, I'm not hurt or anything. I'm okay. Sorry."

Silence. A sigh that changes pitch as a hand passes over his mouth. "Don't scare me like that. Where are you?"

I skip over a pile of fallen rocks and splash into a puddle of unspeakable grossness. "Ugh. No, that wasn't at you. We're on our way there, but we're underground right now. Had a bit of a run-in with the cops at the train station, so we're coming at you via sewers. Apologies ahead of time for getting you up early, and for the soon-to-be state of your carpet. Did you double-check that your keycard will get us into station twenty-nine?"

Davon hums an affirmative. "Yeah, I was scheduled to go replace some servers there in a few weeks anyway. My promotion came with a new level of access. I have the power!" he says, and I can practically hear him shaking a triumphant fist over the call. He clears his throat. "Sorry. Probably not the time."

A million questions and apologies bubble up as a pressure in my chest, an itch on the tip of my tongue. Is he *really* okay with this? Is he starting to hate me? Is he disappointed? Is this going to ruin his career, his life?

"Yeah. Probably *not* the time. See you soon?" is all that comes out.

"Till then."

He ends the call, and I stand there for a tense, silent moment before trotting forward to catch up with the others.

"This tap point work for you?" Remi asks, gesturing one gloved hand at the pipe they've paused beside.

My heartbeat picks up as I look to the familiar panels and valves.

This time is different. No one's expecting us here and now. We're nowhere near station twenty-nine, near either of the spots we've found maz-15 before. There won't be any sabotage. No reason this should be anything less than routine. But even as Remi begins to wind down the flow, finishing the last top-off, I can't shake the growing dread.

The feeling that something is about to blow up in our faces. Again.

TWENTY-FOUR

POOR DAVON. I SWEAR, WE planned to take turns in his tiny shower once we all arrived, washing the stink of fear and sewers from our bodies and clothes.

Instead, while Ania's in the shower, the rest of us crash in a pile of stank on Davon's living-room floor, just like we used to do in the group home. Impromptu nap time. Good thing his roommates made themselves scarce for the day, because Davon would have been kicked out in a heartbeat. Who invites sewage into their home? Someone with terrible taste in friends and family, that's who.

I wake warm and content, feeling better rested than I have in a long time. My neck isn't thrilled about sleeping on the floor with only a throw pillow, though, and I tip my head to try to crack it—

—and gently butt heads with Remi, whose nose is pressed into my collarbone, faint puffs of breath making my skin warm and humid.

I freeze.

Am I still asleep? Or has my sleeping body decided to

be totally mortifying and *as obvious as possible*? It figures I'd have to be literally unconscious to finally be honest about what I want.

Because I do. I *want* this.

I squeeze my eyes shut harder and force my breath to stay even and slow, practically vibrating with the effort to keep my legs perfectly still where they're intertwined with Remi's. Their stomach rises and falls with each breath, gently pressing into my hip bone in gentle rhythm, and I silently beg them to stay asleep. Let me keep this for a few more minutes. My lungs seize, and my breath catches, suddenly burning along with my eyes. Just a few more minutes, please, let me have this, please, let me—

But Remi's breathing changes, one long breath in accompanying a shuffle of legs, a nuzzle against my neck. Awake. I hold my breath, waiting for them to pull away, to avert their eyes and push to their feet. To walk away, the way I've always done.

They hesitate for a long moment, then lean their weight more heavily into me.

Still asleep after all?

I tip my head down, just a bit, just enough to nuzzle into their hair, my lips brushing soft strands.

They shift again with a hum, and tip their face up farther. Their nose traces up from my collarbone, along my neck, the bottom of my chin, until their breath mingles with mine in the scant inch between us. Between our lips. They nestle closer, hips, legs, stomach, arms pressing deeper into the embrace. The closest we've ever been.

Is this really happening?

"Good morning," they whisper, the words a light brush against my lips.

"Morning," I reply, hoarse, my heart racing against my ribs in a desperate half panic. I want to run. I want to pull them closer. I want to roll over and press them into the floor, seal our lips together and give in to absolutely every *almost* I've ruined between us.

I want to take it all back and start over. Me and Remi. The way we could have been all along, if I hadn't screwed everything up so thoroughly and consistently. The way we *should* be.

My breath comes fast, then faster, panic and desire making my hands shake and my mind race. DO IT, my body shouts at me, just lean in, so close. I lick my lips, and that bare flick of my tongue grazes their bottom lip, pulling a gasp from us both—

—and I jerk back like I've been burned, my eyes squeezed shut, breathing like I've just run a marathon. My brain shouts at me in alternating pitch: WHAT ARE YOU DOING? and RUN, RUN, RUN, and I feel Remi shift backward as they make to get up, but my hand darts out almost without my permission. I twine my fingers with theirs and squeeze, hard, then force my wet eyes open. When our eyes meet, I force myself to hold their gaze, though the eye contact is torture, like a continuous shot of adrenaline. I'm laid utterly bare.

But I try. Something about this past week, nearly losing them several times, seeing the professor and his husband together, feeling Remi's sleep-warm body against mine—suddenly I want more than anything not to screw this up again.

For once, I'm actually *trying*.

Remi's expression softens into a smile, and they squeeze my hand back with gentle, understanding pressure. This is the best I can do. But maybe not forever.

Maybe I can do better one day.

When I get out of the shower, Davon is waiting in the kitchen with coffee, a pile of egg biscuits wrapped in crinkly paper, and a mountain of fried potatoes. My cousin is an actual hero. The others have already dug in and are quietly scarfing theirs in the living room.

"Roof?" Davon asks, gesturing with his head toward the fire escape out the window.

"Roof," I agree. I pull my hoodie from the dryer and yank it over my head—still warm, so good—and snag two biscuits and a cup of coffee before following him out the window. The bracing chill and strong coffee drive the last bit of grogginess from my head, and I study Davon over the brim of my mug.

"What are you looking at?" Davon asks. "Did some of your sewer nastiness get on my face?"

I roll my eyes and and finally lose the battle with the questions I've been holding in, all my guilt spilling over into one desperate question.

"Are you sure you're okay with all this? For real?"

He sets his coffee down and looks out over the surrounding rooftops for a moment. "I mean, define okay? This whole thing is awful, obviously, but if you mean am I okay helping you, then yes, of course. Have I ever *not* helped you when you needed it?"

I think back through all the years we've known each other, through all the times I've screwed up, gotten hurt, gotten in trouble, and more. It's true. He hasn't always helped in the way I *wanted* him to, but he's never left me hanging. He's always been there.

"You're right," I say. "Thank you. Really."

"You're welcome. Really," he echoes, then grins. "Now tell me what I can actually *do* to help. You've been having all the fun without me for the past two years. I wanna get my hands dirty."

I shove biscuit in my face so I can avoid the question for a moment. I hate that he even knows what maz-15 is, because even that small bit of information puts him in danger. He really won't like the blackmail portion of our plan, though. It's the one part that involves threatening to do harm to actual people. I trust him completely, love him dearly, but I want him to have deniability if the shit hits the fan. He's not part of this, not *really*. No need for him to go down with us if it comes to it.

"All we really need is for you to get us into station twenty-nine and lead us to the drilling location. Any information you have about the facility and the drill and all that would be helpful too. We've got the rest."

"Come on, Diz, really? That's *it*?" he practically whines. I fight back a small smile.

"That's it. Once we're in, I want you to get out of there and keep an eye on things remotely. If anyone catches on to what we're doing or starts to mobilize against us, we need to know. You'll be our guardian on the outside. Okay?"

He sighs. "Fine. If you change your mind, though . . ."

I nod, though there's no way in hell I will. "I'll let you know."

He leans over to bump my shoulder with his, then I do the same, again and again until we're practically having a shoving match way too close to the edge of the rooftop, biscuit crumbs and coffee-breath laughs flying everywhere.

"Oi, can you not kill her, please?" Jaesin says, poking his head up from the fire escape stairs. "We kind of need her."

Our laughs subside, and Davon offers me a buttery hand.

"So do I," he says with a solemn expression, pulling me to my feet.

And that's my feelings limit for the afternoon. Time to get to work.

We move through the rest of the afternoon with slow, deliberate purpose. Showers finally happen for everyone. Davon invents an IT-related reason for his badge to scan in later tonight, inserting a false tech-support ticket into the system. Remi works on a supply of combat spells for us to use during the break-in. Jaesin works his contacts to source some weapons I hope we'll never need to use. It takes every credit left in our stealthed account, the only thing I feel confident withdrawing from with the police after us, but he manages to get us two maz-fueled stunners. At least they aren't lethal.

My role is the most difficult, the most time-consuming, and the most likely to blow up in our faces. My tiny drone friend is getting a makeover.

"Are you sure this is gonna work?" Ania asks. She sits with her legs splayed out, socked feet occasionally kicking mine specifically to annoy me. A complicated weave of maz lies on the ground between her knees, and she threads new strands into it one at a time, ever so careful, with an occasional consult from Remi. Remi wanted to be the one to work on the spell, it being a "fun" modification of an existing design from a grad-level medical textbook, but Ania is utter garbage at any spell with a bit of an explosive side, so Remi's stuck with those.

"As sure as I ever am about anything," I say. "Which is, you know. Moderately?"

She doesn't deign to respond to that, which is probably

for the best, because I'm at the most delicate part of the operation. It takes every ounce of my control to keep my hands from shaking as I hold a clear glass bubble the size of an egg flush against the bottom of my little drone. The bug needed some significant modifications to be able to carry the bubble in the first place, considering it's twice its size and almost as heavy.

Attaching the thing is a whole other challenge though. The screws are the smallest on the market, barely enough to hold the weight, but there's no room for larger. Every spare millimeter inside the casing is taken up by chips, sensors, and power cells. A quick swipe of adhesive holds the bubble in place long enough for me to get the screws in. I turn the final screw once, twice more . . . then slowly draw my hands away, waiting for the whole thing to explode or spontaneously fall apart.

It doesn't. It sits there, lying on its back like a dead bug with its big round belly exposed, waiting for the final step. The maz.

I sit back with a sigh of relief and prop my elbow on my knee and my head on my hand, running my fingers through the long side of my hair. My gaze lands on Remi, lying upside down on Davon's couch with their head hanging beside Jaesin. Their hands twine threads of maz together almost lazily, not even looking at what they're doing as Jaesin cleans one of the guns and points out its features.

Then Remi looks up, their gaze locking on mine, and my breath stills. Their mouth tugs up at the corner, a faint upside-down smile that pushes a hot flush into my cheeks. I snap my gaze back to the floor, to the drone in front of me, the remembered warmth of this morning like a crackle of static along every inch of my skin.

"What happened while I was asleep this morning?" Ania asks, looking back and forth between Remi and me.

I shake my head, biting my lip to keep the words from spilling out of control. Nothing, really. But also, a lot. It felt like *a lot.*

"Nothing" is what I finally settle on, because it's the truth. Nothing actually happened, externally. Internally, this morning felt like cresting the peak of a mountain, and I can finally see the gorgeous terrain sweeping before me, glorious valleys of rich greens and blue sky and the infinite possibility of horizon.

So many possibilities. If we live through tonight.

"Doesn't look like nothing," Ania says, studying my expression closely. I draw back, practically hissing like a nocturnal animal caught in the sunlight, scrambling for shadow.

"I'm trying, okay?"

That's the best I can offer right now.

All the same, when Remi rolls forward off the couch and heads our way, I duck my head and test each of the tiny screws again, desperate for something to occupy my attention.

"How's the spell coming?" Remi asks, plopping down cross-legged next to Ania.

Ania weaves one final thread into a bare patch in the middle, then severs the flow. "It's ready for your part. You sure you've got this?"

They give Ania a look, one eyebrow raised. Ania holds up her hands.

"I know, I know, I just . . . had to check. It's all yours."

Remi slides their hand under the spell, draping it carefully over their opposite arm like a delicate scrap of silk. It's far too large to fit inside the drone's belly at the moment, but once Remi's done with it, the weave will be compact, layered, and dense with pent-up energy. The spell needs to be powerful enough to affect an entire roomful of people, yet fit in the carrying system I devised—no easy feat. It's a challenge only Remi can manage. For multiple reasons.

I lift my creation slowly, carefully, and deposit it into Remi's cupped palm, our hands touching skin to skin for longer than strictly necessary. They lift their eyes to mine and quirk a little smile.

"Thanks. Looks perfect."

"Hope so," I manage, mouth dry.

Their smile widens, then they step back, heading to the roof to finish off the most dangerous part of the weave.

My gaze follows them the whole time, helplessly glued to their retreating form. I couldn't look away if I tried.

"Definitely not nothing," Ania murmurs.

I close my eyes and sigh.

"Let's try to live through tonight, and then we can decide if it's something or not, okay?"

"Fair enough," Ania says. She reaches out, draws me to her, and wraps me in a hug. I stiffen, a wave of trapped panic shooting straight up my spine, making me want to curl into myself, protect my soft underbelly.

It doesn't have to be this way, Remi said.

I take a long breath. Two. Force my muscles to relax. Soften my shoulders. Let the tension uncoil.

It doesn't have to be this way.

No. It really doesn't.

One more breath, and I let my arms wind around Ania's waist and my forehead fall onto her shoulder.

It doesn't.

After tonight, hopefully I'll have a chance to prove it.

TWENTY-FIVE

OUR FINAL JOB. FOR REAL, this time. Of course, whether it's a voluntary retirement or an on-the-job death that ends our heisting career remains to be seen.

Jaesin crouches in front of me, gun in hand, huddled in the nighttime shadows between two buildings. Behind us, Ania and Remi pull long, velvet strands of plum-colored obscuraz between their hands and pass them back and forth, weaving them together. Ania will never be as good a weaver as Remi, but she knows her ware and can work it like a pro, more than well enough to keep up with their shared spell. Together they weave a giant concealment screen, like a cloak to drape over all of us, much stronger than their usual spells. It won't last long, just long enough to get us across the street and into the alcove holding the employee access, but that's all the time we need.

And me? I sit there and *wait*. Torture. My first bit is already done: a simple message calling all MMC board members to a 12:15 a.m. emergency meeting at HQ, made less simple by the fact that I had to plant it on MMC's servers to make it look like it came from an internal source. I neglected to mention that bit to Davon, just in case his IT manager conscience got in the way.

A notification pops up in my vision.

Davon: We're all clear. I'm right inside the door. You ready?
You: Almost. Sixty seconds.

Davon went in ahead of us about twenty minutes ago, signing into the work log, registering his badge in the server room to give him an alibi, and scoping out the guard situation ahead of time. With a shimmer, Remi and Ania pull their last threads taut to finish our cover. It slithers like purple-black satin over their fingers, the weave tight and even, somehow seeming to glow with darkness instead of light. It's hard to look at; I try to make my eyes focus on it, but they keep sliding away. A good thing, considering its purpose.

"Come on, hurry!" Remi says, beckoning us forward. "The fresher the spell, the better, for this formula."

Jaesin and I dash forward, and the four of us press ourselves together, the crackle of energy from the maz itchy on the back of my neck. We shuffle to the edge of the alley, taking it slow to get the hang of moving together, then step cautiously into the road. Ania has hopelessly terrible rhythm and can't quite march on step and the rest of us adjust to her as best we can. If one of us gets too far away, the strain could cause the whole spell to collapse.

Of course, a car chooses that moment to come diving down from the traffic lanes overhead, angling in to park on this street.

"Look up," I whisper, struggling to keep my voice low. Ahead of me, Jaesin stiffens and hisses, "Double time, now!"

The four of us scurry as best we can to the side of the road, reaching the curb just as the car slams down to hover height on the road and continues on through the next intersection, cruising toward a club that's still open, in defiance of the city's district-wide closure. There's no time to stop and ponder our near death, though. As soon as our boots hit the curb, the staff entrance pops open, Davon's welcome face peeking out from inside.

"Hurry," he mouths, waving us forward as he looks over his shoulder. A cool relief blooms in my chest at the sight of him, and I smile despite the circumstances. He catches my eye and smiles back, then steps out to allow us to slip past him into the hallway.

The door shuts behind us with disturbing finality. We actually have to do this. Our plan for getting back out is vague at best, but we have no choice. It's this or let MMC destroy an entire district of my city. *My* city. Which is not happening.

"Hey," I murmur as Davon brushes past me. I snag the edge of his sleeve and tug. "Everything good?"

He wraps an arm around my shoulders and pulls me in for a quick hug. "Good to go. You all ready?" he asks, turning to address the others.

Everyone nods, expressions serious, focused, nervous. I have the ridiculous urge to throw myself at them all for a group hug, to let Ania fuss and Jaesin ruffle my hair, to pull every inch of Remi's body close to mine. The moment for that is long over, though. Instead, I give Davon what I hope is a firm, confident nod.

"Okay," Davon says. "Follow me and stay close. I've diverted some camera feeds between here and where we need to go. I started in on the security to see what we're up against, but it's heavy duty. Diz, I'll need your help once we get to the restricted area."

Dang. If Davon can't handle it solo, it must be some major ice. Sometimes two perspectives helps, though. We'll handle it. We have to.

We follow quickly and quietly, turning down hallway after deserted hallway. I hold my breath at every corner, expecting someone to jump out and shoot us, to end this whole thing before it even begins. But nothing. Turns out eleven at night is the perfect time for abandoned hallways and silent rooms. I keep glancing up and to the right, waiting for a notification from my little drone, parked on the ceiling of the MMC boardroom. Nothing yet. We still have plenty of time.

"How far in is this place?" Jaesin whispers after about

three minutes of twists and turns, looking over his shoulder every five seconds.

"Not long now," Davon says. "One more hallway. They put the most secure part of the facility in the dead center."

Sure enough, one more turn, the end of the hallway opens up into a larger, darker space, with a door edged in orange warning paint.

RESTRICTED AREA. LEVEL FIVE ACCESS ONLY.

So close.

The lights must be on a sensor, because as soon as we walk in, they flicker on, blinding me for a second. Something in the air changes too, though, like a pressure difference, or movement—

—and when my vision clears, we're surrounded by MMC security, all with maz or guns leveled at us. Not maz-powered stun guns like ours. Real, lethal ones.

Adrenaline hits me like a wave of firaz, burning me from the inside out.

"You've gotta be kidding me," Jaesin says, voice flat. I look over at him, and I've never seen his face like this before—twisted and hateful. I follow his gaze back to the MMC guards surrounding us . . .

. . . and to Davon, standing next to the guard captain at the head of the group.

My mind goes perfectly blank.

I shake my head once, then again, my horrified gaze locked on Davon, pressed and polished in his MMC polo shirt, standing between the barrels of two leveled guns.

"No," I say. "No, this isn't what it looks like. Davon, tell me—"

The head of security gestures to me. "Is she the one?"

Davon nods. "That's the deal. You touch her, they'll have your job."

"Calm down, kid, I know how to follow orders," she says, holstering her gun. "Take the others into custody."

Officers step forward and take hold of Ania, Jaesin, and Remi, forcing their arms behind their backs. My heart lurches painfully, watching them seize Remi's shoulder and force them to their knees, the look on their face. . . .

Jaesin snarls and yanks against the guards' hold, like a bull about to charge. "You complete garbage asshole of a human being, Davon, you godsforsaken—"

His breath rushs out of him in a whoosh as one of the guards slugs him in the stomach. My hands fly to my mouth.

"Davon, you—"

I cut myself off, fury threatening to strangle the words right from my throat. "How could you do this? After everything? After—"

I can't speak. I can't understand. I can't . . .

"I told you, Dizzy. I've *always* got your back," he says, hands held in front of him imploringly. "They knew we were family. They came for me after you left for Jatta-pore. I negotiated for you. Your job offer stands and your warrant gets wiped, and that comes straight from the executive board. You're free. You still get to have a good life. We can get a new place if you want, just the two of us, and finally live like family again. We always wanted to when we were kids, remember?"

I do remember. We used to lie on the roof of Davon's house and imagine what kind of place we'd have as grown-ups, all the things we'd buy for it, who we would marry and how they would totally not mind sharing a house because we'd all be best friends. The fact that we lived in separate houses as kids frustrated us to no end. We wanted to be a "real" family. Because, of course, to a child, family didn't mean the same thing if you didn't share a roof. I dropped my face into my hands and shook my head.

Real family.

He has no idea about real family.

A wave of rage hits me, hot and sudden, and I pin Davon with a fierce glare.

"How could you ever think I would want that?" I shout, the ragged sound tearing itself from my throat. "That I could just pick up and continue my life as if this never happened? As if I could just forget my friends? For-get everything we're here to fight for?"

Davon sighs, exasperated. He has the nerve to be exasperated?

"Dizzy," he says. "You and me, we've always known how the world works. We do what it takes to survive. We look after each other before all others. I know MMC's history is messy, but there's a balance to everything. We can't go back and undo the past, but we can make sure things are the best they can be *now*. We can work to make things better. You would have done the same thing, if it were me in trouble. You know this was the right move."

I shake my head and back away, one step, then two.

"No."

Another step.

"No, Davon. I could never—" I break off, lift my chin, and look Davon dead in the eye. "I could never do what you're doing right now."

I turn to look at Ania, Jaesin . . . and Remi. Kneeling, faces twisted with pain as the guards wrench their arms, bruise their wrists.

I did this to them. It's my fault.

"You have it all wrong," I say, looking back to Davon. "They *are* my real family."

Silence.

"Well," Davon finally says, stone-faced. "I'm sorry you feel that way."

We stare at each other across the room, surrounded by guards who seem to be waiting for something. Waiting to see if I'll turn violent so they can justify taking me down, probably. Waiting for Davon to give up on me so they can take me too.

There has to be a way out of this. There's no way we can come this far only to stop right outside the door. MMC will continue with their drilling, destroy the whole district, Ginny's bakery, the clubs, the factories. More people out of jobs, more maz-15 in the system, more people ill. More people dying. More control for MMC.

I look around the room with a disorienting sense of deja vu. Was it really less than a day ago that we were in this exact same situation at the professor's house, surrounded, no hope of ever . . .

Wait a minute.

"I told you we went to Jattapore," I say, putting it together. "You ratted us out. You're the reason we got ambushed at the professor's house. And at the train station. It's your fault the professor and his husband were almost killed. That *I* could have been killed."

Davon shakes his head. "They wouldn't have hurt you, Diz. They were under strict orders not to."

I snort. "Yeah? Well, it sure felt like they were planning on it when they had me on the ground with weapons and spells pointed at me. Sorry, I'm just not really feeling the forgiving vibes."

But we got out of that situation. I annoyed people, the others fought, and we lived. Barely. There are double the guards here, though.

Can we pull that off again? Do we have another choice?

I turn to the others and take in how they're being held, where they're facing.

They have Remi by the biceps, but their fingers are free. Mistake.

They're clearly favoring Jaesin's right side, expecting the most struggle to come from there. Mistake.

They have Ania's arms much more firmly secured, two hands locked around the ware on her wrists. Her feet though, with their heavy-heeled shoes, are unsecured. Mistake.

There's a chance. Just a chance, but . . .

I pull myself together and take a long, deep breath in through my nose.

"I'm learning all kinds of things today," I say, loud, so every guard can hear me. "Thing number one."

I hold up one finger and meet Remi's eyes. The corner of their mouth quirks, and the faintest, tiniest thread of dark maz slithers out of their necklace, under the collar of their shirt, and down their sleeve. I need to keep the attention away from them, so I spin dramatically and point a finger straight at Davon. The guards all tense at my sudden movement, raising their guns, but I press on, my heart racing. No tremor in my voice, no hesitation in my step, and absolutely no looking back toward the others.

"Number one," I say again, staring into Davon's eyes.

"You're a tool. I thought you were the best person in the world, my brother in all but blood, but I guess you've drunk the MMC poison. Tragic."

I pace to the left, then the right, moving around to keep all eyes on me. How long will Remi need? No way to tell. The guards are twitchy, looking uncertainly from me to Davon to their captain, clearly unsure how long they should tolerate my antics. I draw it out as long as I can.

"Number two," I continued. "Professor Silva, who you may remember as a genius maz researcher who was unceremoniously fired from MMC eight years ago, is an utterly delightful man who knows a whole lot of interesting things about this place. For instance," I say with a grand gesture, meeting every guard's eyes, willing them to focus on me. I'm a mess, look at me, look at me. "Did you know that MMC caused the spellplague? True story! It's caused by this stuff they don't want you to know about called maz-15. A new strain of maz, big deal, right? The world should know! Except for that spellsickness bit."

The guard captain rolls her eyes. "What a load of conspiracy theorist, tinfoil-hat-wearing bullsh—"

"And!" I interrupt. "The same thing that causes the spellplague? Totally responsible for the earthquakes and hurricanes too! Funny how those all started right after the spellplague, don't you think? See, MMC made a little drilling mistake ten years ago, right here in this very facility, and they let something out that was never supposed to be free. But did they clean up their mess?"

The guards on the left side of the room are drifting, their attention waning, eyes rolling, so I twirl toward them with a flourish.

"No!" I declare dramatically, stomping my foot and pointing randomly at one of the guards. "They figured out they could profit off their mistake, so what did they do? They kept drilling for the same maz that killed off your friends and family."

A sure bet. Because everyone in Kyrkarta lost someone in the plague, unless they came to town afterward, and even the newbies have a healthy respect. I risk a quick glance back at the others to make sure their guards are still paying attention. Remi has their hands gently cupped behind their back, and they lower their chin in the faintest nod. *Yes*.

"That drill shaft, by the way, is somewhere behind that door, bringing more and more plague into this world every day," I say, pointing behind me. Who knows, maybe someone here will actually believe me. If we die in this attempt, *someone* needs to know.

"And finally," I say, willing my body not to give the plan away. One . . . two . . .

"Three!"

I drop to the floor, and the room explodes.

The spell goes off at the guards' chest height,

spreading out in a painfully bright disk that throws the guards and Davon back and holds them fast to whatever wall caught them, stuck flat against it like a living mural. Jaesin, Remi, and Ania lurch to their feet as soon as the spell passes overhead, Jaesin snatching his gun back from the struggling form of the guard who'd held him. Remi immediately begins to weave a new spell, this one an odd, intense blend of colors threading together so quickly I can barely catch them, red and gold and violet and black.

"Get to the door!" Remi shouts. "Just blow it open and get inside, Ania. I think we're past trying to be stealthy."

Ania promptly obeys. She's awful at explosives normally, but this time she doesn't need finesse, just raw power. She whips up an explosive cocktail of magnaz and firaz as we run and, twenty feet out, throws the spell at the door.

BOOM!

The door stays stubbornly closed.

The wall around it, however, now features a nice human-sized gap. When in doubt, make your own door.

I shove Ania and Jaesin through first, then turn back to check on Remi. Davon is still pinned to the wall, recovering from the stun hit, but the spell is wearing off enough for some of the guards to reach for their weapons. Remi tosses a furious look over their shoulder at me.

"Get behind the wall!" they shout, whipping their spell into a frenzy over their head, weaving in more and more gold and glowing violet. I crawl through the gap and press my back against the wall next to it. Right as Ania throws a barrier over the opening, the thought right on the tip of my brain finally clicks.

A color of maz I haven't seen much. Only twice, in fact.

The intense violet shade of maz-15.

"Remi, no!" I shout, launching myself off the wall.

Too late.

TWENTY-SIX

THE BLAST FEELS LIKE ALL the air being sucked out of the room, like a sudden vacuum swallowing all of existence. Then—*BOOM!*

A whomp of pressure slams into the wall at my back, the tremor nearly knocking me to the ground even from this side, the flash of violet light shining through the crumbling gap we came through. Debris rains down, dusting our hair gray and coating my throat. I stumble back to standing with a hacking cough and peek around the corner.

The guards—and Davon—are all flat on the ground, sprawled with their various complexions washed out in the pallor of illness, blood pooling around a few who hit their heads in the fall. The onset of spellsickness? Or just an effect of the spell? Their chests still rise and fall, mostly. Davon's does, at least. Stars, Davon . . . is he spellsick now? Do I even care, now that he's completely betrayed me in the worst possible way?

My eyes fixed on the rise and fall of his chest, bile

burning in the back of my throat. I don't know *what* to think or feel, other than *a mess*.

He's alive. That has to be good enough for now. Even after everything he's done, the thought of losing another family member to the spellplague is unbearable.

But that thought came too soon, because in the center of all the blood and bodies is Remi, on their knees and sprawled forward with their face pressed to their folded forearms, sides shaking with coughing sobs that fill the whole room. My heart squeezes hard in my chest, and my foot catches on a piece of broken concrete as I stumble back through the gash in the wall and to Remi's side, falling to my knees beside them.

"Are you hurt?" I ask, laying a hand on their shoulder, running the other through their hair. "Remi, are you okay?"

Remi shakes their head, then shoots up to kneeling, their puffy red eyes wide.

"Dizzy, get out of here! The maz might not have settled yet, and—"

"I don't care," I say, cupping their face in both hands. They're pale, so pale, and their breathing is thready and uneven. I brush my thumbs over their cheekbones and swallow hard. "I don't care. Can you stand?"

They keep their eyes fixed on my face as they take several deep breaths, then nod. "I just caught a bit of blowback from the spell. I was sloppy. I'll be fine in a minute."

Fine is relative, but I'll take their word for it. I sling Remi's arm over my shoulders and push from my knees, staggering a bit as they lean hard on me until their legs steady. Jaesin dashes out a second later, taking Remi's other arm over his shoulders and helping me get them out of that room and its stink and blood and fading, deadly maz.

"Dizzy," they whisper. "I'm sorry. There were so many of them, I didn't know what else to do. I don't want Davon to be ill, I don't think he will be, but if he is—"

"Hey," I say gently, stepping over a groaning guard. "It's not like you're a trained combat weaver. You did what you had to. Where did you even get the maz-15 from?"

Remi looks up at me from the corner of their eye, a bit sheepish. "The professor's stash in his lab. I took a little while I was replenishing our stock, kept it in the smallest chamber in my necklace, sealed up with linkaz. In case of emergency. I thought this qualified."

"This is ridiculous," Jaesin says as soon as we prop Remi up against the wall to recover. "The mission is blown. We have to get out of here."

"And then what?" Remi says. "We just disappear? Never do anything about this giant world-killing problem? Let them destroy this city? Let them continue to exploit the planet, put everyone in danger, and profit off it all?"

Jaesin looks pained, and shakes his head. "But it doesn't have to be us. We retreat, we spread the word until something gets through—"

Remi cuts him off with a weak gesture. "We've already screwed that possibility. Now that they know we know, this place will be a fortress. No one but the most high-level employees will ever set foot in here again. No one else will ever have a chance to fix this without blowing a huge crater in the city and letting all that toxic maz out. It's now or never, Jaesin. I choose now."

"Remi, look at yourself right now. You're about to collapse. I don't think you should—" Ania begins, but I slam my fist against the nearest wall, shaking with all of it— nerves, anger, fear for Davon, sheer terror for us.

"It's their decision." I take a slow breath through my nose and meet Remi's gaze, trying to convey my meaning. "I know I've been a jerk about this in the past, but I really mean it. It's your choice. Only you know if you feel well enough to do this. And you're right, anyway. This is our one and only chance to deal with this. If we don't do it now, it could be years before we can try again, and we'll have to be on the run the entire time. I know that's not how any of us wants to live."

Remi smiles at me, that same warmth in their eyes that I saw this afternoon. Something in my stomach flutters, tightens, but I force it down.

"Time's wasting, then," Remi says, holding my gaze for an extra beat, then looking to Jaesin and Ania. "I promise I feel well enough. I probably won't later, but this is save-the-world-level stuff here. We need to move on before reinforcements show up.

Jaesin reaches out and pulls Remi in for a hug, clutching them to his chest like the big brother he is, blood be damned. Then he lets them go, steps back, and nods.

"Let's do this."

Ania squeezes Jaesin's arm and nods.

"Let's do this," she echoes.

Remi grins and turns back to me with a little bow.

"Well, pathfinder," they say with a wave at the blank hallways beyond. "Find us a path."

"I don't know where we're going," I say, but even as the words leave my mouth, I take in our surroundings. Behind the giant metal security door, this part of the station looks much like the rest of it, much like every other MMC building I've ever wandered in, through, or on. In fact, I've been on the roof of this one before, about a year ago, and with the positioning of the vapor stacks . . .

"This way," I say, and set off down a hallway to the right.

I'm not sure. I'm never sure about anything, and that's part of my constant problem. Sometimes, though, the situation calls for decisiveness. My steps are sure even as my guard is up, checking around every corner before proceeding.

I don't have maz, but this is all me.

The way forward quickly becomes clear, fortunately.

All I need to do is follow the glaring orange signs that warn of potential illness OR EVEN DEATH. Quite dramatic.

We pass two empty security checkpoints along the way. The guards are likely lying passed out or dead in the pile we just left behind, but the comms are still working just fine. Voices chatter back and forth, calling in the report of the bodies we left behind, signs of our passage, and most importantly—our location caught on video. I whip around and spot the offending camera in the upper right corner of the hallway.

Great.

I give them a rude gesture and turn another corner, my mind an uninterrupted litany of swear words. The hallway ends in a decontamination airlock, loudly marked with yet more warnings, and a wall of bright orange storage lockers with—yes, *victory*—eight heat-shielded suits, each with canisters of oxygen and nullaz. I pass three of them back to the others and yank one down for myself, holding the thing out at arm's length. Where the hell is the zipper?

Ania, who can deconstruct any piece of clothing on sight, discovers a nearly invisible seam that hides a zipper running down the center of the suit. She steps into it with impossible grace—but pulling it on is another matter. It's impossible for even Ania to do without looking like a complete jackass. I stumble to the right, hopping on one foot as I try to yank the skintight suit over my shoes. It keeps sticking to me like it wants to strangle me. Remi barks a laugh and falls against the wall, their feet completely tangled.

"Wait, wait," they say, gasping. "These things are spelled. Wait one . . ."

They draw a bit of maz to hand and weave it into a simple pattern, then crush it and sprinkle it over the suit. The gaudy, violently orange thing sags and stretches like a punctured balloon, the arms and legs loosening into wide, floppy noodles. Three more quick spells, and we're all able to maneuver our way into the suits with much more success.

Once we're all zipped up, Remi weaves four more tiny spells that snap the suits back into shape, molded to our bodies in a way that's surprisingly attractive on some and utterly, miserably uncomfortable on me. It's like the suit is trying to give me chest compressions and an all-sides wedgie. Not great.

Masks come next, which are horrifically claustrophobic, then the press of a button to activate the nullaz field. Down the hall, a door slams, and the sound of running boots follows.

"Take the other suits," Ania says. "It'll slow them down. We can destroy them on the other side."

Ooh, smart. We all snag an extra suit and, with no ceremony whatsoever, pull the big dramatic lever and hit the ominous red button. The lights on either side of the door begin to blink, and a countdown appears above the door. Jaesin bounces on the balls of his feet, looking back over his shoulder.

"I swear these seconds feel eight times longer than normal seconds," he murmurs, waggling his gun at me as a reminder to have mine ready.

He's not wrong. Remi and Ania glance at each other, then take up stations on either side of the hallway and draw maz to hand. We're about to travel down to the source of all maz, after all, so the need to conserve our short supply isn't quite so dire. Remi preps a projectile of some kind, holding it at the ready for the first guard to round the corner, while Ania crouches low and threads a slippery weave over the hallway floor. After a moment, an MMC minion rounds the corner at a run and is immediately downed by a golden-red blast to the chest. The man right behind her approaches more slowly, sticking close to the wall with his gun drawn. The second his feet hit Ania's spelled area, though, his legs go right out from under him in ass-over-head fashion. Beautiful. Wish I'd thought to have my lenses record it for the internet to enjoy.

Just as a third guard appears, the airlock behind us hisses and cracks open to admit us into the most secret and most deadly area in all of Kyrkarta. Jaesin and I step in, holding the door open with our guns pointed out into the hallway, while Ania and Remi back toward us, the spare suits held in the crook of their elbows to leave their hands free for maz. Once we're all inside, the airlock chimes cheerfully and slides closed, trapping us in the transfer room.

My breathing picks up as I have a horrible realization: this spot, this airlock, is where we're most vulnerable. There could be anything, any*one* on the other side. Hell, maybe there's a security station somewhere where they could simply cut power to the airlock and let us suffocate in here, or lock us in until more guards arrive. The airlock suddenly seems incredibly small. Another ten-second countdown appears as the door behind us hisses, forming the seal that protects the rest of the station. After a literal eternity, the door in front of us finally slides open, revealing an empty catwalk overlooking a small, dry ravine.

We cross the catwalk with careful steps, wary of the edges. We're on our way toward a drop so long you could call every one of your acquaintances for a tearful goodbye on the way down. Too dramatic. I'd just embrace my fate and spend the time watching funny vids on my lenses or calling up my favorite music on my deck. Because I don't know when I'll die, but whenever I do, it'll be with a deck in my pocket, guaranteed.

I pat my back pocket through the protective suit. Hopefully today won't be that day.

We proceed with caution, Jaesin and me in the lead

with the guns at the ready, looking in every direction for movement. It's still only eleven thirty at night, despite all that's happened since we entered the complex, and the entire area seems deserted. Death drilling is a day-shift-only kind of job, I guess. The catwalk deposits us onto a platform with a large control rig attached to an intricate system of piping, similar to the arrangement we always saw in the sewers. A long line drawn in reflective paint bisects the platform. On our half, machinery and consoles line every wall. The other side is dominated by signage.

WARNING: SHEER DROP AHEAD

HEAT PROTECTION REQUIRED BEYOND THIS POINT

ONLY LICENSED TECHNICIANS MAY OPERATE DESCENT VEHICLES

CHECK IT TWICE, SAVE A LIFE:
1. IS YOUR SUIT'S INSPECTION DATE CURRENT?
2. IS YOUR O_2 FLOW IN THE GREEN?
3. IS YOUR NULLIFIER ACTIVE?
4. IS YOUR COMM UNIT RECEIVING?

PROTECT YOURSELF AND YOUR COLLEAGUES AND REPORT ALL ACCIDENTS PROMPTLY

"Better do as the sign commands," Jaesin says. "Final checks? Everyone good?"

One by one we sound off, all clear. "Though," I add, "maybe we should take those extra suits with us instead of throwing them into the hell pit, just in case something happens to ours."

"It looks like there's extra O_2 tanks here too," Ania says, peeking inside a series of storage cabinets. "Might not hurt, just in case this takes longer than we hope it will. And, worse comes to worst, they're heavy enough to hit someone with."

She tosses one to Jaesin, who catches it in one hand and hefts it, testing its weight. "Yep, that'll hurt. Good idea."

Once the canisters are distributed, we can't avoid it any longer. We have to approach the edge of the drilling tunnel. Jaesin and I take the lead again, shuffling carefully over to the line of maintenance capsules—descent vehicles, they call them—lined up at the edge of the platform. They're silver with loud yellow warning stripes, like some kind of bee, and just as round. A peek through the open doorway of one shows they're clearly intended for only two people at a time, but splitting up into separate pods seems both terrifying and like a terrible idea. We'll make it work.

The yawning edge of the chasm before me makes my head swim, but I force my eyes to the solid floor under my feet and take a deep breath. The contamination suit is hot and sticky, like a second skin that's glued itself to me via my sweat. The heat radiating from the planet's exposed core is suffocating, even though my suit pipes plenty of fresh oxygen into my mask. This whole thing is going to be hell.

And it doesn't matter. It has to be done.

A few feet away, Jaesin and Ania stand close, double-checking each other's suits with lingering hands and intense eye contact. Whoa. Looks like mom and dad are getting back together after all. Remi stands a little way off to the side, seemingly mesmerized by the edge of the cliff, the sheer drop that leads down to a giant pool of exactly what's been trying to kill them for the past ten years. I step over to them and bump their suited shoulder with mine.

"Hey," I say.

I'm terrified for you and wish you would stay here, I want to say, but that's not fair. It's not right.

"Are you okay with this?" I ask instead. "With going down to the source, being so steeped in it? It's got to be weird for you."

"No weirder than it is for you all, I imagine," they say, returning the shoulder bump. "You lost everything to the plague too. You didn't get the same consolation prize, but it doesn't mean this won't be hard for you."

I shrug. The time for getting philosophical and

emotional about the spellplague is long over. Something broke in me, back at the professor's house. But something started to heal a little too, I think. Today is a day for fixing things. That's what we're here to do. No point in dwelling on the rest.

"Everything will be just shiny once we get down there and give the planet a nice Band-Aid. Worth it, right?" I ask, turning to look them in the eye.

Remi smiles and holds my gaze.

"Yeah," they say, tipping their head forward until our helmets touch at the forehead. "Definitely worth it."

I take their hand in mine, swallow hard, and open my mouth, maybe to respond, though I have no idea what I'm planning to say. It doesn't seem fair to take the cheap way out, to plead my case and confess everything in me right before our confrontation with death. But I want to, *stars*, how I want to. I can admit it. And that's a victory of some kind, at least, right?

To my relief and disappointment, Jaesin's hand lands on Remi's shoulder, effectively ending our conversation.

"Hey," he says, his eyes warm and smiling. "Let's go before they show up at the door with some emergency stash of suits and decide pushing us off this cliff is their best option."

I peek over the edge again and wince.

"Yeah," I say. "If I'm gonna die in that giant hole, I want it to be saving the world. Let's get on with it."

Jaesin nods solemnly. "Be real for a second, though. Beyond this point, we have no idea if we'll have a way out. We get down there, do our thing, and if we're lucky our brilliant plans will magically work out. But this could be it. Last chance to back out. Are we all in?"

"Absolutely," Remi says without a second's hesitation.

Ania purses her lips, a hard look in her eye. "I'm in."

I take a deep breath and close my eyes for a moment.

My father is so distant in my mind, his face hazy with memory and time even as I stand in the space where he died. There was no funeral, not for him specifically. The city's funeral industry couldn't support a million funerals in one weekend. But I laid a polished stone for him at the memorial site, like he told me our people do back in his home city, Agara, on the Small Continent. I sat beside my mom as she lit candles and spun what little maz we had into the mourning spell for him, sending points of light into the night sky like a flock of bright, shining birds. And I got Remi to do the same for my mother, once I stopped being mad at her for dying. Or less mad, at least.

Everyone's gone. There'll be no one to send up mourning spells for us. The world has gone to hell.

And we hold the key to fixing it all.

"Yes," I say, squaring my shoulders. "Let's move."

TWENTY-SEVEN

EVEN WITH MY DECK PLUGGED straight into the maintenance pod and the diagnostics running right before my eyes, I can't shake the feeling that the awful thing is going to drop us straight into the fiery pit at the heart of the world at the slightest provocation. Theoretically, engineers have been using these things to descend to core level to perform maintenance and change drill bits for ten years running.

Theoretically, I don't give a shit. My stomach is ready to empty in all directions, and it's not a great feeling. I've never had a problem with heights crawling all over Kyrkarta's buildings, but this is heights on a whole new level.

The rocky walls fly by at nauseating speed, nothing more than a blur at nearly two thousand miles per hour. Even at that speed, the descent takes nearly thirty very uncomfortable minutes, the layers of our planet's thin crust, then the thicker outer mantle, shifting in color and texture as we go. As we near our destination, the pod begins to slow, the heat-shielding spells coating its exterior flaring to life in a spectacular light show. A moment later, we burst from the tunnel into a vast cavern . . . and into the grandest sight I've ever seen.

A vast ocean of maz glows beneath us, strands of every single strain known to humankind twisting and twirling together in a dance far older than our civilization. The colors flow before our eyes, greens, blues, reds, and golds, everything together, but somehow it manages to keep from looking like a tangled mess, a muddy mash-up of colors. Instead, it's like looking at a pearlescent shell, colors shifting in gentle waves. Jaesin and Ania stare, awestruck, but their expressions are nothing beside Remi's wide-open heart worn full on their face, eyes welling with a sort of near-religious ecstasy I can only imagine. With a connection to maz like theirs, this moment must feel monumental. Divine.

Sacred.

But in the center of it all, an enormous piece of machinery like a soaring pillar pierces the surface of the sea. All around it, maz roils in bubbling violet waves, like slowly boiling water. Maz-15, leaking out of the planet's core like an open wound.

The rift. The source of it all.

The pod's maz-powered brakes flare to life, making the final automated descent to a solid steel platform built out from the cavern wall. When it finally comes to a stop, a light winks on as the computer requests further instructions. I do a quick visual inspection of the area and find ten other platforms circling the drilling zone, some nearly a half mile away and at a variety of heights. The one next to us is quite a bit higher than we are, and I zero in on a rather important detail.

"These platforms have maneuvering jets," I say, my fingers flying over my deck. "They're mobile. Let's get out of this clown car and get some breathing room, figure out our strategy."

With that, I command the pod's door to open, and we spill out into the wide-open cavern, steel beneath our boots and deadly maz just beyond the nullifying barrier of our suits.

Inside the pod, it was almost like playing a video game. The sense of scale was completely off. Now, standing on an open platform with nothing but a spindly railing to keep us from tripping face-first into the Maz Sea, the vastness is overwhelming and humbling.

And not just the vastness of the sea. Of the drill. And of our task ahead.

"Any word from the drone yet?" Ania shouts, the noise from the enormous machines in the cavern rendering her words nearly inaudible. I frown and tune in to the drone's feed just to make sure I haven't missed a notification in the middle of all the not-dying business. It's one minute until the meeting time I put in the message to all the board members, but the room is still dark. Did they talk to each other offline and set a new meeting place? Did they figure out the message is a fake? Does *no one* arrive early for these things?

"Nothing yet," I say. "We'll have to start somewhere else. We can't do anything to the drill without the codes."

"First things first," Remi chimes in. "We need to shut down the maz collectors. I feel really . . . just . . . *wrong* down here. It skeeves me out."

Jaesin turns to me. "Maz collectors, pathfinder?"

"On it," I say, syncing wirelessly to the platform's controls. No network security because honestly, who ever thought a hacker would end up down here? I find what we need in less than ten seconds.

"I can shut it down, but we're gonna do something a little more permanent than hitting the off switch, right?" I say. "The control systems for the absorbers are on one of the other platforms, along with the drilling controls. Everyone grab on to something. We're gonna move."

We all pick a workstation and hold on to the handrails, worn dull from years of MMC employees at their daily tasks. Ania kindly weaves us all a quick and simple terraz spell to keep our feet stable as the maneuvering thrusters fire. The kickback almost throws me, but Ania's spell holds fast as the platform accelerates toward the major mechanical controls. Once we near the other platform, ours decelerates smoothly until it docks with a heavy *clank*. We've barely been still for a second before Remi is dashing off to examine the controls. I stay where I am, doing my own inspection digitally.

"Give me one second," I shout over the noise, louder now that we're so close to the source, and get to work on the platform's console. Easy. Some basic security here, a supervisor's password required to give the shutdown command, but I retrieve it from the database and enter it without a problem. Another quick command and—

The vibration of the platform beneath our feet suddenly tapers off with a great sound of powering down, the lights around us flickering for a moment. I grin.

"Extractors are off! Working on the drill now," I call to the others. I can't do much without the executive board's drill codes, but I can at least get the lay of the digital land, see what I'll be working with.

"We're partly here to break stuff, right?" Jaesin says, his voice full of twelve-year-old-Jaesin intent. I look up, scenting mischief on the air.

"Right," Remi shouts back with a grin.

Jaesin hefts a heavy piece of steel piping. "Cool. I'm gonna break stuff."

And with that, he swings the pipe into the extraction system master control, sending up a shower of sparks and a deliciously satisfying *crunch*. Ania's eyes nearly bug out of her head, watching Jaesin's arms, then she seems to shake herself and begins weaving her own bit of destruction. She and Remi take turns hurling spells at the rest of the system, setting small fires and crushing pipes. As soon as I look around for something to join in with, though, a notification pops up in my lenses.

The drone at MMC headquarters.

I flip over to the video feed from the drone and watch as the lights in the boardroom click on, triggered by two women in their fifties entering the room. They take seats on the far side of the table, guessing about the topic of the emergency meeting as they wait for their fellows. The board members trickle in one or two at a time over the next two minutes, and I have to laugh to myself. They're all passive-aggressively trying to be the most fashionably late, like they're *so* important they had other priorities even in the middle of the night. Once they're all seated, an awkward silence falls as everyone waits for someone else to bring up the reason for the meeting. No one does, of course. None of them called the meeting.

I did.

I shout for the others to pause in their destructo party, toggle on a noise filter, and speak loud and clear through the tiny speakers on the drone.

"Hi, everyone!"

The board members freeze. I share the video feed from the drone with the others so they can tune in, and I give Ania mic access too. She's better at talking to fancy people than I am. Once I'm sure we have everyone's attention, I command the drone to fly down from its perch on the ceiling and hover at the front of the room in plain view.

"You must be wondering why we've called you here tonight," Ania says in her best business voice.

"Who the hell are you?" a sharp-looking man in a rumpled black suit demands.

I roll my eyes and jump in. "Before we tell you that, I just want you to know what's at stake here. First off, you might have noticed the maz this drone is carrying. It's a pretty clever spell if I do say so myself, something we created ourselves just for this occasion. I'll spare you the details, though, and be clear about just one thing. That purple glow is maz-15. If at any point you try to leave or we don't like what you're saying, the drone lets the spell loose, and you all spend the rest of your very short lives vomiting your plaguey guts out. Understood?"

The man closest to the door pushes back from the table, and I swoop the drone toward him, cutting off his exit.

"Ah ah ah," I say. "Sit down, Michael. There's a good boy."

"How do you know my name?" the man asks, trying to sound brave despite his pale face and shaking voice. I gesture for Ania to take over again, and she nods gracefully.

"We know everything about you, Michael," she jumps in smoothly. "And you, Antonia, and Koki, and Ceillie, and everyone in this room. Mostly important, though, we know what you don't want *anyone* to know. We know about the mistress, Michael. Those awful, dirty people you're in debt to, Irif." Ania goes around the table one by one, listing the fruits of my insomnia hacking, my terrible habit that I thought would never be anything but a diversion for sleepless nights. Turned out to be more useful than I ever thought. MMC may be untouchable, with their media control and purchased politicians. Their board members, on the other hand, are not. By the time Ania's done, the whole room is silent, everyone's eyes averted, cheeks stained red where complexions allow, everyone sweating or breathing fast or tense with fury.

"What is it you want, then?" a stately older woman with white corkscrew curls asks.

I glance away from the video feed in time to see Ania's lips curl into a triumphant little smile. "The drill codes, please," she says, "and your word, worthless though it is, that you'll stop every awful thing you've been doing to this community. No more doing business with maz-15. No plans to destroy parts of the city. No murdering scientists. But mostly the drill codes."

I pick up the speech from there. "Give us the codes and we'll keep our mouths shut, and this little drone will keep its maz to itself. You all get to walk out of here plague-free. Your choice. What do you say?"

Then a bullet pings off the station beside me, and I

snatch my hand back, blood thundering in my ears.

Another platform drifts toward us, crawling with guards in bright orange suits like ours. I grab my deck off the console and bring it down into my lap, digging into the maintenance pod systems. Sure enough, there are two new pods down here with us, and three more on the way. We're about to have a *lot* more company.

"Shit," I say eloquently.

"Yes," Ania agrees, even as she weaves us a shield, thick rivulets of terraz pouring between her fingers.

"Okay. This is fine," I say, thinking, thinking. "We can't let that other platform reach us. Jaesin, you have a driving license. You theoretically can steer things. Think you can fly this platform?"

He blinks at me. "I mean, I think I'm gonna have to. It can't be *that* different from a car, right?"

I don't bother answering that. In my ear, the board members bicker among themselves, working their way slowly toward the inevitable. Just give us the codes, I think furiously at them, just do it!

"Okay, Jaesin, get us away from that other platform and take us down near the rift so Remi can do their thing. Ania, I'm gonna work from inside the system to stop those other pods on their way down. I think. Can you keep our shooty friends off our backs for a little while?"

"A very little while," she says, adding magnaz to her weave with elegant gestures. "I'm not Remi, I can't just pull in all of this maz around us. Unless Remi has the time to load some of it into my ware, I've got limited utility here."

Damn it to *hell*, she's right, and it's obnoxious. How frustrating to be surrounded by vast stores of power you can't use. But it'll have to be enough. I tip my head back and will my breath to slow, my heart to calm, my brain to just chill the hell out for a minute. Slow down and think.

First things first.

"Ania, at your feet," I say, then slide her my gun. I can't do much with it while I'm working the computer side of things, and this way she'll at least be able to do *something* when her maz runs out. In my ear, the board members are having some kind of vote, but I catch only the last two votes. Both "no" votes.

Ugh.

"Time is ticking away," I say through the drone, forcing more confidence into my voice than I truly feel. "You have sixty seconds before this plague bomb goes off. Your answer."

With that, I trigger the extra dramatic little bit I added at the last minute. The drone starts counting down in a cheerful voice, its beady little eyes blinking with each tick.

"Sixty! Fifty-nine! Fifty-eight!"

With a growl of frustration, the older woman slams her hands down on the table and pushes to her feet.

"The ayes have it, and as board president, I'm giving

my authorization. We're only going to say these codes once, so listen up."

"Yes!" Remi hisses, sending another boulder of terraz at the other platform. It crashes down on the corner, tipping the whole thing at a dangerous angle. They're pulling maz from the air all around us with a fierce joy, reveling in the ability to sling it around without thinking, for once. No rationing needed here. Ania may still be limited by her ware, but Remi is totally in their element.

I prep a recording and tap furiously at my deck, burrowing my way into the drilling system. I enter each segment of the code as the board member responsible for it recites it. The final man hesitates, his reluctance obvious, but a quick glance at the maz glowing in the drone's belly has him rattling off the final string after only a second. With the last bit entered, the drill interface turns green. I'm in.

"Thanks so very much," I say, then rush to add, "there's just one last thing."

And with that, I send the command to release the spell.

The flash is too much for the camera. The feed goes white, then black. My lenses flood with angry red warnings of damage to the drone, critical system errors, impending failure. After a moment, the drone's cameras readjust, showing the aftermath with a giant crack down the center of the lens.

Every single board member sits rigid in their seat, slumped over, expressions locked in frozen horror. The only movement is the faint rise and fall of their breath.

Also, minor detail: they all have floppy rabbit ears sprouting from their heads. What the hell?

A few feet away, Remi cackles with glee even as they sling spells at our attackers from behind Ania's shield.

"What did you *do*?" I ask, baffled.

"Professor Silva gave me a few tips when I asked about the berserker rabbits in the minefield. The maz I needed to add to make it glow purple is pointless otherwise, so I just . . . got a little creative."

I snort and reopen the comm channel to make use of the dying drone's last few seconds of life.

"So, as you may have guessed, you don't actually have the plague," I say. "But now you know just how much it sucks to think you *might*, so maybe consider your life choices while you're stuck sitting there. Because you are *stuck*. Little paralysis spell, like what they use to subdue patients in hospitals. Couldn't have you giving us the codes, then running off to override us or sending the cops, blah blah. The rabbit ears are just for fun. Enjoy! And since I know you'll have a good four hours to plan and plot and rage internally before the morning guard shift shows up, I just want to offer one last little warning. We still have your secrets, and far more where they came from. We'll be watching."

Before I can really nail the threat home, though, the drone gives one last lurch, lists to one side, then crashes into the boardroom table. The feed cuts off with a quick hiss, and I actually feel a quick pang of distress at the thought of my little drone's death. At least it went out in a blaze of glory.

"RIP, little bug," Jaesin says, letting go of the steering controls just long enough to fire a volley of stun bolts at the other platform. I smile to myself, grateful for the tiny recognition, then shove it all away. Time to focus on my next job.

The drilling rig is a complicated system of maz engines, heat management systems, slurry pumps, and piping. It's enormous, several stories tall, and wider at the bottom where the drill bit sits motionless below the surface of the Maz Sea, waiting for orders to dig deeper. Four enormous pylons jut out from its core at forty-five-degree angles, keeping it perfectly balanced above the rift. The controls are complicated—so complicated that for the first time, I feel a pang of dread. People train for years to be able to operate something like this, and they start with much simpler augers and surface-level drills.

I force myself to breathe evenly and go through each menu of the interface one at a time, looking for something, *anything* that might help. Finally, I come across

PREPROGRAMMED FUNCTIONS, and get a *genius* idea.

Well . . . a better-than-nothing idea.

I open the window, and sure enough, it helpfully lists all of the drill's most basic functions and the commands that drive them. Copy, paste, bam, too easy. I can work with this.

First things first—I command the drill bit to back out of the rift. No way we can seal it with the drill still wedged inside. With a hiss and a clank from the enormous maz engine systems, the drill slowly whirs to life and begins its slow ascent—

—and a flood of violet maz bubbles to the surface in its wake, overtaking everything around it.

"Go back, go back!" Ania shouts, rushing back to my side. I reverse the command, overriding the safeties to rush the process, and the flood slows. The damage is done, though. The sea around the rift roils with violet maz-15, a lake of poison right where Remi needs to work.

"We'll have to seal the rift *while* we stop the drill. If we don't do them at the same time, we're just going to make the contamination worse than it's ever been," Ania says.

Our platform gives a sudden lurch, then tips sickeningly, nearly spilling us into the sea. I scrabble for a hold on the nearest railing and clutch my deck to my chest until the platform rights itself, Jaesin clinging to the controls for dear life. Just beyond him, I see the problem—another two pods have arrived, and two more platforms are in motion, slipping around the drill to flank us. We're *so* screwed.

I grab a fistful of my hair and yank, thinking through the problem. "We're going to have to time this super carefully. Remi," I finally say, turning to them. "You and I will have to coordinate. Start on your part and—"

But they shake their head, hands held helplessly at their sides.

"I can't manipulate the maz from up here, Diz. It's too far. I can sense it, but I can't reach it."

"Take us lower then, Jaesin," I snap. We're already drifting lower, but so *slow*, ugh.

Jaesin pounds a fist on the console in frustration. "I'm *trying*," he says, "but there's some kind of failsafe that won't let us get any closer to the surface than one hundred yards. This is as far as we go."

"I'll work on that," I say, already backing out of the pod system to dig into the platform's ones and zeroes. "I can probably turn it off. Remi, how low do we need to get, do you think?"

I turn to look at them, only to find them staring down at the eye of swirling maz at the bottom of the cavern.

"I can fix this," they say.

Our eyes meet, and Remi gives me a sad, lingering smile as they flick off their suit's nullifying barrier.

Then they dive off the platform, straight into the contaminated Maz Sea.

TWENTY-EIGHT

"NO!"

The word tears itself from my throat, following Remi down into the void. But it's too late.

Remi's body falls and falls, a graceful arrow, until they slip into the Maz Sea with barely a ripple, disappearing completely beneath the swirling glow of the most concentrated maz in the world. Right near the rift that's leaking toxic maz-15. The rift that I just flooded with more poison.

I can't breathe, can't hear anything through static in my ears, the crushing tightness in my chest, and my throat is as raw as if I've been screaming for hours. They couldn't just wait? I was working on it, I was going to fix it, between Jaesin and me we could have—

A bullet pings off the platform beside me, bringing me back to the very dangerous present, and I roll away as three more shots come in: two stunning spells and another bullet. Ania crouches next to me, her woven shield flaring bright gold with each bullet and spell that strikes it.

Maybe waiting isn't an option after all.

"Drive, damn it!" Ania shouts to Jaesin over the noise, pushing more maz into her shield. "I can't hold them off forever!"

I get my feet under me and scramble for better cover, ducking behind a low bulkhead. My hands shake over the screen of my deck, the code blurring before my eyes. I take a minute to get my breath back, swallowing great gulps of air to slow my racing heart.

They've done this kind of thing before. When they fell from the rooftop, they caught themself, and that was with only the maz in their necklace. Now they're surrounded by nearly unlimited power. They're fine. Probably.

"Diz," Jaesin says, low and calm. "You need to get these failsafes off, then shut that other platform down. See if you can override it, send them back up the tunnel, something. We need them off our backs so Remi can do whatever it is they're trying to do."

Dying is what they're trying to do, it seems. But as I bring up a command prompt, something starts to change in the sea of maz below us. It begins to shift and bubble, like a great creature is swimming beneath the surface, and the different shades of maz start to separate under the will of some unseen hand.

Remi. Cool relief spreads from my heart. They really

are fine. Somewhere down there, they're doing what they do best: weaving something so intricate and beautiful that it takes my breath away.

The clatter of gunfire intensifies. No time to think about it. Remi will do what they can do. I need to do my part.

I type furiously, forcing my way through layer upon layer of useless subroutines and redundancies, trying my best to get the lay of the digital land on the fly. Manipulating our own platform is easiest, so I focus on removing the limiter from the maneuvering jets first.

"You're going to get a really sudden kick, Jaesin," I shout in warning as I override the safeties. "Get ready to compensate in three—"

My finger slips.

The platform lurches forward, snapping my neck back and knocking me on my ass, and toppling Ania down right next to me. She manages to keep her shield between us and the incoming projectiles despite the tumble, though the guards are still firing in the empty space where we just were anyway. Jaesin catches himself by the edge of the console and just barely keeps the platform from careening out of control, looping us down and underneath the nearest enemy platform.

Okay, task one, complete. Not exactly graceful, but I'll call it a victory. Next up: figure out how to mess with the other pods and platforms. I'm well inside the system now, its architecture nearly as familiar as my favorite buildings in Kyrkarta, but I'm having trouble telling all the platforms apart. They're labeled in the system, but there's no way to know what label goes with which platform when they're named generic things like A-694. I just have to test it. There's no other way.

I find the command for the emergency lighting on the platforms and send a ping, then lean my head out for a second. On the complete opposite side of the cavern, a platform lights up with orange emergency lights in one brief, bright pulse. O-kay. Seven platforms over from the one I wanted. Assuming the labels are in order, that would make the correct one . . .

I send another pulse and lean out again, nearly getting my head taken off by a stun spell aimed right at me. Another platform lights up, seven down in the complete opposite direction.

"Damn it, Diz, hurry it up!" Jaesin shouts, hauling back on the controls. "This isn't the Sunnaz Festival, quit playing with the lights!"

"I'm trying, asshole," I growl, and count seven platform IDs in the right direction. I alter the code this time, then push it out to the other platform with a grin.

The alarm sirens go off at full blast, and the lights strobe on and off in a completely random pattern on the correct platform this time. One of the guys on the platform covers his ears and doubles over, but their techwitch quickly weaves a dampening spell to block the painful sound. Spoilsport. Doesn't matter anyway. It was just a brief distraction, since I was already there. Now, to find the lift controls.

I take a quick glance away from my deck, just long enough to see the maz below whipping into a frenzy, spinning faster and faster in a hurricane of glowing power, with a clear eye at the center. And in the eye, hovering in midair near the bottom, is Remi, using their entire arms in grand versions of the usual subtle gestures they use to weave spells. Something is taking shape in front of them, glowing fiercely and growing larger by the second.

They're doing it. It's working.

I send them every ounce of strength I have. I hope they can last long enough to get the patch in place.

Then, as I watch, a guard on one of the other platforms takes aim at Remi.

Oh, *hell* no.

I identify the correct ID for the platform's thrusters and hastily push through a new command . . . one that fires the thrusters at full power for two seconds, causing their shots to crash into the cavern ceiling as they fall back. Not hitting Remi, that's all I care about.

"Nice!" Jaesin calls back to me, then drops our platform straight down so suddenly I think my stomach gets left behind. I grit my teeth and get ready to send another burst, but half my vision flickers red, and a warning notification popped up. My open blocks of code began to disappear one by one, replaced by a laughing triceratops with a skull and crossbones on its forehead.

"Won't be nice for long," I say, typing furiously. "Reinforcements are almost here, and they have a counterhacker."

"Well, do something about it," Jaesin shouts back. "Remi needs more time."

His voice is harsh and desperate, laced with all the frustration of being a helpless mundie in a maz fight. Driving the platform is taking all his focus, leaving no time for anything offensive. I look around the cavern, searching for anything that could possibly . . .

Then I have an idea.

"Oh, this is mean," I say, throwing some coded shields of my own up against the Great Death Triceratops, wherever they may be working from. I dig back into the controls for the gunners' platform, with extra care to cover my tracks, and take control of its thrusters again. Different tactic this time, though. I lock them out of their own controls and program in a new route, set it on a trigger command, then quickly repeat the whole series with several of the empty platforms closest to the tunnel back up to the surface.

Then, with a gleeful smile, I send the final command.

The platforms' thrusters fire at full strength, safeties off, and the gunners and weavers on the closest platform fall to their knees. All fire momentarily ceases. One man tumbles over the railing at the edge and plunges down into the Maz Sea. I wince and breathe a tiny, useless apology; that guy is almost certainly going to die, but at least he'll be spared what awaits his friends. Angry shouts drift across the cavern as they try to regain control of the platform, but they aren't fast enough. The course I programmed sends them back up the tunnel, where, somewhere in the vast depths, three more pods are descending at max speed.

It won't end well for anyone involved.

Then, just to make extra sure we're covered, the rest of the platforms I tampered with make the ascent up the tunnel as well, blocking them in completely.

They might live. If the Great Death Triceratops turns all their resources toward overriding my lock on the other platforms, they might be able to save themselves. Either way, they're off our backs for a bit.

A violent crash of colliding metal echoes down from the tunnel.

Well, maybe for more than a bit. I've dealt with Death Triceratops, but I've also blocked our only known way out. There are still two platforms full of guards left. And we never did figure out what to do with the drill.

Below, a huge swath of the Maz Sea has solidified into a vast swirling grid, strongly barred with terraz and formaz for structure and interwoven with a delicate lace

of every other type of maz twined together, more color-
ful and powerful and *beautiful* than anything I've ever
seen. Even standing on the sea floor next to the rift,
maybe fifteen, twenty feet below the surface, Remi can
still orchestrate the whole thing. Their power is the key
to everything.

It's time. Time to fix this, to salvage what's left of
our planet, to eradicate the source of the spellplague and
maybe . . . just *maybe*, start down a totally new path
together. As a family.

When I head back into the drill controls and prepare
to do my part, my eyebrows shoot up. There's a whole
category of commands that I missed last time around,
completely separate from its drilling operations. A plan
starts to take shape in my mind—probably a terrible one,
but better than the nothing we're working with at the
moment.

"Ania," I call, even as I pore over the code before my
eyes and pull out a few select commands. "Weave an
amplifier so we can call down to Remi. We have to time
this right. Jaesin, keep those other platforms off our back
as best you can, and get ready to pick up Remi as soon as
they're done."

I trust them both to tackle their jobs, and the faint
white light of songaz shimmers in my peripheral vision
to confirm it. A few more commands, and I'm ready. The
drill whines as I power the engines back up, readying it to

pull free. I blow out a slow breath and turn to Ania.

"Call it down," I say, then cover my ears.

"Remi!" she booms, her voice filling the entire cavern. Damn, girl. "We're ready up here. Can you send us a signal?"

A quick shower of sunnaz sparks shoots up from the center of the woven hurricane.

Ready.

Okay then. Time to back the drill out of the rift. More maz-15 will come pouring out, but it's okay. It's fine. Remi is there to apply the patch. It's almost over.

All I have to do is send the final command.

My throat locks up.

"You have to pull the drill, Dizzy," Jaesin shouts, fighting to hold the platform's controls steady. "Remi can't get out of there until you do."

Another shower of sparks goes up, weaker this time.

I have to trust them. Have to back off, do my part. Watch.

And be here for them when they come back.

I take three deep breaths.

Go.

The drill rumbles as it springs to life and begins to slowly inch its way out of the rift. We have five seconds of relative peace, nothing but the beautiful swirling maz below and the vibration of the drill, almost more of an even, soothing hum—then, all at once, a wave of intense violet maz-15 comes rushing out, flooding the empty eye of Remi's storm. Remi's gestures speed up, whipping the weave into a frenzy and incorporating as much of the new maz-15 as possible, but it's too much, *too much*, and after a moment they're completely swallowed up by the flood of poison. Invisible to us.

No, no, no, no, I chant in my head, gripping the edge of the platform as Jaesin pulls a hard reversal, barely avoiding a ramming attempt by another platform.

Then a bright flash, temporarily blinding in its intensity. A moment of nothingness, like the pressure in the cavern has dropped all at once, like someone has sucked all the air out.

Stillness.

Silence.

Then the brightness fades, and there's Remi, their wards holding the Maz Sea back away from a shimmering, tightly woven patch, perfectly sealed to the sea floor around it. There's no bubbling maz-15, just the calm waves of maz rolling gently outside the barrier Remi erected around themself.

They did it.

"Jaesin, take us down!" I shout, my voice high and unrecognizable. He's already at it, though, practically putting us into freefall as the two remaining platforms plummet after us, spells flying and guns cracking. They must have finally figured out a way to override the speed limiter on their own platforms, because they easily keep pace with us, as if they're herding us toward the sea floor.

Below, the Maz Sea begins to encroach on Remi's circle, their wards breaking down in the face of so much raw energy. Tendrils of glowing, glittering maz lick in toward their crumpled form, casting a mottled rainbow of light over them. A bright green thread curls over their cheek . . . and they move. Just a hand, curling and uncurling as if to reach up and brush the maz away.

But it's movement. They're alive. Barely a second later, their eyes blink open, and they roll onto their front, pushing to all fours, then to unsteady feet.

The guards on the other platforms notice at the same time we do. They angle for Remi, and I didn't think I had any more adrenaline left to give, but apparently I do. I grab the gun from Jaesin's waistband as he brings us down to the seafloor, hovering just a foot off the ground, and I rush forward to pull Remi on board. I reach out and grab hold of their hand, leaving my other one free to fire the gun over their shoulder with no real accuracy, but plenty of intent. I haul back until Remi is securely on deck, wanting nothing more than to wrap my arms around them, but now that we present a single target instead of two, the other platforms are concentrating their fire. We're so close, damn it, just let us win or something.

Jaesin hauls back on the controls, and the platform obeys with a lurch, a clatter of gunfire peppering the deck just in front of me. I stumble back and fall straight on my ass, slamming my shoulder into the console, and something behind me digs hard and hot into my back. I jerk away and grab my deck, ignoring the pain to pull up the drill interface once more.

"Jaesin, head for the drill's core," I shout over the sudden roaring in my ears. The maneuvering jets have gotten a lot louder. That can't be good. Hopefully they aren't about to give out. Just a little farther. Hold it together.

"Dizzy," Remi says, falling to their knees beside me, but I shove the gun at them without looking. If I look, I'll want to touch, and if I touch, I'll never want to let go. There's still work to do.

"I know how to get us out of here. Hold them off until we get to the drill," I say, eyes locked on my deck. I dig through the new commands I discovered and prep a series of them to go off at my trigger. "Jaesin, you think you can land us on a moving target?"

"I think I'm gonna have to, if you're asking," he says. He shoots me a quick glance, then does a double take, his eyes wide. "Dizzy—"

"Get ready to land us on the drill's central platform, then, right next to its control center," I say, and send the commands.

The whole cavern shudders with a clanking groan as, one by one, the four pylons holding the drill upright break free. The first lifts and bends, then plants back on the ground so the next leg can do the same. And the next, and the next . . . until the whole drill is moving, *walking*, like a bug with spindly jointed legs and a very long, pointed nose.

"You've gotta be fucking kidding me," Ania says. Third f-bomb of the week. I like to think I earned that one.

"Not fucking kidding you at all," I say. "Never let it be said that MMC doesn't plan ahead. Why build a single stationary drill to create just one horrific disaster when you can build one for *mobile* destruction? Welcome to your ride home."

Ania keeps talking at me, the pitch rising higher and higher, but it fades right into the background as I line up a series of commands to take us out of this hellhole. We can't go back the way we came in, but there are plenty of other routes to the surface. That's the whole reason Kyrkarta exists where it does; plenty of routes for maz to escape to the surface. I lift a hand to swipe at the sweat stinging my eyes . . . but maybe I don't? My arm stays in my lap, fingers resting on my deck, refusing to obey my command.

Then a drop of blood hits my deck screen, and another.

I look down to find a small hole in my chest, near the junction of my shoulder, blood sliding over the slick material of my heat-shielded suit and dripping when I lean over too far. My helmet is intact, the oxygen flowing fine, but the hole in my suit . . . the heat beyond . . .

The pain hits like a sledgehammer. I gasp, covering the hole with my other hand even as more bullets and spells crash into the deck around me. The wound was numb before, but now that I've seen it, it's like my body can't ignore it anymore. It's hot, so hot, like someone shoving a burning rod through my body while simultaneously beating my shoulder with a club. I drag my functioning hand down to tap SEND on the final series of commands I've queued up, my bloody finger sliding across the screen. It's not enough, though. It'll get us to the surface, but what then?

"Jaesin, you'll have to . . . the drill has controls in the . . . and it . . ."

I break off, gasping through the pressure in my chest. Every gunshot that cracks the air is like a bomb going off in my ears, each several seconds long and hours apart.

"Jaesin, get us . . . to the . . . get us the . . ."

"Dizzy," Remi shouts. I blink, and I'm suddenly horizontal, my head cradled in Remi's lap, their hands covered in blood. Their lips move again, but no sound comes out.

I smile, watching their mouth form my name again and again.

"Hi," I say.

Then I close my eyes and drift far, far away.

TWENTY-NINE

WHEN I NEXT OPEN MY eyes, it's with the echoing memory of creaking metal and rumbling, rhythmic
footsteps. All that is gone now, though, replaced with
gentle rocking and the peaceful sounds of sloshing water.
I blink to clear my vision and take in two facts at once: the
window across from my bed shows nothing but endless
water and sky, and Remi's head is pillowed next to my
hip. They're asleep right on top of my hand.

My hand, which is numb and tingly hopefully due to
lack of circulation and not as an aftereffect of the gunshot.

At the thought of the shot, my chest gives a throbbing
ache, and I hiss, lifting my free hand to cover the wound.
It's dressed with soft gauze, and I slip my fingers under
the neckline of a shirt that definitely isn't mine to scratch
at the tape that holds the edges down.

"Don't," a sleep-gravelly voice protests, and a hand
swats at my elbow. Remi lifts their head from my hand,
a red-creased impression of my knuckles dotting their
cheek. They swipe at a damp spot on my thumb with

an apologetic "Yikes!" look, then sit back, taking in my whole appearance. I cringe, fighting the urge to curl into myself and hide. I opt for lightness instead.

"You look like you're feeling well," I croak, then clear my throat.

Remi nods, smiling faintly. "I slept almost as much as you did. Definitely feeling better, but planning on at least one more week of video games and heavy napping. You should join me," they say with a significant look at my bandaged wound.

"How bad is it?" I try to hold out my arms for inspection. Only the one arm moves correctly, though. The other gives a pathetic half shrug before flopping back on the bed, a hiss of pain between my teeth.

"Stop that!" Remi says. "You just can't sit still, can you?"

"Do you even know me?" I retort.

Their expression softens. "Yeah. I think I do."

I bite my lip and look away, flushing. I know the conversation is coming, but I'm not ready yet. I've only just woken up, haven't gotten my bearings, don't even know where we *are*. I use my one good arm to push myself up to seated, staring out the window at the horizon where blue meets blue.

"Are we on a boat or something?" I ask, steering us onto steady ground. "How did we get here?"

Remi laughs and gets to their feet, coming to stand

next to my good arm. "We are indeed on a boat, unfortunately for Jaesin. It's quite a good story. Too bad you were
bleeding everywhere and didn't get to see it."

A shadow passes over their face, and they take a
steadying breath before moving on. "I pulled a bunch of
vitaz from the cavern before the drill carried us out of
there, and we got you stable. Once we made it onto the
boat, we were able to stop somewhere Ania could pay a
lot of money for you to get treated."

I summon a weak smile. For once, zero bitterness
about Ania and her money. "How did Kyrkarta react to
the drill?"

Remi snorts a laugh. "You so missed out. The footage
was playing on the news feeds until MMC got it taken
down. It's like something out of a movie, that drill climbing out of a crack in the Bridges District like a giant bug.
Since you weren't conscious, Jaesin filled in for you and
got some epic music queued up for our dramatic exit."

My lips curl into a smile as I picture it. "And what,
then Jaesin just drove us out to the ocean? Where is the
drill now?"

"I mean, driving is a bit generous," Remi says with a
snicker. "He pointed the drill in a direction and hit go,
then kept us from running into anything too awful. Once
we got to the water, we figured out how to tell the drill
to keep walking straight forever. It walked around for a
while on the bottom of the ocean, but eventually the salt

water got to it. It fell into a trench and died. RIP, death machine."

"RIP," I echo with a little salute. "But that still doesn't explain where we are."

The door to my little room swings open, and a kindly face appears around the corner. Professor Silva's husband, John.

"Ah, you're awake, good." He leans back out into the hallway. "ARIC, SHE'S AWAKE!"

"DON'T SHOUT IN THE PATIENT'S ROOM!" a voice echoes back, and a moment later Professor Silva shuffles into the room, followed by Jaesin and Ania. "Never trust a mathematician to have a good bedside manner, I suppose. How are you feeling, dear?"

I blink at all the faces crowded around my bed, sudden claustrophobia clawing at the inside of my chest.

"Fine," I say, too sharp, then take a breath and force myself to relax. "Fine. But can I get out of this room? It's feeling a little . . . small."

Professor Silva looks around, then says, "Oh!" as if just noticing the crowd. "Everyone out! Let's set up on the deck."

Jaesin comes around to my bad side and gently scoops an arm under me, while Remi takes my good side and curls their arm around my waist. It takes a minute to get used to having my legs under me again, but I'm in surprisingly little pain, all things considered. More difficult is finding my sea legs, because we are, in fact, on a boat.

I relax. There's no way MMC can get at us out here.

I've never been to the ocean before. Even during our brief time in Jattapore, we didn't really have time to go down and explore. Now it's all I can see, stretching out in every direction to the horizon line, and shining like firaz in the setting sun's light. The boat rocks beneath me, gentle and soothing.

Well, soothing to me. According to Remi, Jaesin spent our first three hours at sea with his head overboard. His olive skin is still washed gray with sickness, and he chugs water to soothe the resulting dehydration, Ania rubbing a gentle hand over his back. Poor guy.

The source of the boat? Turns out *this* is the backup retirement plan the professor had in mind when he literally burned down his own house. That plan essentially amounts to "sail around the world on a giant boat," and they were kind enough to let us hitch a ride for a while. Remi contacted Professor Silva using the information he left with them, they set up a rendezvous, and we apparently transferred to the boat before sending the drill on to its final watery resting place.

Weird. A lot to miss. I was half dead at the time, though, so I think I can be excused.

I drop to the ground at the edge of the deck, threading

my legs under the railing and propping my good arm and chin on top of it. I'm already winded from the short journey from the cabin. Not great. Remi sits down beside me on my good side, close but not touching, while Jaesin and Ania share a deck chair facing away from the water, and the professor and John hold hands over a metal picnic table welded to the deck. It's like a group sigh of relief, everyone resting against one another, hands seeking reassurance where words aren't enough.

I take a deep breath of bracing salty air and let my mind go blank for a moment, willing my brain to catch back up with the present. Part of me is still back at station twenty-nine, baking in my own fear sweat, watching Remi dive into the Maz Sea, and seeing Davon lying on the ground, surrounded by bleeding and dying security guards, pale, sickly . . . ill?

My heart gives a painful clench.

Davon. My family. My cousin, brother, whatever, my closest *anything*. The betrayal aches just as badly now as it did in the moment, driving all that fresh sea air from my lungs and hollowing me out.

I pull up my notifications in my lenses and find two days of ignored messages waiting for me, including several from Davon. That eases my mind ever so slightly; he can't have messaged me if he's dead. His words superimpose themselves over the rolling ocean waters before me.

(private) Davon: Hey
I know you don't want to talk to me
I just need to know if you're okay, though
Please

I hate so much the way my heart reacts to that, the way I crave his attention, the way I need him to be here to hug me and make everything okay. I hate the relief that eases the iron bands around my heart. He's alive, and he still cares about me. That's something. Even with everything that went down, I can't completely hate him. He's my cousin-brother-thing. Always will be. But I'll never trust him again.

In fact, I'm not even sure I ever want to see his face again.

I debate for a long moment about simply deleting the messages. Even confirming that we're alive could be dangerous, if he's still relaying information to MMC. Somehow I don't believe it, though. He may have been an asshole in the end, but Davon always knows when he's beaten. And ultimately, everything he ever did was to protect me. I don't think that's changed. I shoot a quick glance over at Remi's profile, then subvocalize a short message back.

You: I'm alive.
And you?

Several minutes pass as Davon starts and stops his reply, the ellipsis appearing and disappearing repeatedly. Finally, he responds.

(private) Davon: I'm alive for now.

For now. My stomach lurches. I wish so much that those words didn't hurt like they did.

You: I'm sorry.

It's true. Complicated, but true.

(private) Davon: Me too.
I have no right to ask but
Will I ever see you again?

I bite my lip and look over to where Jaesin and Ania are laughing and telling Aric some kind of story with lots of big gestures and interruptions. Ania is practically in Jaesin's lap, an arm curled around his neck. They look happy, happier than I've seen either of them in a long time. Mom and Dad, finally back together again. Warms my tiny heart.

We definitely won't be back in Kyrkarta anytime soon. I need to recover. So does Remi. We need to give MMC's executive board time to sort out their reaction to what happened, see if they'll retract the warrants for our arrest. The professor's sciencey friends say it's far too early to tell anything about the state of the planet, but that there have been no new disasters in the past two days. I'll take it. Apparently the conspiracy theorists on the net picked up on the news story about the drill before it got wiped from the feeds, and John has been systematically flooding every forum and news outlet with ten years of evidence. It's all been taken down within seconds, like an automatic bot is crawling the net specifically to search and destroy any scrap of the truth. Something will make it through eventually, though.

Something always breaks through.

We've got more to do together, this weird little family of ours. Maz research with the professor, maybe even cure research if Remi feels up to it. Investigation into other MMC facilities around the world. Travel to every plague-affected city to see what's been done to them, and how we can help.

I'll miss Kyrkarta, no doubt. But I finally feel like I have a purpose, and I didn't even need Davon to score a job interview for me to get it. Maybe we'll be able to go home eventually. Maybe I'll even see Davon there.

Do I even *want* to see Davon again?

You: honestly I don't know.

And I can't think of anything more to say than that.

(private) Davon: Okay
Well
Take care of yourself, Diz.

I smile the saddest smile of my life at that. His number one priority at all times. Take care of *yourself.* That's always been the problem for both of us. Too busy protecting ourselves instead of living.

You: You too.

Because I know he doesn't have anyone else to look out for him.

I blink the chat away, but don't delete it. I have a feeling I'll regret it later if I do. Instead, I scoot closer to Remi and, with trembling fingers, reach out to lay a hand on their knee. A second passes, two, ten . . . then Remi's hand joins mine, twining our fingers together. When they look up a moment later, I force myself to meet their gaze.

"You okay?" I mouth, mustering up a smile.

They smile back faintly and nod, squeezing my hand gently. I squeeze back, still fighting that awful creeping dread inside me, that bite of the past that works to hold me down. It's easier now, though. It'll be even easier in the future. Every day, I'll work at it. Remi deserves it. *I* deserve it.

We sit together for a while, until the sun is nearly down and the others have gone inside to make dinner. We stay until the stars come out and we can look up and spot our favorites, tracing constellations on each other's legs. Eventually, I lift my hand to Remi's face, drawing a star high on one cheekbone. Another, on the tip of their nose. The corner of their mouth. On their full bottom lip.

When I seal each one into their skin with a kiss, Remi shines brighter than all the stars in the sky combined.

"It's not going to be perfect," I murmur between kisses, hating to say it but needing to all the same, even as our mouths slot together again and again. "I'm still going to mess up all the time."

Remi nudges my nose with theirs, a silent request I'm only too happy to fulfill. I lean in to brush our lips together, featherlight, barely there, that faint touch full of electric promise.

"I'm going to try, though," I whisper.

Their lips pull into a smile under mine, then they sit back to meet my eyes.

"That's all I've ever wanted."

The telltale click of Ania's bootheels on the metal deck draws my eyes away from Remi's face for the first time in what feels like hours. Ania stands at the corner of the ship cabin, one hand on her hip, grinning like a fiend.

"Come inside," Ania says, her eyes shining. "I know what you were up to!" practically radiates from her every smug pore. Out loud, though, all she says is, "It's dinner-time."

"We'll be right there," Remi says, scooting back from the edge and turning to help me up. We take it slow, balancing carefully so as not to put any weight on my half-dead arm. Golden light and deep laughter spill from the open cabin door onto the hard steel deck, drowning out the darkness and crash of the waves.

Yes, I'll miss Kyrkarta. I'll even miss Davon. But my true family is out here. Wherever they go, I go.

Remi's hand slips into mine and squeezes.

"Ready?" they ask.

I squeeze back and take one long, deep breath.

"Yeah," I say. "I'm ready."

Acknowledgments

Second books are *rough*, as every author will tell you, but I've had the most fabulous people on my side.

Anyone would be lucky to have Barbara Poelle, Warrior Agent, in their corner. Thanks for being my fierce defender, keeping me sane(ish), and sharing your wisdom when I'm adrift. You do more than I'll ever know, and I appreciate it so much!

To Stephanie Stein, who gets my nerd references and is so, so smart with her editorial direction: endless thanks for guiding me through the challenge that was this book. I'm grateful for both your enthusiasm and your chill. And to Louisa Currigan, editorial assistant extraordinaire, who keeps the wheels turning like a freakin' wizard behind the scenes. Much appreciated!

And of course, huge thanks due to the entire rest of the Harper team. To the oh-so-talented design team of Alice Wang and Jenna Stempel-Lobell—I know getting to this final cover was a Journey, but I adore it and you both, and I deeply appreciate your talent and time!

To copy editors Shona McCarthy and Laaren Brown
. . . sorry about the hyphens, y'all, and thanks. To the
production team of Kimberly Stella and Vanessa Nut-
try, Shannon Cox in marketing, and everyone else at
HarperTeen whose names and hard work I never hear
about: I appreciate you. Thanks for helping *Spellhacker*
stand out.

I often get asked about advice for writers who are just
starting out, and I gotta repeat the same thing a lot of folx
say: Find your people. I would not be where I am without
the support, love, and ~~shouting~~ gentle encouragement of
many lovely writer friends and groups. The Pitch Wars
2015 Mentee and Mentor Alumni groups and the Electric
18s debut group are so full of wise and lovely people I'm
grateful to know. Some specific love:

Leigh: You were there when this book was born! We
brainstormed the hell outta this thing at a retreat in 2017,
and then you sat across from me at the coffee shop every
week as I swore, cried, and mashed my face against the keyboard over the next year. It literally wouldn't exist without
you. Thanks for the good times, the overcaffeinated times,
the sugar-crashed times, and everything in between.

Jamie: My constant friend, always 100 percent real
and on my side no matter what. No amount of feminist
f-word-filled socks could express my gratitude. I'm so
thrilled to hold your first book in my hands in just a few
short months. You and your words are a gift to the world!

Kat and Steph: Retreat friends, accountability buddies, constant sources of encouragement. You are so talented and you deserve everything.

Kerri: My humble gratitude for your insight. Both my books are better for having had your eyeballs on them!

Mike and Ruby: You're the best cheerleaders and I so appreciate your support. Mike, you are my IV drip line of encouragement and positivity. You deserve your dreams. I'm here for you.

To the Gamefest crew and my local gamer friends: You'd be shocked at just how much creative fuel I get from our table time together, brief and far between though it may be. I appreciate you. Thanks for the support.

And a huge extra shout-out to the *Disasters* launch crew, especially Mike and Vicky. Wouldn't be here without you. I'm eternally grateful.

In Libraryland: I have the best coworkers. Special shout-out to Amy and Hayley for the patience, friendship, and after-work drinks. Always, always, always for my teens: Thanks for the support and constant inspiration. Someday you're gonna blow us all away. I adore you, my ducks.

To my parents, who gave me books, room for my imagination, and a love of sci-fi and fantasy. You showed me what it looks like to bust your ass for the things you want. Glad you're nearby now. Love you both. Take it easy.

And finally, as always, to my partner, Nathan, who fills my every day with the practical and the whimsical, keeping me grounded and silly. Couldn't do this without you. All my love forever and ever until the inevitable heat death of the universe.

Still here? Thanks to YOU, too. Go be kind to someone, and to yourself.